PRAISE FOR THE

"Jade Sky *is a an ass-kicking action-fantasy that takes no prisoners. Lightning fast, brutal and way too much fun. Highly recommended!"*

—Jonathan Maberry, New York Times Bestselling author of *Code Zero* and *Fall of Night*

"Jade Sky *is one of those all too rare reading experiences that just consumes you.... Freivald made a future so rich in detail and so full of life and energy that I couldn't help but lose myself in it. This is a book full of wild invention and even wilder action, yet grounded by a genuinely sympathetic love for the people who live there. Freivald has truly reached a new high water mark here, which is pretty scary considering that he was already so damn good."*

—Joe McKinney, Bram Stoker Award®-winning author of *Plague of the Undead*

"Buckle up and insert your mouthguard because Jade Sky *is a fast ride and Patrick Freivald knows how to write with his fists. Smart, witty, and packed with action and suspense, this is a perfect summertime read. I'm looking forward to reading more Freivald. This guy's good."*

—Ray Garton, author of *Frankenstorm, Ravenous,* and *Warlock*

JADE GODS

JADE GODS

PATRICK FREIVALD

Cohesion Press
Mayday Hills Lunatic Asylum,
Beechworth, Australia

Jade Gods

• • •

eBook: 978-0-9944286-6-0
Print: 978-0-9944286-9-1

Cohesion Press
Mayday Hills Lunatic Asylum,
Beechworth, Australia
www.cohesionpress.com

We are an Australian publisher, and even though we publish many overseas writers, we maintain a certain Australian house style of punctuation.

Also From Cohesion Press

Horror:
SNAFU: An Anthology of Military Horror
– eds Geoff Brown & Amanda J Spedding
SNAFU: Heroes
– eds Geoff Brown & Amanda J Spedding
SNAFU: Wolves at the Door
– eds Geoff Brown & Amanda J Spedding
SNAFU: Survival of the Fittest
– eds Geoff Brown & Amanda J Spedding
SNAFU: Hunters
– eds Amanda J Spedding & Geoff Brown
The Gate Theory – Kaaron Warren
Carnies – Martin Livings
Blurring the Line – Marty Young (ed)
American Nocturne – Hank Schwaeble

Sci-Fi/Thriller:
Valkeryn 2 – Greig Beck
Cry Havoc – Jack Hanson
Forlorn Hope – Jack Hanson
SNAFU: Future Warfare
– eds Amanda J Spedding & Geoff Brown

Coming Soon

SNAFU: Unnatural Selection (July 2016)
The Angel of the Abyss (September 2016)
Fathomless (September 2016)
Primordial (October 2016)
Devil Dragon (November 2016)
SNAFU: Black Ops (November 2016)

CHAPTER ONE

"Do they have her?" Matt Rowley ignored the bead of sweat trickling down the back of his neck and scanned the monitor, where night-vision green illuminated a landscape of buildings outside of Quantico, Virginia. The swarm of Dragonfly-pattern microdrones created a three-dimensional panorama of the target site, with bright orange triangles outlining potential targets – not only sentries armed with snub-nosed carbines wandering the rooftops, but six separate pillboxes scattered across the campus. Far too much hardware for a supposedly-civilian center with an eight-million-dollar annual budget.

The Office of Planning and Development wouldn't have been able to make rent on the facility that bore its name, much less hire rent-a-cops with machine guns. Sloppy for a covert operation, it looked too much like a trap.

Matt shifted his weight in the back of the panel van parked four blocks away and suppressed a curse at the lackluster whine coming from the air conditioner. "I said, 'do they have her?'"

Janet LaLonde held up a finger, lime-green plastic nail jutting toward the roof, and tilted her head, listening. Even with his augmented hearing Matt couldn't pick out the words from her headset. After a long moment she sighed, chest heaving under a matted curtain of straight brown hair hanging in front of her face. "The lab weenies confirmed the blood and hair are Sakura's, but our source hasn't verified that she's there, no."

Seven months. Seven months and eleven unrelated missions since Shane Keene – a supposed FBI agent with perfect credentials but who didn't exist – had kidnapped Sakura 'Blossom' Isuji from the smoking ground of Centralia, Pennsylvania, the only place in the world that smelled worse than this van. Matt unclenched his fist and managed not to put it through the side wall. "And you still haven't dug up any more OPD facilities?"

"The El-Cee would neither confirm nor deny that 'The Shed' exists at all, and seemed more head-up-ass confused than cover-uppy when I pressed him about it, but who knows? Maybe he's a better liar than he lets on. Someone found out we're digging, though, and the attacks on our firewall haven't let up since that meeting. SACLANT's got a hole problem, or a mole problem, or maybe something worse." Lieutenant-Commander Roger Smith earned a paycheck as Head Douchebag in Charge of Douchebaggery at the NATO's Supreme Allied Commander-Atlantic's headquarters, which meant he outranked everyone in the Office of Special Threats, including Matt and Janet, though Smith had learned the hard way not to push his authority too far. Being irreplaceable had its perks, and no one on Earth could replace Matt Rowley.

Except maybe Sakura Isuji. The other of the last two augmented commandos on the Earth, the dour, stoic woman had pulled Matt's ass out of the fire on several occasions, and he both felt like he barely knew her and that they were best friends.

"Any leads on the source?"

Another shake. "You know what I know, bud. We couldn't descramble, but speech patterns put 'female' at eighty-nine percent probability, 'forties' at sixty-five, and she's definitely from the Tri-State area, most likely Connecticut. That plus clearance to know what she's told us narrows it down to, oh, four thousand people or so."

Sweat sheened Janet's high cheekbones, though the

heavy black eyeliner stayed put around her dark brown eyes. Gorgeous and ever-willing to use it to her advantage, in the private confines of the surveillance van she dropped the sexy redneck act but still jawed a wad of pale green chewing gum. Spearmint undercut the body odor and gasoline, both almost overpowering to Matt's enhanced sense of smell.

He waited for her to add more, but she didn't.

"All right, then what's your gut tell you?"

She rolled her eyes. "My gut always tells me to ignore my gut and go off of solid intelligence, which we don't have. If you go in there you're flying blind, and you might not even find her, and if Blossom's still alive that might get them to make that not so true anymore. Our source isn't just unreliable, she's unknown. We got nothing, and it'd be stupid to go all cowboy right now."

Matt put his head in his hands. "All right. Call it."

Janet tapped her Bluetooth with a green nail. "Sorry, toots. Get us proof."

Matt heard the frustration in the reply, which cut off when Janet hung up on her.

"M'kay, bud, why don't you get us home? I could kill a skunk with my underwear."

Matt clambered into the driver's seat and gunned the engine, then pulled out and drove toward Fredericksburg and their home-away-from-home, the Motel 6.

• • •

Marcia Stein removed the SIM card from the burner she'd bought at Walmart, snapped it in half and swallowed it. The phone she cleaned with a Clorox wipe and threw in the garbage.

LaLonde had called her 'toots', which meant at the least that despite the scrambler they knew her gender. How much more did they know? And had LaLonde slipped up on purpose?

She pulled a photograph from her purse and traced her own face, eyes closed, bowing across from Sakura Isuji in an American-style Kimono, their bare feet on the edge of a six-foot circle emblazoned with the eye-and-thunderbolt of the International Council on Augmented Phenomena. Marcia's time at ICAP HQ hadn't intersected Rowley's, but she'd met Janet only twice, and neither had said more than "good morning" to the other.

Slow and dull since her Augs had failed, Stein's desk intelligence job at the Office of Planning and Development had paid the bills. But then the picture of her close-combat instructor had crossed her desk, a bloody shell of a woman secured to a table with steel straps, face blank, murderous eyes clear and focused at the camera. Marcia shivered at the memory of those eyes, and the indomitable will behind them.

No one had ever beaten her so badly, and Sakura hadn't shown her the slightest mercy, in the ring or out, for months on end. Countless bruises and a hundred broken bones later, she'd never once heard a word of praise.

Marcia owed Sakura Isuji a great debt, and wouldn't rest until she'd paid it.

• • •

Flames clawed at the darkening sky, their reflections snaking out across the water of Lake Barnacle. The Georgia heat hadn't fled with the day, and The Prophet Ben Case wiped away a sheen of hot moisture from his forehead. His hand came away red. He rubbed the liquid between his fingertips, hot and tacky and reeking of animal flesh. Stomach roiling, he wiped it on the crude fiber shirt one of his Katies had made him from the wild grasses around his commune.

Three crosses blazed on the shoreline, reducing to ash the symbols of his faith, the Process Church's three-fold god Jehovah, Lucifer, and Satan. Those crosses predated the earliest white settlers and even the oldest native legend. The air shimmered, a protestation at the confines of only four dimensions, a coalescing psychic wail of thetan-space shredding its way into reality. He averted his gaze, and gasped.

A Katie lay on the ground, her pregnant body three feet from her head, which lay in the lap of another Katie, eyeless and armless, sitting Indian-style in the lush green turf. Red-black liquid still gushed from her neck, leaping from the jagged tear across her throat to soak into the lawn and trickle through grass toward the shore. Another Katie lay shattered three feet beyond, her chest a crumpled mess of red meat and jutting white bone, eyes wide, mouth open to the wonders of the sky above. Three Bens lay around her, bodies broken and shredded to shards and chunks of bone and flesh.

Two more piles of three Bens and three Katies littered the shoreline, twisted bodies forming arcane symbols that struck lightning through his brain. Threes and threes and threes, sacred numbers in profane ink, an invocation and invitation to things that had no place on Earth. Not anymore.

Unable to look any longer at the remains of his followers, the prophet raised his eyes to the conflagration, a whirlwind of unknowable colors and incomprehensible sounds around and within the blackened crosses. It stank of shit and coal, the unclean smells of the capitalist world, and of the mysteries of birth and death. His mind shattered, and through the breach a human form emerged, tiptoeing from the flames with the care of a Ben or Katie trying not to crush mayflies during the spring spawn.

Six feet tall – two threes – the naked man's body rippled with muscle and not a wisp of hair as he approached, gliding over the ground with the grace of a cat. He grinned, dazzling white teeth glinting in the firelight. "Brilliant,

brilliant." Conor Flynn's Irish accent hadn't faded with his years in the United States.

Ben shuddered at the unwelcome sound but nodded in greeting, a courtesy he'd give even the worst of mankind. "They told me you'd died, and how I thanked the Jehovah-pattern for it, eh-la eh-la."

Flynn cupped his balls and gave them an upward tug. "Right is right, but you can't keep a good man down. Or me for all that." He stepped forward and wiped his warm hand down Ben's face, then smeared the coagulating blood across his own chest. "Who's 'they' that told you this, hmmm?"

"A colleague of yours. Matt Rowley."

"That's the chap who killed me, sure as sure. What did you tell him?" A fire smoldered behind his eyes, red embers behind light-green irises, before the black, infinite void swallowed it.

Ben met the gaze, and shivered at the mindless, eternal fury within. "I told him you came seeking knowledge of bridges, and took one of my Katies to help you. It seems you found one, eh-la eh-la."

Flynn chuckled, a dark sound in harmony with the stinking carnage and fading flames. "I had a little help on the other side, no thanks to you useless hippy cunts. Eh-fucking-la."

Ben flinched at the profanity, and again at the absurdity of offense at words when surrounded by the broken remains of his followers. "Yet of all places you emerge here, as the trifold Gods—"

Flynn's backhand knocked him to his hands and knees, and left a dark heat across his jaw. "No. Your gods are dead, or fiction. Don't speak to me of gods. I formed the bridge here because I remembered my time so fondly, and this first time I needed an anchor. They got rid of my favorite place, knocked it down and filled it with dirt, turned it into a little park for neighborhood kiddos, stole my trinkets, even that of your Beth."

"Katie." He looked up into those murderous eyes, and stood, head high, defiant. Whatever else happened, Ben wouldn't allow this monster to defame his Katies with their birth names.

Conor's grin widened. "Always Beth to me, even as I peeled her skin and ate it. She hated you, every touch, every whisper, and hated her mother for giving her to you. She asked for escape, so I gave it to her, and she loved me for it."

Ben still woke to her screams in his mind, and the sobbing of his people as Flynn flayed off her skin and then her muscle, treating her with medicines and unholy spells to keep her alive long past human endurance, raping and eating her body and shattering her mind over three days of demonic madness. "That is not what she—"

Conor struck again, too fast to see, and this time Ben dangled in the air, Conor's hand an iron collar around his neck. "I knew her better than you ever could, and she bled her secrets to me one precious cut at a time. We shared a beauty you couldn't even imagine.

"But enough blather. It's time to wake up."

He squeezed, and Ben gasped awake. Crickets protested the death of summer, their chirps an erratic staccato against the stillness of the night. His heart thundered, and the Lucifer-pattern's blessing of adrenaline flooded his body and ensured he'd not sleep again this night.

Three Katies lay around his teepee, their naked bodies a tribute to the beauty of the Satan-pattern's hedonism, a deliberate contrast to the asceticism of a life without electricity, drugs, or furniture. The night smelled of earthy grass and flowers and the subtle tang of algae on the lake. Serene simplicity, separated from the outside world and their maelstrom of thetans and apostasy.

Chest heaving, Ben ran his hand up one Katie's sweat-sheened belly, round with his child, brushing his fingers between her swollen breasts to caress her neck. She smiled without opening her eyes, and spread her legs, an invitation to partake of the Lucifer-pattern's hospitality between. Despite the horror of his nightmare, he felt himself stiffen, and smiled at the universal truth of human existence.

His faith wouldn't let him rejoice in the death of another being, but he couldn't stifle renewed relief, a mirror of the moment Rowley had told him of Conor Flynn's death. Rolling on top of the Katie, Ben kissed her chin and allowed himself a contented sigh as she parted for him.

A voice rang in his mind, friendly warmth smothered in eternal cold. "Brilliant then, on with it. I don't got three days this time."

Ben's fingers dug into her throat. Her eyes shot wide, beautiful and blue and broken with panic and pain.

"My prophet." Her strangled gasp cut off, and she mouthed, 'You're hurting me'.

He tried to pull back, and instead squeezed, black, venomous thought driving his body where his mind would not go. She clawed at his wrist and her heels hammered the ground as he pressed further, fingers splitting skin to dig hot red tunnels in her flesh. A wet gurgle escaped the wound as his fingers met his thumb behind her windpipe, and warm urine sprayed out around his genitals.

"One is done is fun, am I right?"

Someone screamed when he pulled, tearing out her throat.

It might have been him.

CHAPTER TWO

Monica Rowley frowned at the red pickup as it bounced down Turkey Vulture Lane, 'Wilcox Lumber' emblazoned on the side. Cory Wilcox waved, a gesture she didn't return, and in his enthusiasm he almost crashed into a news van parked the court-ordered sixty feet from the driveway.

The Rowleys had moved to the outskirts of White Spruce, Tennessee a decade ago for space and privacy, building their home on the dead-end dirt road with money from Matt's ICAP job, paying cash for the land and managing most of the construction with the help of family and friends. A short drive to town or her parent's house, it backed up to thousands of acres of mountain pines too steep and too rugged to develop. A busy day had meant four or five cars passing, and that only happened during hunting season, if then.

But not anymore.

She closed her eyes and tried to imagine the church going up across the road, a towering monstrosity that would destroy their front view and what little remained of their privacy, such as it was. The plans included a six thousand square foot worship area, four meeting rooms, and a banquet hall, well more than enough space for the eight hundred fanatics who now called White Spruce's their home.

A third of the town she'd grown up in were now strangers, new faces and names that gaped in rapture at

Monica and her son on the rare occasions either of them would escape cabin fever to go out in public. Eight hundred souls didn't count the reporters, part-time pilgrims, construction workers, her security detail, or the raving, sign-wielding lunatics that thought her a soulless monster bent on destroying mankind and consuming their souls.

Gerstner hadn't lied. The fallen angel had told her that in order to escape the plain of needles she had to die, and in fulfillment of that promise Libby Kamen had shot Monica in the head on the Washington Mall, under the cherry blossoms. She remembered the gun, and the flash, and nothing more until Adam, her son, barely a toddler, had cradled her and lifted her on giant wings of feathers and light, brought her to her husband and breathed life back into her.

Unharmed, her shattered mind couldn't hold the memory, but she'd seen the video a thousand times. Everyone had, except maybe a handful of isolated monks in the Himalayas who didn't have YouTube. Half a year of refusing to give interviews or go on shows hadn't dulled the world's appetite for the miracle woman and her angelic son, yet she still couldn't wrap her head around a church built to worship her little boy.

Adam sat in the living room amid a pile of play blocks, extra-large Lego knockoffs as big as his hands that even the most determined toddler couldn't swallow. If he knew of the blasphemies committed in his name, he cared less about them than trying to corral Ted in a wall of cheap plastic. The Bassett Hound, capable of destroying his prison with one shake of his head, instead lay on his back, legs in the air, head flopped to the side, snoring.

The intercom beeped. She pressed the button on the wall. "Yeah?"

"Ma'am," Aaron Walters's deep voice resonated through the hall. Usually assigned to driveway duty, his massive frame and conspicuous pistol kept most people from approaching the house. "Mr Rees is here to see you."

Most people.

"Unca Rees!" Adam clapped his hands.

"What does he want?" She let mere annoyance overwhelm the hurt and anger in her voice. Aaron had no reason to know or care about their history, save that they'd once been friends, that neither Matt nor Monica considered him a threat, and that despite both of those he wasn't exactly welcome.

"He brought a book he says might interest you. Got a weird cross on the front."

She caught herself chewing on the inside of her cheek, stopped, and rested her head against the wall. The cool surface soothed a sudden headache, if only for a moment. "Yeah, okay. Send him in. But just him."

"He's alone."

"Thanks."

She opened the front door and waited, fists on her hips, for Jason to make his way to the porch, feet crunching on the gravel and crushed stone. Graying hair shaved close to his head, he looked more a skinhead than a priest as he climbed the stairs in a tattered denim jacket, jeans, and black T-shirt. His priest's collar had disappeared with his new devotion, his pending excommunication a paperwork formality working its way through the Vatican.

He smiled and she stifled the urge to punch him, to kiss him, to thank and beat him for everything he'd done for her and put her through over a decade of love, lust, shame, and at last, friendship. If the same war raged behind his steel gray eyes, she didn't see it.

Without asking he stepped inside, turning to muss Adam's hair before handing her the book. Heavy, the suede cover had lost most of its fuzziness to leave behind cracked goatskin smoothed with centuries of fats and oils. It smelled of peppermint and cinnamon, warm and sharp.

She read the Hebrew on the front and frowned. "I ain't looking for messengers."

"There's an entry on the nephilim, toward the end, but the language is a bit archaic. You might have to find someone to—"

"I have a guy."

Rees closed his eyes, a hint of a smile touching his lips. "Of course you do."

She set the book on the counter and put her fists on her hips, all too aware of the confrontational nature of the gesture. He wouldn't get the slightest pretext to extend his stay, not while the madness with the church persisted.

He said nothing, so she waited.

His degrees in psychology and divinity might help him play her, but she didn't need a college education to battle an obsessed recovering alcoholic, priest or no. They shared far too much ground on that score.

He broke, as she knew he would. "Aren't you going to look at it?"

"Maybe later." Curiosity burned through her, but she didn't let it touch her face. "I'm a bit more concerned with what made you bring it here."

"Couldn't I just be—"

"No. You don't need excuses to come here, except that now you need an excuse, and this book was it. So what? What do you want, *Father?*" A small part of her shuddered at his hands and lips on her skin, a memory dredged through a long-fought haze of methamphetamines and alcohol, buried by time and guilt and a renewed loyalty to her husband.

"I just thought you might like—"

"What I'd like is for you to stop that atrocity going up across the street."

He sighed. "You know I have nothing to do with that."

A flash of red shot through her vision, as close as she'd come to hate directed at another person in her whole life. "You're their *priest.*"

"Pastor. And you know that church started before I'd

joined, and would go up without me. I'm doing what I can to keep them focused on Christ's love—"

"As evidenced through my son."

"Yes." He stepped forward, breath hot on her face, stale coffee and greasy breakfast sausage lingering under the citrus tang of his aftershave. "Your son, who is a living miracle."

Eyes locked, she just managed not to slap him. "He's just a little boy."

"And you're just a dead woman he brought back to life. If that isn't divine, what is?" He followed as she stepped back, not allowing her room to recover.

"My son ain't God."

"Nobody's saying he's God, or that either of you are saints – nobody anyone's taking seriously, anyway. But he's touched by the divine. Everyone sees it. Everyone knows it. Why can't you accept what's right in front of your eyes?"

Fingertips to his sternum, she extended her hand. Wiry strength from a lifetime of martial arts forced him back a step. "What about those people across town? Those thinking him and me are demon-spawn, rescued by Satan to bring about the end of days? They've seen the same things you've seen, but they don't go thinking my boy's the second coming."

"We don't think he's the second coming."

"But you think he's a messenger."

"He *is* a messenger, can't you see—"

She jutted her finger out toward the door. "You need to go."

"Can I speak with your son for a moment?"

"Unca Rees!" Adam stretched out his arms from behind the baby gate, hands clenching excitedly, unsteady legs straddling the still-snoring Ted. Jason took a step toward the living room.

"No."

"Unca Rees!"

Another step. "He wants to say hi."

"I said no."

He turned toward her and sidestepped toward Adam's grasping hands, and she dropped into a ready stance. Cold rage surged through her, ice cracking and reforming in her blood.

"If your next step ain't toward the door, I'm going to shred your knee so bad you won't never walk right again. Might break a couple bones for good measure. Now go."

He didn't move, though his eyes flickered to her fists and feet. "I just want—"

"GET OUT!" She advanced and he scrambled back, jerking open the glass door to stumble onto the front deck. Fingertips on the handle, she forced a hostile smile. "Thanks for the book. Don't come back."

He opened his mouth to protest and she shut the door, jerking the new curtains in place to block the view to – and more importantly from – the outside. Leaning her head to the side, she pressed the intercom button as the ice in her veins thawed. "Aaron, make sure Jason makes it safely off the property. Don't hurt him unless he gives you an excuse."

"Will do, ma'am."

With a sigh she rolled her head toward the living room, where Adam pouted at the closed curtain.

"I know, little man. I like him, too, maybe more than I should. But he's gone crazy, and you don't need none of that, least not until you're older."

Adam looked at her, nodded – a gesture filled with far too much adult understanding – and flopped down next to Ted. The plastic blocks burst apart, scattering across the floor with the force of his frustration. Ted opened one eye at the telekinetic display, yawned, and closed it again.

"I know, baby. Now pick those up. Being mad ain't a reason to make a mess."

Unless he learned to control his outbursts, and they went into hiding, Adam would never have a normal life.

But she'd be damned before she let him become an object of worship.

• • •

George Needel set down his hammer and watched with everyone else as Jason Rees pulled his arm out of the jacked security guard's grip and stumbled across the street. Workers and parishioners on the ground mobbed the fallen priest, hoping for word of Adam Rowley or his blessed mother. Though obviously flustered, Rees calmed their fervor and set them back to work, the model of an effective leader with a clear mission. But George didn't care about any of that.

He kept his eyes turned toward Rees and used the excuse to track the guard. Seven steps back to the mailbox, another thirty-four to the front steps. He didn't speak into his earpiece, but did double-check the pathway around to the side deck before returning to the porch, just like after the FedEx man two days earlier and the babysitter the day before that. Routine, routine, routine.

Needel picked up his hammer with his right hand, and thrust his left into his pocket. Without looking he sent a message to Shane Keene at the Office of Planning and Development: "Mission is go."

CHAPTER THREE

The phone rang four times before it picked up, and Matt tried not to worry with each successive beep.

"Hey, baby." Monica's voice filled him with relief.

"Everything okay?"

"Sure, why wouldn't it be?"

He let out a breath. "I don't know. I just wish I could be there, what with all the commotion."

Through the wall the shower turned on, Janet making good on her promise to clean up. The flowing water garbled her voice, a murmured undercurrent punctuated by pauses – a conversation, not talking to herself.

"It's fine," Monica said, interrupting his eavesdropping. "I miss you, and the boys miss you. Ted piddled on the kitchen floor again, and Adam keeps asking where you are. Jason brought me a book with some interesting stuff in it a couple days ago, but none of it pertains to egregoroi in particular, just messengers and heralds and the like. Interesting reading, but nothing we haven't seen before."

The nephilim that had called herself Gerstner had not only freed several of the Watchers, the egregoroi condemned to the eternal pit of Tartarus for laying with human women in the time before the Great Flood, she had snapped a spell that had sent Monica to her own personal hell – or maybe someone else's hell, if she could be believed – and brought his wife back only to have her murdered weeks later. Saved by their son, Monica had poured herself into learning as much as she could about these insane, powerful beings that only Matt could stand up to and survive.

As much as he didn't want to involve his delicate wife in the violence of his job, he needed help more than ever, and of all people on the planet he knew he could trust her. And maybe Jason. Maybe. To a point.

"Well, tell him I said thanks next time you see him."

"Yeah, I'll send some muffins across the street. Or something." The flat anger in her voice made him smirk. "Hey, little man! You want to talk to daddy?"

He spent the next few minutes responding to Adam's nonsensical babble, said goodbye to his wife, and hung up. Through the wall Janet had stopped talking, instead humming through the slosh of water.

Matt the Tennessee State Trooper would have taken the downtime as an opportunity to exercise, perhaps go for a jog or visit a nearby gym. Since his augmentations had returned after Gerstner's destruction – or temporary destruction – he remained a wall of muscle well beyond the peak of human perfection without lifting a finger much less a barbell. With a sigh he sat on the bed and turned on the TV, flipping through channels to find something worth watching.

He stopped at an attractive black woman in her forties, sitting on a loveseat between two men he recognized. Ronald Kellett, a tall, wispy ghost of a man in his mid-eighties, spoke in a discordant blend of proper British and Texan drawl. "I'm not trying to be insulting, but Mr Rush is nothing more than a cult leader, and with the developments of the past months this is as irresponsible as it is dangerous. Humans must stand up for humanity, and against the inhumanity that beckons men like Mr Rush to its demonic embrace."

Matt recognized the redheaded bombshell that stood behind the leader of Humans for Humanity, the same woman that had given him a bottle of water in Kellett's office more than a year prior, and wearing the same stark white, thousand-dollar skirt-suit that showed off far too much cleavage and legs for a church-based organization.

Nigel Rush squirmed in his seat. Too tall, too thin and as pale as milk, his skin gleamed under the TV lights in contrast to his rumpled brown suit. The Ul blazed from his white tie, a circle cut with a line, each half filled with a sinuous squiggle, in embroidered red. Rush had given the symbol a name to Matt, though Matt had seen it on the head of the first egregoroi he'd encountered, before he knew about or believed in damned angels or nephilim, before he'd seen the Ul on Ben Case's crosses at Lake Barnacle, or on the tattered skin of Conor Flynn's victims.

"Y'all can call something a cult just because it's new, but naming it such doesn't diminish its power." Rush smiled, his teeth still brown and rotting despite his increased public profile, his south Georgia drawl a stark contrast to the charisma behind his voice. "More people witnessed the multiplicitous Ramiel's death at the hands of Matthew Rowley, more people witnessed his wife's death and resurrection at the hands of her divine son, more people have seen these things in real time than believe in all of Christianity. Whether or not they have embraced the truth is only a matter of time and increasing revelation, so it matters not to me whether Mr Kellett and his ilk call us a cult. His misguided prayer group is of increasing irrelevance in an age of miracles."

The moderator turned to Kellett. "Mr Kellett?"

The redhead bent low to whisper in Kellett's ear, her blouse just managing to keep the program PG-13. Kellett nodded, then creased his lips in a thin smile before speaking to the moderator, not his opponent. "And this kind of fervor is exactly why we need Humans for Humanity. Mr Rush is so convinced that these creatures are divine, but has his own research not shown us their true nature, that they are outcasts from heaven, banished for eternity by Almighty God? It has."

Rush's smile widened, revealing red sores on his gums. "Banished by God, yet here they are. If the banishment were God's will, then surely so is their return."

Kellett opened his mouth, closed it, then tried again. "You seem to take their rule as desirable—"

"Inevitable."

"—and that, Mr Rush, is why all men and women of God must oppose you. These creatures are Satanic, and you—"

Matt turned off the TV. Nigel Rush hadn't yet shown up in White Spruce, though Jason had indicated that the strange man intended at some point to make 'a pilgrimage'. In words and action Rush had yet to do anything Matt would call dangerous, but Matt would never forget the wisp of blackness writhing behind the man's pale irises.

He stripped off his shirt and tossed it to the floor on the way to the bathroom. If he hadn't needed a shower, he did now.

• • •

He emerged from the steam-filled bathroom wearing only a towel, and grunted in surprise at Janet, who sat on his bed in a cream blouse and pale blue miniskirt, legs crossed to provide the illusion of modesty while propping up her laptop. They'd given each other their room keys on a 'just in case' basis; despite each being a model of physical perfection – hers genetic, his through the magical science of Gerstner Augmentation – the attraction went nowhere beyond appreciation, and their relationship had never threatened to go anywhere past work. Matt would never cheat on Monica, and to Matt's knowledge Janet had never shown the slightest sexual interest in anybody.

"A little privacy?"

She glanced up and back at the screen. "Nothing I haven't seen. Get dressed, we're going to dinner."

He turned around, let the towel fall, and slipped into a pair of clean blue jeans. "T-shirt or polo?"

"Whatever blends in better at Denny's."

He pulled on a T-shirt and a light gray windbreaker emblazoned with the Special Threats Bureau logo, three plain letters on the Homeland Security shield. Anyone who knew of the STB would recognize him by face – despite their extraordinary funding the office consisted of Matt, Janet, and three dozen minions, and reported directly to the Director of Homeland Security. Tasked with isolating and destroying supernatural enemies of the United States, they outsourced ninety-nine percent of their intelligence and, thankfully, almost all of their paperwork to other divisions in DHS.

"All right, let's go to Denny's."

She held up a finger, then ignored him to type, nails clacking against the keys.

He knew she'd finish on her own time, so he sat on the bed and looked at the screen.

A military drone with a forty-seven-foot wingspan soared high above the Fredericksburg metro area, and from it spilled hundreds of tiny objects. Light blue, they deployed tiny iridescent wings and scattered, buzzing rooftops and clinging to walls and under windowsills to map out the area around the restaurant, including the Motel 6 where they now stood.

"I didn't realize the food was that bad."

Janet rolled her eyes. "Our contact said she'd meet us there in an hour. I assume she'll be early, and unless she's either honest or an idiot she'll bring backup. I want to know what we're walking into before we walk into it."

"That's, like, less than a half-mile from here. Coincidence?"

She shook her head. "She let me pick the venue."

"And you chose Denny's?"

Janet's glare held no humor. "The reviews for this place are wretched, even for a Denny's. Bad service, sticky tables, no soap in the restrooms. I figure we'll have a half-dozen employees and maybe that many patrons. Public enough to be a pain in the ass, but not a lot of collateral to worry about if things go south. So let's drive a while, turn around, and go to Denny's."

"How will we know her?"

She shrugged. "She said I'd recognize her."

"ICAP, then."

"I'd bet on it. She knows me and Sakura and trusted you enough to reach out. She's got to be either a former Aug or an office weenie... which narrows it down to two hundred and eight people, incidentally."

"Well," Matt pulled on his belt. "Let's go find out which."

• • •

The Dragonflies had indicated no hostiles as Matt waited a block away for their quarry to arrive. The only gunpowder residue came from a few cars and nearby hotels, and no more than you'd expect for an urban area in Virginia. No snipers hid on rooftops, and no getaway cars or spotters idled with binoculars on the restaurant.

An early-nineties Chevy Corsica pulled in, blue paint peeled back in patches to reveal white primer beneath, a clunker for which someone received no government cash. It idled in a parking space long enough for a Dragonfly to land and video the occupant. Janet tapped the screen, zooming in on the face, and thrust it into the front seat so Matt could see. "Looks familiar."

Matt nodded, pulling details from his eidetic memory as he set the car rolling. "Marcia Stein. Two classes above me. Level three musculoskeletal enhancements, five on neuro – almost as fast as Sakura. Trained at Quantico for game theory and Monterey for linguistics, took a desk job at the Farm before ICAP picked her up for field work. Stationed at ICAP HQ NYC for Augged combat, armed and unarmed; want to guess who her instructor was?"

"All right, let's do this."

Marcia had made it halfway across the parking lot before they pulled in, her gray wool pantsuit out of place against the venue and her vehicle. The whispers screamed in Matt's head, urging him to jerk the wheel sideways and run her down, then leap out and gorge on the crushed and splattered entrails. Instead he cut her off and let Janet reach forward and pop open the passenger's-side door. Even the parking lot smelled of old, half-rancid grease.

"Get in, Marcia." Janet pulled back, out of her way.

Marcia hesitated, hands clasped in front of her waist. "How long have you known it was me?"

"About twenty seconds. Now get in the car."

She got in, head brushing the ceiling of the SUV. Janet stood almost six feet, and Marcia had her by a good four inches. She kept her hands on her knees, in sight, almost relaxed with a slight quiver in long, delicate fingers.

Matt turned forward and hit the gas, letting inertia close the door, and letting Janet handle the interrogation as he pulled onto the highway heading north, toward nowhere in particular.

"Who are you working for?"

"The Shed."

"For how long?"

"Over a year."

"And in what capacity?"

"At ICAP I'd taken over for Isuji Sakura assessing new recruits in their combat abilities, grading their capabilities as they got used to their Augs. After... after she'd been reassigned to your team, Mr Rowley. I have a... similar role at OPD."

"OPD has Augmentation technology?"

She shook her head. "No, not really. They're doing a lot with exosuits and endoneuropathic implants, real clunky stuff compared to Augs but without the whispers. DNSP allows for a certain level of control—"

"DNSP?"

"Direct Neural Signal Processing. Computer-aided reflexes and muscle control. When the shit hits the fan the computer overrides your instincts to make you better, stronger, faster. Combined with a hydraulic exosuit you get—"

"Murdock Yardley." Matt kept his voice neutral.

She grunted. "What about him?"

"He had a big suit like that, and incredible reflexes."

"Huh. I thought he was in the hospital."

Janet took over again. "Do you know anyone named Keene?"

Marcia raised an eyebrow. "There's a tech named Keenan in the neurointegration lab."

"How about Shane?"

She shook her head.

Janet produced a full-color photo from a manila envelope, Shane Keene's fake FBI badge with the credentials scrubbed. "What about this man?"

"No. He might work there, but I haven't seen him."

"All right," Janet said. "Enough of that. We're happy to debrief you on everything OPD is doing later. The real reason we're here is because we want Sakura."

"I confirmed where they're holding her."

"Can you get Matt in there?"

"Not a chance. Everyone there knows what he, and you, looks like."

"Why the hell would they know me?"

Marcia shrugged. "Why wouldn't they?"

Matt stifled a growl of frustration. "Then what's the plan?"

"The place is like Raccoon City. She's on R&D, third floor below ground. They've got her restrained, but she's healing, and she's fast, and they don't even know I know she's there. You make enough noise topside, I'll get into the lab and get her free."

"They're packing a lot of hardware."

She shrugged. "Most of them are normals, and while they think they're prepared for the eventuality, they won't know you're coming. Off-site response will be at least ten minutes, maybe longer. I'm on shift tomorrow night, and the forecast calls for thunderstorms. You bring the noise, we'll meet you outside."

Janet exchanged a look with Matt through the mirror. "Sounds okay. Last question for now: you and Blossom weren't exactly friends. So why are you helping us?"

Marcia closed her eyes. "Isuji Sakura is the most formidable woman I've ever met. She broke me and built me back up like no one ever could, made me a thousand times more than I could have been without her. She's a good agent and I owe a great debt to her, and..." She swallowed. "...and no one deserves to have done what they're doing to her."

Matt closed his eyes just long enough to swallow his rage, then turned his attention back to the road.

"Okay, we go in tomorrow night."

CHAPTER FOUR

Lightning flashed as Matt released the harness and fell the last twenty feet. He extended his hand as his feet hit the rooftop, taking the first guard in the throat with the tips of his fingers before the normal had opened his eyes. The guard fell to his knees, clutching at the blood gushing from his ruined throat, as his partner finished his sentence.

"—wouldn't even call me!"

Matt spun and caught the talker with a boot to the side of the head, steel toe caving through his temple and out the back of his skull. Two orange double-triangles blipped to light gray on his HUD as thunder shuddered across the rooftop of building three, the tallest in the OPD complex.

He crumpled his parachute into a ball and stuffed it into the air vent, then spun left around the large metal to take in his next targets. Lightning flashed so he fired twice, whirled, and fired twice more, each puff of air no louder than a staple gun. He didn't care for the pre-charged pneumatic rifle, but the PCP beat conventional suppression for stealth every time, and without bothering with more than cursory aim the Dragonfly-guided smart bullets found their own targets with better accuracy than most expert snipers.

Four more triangles turned gray, the last of the rooftop snipers.

He took cover and waited, but heard no alarm, no sounds of pain or panic.

"I wonder if killing everyone counts as a diversion."

If Janet heard him over the COM, she didn't bother with a reply.

Marcia Stein took a long gulp of coffee as the clock hit nine twenty-four. "This stuff is going right through me."

Jack Castleton looked up from his computer. "Sheesh, Stein. A man's man's bladder can hold six hundred ccs. You've got to be rocking out at what, two-fifty?"

Three minutes early, but worst-case she could always visit the bathroom. "Yeah, yeah, 'man's man', all this talk of bladder size is making you irresistible."

She set down her mug and walked out as he called, "So Friday, seven-thirty? Your place?"

"Your *dreams!*" Some rumors didn't spread fast enough.

With a wave to the security guard she walked out of the training area, into the common hall, and instead of turning left to the bathroom she cut right into the stairwell. No alarms beeped, and the doors weren't locked.

To get this far you had to have passed through four layers of security and a background check invasive enough to make a proctologist squirm. Somewhere between here and Sakura's lab she'd hit a roadblock, but at that point Matt better have created her diversion.

She came out of the stairwell into a long hall blazing with fluorescent lights, peppered with sporadic doors for a hundred-odd feet before hitting a T-intersection. It smelled like hospital antiseptic and microwaved macaroni and cheese.

End of the hall, to the right, down two more flights of stairs. Sixty more feet to Gina's lab, and one more door to Sakura.

A pang of guilt tugged at Marcia's conscience. Gina meant nothing to her, but over the past month she'd come to mean something to Gina, and tonight one way or another that façade would come crashing down. A blood tech, her 'girlfriend' didn't appear to know anything about the source of the miracles she'd uncovered in her tests, had no idea of the cruelty wrought to get those samples.

She took the right and smiled at a pudgy man in blue suspenders, his wisp of a comb-over doing nothing for his frumpy appearance. He smiled back, and his head turned as she passed by, though from suspicion or a desire to check out her ass she couldn't be sure. At the bottom of the stairs Jake Farmers leaned against the door, sucking on an e-cigarette. Mint filled the enclosed space, mingling with too much aftershave.

"Hey, Jake." She stepped up to push past him and he didn't move, instead blowing vapor in her face. Her height, Gina's boss outweighed her by a good eighty pounds and liked using his physicality to intimidate everyone.

"Hey, back. Your girlfriend's not here. Might as well go back upstairs."

Marcia frowned. "She said she's working tonight. Excuse me."

Jake rolled his eyes and didn't move. "I said she's not. So why don't you take your dyke ass back upstairs where it belongs?"

Heat flushed her face. "*Excuse* me?"

He stuck the e-cigarette in his shirt pocket and spread his stance to better cover any avenue through the door. "Look, you want to munch rugs on your own time, company policy says we turn the other way. But you distract my employee when she's on the clock? Now we've got a problem."

She put her finger under his nose. "Now you listen to me: our relationship is none of your damned—"

He grabbed her wrist, smiled. Then he squeezed.

Pain shot up her arm as his fingers dug into her wrist, red-hot shockwaves over the duller throb of grinding bones. She tried to jerk free and he didn't budge – the little shit had to be more than just a middle-management employee. Through gritted teeth she said, "You're hurting me."

"Am I?" He squeezed harder, and she gasped. Jagged memories of broken wrists filled her mind, the countless times Sakura had put her down on the mat, shattered, and let her heal just to do it again. Only this time she wouldn't heal, couldn't regenerate bones in hours or days.

Through wet eyes she stared at him, pleading. "Please let go. I'll go back upstairs, leave Gina alone. Just please let go."

Instead he pulled her close, inches from his hot breath on her face. "Maybe you will and maybe you won't. Maybe instead I'll show you what a man can do for you. You have no idea what it is we—ah."

The last came out a faint gasp as hot red fluid gushed over her left hand. He looked down and she twisted the razor-sharp knife, pulled it up, jerking to draw the four-inch blade through the abdominal wall and the intestines beneath. His grip slackened even as his face deformed into an inhuman snarl. Strength, reflexes, mental acuity; the OPD had been able to recreate some of what Augs could do, but hadn't gotten anywhere close to regeneration.

"You bitch. You fucking stabbed me."

She patted his face with her now-free hand and forced the knife up further, between his lungs and under his sternum. "Sorry, Jake. I don't have time for your shit today."

Blood dribbled from his bottom lip, and his voice gurgled, speech slurred. "You fucking stabbed me."

She tore the knife free as he sat, hard, legs splayed out, back against the door. Two swipes on his shirt to clean it, she flipped it closed and put it back in her pocket. Grabbing his head with both hands, she dragged him out of the way and pushed through the door.

The blood lab sat almost at the end of the hall, and the room where they'd held and tortured Sakura for months on end just beyond it. With nowhere to go but forward, she took a step, then another, then stalked down the hall, trying to ignore the red stain soaking her blouse and pants.

A security guard stepped out of the break room, tall and dark, his lips covered with powdered sugar, a doughnut in one hand, coffee in another. His eyes widened when he saw her and his meal tumbled to the floor. He reached for his pistol.

• • •

Crawling to the rooftop, Matt took in two more targets through his sights, and waited for another flash of lightning. The whispers chittered their insatiable glee at hot metal shredding his skull and brain and he rolled to the side, warned by their psychotic precognition. Light erupted from one of the pillboxes on the ground, and bullets chipped brick from the roof where he'd been laying.

Stealth moot, he dropped the PCP and unslung his AA-12, the fully-automatic combat shotgun at home in his sure grip. The drum magazine held thirty-two rounds of fin-guided, directionally-triggerable fragmentation rounds, networked to the Dragonflies and his Friend-or-Foe system to explode behind, over, or around cover for maximum casualties with minimal fuss. And in close quarters it made an excellent club.

"Janet? Hit it."

"Roger."

The whispers urged him to kneel, back turned to the roof access door, to take the high velocity metal and bleed out on the roof. Instead he charged the door as it opened, firing two rounds through the widening crack. The twin explosions blew the metal door wide open in a shower of red meat and pink mist the moment before he leapt through.

A string of bodies lay in tatters down the first flight of stairs, urban camo smoking in the astringent air. He leapt through the acrid smoke, slid down the bannister, and took the next flight four steps at a time before bursting through the fire door into an expanse of cubicles.

"Brace for impact." Janet's voice carried with a cool lack of passion, helped by the fact that she had arranged the Air Force strike on a 'terrorist cell' from the Motel 6, where she currently sat.

Matt opened his mouth as the building rumbled, and orange flames blossomed in the distance even as the night sky brightened much closer but out of sight. He ran toward the wall of windows even as they shattered from the explosion, peppering his visor and armor with shards of high-velocity glass. His boots crunched it to pieces as he reached the edge. He leapt, crossing eighteen feet over a rising fireball to crash through into the next building.

He stepped back the moment before a man rose and fired a handgun at where his head had been. Matt snaked out and crushed the man's upper arm with one hand, turned, and threw him screaming toward the next target. A dark-skinned man in a plaid shirt collapsed under the writhing weight.

Matt leaped onto the dog-pile and punched, crushing through both bodies into the floor below. He pulled his fist from the hot, sticky mess, dusty red streamers of gore sloughing off of the hydrophobic coating on his gloves. Nothing moved.

The four Predator-pattern drones had four Hellfires apiece, and by his count each had fired one.

"Janet? Status?"

"Uh... we're getting cross chatter from Anacostia-Bolling. Someone's not happy about us commandeering their airspace. They're being ordered to stand down."

"Belay that order."

"Yeah, bud, trying." Her muttered, "dumbass" carried loud and clear through the COM.

The building shuddered, and shuddered again. And again. Footsteps.

Crouching low, he ducked behind a cubicle and took aim under the desk at door to the main stairwell. "I've got company. See what you can do."

The door exploded inward. His FoF lit up two human forms in the cloud of dust, sleek and black under infrared light. In the ultraviolet they glowed much as a human or statue might, with goggles scanning the room over raised carbines of an unfamiliar make, with short, fat barrels something between a rifle and a grenade launcher.

• • •

Marcia stumbled into the wall, bloody left hand clutching her bloody abdomen, and pointed to the stairwell with her right. "Hurry! She's getting away!"

A shrieking wail blasted thought from her consciousness, and through eyes clenched shut against the cacophony it resolved into an alarm loud enough to wake the dead. The door at the end of the hall burst open and four guards ran out, bolting past them toward the stairs.

Sugar-lips kneeled next to her. "Miss, let me see the injury. I'm an EMT."

She tried to wave him off. "No, no, I'm okay. Just go get the bitch."

He grabbed her by either side of the head, forced her to look at him. "Ma'am, I'm not asking. We're going to get you patched up, but you need to work with me."

With a deep breath she nodded. "Okay." Settling back, she took her weight with her right hand and reached into her back pocket with her left.

He tore open her shirt and scrunched his brow at her bloody but whole abdomen. Steel flashed, and his hand didn't make it to his pistol. A line of red erupted from his neck, splattering her with a stream of hot arterial blood before she shoved his twitching body to the side.

A high-pitched scream tore through the alarm, and Marcia looked up into Gina's eyes, so caring and innocent, now wide with terror and shock. Marcia jerked the gun from the guard's holster, a 9mm Glock with a detachable magazine, and choked it up.

"Gina, baby, I'm not going to hurt you. But you need to run. Now."

Gina didn't move.

Marcia stood. Gina bolted for the open lab door.

She ran. "Gina, wait!"

The door slammed closed, and the LED on the swipe-card lock went from green to red.

"Fuck!" Gina had been her ticket into the lab – an ID without a code couldn't do it, nor a code without an ID. She banged on the door with a fist. "GINA! Gina, listen to me! I need to get in there!"

The alarm cut off. She closed her eyes, listened at the door. A sob, then nothing but hyperventilation.

"Gina? Babe? I need you to open the door."

Matt fired two shots and rolled left, the triangles splitting wide on his HUD. One dove to the corner and ran straight up the wall, the other bolted right, both much faster than a normal. The microgrenades detonated, shredding drywall, rolling chairs, and computers, tangled bits of red-hot metal pinging off of cubicles and ceiling tiles.

Both men – if they were men – came up firing. Projectiles sailed from their weapons, expanding into webbing as they reached where he'd just stood. Matt fired twice around a pillar to keep them down, then rolled out and fired twice more, his foot landing in the sticky mess left behind by their weapons.

A microgrenade detonated on impact with the left man's chin, another in his torso. Chunks of bloody meat and bone splattered the ceiling and walls, leaving most of his legs and pelvis the only indication he'd once been human.

Matt ducked another web. A thin tendril of goo nicked the side of his helmet and the mass jerked him back half a step. The rest of the net fell, adhering to his left arm and back. He stretched out and it pulled like taffy before hardening. He fired another two rounds and then jerked, tearing the sole from his boot to separate it from the floor.

"Are you getting this?" He ducked behind the pillar at another shot.

"Looks like they want you alive."

"Not mutual." He rounded the corner, dove under two shots of webbing, and came up under his opponent's weapon. The barrel of his AA-12 punched through the man's abdomen and out his back, and as the body fell to the floor intestines spilled in a reek of shit and cumin that permeated even through Matt's helmet.

He slammed the hardened resin against the pillar. Twice. Three times. The concrete chipped, but the hardened goo didn't budge. The Dragonflies indicated two hostiles, large, coming up the elevator three floors below. Leaning the AA-12 against a filing cabinet, he pulled a combat knife from his belt and cut away his suit at the shoulder, hissing as the line of red appeared across his skin and then healed. He grabbed the ruptured seam and tore, peeling the hardened gunk off like a glove.

The elevator dinged, and he choked up the shotgun and fired. The projectiles entered the opening doors and exploded, showering the inside with high-velocity shrapnel. A figure stepped out, a ten-foot monstrosity of steel and hydraulics, construction-yellow paint scraped here and there from the explosion. Huge claws scissored at the end of each hand, each big enough to cut a man in half, and a .50 caliber machine gun tracked the room along with the gaze from the thing's helmet. Smaller, sleeker cousins of the suit worn by Murdock Yardley, with inch-thick armor and a portable generator it might as well have been a humanoid tank.

Which meant with a little luck he might be able to exploit its weakness before it killed him. He braced himself to charge, the whispers already keying up to the path of the incoming bullets.

It stepped out, making room for a twin behind it. Matt turned and bolted for the windows.

• • •

The bruise on Marcia's palm ached as she banged on the door. "Gina, babe, look around you. What are they doing to her in there? You have to let me in."

Something clattered to the floor, metal shelves or trays and instruments. A muffled male voice carried through the door. "Ma'am, put down the knife." He repeated himself, then, "I'm not going to ask you again."

The door beeped and the LED flashed green.

Marcia yanked it open and Gina stumbled back into her arms, narrowly missing the knife Marcia held in her right hand. She caught her, so familiar a feeling, the panicked tension so alien. A technician in a blood-spattered white coat held out a pneumatic mortician's saw, the air hose snaking up to a gantry in the ceiling.

Between them lay a steel bed, and on that bed lay suffering. Sakura's skin had been peeled back to reveal muscles underneath, and filaments of new tissue wormed their way across the bloody, naked meat. Her breasts lay in a tray to her right, misshapen light brown blobs in a pool of blood. A crack in her sternum – a thick plate three times as wide as an unaugmented human's – knitted closed as Marcia stared in horror.

Blood-slicked shackles bound her wrists and ankles, held in place with spring-pins, so easy to remove if you could push the button, impossible if you couldn't. The quarter-inch thick steel had warped over who knew how many escape attempts, and Sakura's flesh had partially healed around the metal.

The tech revved the saw and stepped forward, the blade's whine a dagger through Marcia's throbbing head.

She let Gina fall to the floor and flipped up the butterfly

knife, holding it out to the side in a stance more dramatic than practical. A sluggish shadow of her augmented self, she could still go toe to toe with the world's best normals, and the tech's shaking hands didn't radiate confidence. "I'm going to give you one chance to drop that cutter and run. If you're still here in twenty seconds, I'm going to gut you. One… Two…"

He bolted for another door as Marcia rushed the table.

She jerked one pin free, then another. Sakura sat up with a sticky, wet tearing sound, yanked the pins from her ankle shackles, and slid off the table. She put her hands together, gave a small bow then bolted for the closing door.

The tech screamed as Sakura jerked him back into the room by his hair, straightening her arm to force him down to his hands and knees.

"Please! I was only doing—"

She dropped to the floor, pulping his skull beneath her fist, and disappeared out the door before it shut, leaving only bloody footprints in her wake.

"Sakura, wait! We need…" Marcia looked down at the broken body, and back to the exit door where Gina huddled, knees to her chest. "…we need to get out of here."

The tile floor ice cold on the new skin of her bare feet, Isuji Sakura flashed through the lab, shattering refrigerator doors and demolishing centrifuges with her bare hands. She didn't bother with the computers – anything important would be backed up off-site.

Stein's voice buzzed in the background, a distraction as she shattered the next security door and tore it from its hinges. A startled guard fired two shots, slow and clumsy. She sidestepped and struck his temple with iron-hard knuckles, shattering his skull and turning his frontal lobe to useless jelly.

Snatching his pistol as he fell, she whirled and fired three shots, one each at the forms cowering behind gurneys and sample racks. Another door led to a freezer. She tore the power plug from the wall and turned, weapon raised.

Marcia Stein stood before her, hands raised.

"How many times have I put you down?" The English came to her lips unbidden, a welcome reminder that she could think and feel beyond pain and the table.

Marcia closed her eyes and gave a small bow.

"Too many to count, sensei."

"And how many times did you stand back up?" The Japanese accent rang too strong in her mind, an unwelcome side-effect of too much time without practice.

"All of them, sensei."

Sakura returned the bow. "I'm going to kill everyone here."

Marcia held up her hands. "Please, not the girl in the next room."

Sakura ran forward, too fast for a normal to see, and brought herself up beneath the white woman's gaze. "Why not?"

"Because I care for her."

Sakura closed her eyes, and only saw red. "Not good enough."

The wind from Marcia's grab brushed her hair, and the scream erupting from her throat followed Sakura into the next room. The young technician still huddled next to the door, wide eyes pretty even in her terror. She didn't have time to react before Sakura's knee crushed her trachea.

Through the door, she swept up the dead guard's pistol and swept room after room, killing seven, three with her bare hands, before reaching the stairwell up and the dead man guarding it.

"Blossom, *please!*"

Sakura turned on the balls of her feet.

Eyes filled with tears, Marcia held out both hands from

the far end of the hall. "We need to get out of here before they call reinforcements. Matt Rowley is upstairs. And he's in trouble."

• • •

A bullet grazed Matt's ankle as he hit the ground, rolled, and dove behind an industrial dumpster. The fully-automatic .50 caliber weapons overwhelmed all other sound, including his own breathing. The wound throbbed, the warm pulse turning to a burning itch as blood vessels rejoined and muscles knitted. A quick stretch told him he had full mobility.

His back to the cold metal, Matt popped the fragmentary rounds out of the AA-12, dropped the drum magazine in a satchel, and pulled out another. He slapped the UHVAPTS – ultra-high velocity, armor-piercing tungsten sabot rounds – home and chambered the first. They lacked the guidance systems of the fragmentation rounds, but a razor-sharp tungsten dart at two thousand feet per second could punch through the depleted-uranium armor of a tank, come out the other side, and lodge in the tank behind it.

He turned and aimed straight through the dumpster. Lights on his HUD directed him left and up from his initial guess, and the crosshairs flashed when the FoF locked with the Dragonfly data. He pulled the trigger and held it a full second, sending five rounds into and through the steel barrier.

The deafening roar of the .50s vanished. The ground trembled. Matt backpedaled as the dumpster crushed inward, a huge metal claw reaching over the top to shred the air an inch from his face. He spun left just before the metal smashed into the brick wall, ducking under a crushing claw and taking a metal knee to the stomach. He choked up the shotgun and got off one round before hydraulic pincers sliced the barrel short.

One exosuit stood silent and still, dark red blood spurting from its abdomen. The other body-checked him through the wall.

Bones creaked. Brick and rebar tore at his bare arm. He stumbled back and pulled out his Barrett WildStang .50 caliber pistol, a tiny smirk turning up the corner of his mouth. The metal behemoth had him dead-to-rights, but this time hadn't fired its machine gun. They wanted him alive, a critical handicap in any combat situation.

Screaming, he charged. A huge metal arm batted him to the side. He rolled with it, placing the pistol against its elbow and firing. The weapon bucked. Sparks flew.

He hit the ground in a roll, came up on his feet, and met its lumbering charge head-on. A metal claw grabbed his left wrist, jerking it wide, and held.

He fired again, same spot, and the metal dent grew.

No prisoners, asshole.

The claw closed, and blood spurted from the bloody stump that remained of his arm. Endorphins and adrenaline flooded his system, muting the pain without hiding it. A dull sheen of suppressed shock overlaid his reality without slowing it down.

He shoved the bloody mess of his wrist in the thing's faceplate, covering the bullet-proof visor with red mess, and fired again. The covering sheared free.

Flailing, blind, it clipped his bicep, shearing off a chunk of meat. He accepted the punishment and reached into the exposed gap. His fingers closed on a warm, pulsing hose. He yanked, and hot, orange-yellow fluid spurted from the ruptured tube. Its arms lifted as if to crush him to the ground, then sagged.

Matt put the pistol against the visor and pulled the trigger. A spiderweb crack spread across the reinforced polycarbonate. He fired five more times, shredding the plate and pulping the head beneath.

With a grunt, he holstered the pistol and picked up his

left hand and the chunk of meat next to it. The claw had sheared his wrist in two places, crushing the bones clean through by sheer force.

"Dammit." He schooled his breathing, forced his mind away from the maddening itch. "Status?"

"Choppers incoming," Janet said. "You've got four more of those behemoths on the south side, heading your way. They look grumpy."

"What about those drones?"

"Ordered B2B. Someone above my paygrade."

"Sakura?"

Marcia's voice broke in. "I've got her. We're coming out the East entrance, hot."

A grin split his face, and excitement coursed across his skin. "I'll meet you there."

He took off at a run, long strides eating up the rain-soaked pavement, meat held against the ruins of his wrist. Ropy tendrils of shredded flesh grasped, connected, sought their like.

A Vietnam-era jeep shrieked out of an underground garage, Marcia's double-green triangle highlighted on his HUD. Sakura stood in the back, manning an M240 machine gun wearing nothing but heavily-stained a lab coat and a lot of someone's blood. Muscle glistened in exposed patches under her light brown skin. Tracers streaked across the campus as she found a target and opened fire.

Matt veered as Marcia approached without slowing, and he dove into the back. Lurching against the seat as the jeep accelerated, he found his feet and stood, still holding the barely-connected hand against his stump.

"It's good to see you, Blossom."

She shifted sideways. "Take this." As he tucked his injured hand into his armpit and grabbed the gun she kneeled, coming up with a Stinger missile.

She readied the SAM, and he yelled, "Marcia, open your mouth!"

He hollered, "Ease!" as Sakura pulled the trigger. The force of the launch buffeted his helmet as he turned the M240 on the truck approaching from the left. The belt of ammo disappeared into the machine as the metal hammered bullets through the feed. Streaks of white light walked across the ground and along the side of the truck, painting the drab green with pinpricks red hot in the infrared.

He'd aimed for the cab, but between the careening jeep, recoil, and his severed hand, he couldn't quite manage the aim.

A fireball blossomed in the sky half a mile back. In the billowing orange light he could just pick out rotors coming free from a fuselage, and another helicopter banking wide to avoid the shrapnel. Sakura grabbed the machine gun and washed the cab of the truck in hot lead.

Their jeep skidded out onto the highway and took off, engine humming with clean efficiency as they streaked past a tractor trailer. The driver gaped at the afterimage of the fireball in the sky, and Matt searched for the other chopper behind it.

"We're not going to outrun a helicopter."

Sakura tilted the M240 up. "Don't have to. It pulled off."

Janet broke in. "I got SACLANT to pull surveillance satellites offline, thank you Roger Smith, and Anacostia-Bolling grounded the drones. They're flying blind, and so are we."

Sakura closed her eyes. "But only we know we had only one missile."

• • •

Matt gritted his teeth as Sakura scraped muscle away from the last bone. He flexed his fingers and she slapped the back of his hand.

"Be still."

He knew better than to complain. Even before her

ordeal, Sakura 'Blossom' Isuji had endured more than most could survive with a grim stoicism that rivaled that of any tree. The former Tokyo PD officer had gone undercover as a drug runner, a courier, and eventually a Yakuza enforcer, living lives filled with untold violence and pain as a ruse to destroy some of the world's worst criminal enterprises. She had no patience for complaints and even less for whines.

They'd smuggled her up the back stairs and let her shower. Janet's pajamas dwarfed her short, stocky frame, and though most of her chest had healed the flannel top still hung off her like a fuzzy blanket. The light blue penguins did nothing to offset the cold flatness in her eyes.

He let her finish and blot the wound with toilet paper, not bothering to dress it or use antibiotic cream, then flexed again. Everything worked, so he stripped down his WildStang, spreading the parts across the bedsheet to clean and oil them. Sakura stood by the window, watching the storm through the crack in the floral curtains.

"Are you okay?" He broached the subject with tactical precision – sudden and to the point.

Her eyes didn't leave the window. "I am alive."

"That's not what I asked."

"Arigato. You honor me with your concern, but it is unnecessary. I will be okay when Keene is dead and the OPD destroyed. Meantime, I am alive, and that is enough."

Nothing in his experience would ever make him think she might go to counseling. He licked his lips. "If you need to talk—"

"I don't."

"But if you do—"

"I won't. I need my knives and a replacement rifle and sidearm to my specifications, I need my standard field kit, and I need a place to sleep."

He couldn't bring himself to smile. "We can do that."

CHAPTER FIVE

Matt smiled. Monica collapsed on top of him, chest heaving, slick with sweat, her naked body quivering and tensing around him. After a long moment she settled, giggled, then nibbled his chin.

"Welcome home, baby."

He stroked her hair and breathed her in, strawberry shampoo and femininity and an undercurrent of stark worry. "It's good to be back."

They lay together, basking in the closeness another several minutes before Monica rolled off of him and padded toward the master bathroom. He watched her go, smooth curves and tight muscle, a crystal lioness, hard but brittle and so, so soft.

She kissed her fingertips and slapped her ass on the way out of the room, shattering his musing.

"Bring it back here and I will!"

She stepped back into the doorway, rolling her eyes at him. "Shush. You'll wake the little man." With a quirk of her eyebrows she disappeared around the corner.

A few hours later her mother came over for dinner, and after dinner talk turned to the growing church, as it always did.

"Those people are dangerous." His mother-in-law helped herself to another glass of chocolate milk in lieu of her typical nightcap – Monica's parents still drank, but since her recovery they never did so in front of her, and never brought alcohol to the Rowley household.

Matt nodded, as much to fill space as in agreement.

"That Rees boy ain't done nothing to slow them down, neither." Momma Walters's unapologetic white trash twang clashed with her general intelligence and insight into human nature, and traces of it still infected her daughter's speech, more when agitated. She plopped down on the couch and stretched out her stockinged legs next to Adam, who pushed a fire truck in circles on the floor.

"I wouldn't say he's done 'nothing', Momma." Monica poured another cup of coffee, decaf, cupping it in her hands and blowing on it before taking a sip. "It's smaller than it was going to be, and shorter, too. That was his doing."

Momma shook her head. "A sacrilege no matter the size. That boy should know better, raised Catholic or no. His mother must be rolling in her grave."

A thousand replies raced down Matt's synapses, only to be strangled by his brain before they blurted from his mouth, not the least of which that Jason's mother still lived on the other side of town. Instead he took a sip of coffee and let Monica handle it.

"He's just misguided. He'll calm down one of these days and move on to another project, just you wait."

Momma snorted. "I'm too old to wait."

"You're fifty-one."

A lifelong smoker and hard drinker, Monica's mother looked closer to seventy everywhere but her eyes, sharp and bright green if a bit bloodshot.

"Old enough." She leaned down and mussed Adam's hair. "You get to be old when you're a grandma, no difference how many years you seen."

Adam reached up and grabbed her finger.

She grinned.

He grinned back. "You have a little time, Nana."

Monica stiffened. Her mother froze. Matt watched her extract her hand and wipe it on her shirt. Adam steadied himself against her legs, eyes wide, a bright smile on his lips.

"What do you mean by that, child?"

"You'll get older for a while." He held her gaze, still grinning, as her perplexed look turned to a frown.

"Well I should hope so."

He let go and plopped down. Grabbing his truck, he made siren noises as he pushed it toward the cold fireplace.

Monica and Matt exchanged a look as her mom wiped her hand on her pants, a flash of distaste adding another decade to her prematurely-aged visage. "From the mouth of babes…"

Matt's work phone buzzed, so he excused himself and walked into the hall leading to the rear deck. Ted looked up from the middle of the floor, tail thumping twice before settling back into a light snooze. He stepped over the dog and swiped his thumb over the fingerprint reader.

Unknown Name. Unknown Number.

His government-issued, CIA-grade antivirus and anti-spyware program nuked anything that even looked like a cyber-threat from orbit, so he opened the message.

WISH U WERE HERE

Three crosses burned, each with the crossbar set at a different height. The highest for Jehovah, the middle for Lucifer, and the lowest for Satan, his throat hitched at recognition of the idols of Ben Case's weird Process cult in flames. Illegitimate son of Manson devotee and lover Katie Krenwinkle, Case had founded his pacifist, ascetic, free-love religion as a spinoff of Manson's spinoff of Scientology, rejecting his mother's violence to live in weird, vegan peace on the shores of Lake Barnacle, Georgia. He'd run his family for decades without much incident, with only occasional harassment from law enforcement and a murderous visit from Conor Flynn as exceptions.

Whacked-out freaks who all took the name Ben or Katie, still it pained Matt to see their crosses on fire. The ancient wood had borne the Ul, the mysterious symbol that had come to identify Gerstner's influence through the ages, from ancient Mesopotamia to the murder cults of the Aztecs, and they had stood for as long as records went back.

He stepped out on the deck, holding the door as Ted dashed past him to bark at squirrels in the underbrush, and pulled up the number for the Lake Barnacle PD. A two-man operation happy to cooperate with federal agents on the once-in-a-blue-moon occasions they might call, he'd dealt with them only once before. It rang six times before a male voice picked up, heaving and out of breath.

"Sheriff. Sheriff's office. Sheriff speaking."

"Hi, Sheriff Jaus? This is Matt Rowley from the Special Threats Bureau. I came down last year—"

"I remember. Murder at the Compound. We dug them up, but didn't find enough evidence of a homicide."

Matt already knew, and hadn't been surprised when the results had come across his desk. With years to decompose, a raped and skinned body would have been nothing more than bones.

"Thanks, but that's not why I'm calling. Is there any evidence of a fire out there tonight?"

A pregnant pause, then, "Tonight? No sir. Sky was pretty bright out that way a few nights ago, lots of smoke and so forth, but nothing tonight, no."

He closed his eyes. "Did you… investigate?"

"No sir. If the Prophet wants an investigation, he'll invite us in. Otherwise they handle their affairs in-house and we leave them right alone. Figured they was having a bonfire is all."

"Do me a favor and make a run by, see if everything's normal. As normal as they get."

"Can do. Take maybe thirty minutes. Call back at this number?"

"I'd appreciate it."

The line clicked dead, and Matt opened his eyes. A splash of color in the infrared spectrum, Ted frolicked on the edge of the yard, rustling in the leaves, sniffing after rodents he'd never hope to catch even if he lost five pounds.

"Ted! Come!" He used to let the dog roam the property, but recent reports of cougar sightings made Matt wary of leaving him out at night too long. The Tennessee Department of Environment and Conservation claimed cougars no longer existed east of the Mississippi, but Kevin Bartell and Deputy Broadbent had both claimed sightings in the county, and he'd never known either man to be a liar.

Ted charged the stairs, tripped on his ears on the way up, and landed sprawled out on the deck, tongue lolling out the side of his mouth.

"Good boy." Matt scratched him behind the ears and let him scramble inside, following the berserk tail around the corner into the living room.

Monica raised an eyebrow, her expression an exact copy of her mother's.

He shrugged. "Work."

"Of course," they said in unison.

Monica frowned. "You just got home."

He rubbed his temples, glad that his wife didn't know one of the hands rubbing hadn't been attached two days prior. "Don't I know it."

"They work you too hard, young man." Momma's voice cut like a knife through what little peace the rubbing had brought him.

"You're not the first to think so."

They put Adam to bed and finished dessert. Momma said her goodbyes before Sheriff Jaus called back fifty minutes later, his voice shaking over the line.

"Rowley? I think y'all want to come down here."

"Oh?" He snuffed any concern from his voice, lest Monica overhear while brushing her teeth.

"Yeah, they're dead. All of them."

"Roger that."

Silence carried for a moment, then, "You don't sound too surprised. Maybe you want to tell me why that is?"

"A bad feeling, I guess."

"So what prompted the call about the fire?"

"We'll debrief on-site. Tomorrow morning work for you?"

"All right. We'll be here all night. My best to your wife and son."

"Sure." Too many people knew too damned much about his family, thanks to impossible events, ever-present video-recording devices, and an exuberant press. He hung up the phone and texted Blossom. "Helipad at 05:00."

Then he called Janet. "Hey, something happened at Lake Barnacle. A lot of people dead. You want to come down, or handle things from there?"

Janet lived in Maryland a short jaunt from DC, but the Special Threats Bureau owned three demilitarized attack helicopters for transport purposes and could commandeer whatever else they needed on Matt's authority.

"I'll meet you there. Tonight, or tomorrow?"

"I'm meeting Sakura at five hundred hours, to get there at dawn."

"You bastard."

"G'night."

Hands wrapped around his waist, gentle and freezing cold. "Leaving so soon?"

The whispers urged him to leap back, smash her to jelly against the stonework fireplace and feast on the twitching remains. A softer set of voices, cool white and full of love and compassion, intertwined with them. Jade and white, they filled him to bursting.

He leaned back into his wife's embrace, careful not to press her into the wall. With his augmented strength every movement had to be scripted, from petting the dog to making love to shaking hands. "Sorry, Mon. This shouldn't take too long."

She buried her head between his shoulder blades. "Days or weeks?"

"Hours, if I'm lucky."
"Just come back safe."

• • •

The helicopter touched down on the far side of the shoreline next to its twin, a jet black Zulu Cobra emblazoned with STB in plain letters, lacking only the weapons systems of its military-service counterparts. Janet wandered through the charred remains of tents and lean-tos, tiptoeing around severed limbs and chunks of bodies in a windbreaker and combat boots. Thousands of small yellow flags littered the ground, the droppings of a flock of forensics technicians, some of whom stood at the edge of the water with Sheriff Jaus and his deputy, a buff twentysomething whose name Matt had never learned. Their pale faces and haggard expressions betrayed a night of unrelenting horrors ground down to monotony by the sheer scale of their task, and their blazers bore the marks of six different counties.

Sakura beat him out the door and around the pond, flashing from scene to scene, a blur in human form not bothering to hide her abilities. The normals watched her with a mix of curiosity and awe – everyone 'knew' Augs were a thing of the past, as useless as Jade, with the sole exception of Matt Rowley.

Jaus put out his hand as Matt approached through a stinking miasma of shit, rot, and smoke. The sheriff squeezed too hard, and Matt returned it pound-for-pound.

"No press?"

Jaus spat. "We're keeping them outside the gate. Caught two sneaking through the woods around three. They know it's bad from the birds, just don't know how bad, yet." As the helicopters powered down, hundreds of crows and dozens of vultures closed in, circling above or diving down from the trees.

"How bad?"

"Sixty-seven casualties; men, women and children. No sign of Case, far as we can tell, though some are harder to identify than others. Most died of some combination of blunt trauma and dismemberment. Long with the birds, coyotes and foxes been working the mess a few days, which don't help the lab techs none, but bug analysis puts time of death at four days ago, same time as the fire."

DHS put the text message at an hour before he got it, from a pre-pay cell phone purchased at a Walmart in Columbia, South Carolina. Surveillance records showed a white man in a gray hoodie that couldn't manage to contain a giant light-brown afro. Ben Case. After the purchase he'd smiled straight at the camera and blown a kiss.

Matt told Jaus what he knew, and showed him the security footage.

Jaus grunted. "I've known Ben Case since he was your age, Rowley, and he ain't never smiled like that. Never."

"What do you mean?"

"Weird a bug as you're ever like to meet, but that boy didn't have a cruel bone in his body."

From their one meeting, Matt couldn't disagree with the assessment.

Matt pocketed his phone. "So what's your take?"

Jaus raised his eyebrows, eyes locked on Matt's. "You're the man's got an inside track with the almighty. Why don't you tell me?"

Feeling himself flush, Matt suppressed a snarl and instead shook his head. "You've got that wrong, Sheriff. My boy's just a boy, and as grateful as I am that she's safe and sound, my wife is the same woman she's always been, proud and stubborn and just a woman."

Jaus broke his gaze. "Not what I've heard."

"Then you've heard wrong."

"I guess I'll have to take your word for it." The Sheriff picked up a flat rock, hefted it, and spun it out over the lake. It skipped four times before disappearing into the water, and in that moment Matt remembered the alligators and took a step back.

"What you worried about?"

Matt nodded at the water. "Gators."

"Ain't no gators in Lake Barnacle."

"I saw one take a bird on my last visit."

Jaus spat. "You saw wrong."

Matt conjured the image, a perfect recollection from his eidetic enhancements. A sudden ripple, a flight of squawking birds, bloody white feathers on the water. Ben Case had seemed unperturbed by the disturbance, but had confirmed his suspicion of alligators. "Maybe I did, but Case thought so, too."

Jaus spat again. "Case thought lots of things. Ain't but two or three were true."

Janet peeled off blue latex gloves as she sauntered up, returning the sidelong looks from the techs and young deputy with just the right amount of totally inappropriate and out-of-place interest. She blew a purple bubble, sucked it back into her mouth, and chewed it a few times. "Morning, Rowley."

"Janet." He nodded. "How long have you been here?"

She shrugged. Jaus answered for her.

"Miss LaLonde arrived not three hours after your call last night. She's been here all night, helping the forensics crews tag and catalog."

Matt smiled a smile he didn't mean. If Janet had any forensics training, he hadn't been aware of it. "Good of you. What have we learned?"

"Dead people smell bad."

"Sure. Anything useful?"

Pointing at one of the techs, she blew another bubble, pierced it from the inside with her tongue, and let it deflate before chewing it back in. "Mac here figures the wounds were caused by bare human hands, and the only people we know of capable of doing that kind of damage are you and Sakura, and both of you have firm alibis."

Jaus grunted. "There's a dog loose in the wood."

Matt turned to him. "What?"

"Watership D— never mind. Book reference."

"Okay." He turned from the sheriff back to Janet. "Anything else?"

"Nope." She turned so that nobody else could see her, and winked. "Pretty fucked up."

"Yeah, okay."

They spent the next fourteen hours going over the scene, analyzing pictures, discussing theories, and dealing with the FBI, who'd shown up just after midday and tried to pull rank before Matt shut them down and relegated them to an advisory and assistance role. The evidence pointed to superhuman or supernatural threats, and that made the scene Matt's jurisdiction.

That night they sat down to dinner at the closest diner, fifteen miles away, the Alligator Moon Hotel long-since out of business despite having been the only place for lodging or food in Barnacle Township. Katie's Koffee Kup offered a simple menu of southern comfort food. Sakura ordered enough food for three people, and Matt enough for five, including three chicken-fried steaks and two baked potatoes.

Janet came back from the bathroom and slid in next to Matt, leaving the other side of the table for Sakura. Janet ordered a Coors Lite – the only beer on the menu – a chili dog, and collard greens with black beans. As soon as the waitress left she tapped the table with a fingernail. "Kanji, right?"

Sakura nodded.

"What's it say?"

Matt looked from Sakura to Janet. "What's what say?"

A paper appeared on the table in front of Sakura, too fast for Matt to follow. "The bodies make a poem. It's not right, like a new student who translates a song. The Japanese is very bad."

"What's it say?"

"It says four lines, with one repeating between. It even sort of rhymes before translation, in a Western manner. 'The boy will join the parents in death; prepare, the master will arrive; the prostitute's brother will leave her in dishonor and shame; prepare, the master will arrive; power will not withstand true power; prepare, the master will arrive; the correct way is the correct way.'"

Janet snorted. "What the hell does that mean?"

The waitress arrived with their drinks: coffee, Coors, and hot water. Matt sipped his coffee, dark and robust and much better than he'd expected.

"You both remember Conor's tattoos." It wasn't a question. Conor Flynn's body had been covered with human-blood tattoos under his clothes, one for each victim, including his wife and son. In dozens of languages, each one had read, "Be ready, the master comes."

Sakura nodded. "Yes, the repeating line could interpret the same."

"Right is right," Janet murmured, Conor's favorite saying.

Matt grew cold. "Blossom, could the last line mean, 'Right is right?'"

She shook her head. "Only if the person is very bad at Japanese."

"Conor had some vague proficiency," Janet said. "Maybe he—"

"Conor's dead." Matt turned to glare at her. "I crushed his brains with my own hands, and I watched as they autopsied and then incinerated his body. He's very, very dead."

She sucked in a breath through her teeth. "I think we both know that's not as permanent as it used to be, bud."

Matt scowled. They ate in silence, aware of but ignoring the stares from the customers and employees, who seemed to think strangers a special form of entertainment. After dinner Janet excused herself to the restroom, and Sakura slammed her hand down on the table.

"She was there, many hours. Why?"

Matt raised his hands, defensive. "I don't know. Keeping an eye on the locals, I guess."

"No. She would have said before she left."

"She's had our back since day one, Blossom."

"She is secretive. Do not forget why she joined ICAP, who she worked for and with. She knows many things she did not reveal, and I am certain she knows much more. Her agenda is not ours, and her loyalty lies with her brother."

Matt opened his mouth to say that Dawkins was dead, and closed it. Janet had never done anything to make him doubt her loyalty, and though her allegiance lay first and foremost to her brother, Dawkins had, in the long run, turned out to be right about the demonic corruption behind Jade and ICAP. "You're right."

"So you don't trust her."

He shook his head. "I do."

"A mistake."

"I'll be careful."

"You must."

• • •

Janet locked the bathroom door and pulled a vial from her purse, setting it on the chipped tile next to the sink. Scooping a nail-full of gray powder from the plastic bottle, she held it under her nose and snorted it. A black haze filmed over reality as the dried, mummified flesh poured its psychic energy into her, forming a fragile, tentative bridge between life and death.

"Sister, help." Her brother's voice cracked with pain and desperation, a ghost of will broken down by madness and loss. "I need… I need something to take the edge off."

"You need to fight, D. Someone made a bridge, found his way back. If he can do it, you can do it."

"We tried. We tried and it didn't work. I just need something to take the edge off."

The trap Janet had laid to free her brother had been designed to trade Matt Rowley's soul, but had instead ensnared his wife, plunging Monica into a hell meant for Janet's brother, an endless plain of broken hypodermic needles with just enough smack to taste, but never enough to remove the desperate craving. Janet had seen it, felt it, drowned in it for the split second before Gerstner had shattered the spell, freeing Monica and plunging Dawkins back into the hell she'd reserved for him, an act of spite from a creature with eternity to waste.

"We almost made it, D. And we can again. You can escape from that side."

"I don't need to escape, I just need—"

"GODDAMMIT." She flinched, pulling her fist back from the broken mirror, knuckles a bloody mess from the impact. "You don't need drugs, you need to come back to me."

His sensation faded, and as it did she took a moment to clean up her bloody nose, powder her face and wash her hands. How the strongest man she'd ever known had become such a useless coward she would never understand. But coward or no, she would free her brother, no matter what it took.

• • •

Straddling the man tied to the chair, Conor Flynn grabbed his victim's nipple with a pair of pliers and twisted, tearing the soft flesh from the muscle beneath. Blood welled in the open wound and Conor sucked at it, chewing through exposed meat with Ben Case's half-rotten hippy's teeth. It tasted like chicken-fried steak and baked potatoes, a living man's banquet on a dead man's tongue.

Writhing and screaming through the towel duct-taped over his mouth, the man's anguish shuddered over the psychic bridge, shoving back the crushing weight that threatened to snap it. Conor did the other nipple, then seared both wounds closed with the soldering iron, flicking red droplets onto the living room rug between passes to let the metal tip come back up to temperature.

Hot smoke wafted up, succulent charred flesh and acrid burnt hair, and Conor sucked it in, fed it to the bridge, always hungry, drowning in thirst. He had had no idea it would be so demanding.

The woman – wife, girlfriend, or mistress, Conor neither knew nor cared – lolled in her own chair, the remains of her face a gnawed, ruined mass of cauterized red. The dark sockets of her eyes didn't even twitch, and her breathing came too soft, too regular. Useless until she woke up. Their boy lay crumpled on the floor, limbs twisted at odd angles, eyes staring at the black nothing the righteous and innocent got when they died.

Useless forever.

The bridge didn't care about life or death. Only pain kept it open, and every day it demanded more.

He patted the man's cheek then drew the pliers in a line down his jaw. "Sorry, pal, might is right is might, and you're the awake one so it's still your turn."

The man murmured. Flynn leaned in, tore off the tape, and pulled the cloth out of his mouth. "Try again?"

"Just don't hurt her anymore."

The revelation smacked him upside the head. Flynn smiled. "Thanks. Brilliant idea. I hurt her, you do the suffering, the bridge stays open."

"No, please. I—"

He stuffed the gag back in place, ignoring the vain attempt to bite his finger, cut the rope holding the woman's left hand, and lifted it to his mouth. The man whimpered as Conor sucked her index finger, and screamed through the gag as he bit down, grinding his teeth until the first knuckle gave way. He pulled back, swallowed the meaty nugget whole, and giggled.

She felt nothing, but her lover's anguish bled through like an open wound.

The bridge sighed in pleasure, and strengthened. Across its expanse, figures moved in the darkness, attracted to the light and life on the other side. Flynn shooed them away with a flick of his mind, and took another bite.

After a moment's thought he closed his eyes, stretched his mind across the bridge, and called them back. "Right is right, boys. Maybe I've got a use for you."

CHAPTER SIX

"What do we have?" Matt shifted his weight to accommodate the helicopter's sudden bank.

Though Janet sat right next to him, her voice carried through the headset more than through the air. "Local PD put someone matching Case's description on Ambrosio José Gonzales Court last night at eighteen hundred hours while we were finishing up at Lake Barnacle. It's hard to miss that hair."

Seven miles from the Walmart where he'd purchased the phone, Gonzales Court continued the century-old tradition of naming cul-de-sacs, highways, and bridges after heroes of the American Confederacy, only in this case the cul-de-sac consisted of a quarter-mile loop enclosing a small park little more than half a basketball court and a shoddy, rust-studded playground. Single and double-wide trailers ringed the loop, half hidden under a canopy of trees just beginning to turn.

"Anywhere from there?"

She shrugged. "Not that they know."

The helicopter touched down in the center of the track, and they disembarked to a growing crowd of curious onlookers ranging from naked toddlers to gray-haired men stooped with age, all spilling out onto stoops and into lawns to gawk at the commotion. A pit bull charged, a black and orange brindle dragging a chain still attached to a pinch collar, a shirtless black kid in his early teens chasing after it. It reared up under the rotors, barking and snarling and leaping into the air.

Matt took one look at the berserk nub of a tail and grinned, holding out his hand and stepping forward. The dog barked again and shied back, dropping low on its front legs before bounding a few steps back. The boy skidded up and grabbed its collar, jerking the animal away from the dying noise of the rotors. His suspicious brown eyes darted from Matt's pistol to Sakura's, and down to the dog.

Matt crouched to his haunches. "He friendly?"

"Yeah. Ain't never seen a helicopter, though. You a cop?"

Matt shook his head. "Federal Agent. But don't worry, I won't hurt him. What's your name, boy?"

The boy approached, the pit pulling at the chain despite the collar until he could slobber his wide, pink tongue over Matt's fingers and palm. "He's Booger, I'm Chris."

Matt let the dog lick his face, then stood. "Nice to meet you, I'm Matt."

"You're the guy with the kid."

Biting his tongue, Matt pulled his phone from his pocket. "That's me." He brought up the image of Case smirking at the camera. "Have you seen this guy around?"

Chris shook his head.

"You sure? Cops spotted him out this way last night."

Chris shrugged. "You don't forget a fro like that on a white man. He dangerous?"

"Very. Thanks." Matt approached the gathering crowd, phone in the air, while Sakura circled toward the trailers behind them. "We're looking for this man. Caucasian, six feet, brown curly hair. If anyone—"

"I seen him." A scrawny white man with hair the color of corn silk stepped forward, thumbs hooked in the belt loops of his dingy jeans, torso almost covered by a threadbare Confederate Flag T-shirt emblazoned with 'Keep It Flying' in peeling white letters. "On my way back from the store, hitching a ride from Terri Deuel."

"Which way?"

"North."

"And what do they drive?"

"Minivan. Kind of dark red."

Matt asked for the spelling and put 'Terri Deuel' into his phone, leaching information from government databases and public records in a fraction of a second. He looked at the pilot and spun his finger in the air. As the rotors started churning he thanked the man and got on-board, pulling on his headset to relay information to Sakura and Janet even as they boarded and took their seats.

Bobby Deuel, eight years old, had been marked absent at school that morning. A phone call home resulted in no answer. Matt tried, then called Jason Deuel's work. He hadn't reported in to work, a first in three years of employment.

As the chopper landed in their yard a few minutes later, Matt took note of the Deuel's maroon minivan and gray sedan in the driveway. A yellow, vinyl-sided two-story colonial with black shutters on a half-acre yard, they had no neighbors within a half-mile, and a small, rusty playground in their back yard complete with a sandbox and slide. No one came out to look at them as they circled twice.

Matt left his helmet under his seat in favor of an ear bud – without a swarm of Dragonflies relaying data to it, the helmet would do more to restrict his vision than protect his head – and with the possibility of collateral targets he opted for the REC7 rather than the AA-12.

The 5.56mm rounds of the NATO-issue REC7 didn't have the impact or versatility of the AA-12's multiple loads, but at Matt's insistence the STB still used ceramic composite 'bonk killer' rounds. ICAP's collapse left several million boxes on shelves all around the world, and Janet had managed to appropriate most of them before the reality of the egregoroi threat had quashed any relief at the disappearance of bonks. Every round had been blessed by as many religions and creeds they could find, with no idea whether any of it helped.

Sakura opted for a REC7 as well, supplemented by a .357 and a pair of monofilament knives, sharper than the sharpest steel.

They hovered next to the driveway, downwash scattering leaves across the well-manicured lawn in eddies of mixed brown. Matt and Sakura leapt out, then the pilot banked upward, carrying Janet away from any potential hostilities.

He approached the front door, scanning for threats, while Sakura disappeared around the back.

"Back is clear, door is locked."

He peeked inside, and didn't bother to ring the bell. Congealing blood slicked the floor in a smear of black-red. At least three bodies lay in heaps in the living room, entrails strewn about the furniture like holiday garlands. They shimmered a dull red-black in the infrared, no warmer than their surroundings.

"Sakura, to the front."

She appeared at his side a second later. "I see it."

"Janet, we have multiple casualties. Call FBI for forensics support, and get local PD to set up a perimeter. Tell them no leaks."

"Roger. Tactical assist?"

"Hold off." Since augmentation, he'd never found a hostile situation that would be improved by the addition of normal friendlies, but to the book Janet asked him every time.

He tried the doorknob. It turned, so he opened it and spun inside, raising the REC7 as Sakura passed him, disappearing into the kitchen area in a blur. He rolled right, cleared every room on the ground floor, and met her at the bottom of the stairs.

Nose crinkled at the acrid, almost burnt smell overlaying the blood and shit, she looked down at the bodies.

"Upstairs is clear."

Blood covered the wooden floor, soaking the woven

rug under the coffee table and running under the couch, TV console, and bookshelf. Two wooden chairs sat in the middle of the room, facing each other, loops of wire around the front legs and armrests. The mutilated bodies lay in pieces, so mangled that only the general shape remained to identify a leg, a torso, or a skull. Red-brown streaks covered the walls, occult symbols and archaic or made-up writing in human ink.

"Meaning?" Sakura asked. Though brilliant and quick-thinking she didn't possess Matt's eidetic memory enhancements.

"It's gibberish. Wiccan here, Druidic there, a little Aztec, even some Process Church, but none of it goes together. It's like something you'd find in a high school poser's notebook."

"So we go outside."

He took another look around. "Yeah. Wait for the techs to tell us what happened, here."

The mutilated skull next to the couch opened its eyes.

Matt shied back, raised his rifle. "Watch it!"

Sakura spun left, weapon up, and scanned the room. "What?"

A bubble rose out of the bloody mess, expanded, growing ever more translucent, then popped. The curtains danced, pushed around by an impossible wind. The blood receded, pulling in toward the skulls lying in the red pool.

"Fall back." He backpedaled toward the door, careful not to step in the shifting gore.

Meat surged upward, pulsing and solidifying around a growing column of blood topped by the three skulls. Jaws flexed and silent screams pierced Matt's mind, an unheard shriek of mad suffering. He opened fire, and Sakura joined him.

A skull shattered in a mess of brains and bone. Holes appeared in pink muscle, punching straight through to pepper the wall behind, and red-brown liquid leaked from the wounds.

Brimstone filled Matt's nostrils, burnt matches and rotten eggs, and the psychic shriek became physical. Jarring dissonance filled the house, shooting through his teeth and up his spine, a white-hot dagger to his temples.

A ropy mass shot from the pillar of meat, and Sakura moved. Her form blurred around it, and streams of old blood splattered the ceiling before her rifle hit the floor. Matt fired at the base of the tendril, punching black holes through the knot of tissue.

The thing twisted, four more arms springing free from the growing tower, which now brushed the ceiling. Chunks of recognizable flesh stuck out of the amorphous mass, bone and gristle, ribs, a small hand with dirty fingernails. Matt fired into it, and direct hits on the column did nothing. He took aim at an unrecognizable face, ears, nose, and lips cut off, skin burned away in blackened lumps.

His rifle barked. The head disintegrated, but the wailing didn't quiet. "Sakura, get out of there!"

Sinuous ropes lashed out, wrapped the muzzle of his REC7. Meat sizzled against the hot metal. He pulled the trigger. With a sharp hiss the weapon bucked. Streams of metal peeled away from cooking flesh, the barrel a wasted ruin. Hot muscle enveloped his wrist as he grabbed his WildStang. It squeezed, grating bone against bone, the sharp pain a reminder of his injury earlier in the week.

Blackness blurred across his wrist, and monstrous flesh fell away in bloody strips. Before he could react Sakura had already moved on, spinning and ducking, black-bladed knives leaving trails of devastation in their wake.

He raised the pistol and fired, .50 caliber bullets blasting holes in the inhuman form. A tendril grabbed his ankle. Then the other. Still firing, his muscles strained against the pressure, but it pulled him closer to the wall of meat.

The pistol clicked dry. He let go and it sucked from his hand, disappearing into the creature.

Boots hard against the floor, he pushed back. A wet ripping sound accompanied renewed freedom, and he shifted back half a step, and then another. His legs burned with the effort, cramping with the effort to shift back again.

It released him, and he fell backward.

The column fell with him, a thousand pounds of dead weight pushing, reaching, tearing at his armor, clothes, and flesh. Warm, squirming tentacles wormed their way up his nostrils, pushed past his teeth and tongue down his throat. The slimy film on them tasted like rot and shit. His lungs burned as he tried to suck in a breath, eyes squeezed shut against unrelenting pressure, trying not to throw up.

Stars formed in his vision. Fire scorched his lungs as he wormed his left hand toward his belt.

His chest armor tore free, composite plates coming off in sections, replaced by hot, pulsing meat. Skin split as tendrils writhed over his fused breastbone and ribs, worming their way across his body, searching for purchase, tearing his clothes and weapons from him. A shudder wracked him as a knot of gristle punctured his abdomen.

Red cracks formed across his vision, and the shrieking wail turned to triumph.

His thumb hooked a metal ring as the pulsating wall of meat sucked in the orb attached to it. Tension pulled at the ring, then released.

A shockwave pulsed through the fleshy thing.

It shuddered, and its grip slackened. Matt forced his arms up, grabbed at the slick, ropy masses smothering his face, and pulled. Fire blazed up his throat, sliding out his mouth and nose. He gagged, turned, gasped in a breath.

The air reeked of body odor and blood, a salty funk that clung to his nose and tongue. He sucked it in greedily, took another breath, and squirmed up, boots clawing for purchase against the wooden floor.

Hands grabbed his, small but strong, and heaved him half of the way out.

Sakura stood above him, face drenched in blood, and re-drew her knives. Missing her left ear and half her scalp, white bone shone through a sheen of red that spilled down her face and neck to drench the tattered remains of her shirt. Without looking away from the monster she said, "You're alive."

He nodded, rolled to his stomach, and did a pushup, hauling his body from the floor and out from under the gelatinous, disintegrating mass. Flatulent bursts of air escaped from it as the meat softened and collapsed into a steaming, sticky-looking goo. "Only just."

Her eyes flickered up and down his drenched body, from his shredded jeans to his missing shirt and everything in-between. "Grenade?"

The ring, still around his thumb, fell to the floor. "Yeah. I don't think it had the stomach for food that spicy."

"It. Was that Case?"

"I don't think so." He nudged a skull fragment with his boot. "I think it was the Beuels. But Case was here."

"We think."

Nodding, he leaned his head against the doorframe, careful not to disturb any of the writing more than they already had. "Yeah. We think."

They kept watch on the collapsed mess until forensics showed up, Janet handling the local PD in the meantime. Five hours later a mob of men and women swarmed the house behind the forensics photographers, clear plastic coveralls protecting every inch of skin, hair, and clothing as much as the crime scene.

At last satisfied the creature wouldn't spring back to life, they rode to the local PD in the back of a prisoner-transport van, showered, changed into borrowed clothes, and debriefed.

Three days later they'd bagged, tagged, photographed, sampled, and compiled every piece of evidence. The writing on the wall meant nothing as far as anyone could tell, and no clues led to Ben Case's whereabouts. With no leads and a national APB out on Case, they headed home.

CHAPTER SEVEN

Monica frowned at the small TV under the kitchen cupboards, eyes locked on the captions scrolling across the screen. Hands covered in flour, she stopped cutting Crisco into the biscuits to watch as picture after picture showed the gory scene and occult writings from South Carolina. As they wheeled out to the waiting ambulances, nothing in the body bags resembled bodies.

When they switched to commercial she turned to Matt, leaning against the counter, cup of coffee in his hands, and spoke in a low voice so as not to wake Adam. "That was you, wasn't it? Why you were gone?"

A sip of coffee gave him a moment to formulate a reply, and swallow his anger at the sloppiness of the FBI investigators to let the pictures leak. Strong enough to strip paint, the black brew didn't quite burn his tongue. He settled on the truth. "Yup."

"My God, baby. What happened?"

He shrugged. "Some bad things. The news has a lot of it wrong, and what they don't know, I—"

"—can't talk about." She wrapped him in a hug. "This is getting crazy."

He took another sip, careful not to spill it on her head. "What?"

"Everything. It's like the sky is falling in slow motion and there's no way to stop it."

A well-timed grenade had stopped some of it, but he couldn't tell her that. Instead he kissed her forehead, set down the coffee, and wrapped his arms around her. Over the tree line a crane swung another six-by-six in place. They'd been pouring concrete footers for two days, sinking the posts into the ground as a foundation for their steeple. Or watchtower.

"The only thing that's important to me is that you and Adam are safe. If the world burns around us, then it burns. But we're going to be okay."

She squeezed harder, then let him go. "Yeah, we will. So what's next?"

He shrugged. "I have a meeting with Sakura and the woman who helped us get her out this afternoon. There's going to be fallout, and it's hard to say when or what."

"Is she okay? I mean, from what you said they did terrible things to her. She has to have PTSD."

He shrugged again. "If there's anything I know about Sakura, it's that she's the toughest bitch on the planet. She's had PTSD her whole life, and channels every stray emotion into duty. Her sense of selflessness is stronger than in anyone I've ever known."

Monica rolled her eyes. "Baby, they kidnapped and tortured her for months right after she lost her daughter. There's no way she's okay."

He held up his hands. "You want to talk to her about it?"

"I could." She raised her voice at his smirk. "I *could.*"

"You're going to wake the baby. And any time you want to have Sakura over to talk feelings, let me know and I'll invite her."

"Maybe I'll do that, and then we'll have a girls' night out."

"Riiiight. And I'll go out with the Pope and Dalai Lama for some hookers and blow."

Her slap caught him off-guard, and the whispers urged him to channel the sting in his cheek to a murderous rage, to take off her head and beat the dog and their son to death with the skull. He raised his fingers to his cheek and lowered his eyes.

"Sorry, Mon. Not something I should joke about." The callous sense of humor popular among the military and law enforcement didn't mesh well with marriage to a recovering addict, and he had no one to blame but himself.

Tears in her eyes, she gave a curt nod. "Yeah. I'm going to get the baby."

When the bedroom door closed he muttered, "Dammit."

Ted snoozed next to the fireplace, flopped on his side, ears splayed across the stone. Matt kneeled and picked up a tennis ball, the green felt rubbed almost smooth over most of the surface.

"Ted, you want to go outside?"

His head snapped up with a sneeze, and he rolled to his feet. Little legs carried him at high speed toward the door, which Matt opened just in time to avoid a collision. He stepped out and winged the ball toward the bushes, and Ted trundled down the stairs after it, baying in excitement.

• • •

Sakura slammed her hand down on the conference room table. "I said I don't want this."

Marcia's frown hadn't softened in twenty minutes, and the tension between the two women sang like a high-wire. "This isn't about what you want, this is about what has to happen. If the media gets these files, the OPD will never recover. The press will eat them alive, and the president will have no choice but to shut them down."

"The president will shut down the OPD and pay the same men to do the same job under another name. You know this. I know this. Releasing this information will do nothing that matters."

"Blossom's right." Janet tapped the picture. "Even if this could be substantiated, that opens us up to, what, attacking a government installation on American soil? Killing soldiers and contract employees? Plausible deniability is all we've got, here."

Sakura frowned. Matt figured the only thing she disliked more than a breach of her privacy was Janet LaLonde agreeing with her.

Generals, congressmen, and executives in weapons companies had all toured the OPD facilities, caught on digital feed watching as men in white lab coats tortured Sakura and other test subjects to demonstrate what they had and hadn't been able to reproduce from her blood and body chemistry. Some had even joked while watching, their comments captured by a wire worn by someone Marcia wouldn't reveal.

The victims' bodies had been cremated, but several visually matched with missing persons, captured terror suspects, supposedly-executed criminals, and homeless people from all over the country. Dozens of counts of first-degree murder, conspiracy, torture, and countless other crimes, all done with taxpayer dollars and on American soil.

"I will not agree. The world does not need to see my shame."

Marcia sighed. "Blossom—"

"Don't call me that anymore. I am Isuji Sakura; call me Sakura, or Miss Isuji if you must be formal, but my name is my name."

Marcia spread her hands on the table. "Sakura, please, this is bigger than you. We need to expose these people, bring them to justice."

She crossed her arms. "We know who they are. We find them and kill them. Justice enough."

Matt shook his head, harder when Sakura glared at him. "We're not killing six congressmen, three senators, and the Undersecretary of Defense."

"Why not?"

"We don't have the prerogative. They're not a supernatural threat. No matter what they did to you, we don't have the jurisdiction."

"I am not concerned with jurisdiction."

He folded his arms to mirror hers. "I'm not a murderer."

Janet snorted.

"I'm not. I'm a soldier, and a killer, but not a murderer."

She ran her tongue over her teeth. "I think a couple dozen bodies might not care too much about that distinction, bud."

Sakura stood tall – a head shorter than Matt, and half a head taller than most of her countrymen – her chest puffed out, hands at her sides clenched into tight fists. "You confuse us with your brother, killer of millions."

"My brother saved the *whole fucking planet.*" Despite the murder in her eyes and flush in her cheeks, Janet maintained careful body language – leaned back in her chair, legs crossed, hands in her lap. The notion of the two women coming to blows couldn't be more ludicrous. One worked in an office and never exercised, and the other could kill a bull hippopotamus in unarmed combat without breaking a sweat. Only Sakura's restraint kept Janet from harm, and the murder in her eyes betrayed a limited reserve.

Marcia raised a hand, like a timid girl in grade school. "Can we calm down, please? I know this is emotional, and I brought it to the table, and for that I'm sorry, but it's too important for personalities to interfere."

Sakura glared at Janet, then at Marcia. "Fine, go. Do it."

"Send the information?"

"Yes. I give you my permission."

Janet scowled.

Marcia crumbled in her chair, the tension bleeding out of her. "Oh, thank God."

"What?" Matt asked.

"I sent everything to the major news outlets this morning."

Sakura opened her mouth, closed it, then stormed out

of the room. The doorframe split as the door slammed closed.

Monica's concerns reverberated in his head as he exchanged a worried look with Marcia. "I've never seen her like that."

"She's been through a lot." Without waiting for a reply she turned to Janet. "And I know you don't agree, but—"

"Oh, I agree."

Marcia opened her mouth, closed it, and opened it again. "What? But you were—"

"Hey, if I come out in favor of something, Sakura doubles down against it. I haven't done jack shit to her, but she'd rather eat a bullet than let me have my way." She leaned forward and patted Marcia's hand. "You did the right thing, except maybe admitting it."

"Wow," Marcia said. "Remind me not to get on your bad side."

Janet patted her hand again. "Don't get on my bad side, toots. Really."

Matt closed his eyes and rubbed his temples.

"What?" Marcia said. "You can't get headaches."

"No, but sometimes this feels good anyway."

"Phone call."

Janet's voice shattered Matt's concentration, so he pulled his hands from the keyboard and triggered the intercom, speaking around the toothpick between his teeth.

"Pardon?"

The STB had a dozen office staff, men and women cleared for the highest level of government secrecy tasked with all the filing, phone calls, public relations, and scheduling they might need. A former data systems administrator for ICAP and now Matt's field coordinator, Janet's pay grade dwarfed answering phones. She emphasized every word, as if speaking to a confused child. "You have a phone call. Line Two. Answer it."

He picked up the phone and pressed the flashing button. "Hello?"

"Sergeant Rowley, this is Eugene McGrath, Deputy Undersecre—"

"I know who you are, sir. Go ahead."

The Deputy Undersecretary of Defense, or at least his underlings, approved all budgets and weapon requisitions for the Special Threats Bureau. A former Army Colonel with a dozen decorations, he'd lost a leg and half an arm in Enduring Freedom and had manned a civilian desk ever since. Nobody ever called Matt 'Sergeant' unless they planned to order him around, and with recent developments the likelihood of McGrath making a social call hit zero and started digging.

"What can you tell me about this media story that I can't see on my fucking television?"

Matt had never spoken to McGrath directly, and the cursing caught him off-guard. Schooling his voice to neutrality, he pulled the toothpick from his mouth and replied, "It's pretty much all out there. A man calling himself Special Agent Shane Keene with iron-clad credentials kidnapped my agent Sakura Isuji and tortured her for most of a year, in front of a lot of really important people. We got her out last week along with a data dump."

"You need to control your personnel. Leaks like that can't happen."

Matt chuckled, and made sure McGrath heard it. "The Office of Planning and Development is an illegal organization guilty of kidnapping, torture, and murder. I *authorized* the leak." True, if after the fact.

"You should have reported it to me."

"Begging your pardon, sir, but your boss is on those tapes. I don't know how high the OPD—"

"Nobody here has heard of the Office of Planning and Development."

"Begging your pardon, sir, but it's not my fault if you've been mushroomed. They've got a modest budget and a huge campus with a hell of a lot of hardware. It's all in my report, which I sent to your desk three days ago."

"I... you're going to have to report to Washington. Today. Like right now."

Matt rolled his eyes to the ceiling and put his feet up on the desk. "I'm in the middle of an investigation. We have dozens of dead bodies and a suspect still at large. It's going to have to wait."

"This isn't a request, Sergeant. A congressional subpoena is going out this afternoon, and the President wants to talk to you, Miss Isuji, and Miss LaLonde before you open your mouth on Capitol Hill. So get in one of those helos I pay for and get your ass to D.C. We'll clear space for you on the White House helipad."

"Roger, wilco. Sir."

The phone clicked dead, so he set it down and hit the intercom to Janet's office. "You get that?"

"Yeah. I'll spool them up."

• • •

The size of a high school classroom, the Oval Office sure beat a cubicle, but with seats for eight, not counting the President's desk, the eighteen men and women – mostly men – in suits or military uniforms filled the couches and chairs and every bit of standing space besides. President Robert Williams, handsome despite his graying hair and scowl, eschewed his chair to lean on the desk, forcing Matt and his team to turn their backs on most of the crowd.

Now that the story had broken, Sakura refused to be anything but completely honest, recounting the physical, sexual, and psychological tortures she'd endured at the hands of the OPD, spilling out gruesome details in an efficient monotone until the President had asked her to stop.

Matt flushed with rage at the story, worse than he could possibly have imagined – they'd seemed intent on seeing how close they could push her to the brink of survival, for no sane reason.

She identified dozens of government officials and employees as observers, ranging from the FBI and CIA to all branches of the military, Congress, and the Executive Branch, some by name, others by their picture. Raising a hand, she pointed it behind her and to the left.

"This man was there."

A sandy-haired man in a dark blue suit took a step back, eyes wide. "What? No!"

Sakura turned, and Matt tensed. All eyes fell on the man in the suit, who hit the wall and kept his hands spread, out from his body.

"On August twelfth he observed in hospital scrubs as they removed my leg at the knee. He complimented me on my stoicism, and thanked me for my sacrifice."

Matt put a hand on her wrist. "Don't kill him."

She stood unmoving, unflinching, as the Secret Service crept their hands to their weapons. They had no chance against an Aug, and if forced to choose sides Matt knew where his loyalties lay – but he had no desire for a bloodbath in the White House, with loyal Americans the victims.

"Not here. Not right now."

She relaxed a hair, just enough, and he took away his hand.

"Stand down, Agent Isuji." The President's voice reverberated through the room, hale and strong. She turned back to him and he smiled, a bead of sweat on his forehead. "We can't have you hurting anyone here. I'm going to place you into custody for your own—"

"No."

Williams stood there, mouth open. He licked his lips and started again. "Just tempor—"

"No. I will not be detained."

The door opened and another four guards squeezed inside, weapons out but at their sides. They looked from the President to Sakura and Matt, while the previous guards kept their focus between Sakura and the man she'd accused.

Matt raised his hands in a defensive posture he didn't feel, drawing attention. "Mister President, there's no reason to detain my agent."

Williams shook his head, lips pressed in a white line. "Not your call."

Matt cracked his neck. "It is, and I'm telling you that we will not allow it." Faced with six Secret Service agents and twenty unarmed civilians in an enclosed space, Matt had no doubt how two Augs would fare. "You're going to take that man in custody and when this meeting is over we're going to leave, and nobody's going to try to stop us."

Flushed, Williams snarled. "I am the President of the United States!"

"So you are, sir. But you're desperately outmatched, and we're not letting you take either of us into custody. Please. I don't want to hurt your men."

He glared at Matt and Sakura, bright red face turning almost purple, then leaned back on the desk again. "All right. Take Jones into custody, and everybody else get out."

The accused man – Jones – allowed the guards to handcuff him, shuffling along behind the fleeing crowd. The last two guards closed the door behind them, leaving only Matt, Janet, Sakura, and President Williams in the room.

The President walked past them, turned, and plopped down into a chair. Gesturing to the couches on either side he said, "Please, sit."

They sat, Janet across from Matt and Sakura, turned to half-face the President.

"You can't just defy my authority like that."

Sakura leaned forward. "I can. I will. You will not take me into custody."

He leaned back, feigned relaxation betrayed by his stiff movements and the hand clenched in his lap. "Were you going to hurt Jones?"

A nod. "I'm going to kill him."

"We are a nation of laws, Miss Isuji."

"Yes. And a nation of corruption and terrible men who go free because they are useful. I will not allow this to happen, to any of them."

Williams smiled, a friendly gesture that held no mirth. "And I won't let it. But you have to let the justice system run its course."

Sakura said nothing.

Matt shifted in his seat.

Janet stared at the TV in the corner, news ticker scrolling past under a muted anchor with bottle-blonde hair. "Matt, you're on TV."

Matt turned. Pictures splayed across the screen, close-up shots of Matt and Sakura covered in blood, heavily-cropped photos of occult symbols in blood and shit on the walls. Ronald Kellett appeared, the leader of Humans for Humanity standing tall behind a podium, then was replaced by Matt and Janet exiting the helicopter on the White House helipad. The headline underneath read, "KELLETT: PRESIDENT HOSTING CULTISTS."

"How the hell did they get that footage? You just got here!"

Matt shook his head. "That's two years old. From the ICAP hearings."

"But they know you're here."

"And OPD isn't going down without a fight."

The President rubbed his face with both hands, peering at them with eyes stretched downward from the tension. "And you're due on the Hill in three hours."

"Yes, sir."

The impromptu and hastily-thrown-together hearings took four grueling days. In that time the FBI arrested over two dozen people, another dozen disappeared – including one senator, two representatives, a general and three CEOs – the first of which washed ashore on the Canadian side of Lake Superior with a bullet lodged in his brain. Matt burned in frustration, flying back and forth to Washington D.C. every day so that angry politicians could ask him the same questions over and over, and all the while Humans for Humanity agitated against the president and congress for associating with 'Warlocks and Devil-Spawn'.

Case's trail grew cold, and with it, any hope of figuring out what happened at Lake Barnacle.

• • •

Sobbing, Conor Flynn drew the knife down his – Ben Case's – forehead, arcing out to the side as the razor-sharp steel grated against the bone beneath. The blade sliced his eyebrow in half, punctured and destroyed his left eye, then curved inward to meet his lips at the corner of his mouth. Another line repeated the motion on the right side.

Blind, he turned the knife upside-down and plunged it between his knees. The girl held there shuddered, and her screams of terror softened to a choking wail of shock and fading life. The bridge sucked at her suffering, and he screamed in defiance. Reaching up to peel away the flesh from his skull, he denied the bridge his sacrifice, neither his pain nor that of the girl beneath him going to sate its all-consuming need. Instead he focused the pain into his new body, his rebirth.

The bridge shuddered, an earthquake through his soul, rocking foundations and seeking cracks to pour through. Creatures tittered and squirmed on the far side, desperate for a taste of what dribbled from its maw.

Conor denied them all, and fell upon the girl. Sixteen,

maybe. She'd claimed nineteen when he'd picked her up at the bus stop, with a promise of a hot meal and place to stay in exchange for a hot night. Her life gushed from the wound as he pressed his hot flesh against her bony frame, too-short years of sex and blood and bruises and empty eyes given succor through needles and pills. Case's skinless body collapsed inward, crumbling and crawling, writhing into and through her, merging their agony into a single, perfect whole.

Flynn sat up in the darkness, opened his eyes to the orange haze of sodium vapor. He licked the blood from the blade, held it up to look at what his power had wrought. Green eyes, shaved head like the day he'd gotten his second-generation regenerates, perfect teeth and a bright pink tongue. He looked down at lean muscle tufted here and there with fine blond hair, and the crop of fuzz around the scabby stump between his legs. He'd removed that long ago, in a life before death and the life that came after.

The bridge roared.

True power required sacrifice.

"Right is right."

CHAPTER EIGHT

Matlal crested the ridge, looked out across the desert and wailed, the sound wrenched unbidden from his heaving chest. His heart hammered against his ribs as he ran toward the slaughter, misery and desperate hope cutting off his ability to breathe.

The mammoth lay on its side, leather skin stretched tight across enormous ribs, brown-red liquid staining the scorched earth beneath. His men surrounded it, hunters chosen for their skill and bravery, with straight spears topped with sharp stone. They lay in crumpled heaps over their own red-brown stains, bellies and chests torn open to reveal shriveled organs beneath.

Around them the sand had shifted, forming spirals within spirals, an endless altar to the forces of wind and water.

No vultures circled, and despite the banquet the bodies showed no sign of ravage by the Great Jaguar or his children. Not even flies disturbed his brother's corpse, leaving bloodshot eyes to stare into the naked sun. Forgetting caution, Matlal charged forward, his spear dropping into the dirt.

Cradling his brother's head in his arms, he let tears flow. Anguish poured from him for the sibling and friends he'd leave behind, for the wasted meat that would not feed his people. Disaster, for his family, for his tribe.

A shadow crossed his vision. He looked up.

She stood between him and the endless sky, a dark

beauty with blazing emerald eyes, her body wrapped in wings of translucent jade. They drowned the sunlight, refracting and intensifying it into shadows of visions, the history of his people laid naked and drowned in the great salt oceans that divided the world. Her voice reverberated in all languages and none as she reached out her hand. "Come, father, this is not your fate."

"I have no children." He held out his hand. Her touch blazed on his fingertips, her strength unimaginable. She hauled him up and her smile filled him with the memory of memories, an inkling of a time and space beyond. "Who are you?"

"I am your daughter. You are one of my fathers, and because I love you I have come to pull you from this Pit."

He followed her eyes up, to the blazing, black maelstrom he'd mistaken for the sun. A swirling mass of billions of souls screaming for the light, it blotted out hope and washed the world in un-light. He looked down at his brother, the scattered bones little more than dust, like the mammoth and the men who'd killed it, all but lost to wind and time.

The remains of men he'd killed, striking from the sky to take their souls and ravage their women, to feast on their bones and laugh at their plight. He looked around, confused, and spoke in the language of man. "Pit? I see no pit."

"You are not this weak flesh, this hollow shell. You are a shard of divinity, brother to Shemyaza, father of thousands, breaker of time. You are the world-dragon, who these men would come to call Ometeotl, the father of gods, among other names." Her knuckles brushed his cheek, sending a tingle of lust through his body. "You are not this pathetic creature. Let it go."

How many times had he relived the memories of his victims? How many countless eons had he rotted under the un-sun at the bottom of Tartarus, condemned to this meager torture by the jealous One beyond because He coveted the pleasures of human flesh for himself? Ometeotl bore his fangs, and a rumble in his chest rocked the earth.

Her smile blazed. "Now you remember." Her foot crushed a bit of jaw into powder, not his brother at all, only a meal from millennia ago. "Above they call you 'egregoroi', a Watcher. But the time for watching is past."

Mist curled from her open mouth, and tendrils of green light groped from her eyes. They found his, and an eternity of suffering poured through him, thousands of stolen years. Human misery arced down his nerves like lightning, disintegrating flesh and bone, replacing it with something stronger, something *real*, the divine vitality of his making, pleasure and wrath given form.

He shuddered, gasped, as the weak, human body tried to contain his new majesty, his old majesty, his birthright and inheritance from the time before time.

She stepped back and spread her wings to reveal dark skin without blemish, desire made flesh. His flesh, their flesh, the spark from the loins of an egregoroi and a human woman. His child, another's child, he couldn't know. There had been so many women, shared so many ways, and only one daughter. How he wanted her. "I know you. Where are your brothers?"

A dismissive flick of her fingers pierced his heart. "Dead, the last centuries ago. Only I remain, and I but a shadow of my former self."

"A shadow of such beauty." He stepped toward her, unable to contain his lust.

She faded to mist, a distant memory, and her voice rang in his ears. "I am not for you, father – I've given too much already. There is a whole world above. Take it."

He spread his wings, feathers of a million colors, and his skin parted, sloughing off to reveal a rainbow of scales. His legs twisted, merged, formed a great tail, and with it he launched into the sky, into the maelstrom, up and up toward the bright world above. The souls shrieked around him, and he screamed in triumph.

• • •

Cat shit, cumin and Old Spice. The filthy trailer reeked beyond even his own stinking humanity. A 'shaman' at twenty-seven, what a joke. Aaron Albonico wiped the drool from his mouth and sat up, and the pounding in his head punished him for it. Beer bottles tinkled as he stood, nudging them to the side with brown feet stained white with chalk dust from last night's 'ritual'. Tourists looking for a taste of authenticity paid him just enough in tips to maintain his shithole trailer, as long as he didn't want anything crazy like running water or electricity. And it only cost him time and the unbearable shame of his parents and ancestors.

The cat bolted inside as he stepped out to pee, eyes hovering with disinterest past the ghettos of Cholula to Popocatapetl, the Smoking Mountain made famous by postcards around the world, and Iztacchihuatl, the White Woman, on the horizon.

Ometeotl chuckled. He knew the mountains, and had thought the snow-covered one looked like a woman on her side long when he'd first seen it, too. But nothing else looked familiar, not the strange structures nor the wide ways of gray stone snaking around them in lines too straight for nature.

Aaron froze mid-piss. "Yo, is someone there?"

With none of the beauty of the language Ometeotl had taught the mammoth-hunters who had roamed this land, this pathetic creature spoke in mushy bird-noises. They grated, but the meaning came clear enough.

Aaron squeezed his eyes shut. Yellowcrest tea gave a trippy vibe to his performances, which is why he served and drank it at his 'ceremonies', but he'd never hallucinated the next morning. He leaned his head against the side of the trailer, metal already hot in the morning sun, and spattered his toes with another burst of piss.

"You okay?"

The world hazed back into focus. Maria Aguilar stood, fists on her hips, brow furrowed with concern. An archaeologist, Aaron always figured her for older than the pre-Columbian ruins she studied, her head twice as hard as the stones that made them. Wrinkled and cracked like old leather, the skin on her face and hands sported warts and liver spots.

Hideous, and the first real woman he'd seen in thousands of years.

Omeleotl-Aaron advanced, grinning, arms wide. With a casual rape of Aaron's mind the egregoroi seized the man's ugly language to use on this ugly woman, taking his memories, knowledge, and spirit with it. His heart burned, and his erection throbbed in his pants.

Maria screamed, and he screamed with her.

• • •

"You can't be serious." Matt blinked at the orders, then looked up at Janet.

She shrugged.

"Mexico is on fire, and they're sending us to Cape Cod."

"You're not a fireman, and Omelet-man isn't our problem. SACLANT's sending in an entire carrier group for support."

At least eight thousand men had killed their families in Cholula at the command of Omeleotl, a fake shaman named Aaron Albonico who had formed a rape cult four days earlier. The Mexican president had declared a national emergency and called in the army, but the first squads in had turned on their brothers in arms, killing and raping fellow soldiers in an orgy of bloody violence, so focus had shifted to long-range containment. The Mexican government had requested US and UN support, specifically the Special Threats Bureau, and the president had turned them down, though surveillance support had been offered and accepted. While news helicopters lay in ruins on the ground, the cultists couldn't reach satellites.

On the live feed Matt forced himself to watch as five men poured out of a pickup truck and into a house. They dragged a man into the street by his hair, cutting and tearing off his clothes with no regard to the flesh underneath. Blood spurted from his arms and legs as they forced him down on his stomach, and Matt thanked God they had no audio feed. The men – if they were still men – took turns raping their victim in the street, each stabbing him once in the back as they rode him. He stopped moving. They didn't.

A fight broke out between the rapists, and moments later only two still stood, the others spraying their blood into the street. The victors fell on them, thrusting into holes made by knives and tearing fingers.

Matt forced himself to keep watching, to internalize the brutality on the screen, so that he might unleash it without qualm when he got there. "Screw this. I'm going to Mexico."

"Not unless you're jogging. There's something weird going on in Massachusettes, and you're on point. Sakura, too, if she's ready."

"She's ready."

He turned off the monitor and closed his eyes. "Tens of thousands of innocent people are dying. Right now. And I can stop it."

"Some Aboriginals in New South Wales just seceded from Australia. Their representative crumpled a police car into a ball and crushed it into another police car. There were cops inside both vehicles. Two SWAT teams are dead, and dozens of civilians. And it's getting worse. The Russians just firebombed one of their own towns and called it a 'training accident' – at least four thousand dead, and our intel says it wasn't an accident. A whole city in China just up and stopped eating last week, said the cloud dragon told them to – not very many casualties yet, mostly children and elderly, but it's going to get real bad in a week or two. In South Africa…"

Sitting, he picked up the folder. "So what's in Provincetown?"

"Hostage situation. Bunch of tourists are stuck in a hotel on the beach, and the staff won't let them leave. Said they're holding them for Dagon."

"What do we know about Dagon?"

"Mesopotamian god of fertility, grain, and fish. His history is a mess from a bunch of cultures from that area, Amorites/Canaanites, Assyrians, Babylonians. Philistines in the Bible – Solomon destroys his temple, and his statue is humbled before the Ark of the Covenant in some kind of miracle. He's also a made-up name from early twentieth-century horror novels. The crazies have talked to the cops, and they've renamed their hotel E-Mul, or 'House of the Star', and keep babbling stuff about HP Lovecraft. Heard of him?"

"Vaguely. Weird tentacle-gods and stuff, right?"

"That's the guy. Pretty popular in modern culture, if you're a weirdo."

"So… there's a chance we go there and these are just plain-old nutcases."

She shrugged. "Sure."

"And what are their demands?"

"They aren't making any, except that nobody crosses the beach or parking lot. They're holding the hostages for Dagon, and will kill them before letting them go."

"Has anyone seen anything supernatural about any of them?"

"Nothing verified. Eyewitnesses report them as very creepy, but couldn't really elaborate on why."

"So we're wasting our time on this because…"

"Because the president's poll numbers are tanking in

response to H4H's attacks, and he needs to look strong on cults. You're the cult guy, so you're on deck."

He stood and walked toward the door. "Call Sakura. Wheels up in an hour. We'll study layout and tactical en route."

"Aye, aye."

• • •

Unarmed, Matt stormed past the police line toward front steps of the hotel, ignoring the alarmed cries behind him. The cultists had fired on the cops, twice – or at least on the ground at their feet – and had refused to negotiate. IR surveillance put them at three hostiles and thirteen hostages in the lobby, two sentries each at the back and side doors, and two on the roof.

A shot rang out and sand spit at his feet. It hadn't even triggered the whispers, except for their usual murmurs. He kept walking, and another shot blasted a puff of sand to his left.

"Don't come any closer! Next one's in your head!" A male voice, deep but shaking, it came from next to the air conditioner on the roof. Well-camouflaged from standard human vision, in the infrared the man stood out like a dandelion in a mowed lawn.

Matt stopped, lifted the bullhorn in his right hand. "Look at me. Do you know who I am?"

A pause, then, "Yeah. You're the ICAP guy."

He nodded, exaggerated for effect. "Special Threats Bureau, now. You've been classified as a special threat. Do you understand what that means?"

The whispers flooded his mind with an orgy of violence, crunching bones and pulsing arteries, screams and cries for mercy that wouldn't come.

The man whispered to his companion, head ducking behind the metal unit, then shouted over the roiling surf.

"No."

"It means you're going to put your guns down and come out with your hands on your heads, or you're going to die." He looked at his watch, which he'd bought just for this bit of theater, the unfamiliar weight a cool annoyance against his skin. "You have ten seconds... nine... eight..."

His eyes flicked up. Above the men on the roof, Sakura detached her harness.

"Seven..."

The parachute jerked, collapsing as it headed out to sea.

"Six..."

She plummeted, a baton in each hand, as the men stood. A pair of wet impacts dropped them to the roof as the front door opened.

"Five..."

Three men hustled out, hands over their heads. Sakura leapt off the roof toward the back, sailing in a clean arc, arms raised, batons extended, and disappeared out of sight.

"Four... three..."

Two sentries ran from around the side entrance, hands on their heads, eyes wide. Sakura followed, dragging another two, limp and dead weight, by their shirts.

Matt lowered the bullhorn then dropped it into the sand. Turning, he walked back toward the police and said to no one in particular, "All yours."

He triggered his COM as people rushed past, weapons raised, yelling orders. "Saddle up. We're going to Mexico."

• • •

Across the beach, Conor lowered the binoculars and sighed, taking the moment to shove half a McDonald's cheeseburger into his mouth. Those deaths would have triggered an incursion over the bridge like nothing seen in hundreds of years, a wholesale slaughter that would have consumed half the town and maybe, just maybe, given Rowley a run for his money.

He swallowed, ate the rest, then munched on a French fry. Limp, lukewarm and over-salted, it mirrored his discontent rather too well. A nagging thought troubled him. Killing Matt seemed fair play of the best turnabout sort, but the rest of it, the incursion... he didn't know why he wanted it. He dropped the other half of the fry in the bag and tossed it in the waste receptacle, scowling.

"Brilliant. Just brilliant."

CHAPTER NINE

Matt followed Sakura toward the waiting group of uniformed officers, a hodgepodge of men and women in dress blues or SEDENA digital camouflage, shuffling feet and fidgeting on the tarmac. They sweated under the oppressive Mexican sun, though not as badly as Matt. Setting down his operations case – thumbprint-locked and five feet long, it held his combat shotgun with high-explosive, fragmentation, and armor-penetrating microgrenades, REC-7 assault rifle with ceramic composite 'bonk killer' rounds, plus an assortment of more traditional grenades and monofilament combat knives – he shook hands and introduced himself and Sakura.

General Marco Valdez looked like a half-dead version of his dossier photo. A tall man, his close-cropped silver hair popped against his dark brown skin, and the smile on his rugged face didn't reach his haggard eyes. He spoke in rapid-fire Spanish, and a young woman next to him in a dress blue skirt-suit translated in unaccented English. "Mister Rowley, Miss Isuji, thank you for coming. You've seen the news so I won't waste your time explaining the obvious: we're in deep trouble, and we don't know what to do about it. If the threat isn't contained in seventy-two hours the president has authorized the use of strategic fuel-air bombs to eliminate it. We would like to avoid—"

Sakura interrupted, her voice clipped. "When did the Mexican government get strategic fuel-air bombs?"

General Valdez turned to her as his interpreter

translated, and replied through her. "We have been exploring all options for dealing with the cartels. When the civilian populations live under the terror of madmen, sometimes you do as you must."

She nodded, face a blank mask, and he continued as an aide brought up a map of Cholula on a tablet.

"The effects seem to be centered on the pyramid, and extend just over eight kilometers in every direction. Beyond that range people have fled, most of them, though aerial reconnaissance has picked up too many instances of civilians trying to flee the afflicted zone. After some unfortunate incidents we..." The interpreter swallowed. "We are killing all who seek to escape the quarantined area, and cannot send any more in. We've lost too many soldiers already, to friendly fire."

"Mind control." Matt frowned.

"Something like that. Our best and trusted soldiers turn on one another when they get too far inside the quarantine zone. We've lost a battalion, and six helicopters."

Sakura pointed toward the sky. "Eight kilometers, pretty high. High as a bomber."

"We've considered that, and have mobilized long-range assets. Your president denied our request for strategic support."

Matt put his hand up. "Wait. You can't possibly be considering bombing your own city."

The general shrugged.

The interpreter grimaced. "If you can't help us we're going to have to."

• • •

An hour later, Matt approached the quarantined zone around Cholula. The dense line of military trucks, makeshift barricades, and now-abandoned buildings ringed an enormous area. Thousands of soldiers patrolled the perimeter, armed with FX-05 Xuihcoatl 'Fire Snake' assault rifles and carbines, some with underslung air-burst grenade launchers. Pillboxes dotted the rooftops outside the barricade, the barrels of tripod-mounted machine guns poking out from piles of sandbags. In the midday heat Matt couldn't see the mountains behind a yellow-gray haze of dust, smog, and humidity, so the pyramid and its church dominated the skyline.

Soldiers made way and saluted the general, Matt and Sakura in his wake, the interpreter and two aides hurrying by his side. Matt ignored the excited whispers and awed looks, the signs of the cross and damning scowls, instead focusing on the carnage beyond the barricade.

Bright-red blood streaked the asphalt and spattered buildings. Dozens of bodies lay in the street, twisted or slumped, dark stains on their clothing, some missing limbs, others heads. Makeshift weapons littered the ground around them, pipes and axes, chains, wrenches, nail-studded chunks of construction lumber, even a few firearms – hunting rifles and old revolvers, and the occasional military-issue Fire Snake.

The whispers cackled their sadistic glee, and the sound reverberated down streets and alleys, echoing off of silent buildings. Something black mingled with the jade, filling Matt's nostrils with a burnt mix of cinnamon, coriander, allspice, and cooking flesh. It throbbed in time with his heart, each pulse a rush of violence straight to his frontal lobe. Sakura grunted, and Matt turned to assess the murder in her eyes, the promise of sex and death and sex in death, and restrained himself from knocking her down and gouging out those furious eyes and fucking her still-screaming skull. As the white whispers shocked down his synapses, his son and Akash and a million other souls muffling the jade whispers and the dark power amplifying them, Sakura's eyes softened.

"You feel that."

He nodded, though it wasn't a question.

"My Kazuko is protecting me. Same for you?" Sakura's daughter's voice had become her white whispers the moment she'd died from cancer, the same moment Sakura's augmentations had returned.

He nodded again, throat dry from wanting to scream. "The gang's all here."

The soldiers hadn't reacted. As the whispers clawed at the insides of his skull, Matt wondered if the egregoroi's powers keyed off of Gerstner's, and if they'd fight or play nice in his head. For the moment the white contained the jade and black, so he turned to Valdez.

"I've seen enough. We'll go in by foot." They didn't have the ESG Gryphon winged gliders they'd used to infiltrate Dawkins's stronghold on Lake Kivu, and gearing up a plane for a HALO jump would take too long. Matt could cover five miles in just over fourteen minutes without tiring himself out, and Sakura could do it in half that time. "You understand that there could be massive civilian casualties, even if we do this right."

Valdez nodded. "Our options are bad and worse."

"And we have full authorization to use US and NATO forces to contain and eliminate the threat."

"Si. Yes," he said without the interpreter.

Matt keyed up his COM. "Janet?"

"Go ahead."

"Deploy Dragonflies, and put two Reapers up. General Valdez will make sure you have clear airspace."

"You got it, bud."

The Mexican army didn't have any combat drones, but Matt had direct command of up to four, only usable outside the United States and its territories. Sleeker but well bigger than a car with a twenty-meter wingspan, each Reaper carried four Hellfire Romeo missiles – armor piercing munitions capable of leveling buildings – and two GPS-guided JDAM BLU-97/B Combined Effect cluster bombs, dozens of individually-guided smart munitions designed to make everything in a half-block area go away. For fighting an egregoroi and an unknown number of hostiles, Matt would have preferred gunship support.

They kitted up, ignoring the stares as they loaded hundreds of pounds of weapons and ammunition into pouches, packs, and straps. Sakura carried her REC7 with a satchel of 'bonk killer' ammo in spare magazines, at least four combat knives, and a bandolier with fragmentation, incendiary, and flash-bang grenades. Matt skipped the knives and assault rifle in favor of the AA-12 and his own bandolier of grenades.

Pulling on his combat helmet, he switched the visor to black and took in the Dragonfly feed, a composite overview of the city in full color projected on his heads-up display. The cloud of information spread out as the robotic insects flitted deeper and deeper into hostile territory, replacing the fog of war with a coded overlay identifying potential targets. Buildings, streets, and individual stories shaded green if clear, red if potential hostiles were present, and light blue if the Dragonflies couldn't assess for threats.

Default settings labeled every living human as a potential hostile.

Target designations popped up, giving the team a common language in the blink of an eye.

The closest hostiles crouched behind a dumpster three blocks away, just out of sight of sniper fire, their bloody hands clutching improvised weapons, clothes a torn mass of red-brown gore. Behind them a brick building stood three stories high, windows shattered, top floor smoking, with at least sixty hostiles inside, waiting. The Dragonflies called it A-1, the first target.

"Sakura, cut right. We'll circumvent A-1, go left around A-2, then punch straight for B13 through that open market. If we hit any surprises, flank them. Janet, if A-1 comes for us, knock it down."

Sakura dodged to the right, a wide loop that kept her out of sight of A-1. Matt did the same on the left, dashing from cover to cover, eyes and ears alert for anything the swarm of microdrones might have missed. His visor dimmed the visible light enough for his infrared and ultraviolet vision to work through it, providing more detail that supplemented the Dragonfly feed. The whole town reeked of blood and shit, overwhelming the underlying aroma of dust, corn flour, and cinnamon. He made it four deserted blocks before Janet piped up.

"Sakura, you've got four hostiles on your six. Matt, eight on your ten, closing fast."

"Yes," Sakura said, as Matt replied, "Roger."

He watched the bedraggled, bloodstained octet approach on the HUD, creeping up on his position, their clumsy attempts at stealth rendered moot by the Dragonflies. He zoomed in – improvised clubs and machetes, nothing that would require a gun. Matt dashed across the street and took cover behind an overturned pushcart, feet skidding across the mushy remains of apples baking in the sun.

They approached at a crouching run, covering the ground in loping strides more like animals than men, shoulders hunched, weapons dangling from their hands. The feed from Sakura's helmet camera flashed, a blur of motion as she took her assailants apart. Footsteps slapped across the pavement, stealth abandoned in favor of an all-out charge.

Matt rose, caught an overhead swing from an aluminum bat on his left forearm, then chopped down into the man's leering face. His cheek and nose exploded toward the sidewalk, and Matt turned into the blow, ducking low to avoid a swing from a second assailant.

Air whistled overhead.

Still turning, Matt chopped the side of his hand into the second man's ribs. Stumbling sideways, machete falling from his hands, the man dropped to his knees and looked into Matt's eyes with unbridled hatred. Blood dribbled from his assailant's mouth and nose, and Matt turned to meet the next four head-on.

He shattered a skull with his helmet, snapped a neck with a kick to the side. A machete scraped down the armor on his bicep without fraying the Teflon-coated fabric, much less damaging the carbon fiber-reinforced ceramic underneath. Matt grabbed the arm and swung, hurling the machete-wielder into another man hard enough for blood to erupt from both their mouths. A board bounced off his helmet. Spinning, he crushed a throat with a punch, then turned to the last man.

Flexing his fingers, he circled around the pushcart and the bodies strewn around it. His opponent gripped a bent piece of rebar, his yellowed teeth exposed in a soundless snarl.

Hands upheld, Matt took a step back. "Walk away. You don't have to die today."

Circling, passing the rebar from hand to hand, he babbled something neither English nor Spanish, a rapid-fire string of syllables none of which Matt recognized.

He tried high-school Spanish. "Put it down. I don't have to kill you."

Snarl unchanged, the man charged. Matt sidestepped a clumsy swing, and another. The best martial artist in the world stood no chance against an Aug – this man probably sold street food or ran a bicycle repair shop.

Matt tried again. "Please stop."

The air shuddered, the enormous noise muffled automatically by his helmet, and building A-1 flashed on his HUD, then disappeared.

"Quit dicking around," Janet said. "You've got more incoming. A lot more."

Matt stepped inside a clumsy swing and brought his elbow into the man's temple, hard enough to knock him senseless but not hard enough to kill. The man fell to all fours, then lunged, his full-arm tackle wrapping Matt's waist without budging him. Matt chopped the back of his head, again hard enough to render any normal person unconscious. The man bit down, trying to chew a hole through his armor.

"Matt..."

Skull crunching under the impact of a downward punch, his opponent finally collapsed.

Matt ran.

Sakura joined him halfway to the open market, matching him stride for stride, a black combat knife in each hand. "You see this?"

Hundreds of hostiles closed on their position, maybe a thousand, matching speed and direction to intercept them though they were out of sight and several blocks away. He grunted. "I think it knows we're coming."

"C-9," Sakura replied, changing course. He followed her toward the vacant five-story office building with huge glass windows on every floor. Red blips surrounded by double-triangles shifted to match their new trajectory – farther away, they'd reach the building seconds before the mob.

"What's the plan?"

"Up, then jump to C-6." C-6 stood across the street from C-9, a brick-façade hardware store three stories tall with a terracotta roof. A shed in the back made for a fifteen-foot drop, then another to the ground. The initial jump would leave a bruise, but they'd both survived much worse.

"Won't buy us much." They rounded the corner and bolted across a small park, skirting a wading pool turned pink with half-floating bodies. A roar erupted as a growing mob sprinted across the open space to cut them off, a boiling tide of filthy men, women and children screaming and hissing in unbridled hatred. They filled the streets and alleys, loping gaits turning to outright sprints as they caught sight of their quarry.

Two Augs against a thousand people – nobody could survive that. The whispers, Jade and black, told him not to, told him to join them in the naked, bloody revelry that defined mankind.

At a dead run Sakura fired the REC7 at the front doors, shattering the glass. Her voice carried over the COM as she disappeared inside. "Slow them or you won't make it."

Matt raised the AA-12 and put his finger on the trigger, still sprinting. His Friend-or-Foe picked two dozen targets, each five to ten feet from the next. Three of them children, no older than ten. Gritting his teeth, he fired. The weapon bucked, and fin-stabilized grenades hammered the front of the crowd. Bodies burst, bodies fell, people staggered to the side holding faces and stomachs and shredded limbs.

The mob ran over the top of them, barely slowed.

Matt rushed through the broken glass and backed into the lobby, indiscriminately spraying the crowd with frag rounds. People burst, spraying those behind with steaming red blood and chunks of meat and bone. As the entryway choked with hot, messy remains the mob pushed, using sheer mass to slide the smoking remnants forward.

Matt reloaded on the run up a spiral stair to the second floor where Sakura fired controlled bursts into the hostiles, prioritizing those who'd made it around the growing pile. The mob flowed across the entryway like grasping tentacles, each sucker a human soul enslaved to the egregoroi's will.

Sakura threw a pair of grenades down the stair and disappeared into the fire exit. Firing, Matt followed, slamming the door behind him before running up after her. Taking stairs four at a time, he pulled the pin on a frag. The door below banged open, so he let the grenade fall, spoon tumbling from his fingers after the explosive. He pulled another, still running, and dropped it.

One detonated, the second moments later. Ears ringing, he made another two floors before his eardrums healed enough to hear again. Footsteps hammered up toward him, so he dropped two more grenades before hitting the crash bar on the top floor and rolling out into a hallway carpeted with drab industrial gray-brown.

Sakura kneeled between executive offices with massive windows that looked out over the city and toward the haze-obscured mountains beyond, her REC7 trained on the far exit. Above her, a ladder led to a hatch. "It's open. Go."

Backing toward it, he opened fire on the exit door as it opened, blasting the first through into smithereens. The far door banged open and Sakura dropped one man, then two, then five.

Matt fired three more shots, shouldered his weapon, and leapt. His hand closed on the bottom of the maintenance ladder, metal cool against his skin. He hauled himself up, shouldered open the roof access and clambered out into hazy sunlight. Sakura's rifle popped below. He took aim into the hole and yelled, "Clear!"

She appeared at his side before he could pull the trigger, sending a trio of fragmentation grenades down the hole. The access door slammed closed under its own weight. It had no lock.

"Let's go." He took a step and she grabbed his wrist.

"Not yet."

She nodded toward the mob on the street, hundreds of people still flowing into the building, faces twisted in inhuman rage but without the slightest sign of pushing or shoving. A green circle appeared on his HUD, high in the sky and approaching fast.

"Oh, shit. Sakura, these people are innocent."

She nodded, almost more of a bow. "Yes."

"Goddammit." They didn't have the ammo, even at a bottleneck, to deal with thousands of fanatical civilians. Even if they did, they'd never kill them all before more arrived, and General Valdez would run out of options.

Sakura fired as the hatch cracked open. It shut, then opened again a moment later. The first body erupted out of the hole, and though she shot the woman in the head two more spilled out, barely slowed by the bleeding meat obstacles in their way.

"Fuck," Matt said, bowling a grenade into the hole as Sakura double-tapped the three on the roof. Red mist puffed from their heads, and they dropped.

"Now." Sakura disappeared in a blast of wind, and he turned to follow her blur as she disappeared off the roof, flying out toward the hardware store.

"Incoming," Janet said.

Feet crunching across the gravel, Matt reached the edge and leapt. A concussive wind knocked him forward, the rising fireball from the Hellfire Romeo turning the world orange red as he sailed over the street.

Legs churning, he hit the terracotta tiles and tumbled forward, using his momentum to roll from his shoulder to his hip before regaining his feet on the precarious slope, taking five more steps and leaping again, skidding off the tin roof of the shed to land on the ground, weapon raised, scanning for hostiles.

A cloud of concrete dust rose above them, billowing out to blanket the neighborhood.

His shoulder burned.

Janet chimed in. "About a thousand down, but there's a lot more where that came from. If you're going to make that temple, you need to hoof it."

Matt took off at a run, Sakura at his side. "What have you got left for armament on those Reapers?"

"Five Hellfires and four whatever the hell those others things are. But the Powell has moved into position in the Gulf, and can provide us with some other options." A US Navy Destroyer in weapons range opened all kinds of possibilities.

"Like what kind of options?"

"High Speed Strike Weapons, bunker busters, if the Mexican government authorizes it." Still experimental,

HSSWs traveled at six times the speed of sound and used compression shockwaves to provide lift. The four thousand-pound missiles slammed tungsten rods into their target with the energy of a ton of TNT each, a tiny fraction of even a small nuclear warhead, but concentrated on a tiny area. The shock of impact would obliterate reinforced concrete and ravage living bodies before the explosives even detonated.

"Tell them General Valdez authorizes it, and when we're a quarter mile from that temple, have them level it. Then use the Reapers to play crowd control while we find Mr Happy, if there's anything left of him."

• • •

The church – and the pyramid below it – disintegrated a split second before the sonic boom hit, slamming Sakura against the wall of the building behind her. She took off at a dead run, straight toward the collapsing ruin, covering half the intervening distance before the ground had settled.

A figure rose from the rubble, ten feet tall and radiant. His almond eyes accentuated rugged skin tanned a deep brown, and his pronounced forehead and protruding jaw proclaimed him a creature from an earlier epoch. A cloak of woven corn husks trailed down his back and across the ground as he stalked forward, his enormous, muscular body bedecked with jewelry – simple beaded necklaces, bracelets, and anklets of green jade connected with fine silver links – and nothing else. His eyes burned with an all-consuming black fire.

Her gaze traveled down to his comically large penis, engorged and swinging with every step, and back up past oversized hands and giant, square teeth to meet his eyes.

Desire bloomed in her abdomen, and lower, a physical need more powerful than any drug. It consumed her, and for the first time in her life she wanted a man. She wanted to be violated by this heinous monstrosity, consumed, broken and used.

Kazuko laughed, and Sakura laughed with her, an American laugh made for effect, and the daitengu scowled. Rowley called them Watchers and rolled them into his Judeo-Christian mythology, but Sakura recognized a demon when she saw one, and didn't need Rowley's monotheistic trappings to see through this one.

It spoke, nonsense words in a pre-Olmec tongue. Guttural and low, they reverberated in her bones, and she stumbled to a stop.

Another wave of desire shuddered through her, her body wet and ready and wanting him to destroy her. Her uncle had wanted her like this, as had oyabun Kasahara Noboru. The first had taken her innocence at far too young an age, while the second she had used for three years to decapitate an ancient dynasty of boryokudan, what the westerners called Yakuza. Both had wielded the pathetic flesh between their legs to stake a claim, to subjugate beyond all human decency and reason, to enslave and to own. One dead, the other in prison, she'd shown each their folly, but not before Kasahara had given her a daughter.

She laughed again, and spoke to the giant creature in formal Japanese. "Surely you understand me, daitengu, at least in speech." Head raised in defiance, she drew her combat knives. "But I understand you so much more."

It spoke again, and she flushed again, this time with rage. The desire to kill, to take its life – to take any life – a raging fire in her breast threatening to burst forth and consume all around her in an orgy of never-ending violence. She wanted nothing less than to paint the ground with its blood, and gorge on the remains.

Her first kill had been a john beating her mother. She'd picked up a kitchen knife and slid it into the side of his fat belly, sawing forward as he pulled away in shock and horror. His entrails had spilled out onto the bed, coating her mother and the sheets beneath, a seppuku borne by choices without honor. Instead of incarcerating her, the police had used her, and she had lost count of how many she had killed while undercover as Kasahara-san's mistress and enforcer, nor how many more as an augmented soldier for ICAP.

And not one of those murders had come from rage or desire, but only duty and honor.

She laughed again, and stepped forward. "Perhaps you do not understand me at all, daitengu. Perhaps you are just a pathetic thing in want of an audience."

His arrogant scowl deepened, lips twisted into a snarl, the paragon of the expression worn by his murderous followers. It spoke in all languages and none. "I am Ometeotl, the father of Gods, and I will not be mocked."

Shaking her head, she advanced on the balls of her feet, ready to spring, keeping the wry smile on her face. "It is not my fault that the truth mocks you, daitengu. You are a relic, sad and old, deserving only of pity, a wounded dog lashing out with mindless, misplaced fury. It is fortunate that I am here to put you down and end your dishonor."

With a roar, Ometeotl charged.

• • •

Matt hefted the sign, a seven-foot chunk of metal with a ball of concrete on one end and a red octagon with 'ALTO' in white letters on the other. Almost well-balanced, it packed a much heavier punch than his combat knives and carried a significantly smaller chance of injuring Sakura than the AA-12.

Their conversation over, she stood in the middle of the square as the egregoroi charged, knives at her sides, an actual, honest-to-goodness smile on her face. She'd kept her visor clear, so she meant the fallen angel to see it. To make it angry. Matt ran, and timed his swing for the moment before it hit her.

Concrete shattered against Ometeotl's ribs, the blow knocking the fallen angel sideways. It grasped for Sakura and she whirled in a blur, severing two of its fingers in a spray of hot black blood.

Matt swung again, bringing the sign down in a vicious overhead chop. The demon dove to the side, and shock ran up Matt's hands as the sign sparked off of the concrete. He swung the makeshift axe again, then backpedaled as Ometeotl's hand gushed blood across his visor. Wiping it away, he grunted as a punch shattered his ribs and sent him tumbling, chest aflame.

He landed on his back and skidded. Sakura's REC7 chattered, a welcome distraction from the itching fire as the fused bone that made up his ribs knitted. He kipped to his feet, reached for the AA-12 and met air.

Ometeotl held it like a baseball bat, hands around the barrel, as he charged Sakura.

Both figures blurred, too fast to differentiate. Blood sprayed, red and black, as Matt approached, flexing, giving his body time to heal enough for round two, scooping up the sign along the way. In the distance a missile popped like a star flower on the Fourth of July, raining countless tiny objects like falling bees onto the ground below. The earth rumbled as the cluster munitions detonated, and Matt wondered how many innocent lives this egregoroi had made them take.

A heft of the sign told him what he needed to know. Walking up behind the thing, he spun, putting all his weight and might into the blow. Metal bit deep into its bicep and the egregoroi stumbled, white bone showing through the dark red flesh.

Sakura stepped in and her knives flashed, dull black streaks punching in and out of the thing's neck and upper torso. She ducked under its arms and rolled between its legs, coming up behind it, both knives buried in its kidneys.

It whirled, ripping them out of her hands, and back-handed her. Her visor burst sideways in a mess of reinforced glass, teeth, bone, and unidentifiable chunks of bloody meat.

Matt chopped down, severing Ometeotl's arm at the shoulder. It fell next to Sakura's limp body, both gushing blood across the sidewalk. Red mingled with black and sought cracks and crevices, the greedy earth sucking up the warm liquid.

The demon roared and lashed out with the AA-12, a clumsy, noncommittal swing. Matt grabbed it and stumbled sideways, alert to the new limb snaking forth from the gushing hole in its shoulder. Ometeotl spun him as he stretched his finger forward. As the biometrics read his fingerprints he pulled the trigger.

Its lower arm exploded. Hot, bloody shrapnel pinged off of Matt's helmet as he fired again and again, sinking four more rounds into the demon's torso. It fell in a black-red heap. Wiping steaming mess from his visor, he stalked forward and stomped down on the thing's exposed spine, crushing vertebra and severing connection to its legs.

Another cluster munition carpeted the neighborhood to his left, and in the burst of light, fear shimmered in the creature's eyes.

It spoke, black words that shocked through Matt's mind, pulsing with the murderous whispers and commanding him to take his own life. He crushed Ometeotl's throat with his boot, then kneeled next to the gaping, struggling head, plucking a thermite grenade from his bandoleer – designed to destroy enemy vehicles and melt through enemy bunkers, it burned at over two thousand degrees Celsius, hot enough to vaporize steel. "You don't belong here. This was never yours to take. Go back to the hell you earned."

The thermite grenade just fit between its large, square teeth, and he shoved the canister back, hard, putting his weight into it. He pulled the pin, stood and stepped back. A second later the white-hot fire reduced Ometeotl's head to ash, and Matt's eyes ghosted despite Augmentation and his auto-darkening visor.

He turned on his heels and kneeled down next to Sakura, her head a mass of blood and hair. He plucked glass from the remains of her face, and breathed a sigh of relief as they pulled away from newly-forming skin. Gently, his fingers sought the extent of the damage – a burst eye, missing teeth, most of the bones in her face crushed beyond recognition.

Her jaw worked up and down, and her tongue writhed in a mouth she couldn't close. He shushed her, then triggered the COM. "Janet, report."

"Hostiles are standing down. They seem pretty confused."

"Good, 'cause Sakura's going to need a while."

"Mmkay, I'll hold off the locals. The paperwork on this one's going to be a bitch."

He stroked Sakura's hair and pulled off his helmet. "Let Valdez do it."

CHAPTER TEN

Monica Rowley watched her husband sigh and lean back from the papers scattered across the kitchen counter, the breakfast nook where they took almost all of their meals.

"If I'd wanted a desk job I'd have become an accountant." She mouthed it with him, the familiar frustration a balm to her soul. Their counter made a poor office, but Matt worked from home as often as he could, which usually meant days and days of paperwork he hated after every mission – and it had only gotten worse since the dissolution of ICAP. A man of action, he needed to create or destroy, to fight, to protect.

Ted bellowed as Adam pulled his tail, both running in tight circles on the carpet by the fireplace. He let go, and Ted bellowed again, tail a joyous fury against the couch, loveseat, mantle, and floor. The TV blared a nonsense show that could only have been designed by people who hated parents and Monica in particular; Adam loved the music and colors and didn't seem to mind the utter lack of plot or coherence.

The house phone rang, and Matt banged his forehead into the table.

"Got it." Monica hurried to the charging station and plucked it up on the third ring. Adam fell silent, and Ted followed, content to scratch his back on the floor and let his boy rub his belly. She hit 'Send' and spoke. "Hello?"

"Hey, Button. Your husband home?" Only her dad called her 'Button', the origin of the nickname lost to time and memory.

"Sure is, Papa. What's up?"

"Dick dropped twelve face right in front of the barn. I was hoping for some help getting it moved to the shed." Twelve face cord of wood in the wrong place would be a terrible backache of a problem for an old man, and maybe two hour's work for her husband – somewhat longer if Papa helped out, which of course he would.

"I'm sure he'll help."

Matt's head jerked up, eyes wide, a smile on his face. His cheeks jiggled with his frantic nod.

"I'll be around all afternoon if he can stop by."

"Let us grab some lunch."

"You got it. Love you."

"You, too."

Matt stood as she hung up, grin bigger than a moment before. "Physical labor? Please tell me it's physical labor."

Adam took his hand off of Ted's head and the dog flopped over, squirming and biting at the air, a contented, whining groan erupting from his throat. Adam squealed and dropped to his knees, hands on Ted's belly, rubbing furiously. Matt squinted at the noise, his face scrunching around his left eye, and Monica laughed.

"Okay, you two outside. A few minutes of running around will be good for you."

She marched them to the back door as Matt called out, "I'll make lunch!" They piled onto the deck, galumphed down the stairs as she plopped into a deck chair and chased each other through the yard, squealing and barking in frenetic spirals until Ted bolted around the side of the house.

Adam ran after him, and Monica shot to her feet. "Adam, in sight!"

The bellows and squeals got farther away, so she shot down the stairs and across the grass, still damp from the morning dew. "Hey! Get back here!"

Her hand went to her mouth as Ted bolted into the road, Adam two steps behind. Aaron Walters ran for them, thirty feet away, suit coat flapping like a superhero's cape. Too far.

Tires squealed, the loaded, bright yellow construction truck locking its brakes ten feet from them. Aaron cringed, turning his head.

Adam fell on Ted, head down, and disappeared from view with a sickening thud.

A scream erupted from her throat, half her son's name, half a mindless wail, as the truck ground to a halt. She covered the ground before the trucker's boots hit the asphalt, and rounded the front of the vehicle.

One hand on the dented bumper, Adam still crouched over Ted, wings of ice enveloping them both in a shimmering field of silver and white. A deep rut dug into the pavement, chunks of asphalt skittering across the road. She blinked; the wings vanished.

Ted barked as the trucker came around the corner of the vehicle, tail a whirlwind of oblivious joy. Adam stood and held up his arms, a worried grin on his face, as Aaron stumbled up.

"Ma'am, we should get back to the house."

She picked Adam up and squeezed him, maybe too hard, never hard enough or long enough. He shushed her and stroked her hair, whispering through her sobs. "Ted's okay, Mom. Ted's okay."

Matt appeared behind her, wrapping them both in his massive arms, the scent of gun oil and aftershave mingling with burnt rubber and diesel exhaust. "Come on, let's go."

Through panicked tears she resolved the crowd, open-mouthed, staring, dropping to their knees one by one.

"Let's go." He pulled them, turning her, putting her back to the crowd. "Let's go, Ted."

Ted chuffed and heeled, a good dog. Aaron's footsteps crunched behind them, followed by lighter, faster ones.

"Sir," Aaron's baritone reverberated through her. "I'm going to have to ask you off the property."

• • •

Matt turned. "Aaron, I got this. Return to your post."

Jason slowed, eyes wide, the unbridled awe on his face fading to guarded hostility as Monica disappeared through the door and Matt blocked his view. Aaron retreated, leaving them alone in the driveway. Behind him a hymn broke out, *A Sovereign Protector I Have* set to that same damned melody as dozens of other hymns.

"Go home, Jason."

"I will in a minute, but—"

"Not across the street." Matt crossed his arms. "Home, home. Go back to your parish in Kentucky."

Jason shook his head. "Not my parish anymore, not my church. I'm here because I belong here. Because your son is a divine emissary."

"He isn't." Matt just managed to keep cold fury in check.

"You can't deny what you just saw. What we just saw."

"It happened. That doesn't mean it means what you think it means."

Jason smirked. "Say that ten times fast."

"Do I look like I'm joking?"

The former priest closed his eyes, breathed out, long and low. "No. I'm sorry. Look, man, your son is special. Very special."

"I know—"

"Let me finish, please."

Matt scowled but said nothing.

"Your son is special, and these people across the street, they're just the beginning. Tens of thousands of people send letters and e-mails every day. The video from DC has over two billion hits. This one will go even higher."

"This one?"

His eyes flicked away, then back. "Yeah. Someone's bound to have caught it on camera."

"So you're filming my property."

His grimace spoke for itself. "We're looking for miracles. For miracles like this."

Matt spread his arms, a threatening gesture borrowed from NFL players. "Am I a miracle? Am I divine? Am I an instrument of divine wrath?"

"Was Saint Martin?"

Matt sneered as Jason continued.

"You know who he was. I knew. That's how we managed to free him. Or would you rather forget that?" Jason put a hand on Matt's shoulder, and he forced himself into a facade of relaxation. "Why is it so hard to believe in a God you have direct evidence of?"

Matt gritted his teeth. "The things in my head aren't divine. They're old and they're powerful, but there are other things, too. So many voices, sadistic and cruel, but millions of others, every Jade user on the planet somehow linked together inside me. Just because we don't understand it doesn't make it God."

"Your son has angel's wings."

"Yes, he does. But he's not an angel, and he's not an egregoroi. He's a little boy who likes Captain America and the Wiggles and peas with peanut butter."

"And stopping a truck with his bare hands."

Matt closed his eyes, silenced the murder lurking there, then opened them and met Jason's pleading gaze. "You believe what you believe, but leave my family alone. You're no longer welcome on this property, and will be considered a threat."

"Oh, come on! We were friends!"

"Were. I don't know what we are now, but I'm keeping you the hell away from my family. Further trespassing will be met with violence."

Jason sneered. "You can't punch your problems away."

Matt pushed him back a step, then another. "I shouldn't have to."

Once he'd removed Jason from the premises, and had

instructed the guards to make him persona non grata, he went back to the house. Monica sat on the couch, cradling Adam, Ted curled up against them. Red streaks marred her beautiful face, and her hands trembled as she stroked their son's hair.

His augmented hearing picked up continued psalms – they'd graduated to 70s hippie church music – so he walked to the mantle and turned on the radio before sitting next to them. They sat while talk radio prattled about immigration, and instead of trying to read his wife's mind Matt scratched Ted's ears and stroked his fur until he fell asleep with a contented explosion of gas.

When she finally spoke it startled him. "You going to help Papa?"

He caressed her neck with his knuckles. "Is that okay?"

She shrugged. "It's got to happen. You know he'll do it himself if you don't show."

"Want to come with? You can bring Adam, chat with your mom. We'll let Ted terrorize the rotties." Ted's tail thumped at the mention of his name.

"I don't think so. I think I want to stay home and just be with my boy."

"Sure?"

"Sure. I'll put some dinner on while you're gone."

"Okay."

• • •

Marcia Stein took a gulp of cabernet and ignored the well-dressed waiter's widened eyes. Cute in a too-young and too-pale sort of way, he averted his gaze by way of looking at Isuji Sakura. Her former mentor warmed her hands around a huge mug of green tea and ordered a bacon double cheeseburger in fluent French.

"I'm sorry, ma'am," he replied in English with an affectation of superiority, "but this is Le Bistro Laurence. We do not serve American cuisine."

"Then put foie gras on it and hold the ketchup."

"I'm afraid you don't understand." He opened his mouth to continue, assessed the look on Sakura's face, and swallowed. "I'll see what I can do. Side?"

"Mashed potatoes. Butter and sour cream."

He closed his eyes, sighed, and opened them again. "We have crème fraiche. I'll have to see about the potatoes."

She nodded, a sharp downward jerk of her head. "Arigato."

Marcia ordered from the menu – something from the fish menu she could barely pronounce and didn't understand, biting off a wicked grin until he left with their order. "Was that necessary?"

Sakura sipped her tea. "These Americans are so rude about everything all the time, I don't have the capacity for polite anymore. I ordered what I want. They'll make it or I won't pay."

"That's how you get spit in your food."

"Better than snails."

They drank in silence. Marcia formulated a dozen conversation starters, and every one struck her as lame and unimportant. In Marcia's experience Sakura didn't engage in small talk, and limited important talk to lessons and mission parameters. She hadn't asked why Marcia had invited her to lunch, and if it made her uncomfortable she made no sign of it.

Their food arrived – Sakura's a chopped beef on baguette with white cheese and bright yellow foie gras that almost but didn't quite resemble a cheeseburger; Marcia's a smattering of chopped white something in yellow-brown sauce that smelled of butter and saffron and tasted like three-thousand calorie heaven.

Sakura covered her mouth with her left hand while she chewed, as close as Marcia had ever seen her come to anything that might be called dainty. "Is he there?"

The question spoiled the effect, but Marcia didn't let it

trip her up. She took another bite, chewed with gusto, and flashed a 'yes' as she reached for her glass. All ICAP agents had trained in American Sign Language as a part of their covert ops training, harder to learn but significantly more versatile than the hand signals used by most American and NATO military personnel. She scratched her head with her index finger and thumb, then brought her hand down, thumb and pinky extended just enough to convey the message: blond hair. The day before he'd had long brown hair in the grocery store, and the day before that a Dodgers cap had just covered a tangle of curls as he walked by the gym.

Sakura took another bite, and muttered with her hand over her mouth. "When you leave, go home. I'll tail him from there."

They finished their meal discussing post-Aug life, and Marcia suppressed a twinge of jealousy at Sakura's renewed powers. As much as Marcia missed them, she wouldn't trade for the whispers again. They skipped dessert and skipped the check. Sakura went to the bathroom; Marcia left the restaurant into the blinding light of midday.

He followed a moment later, pausing at the entrance as she cut right around the side of the building toward the gated parking lot in the back. Two stories sided with tan vinyl, across the alley a brick wall narrowed her escape route to a black iron fire escape beneath which squatted a bright green dumpster. Footsteps closed behind her, soft shoes crunching on loose gravel. Clutching her purse, she reached the small parking lot and turned.

Her follower stopped short, an awkward smile on his face. "Excuse me, miss. Do you have a light?"

Marcia didn't smoke, but she reached into her purse anyway. Her Sig Sauer p320 Compact felt cool in her grip, and the thirteen-round .357 packed an enormous punch for its size. She let the purse fall as a white panel van rolled to a stop on the curb, blocking the only exit from the parking lot.

Instead of backing off, her tail smiled. "Now, now, no need to get violent."

Nobody smiles at the business end of a .357, except maybe an Aug. And there weren't any Augs anymore, not really.

A shock ran up her hand and the pistol skittered across the parking lot. Strong fingers throttled her neck, lifting her from the ground with effortless ease. He'd moved so fast she hadn't registered the blurring form, and his hands clutched like iron.

Stars exploded in her mind as he bounced her head off the car. And again.

Darkness fell.

• • •

Sakura exploded out the back door, leaping down the steps with a chef's knife in each hand. Gravel crunched under her boots as the man dragging Marcia looked up, let her go, and cracked his neck.

The world slowed as her augmented reflexes kicked in, the ambient city noise Doppler shifting into lower octaves. A bird took flight from the fence, wings beating in slow motion as it fell then rose, a war between the pull of Earth and the freedom of the sky above.

The knife left her hand at almost the speed of sound. Her assailant jerked to the side and it grazed his neck, red blood welling at a fraction of the speed of his dodge. Faster than Rowley, he almost moved in real time to the neurons screaming in her head. The whispers joined them, mocking her confidence and proclaiming her death at this stranger's hand.

He met her charge, and the impact sent them both flying. She flipped and landed on her feet, shoes skidding across gravel-strewn asphalt. He smashed into the car door, shattering the window and crumpling sheet metal, and leapt off toward her before the glass had time to fall.

Rolling her left shoulder back, she let his punch glance off and drove the knife toward his kidney. The heel of his left hand deflected the blade so she dropped and punched up in a knife-hand strike to his groin.

Limping back, his condescending smirk had twisted into a snarl. "They said you were fast."

She flicked her eyes down and back up, as close as this thing would get to a bow of respect. With nothing to prove, she had nothing to say, so instead switched the knife to her right hand and flipped him the bird with her left.

He attacked, the predictable, undisciplined response to a taunt – much faster than a man, still slower than half the bonks she'd fought. She spun out of the way, drawing the knife across his right bicep on his way by. The blade dragged against the cloth but didn't cut. She ducked a roundhouse kick and punched the knife into the side of his knee, blocking out his scream as she pushed off the ground into the cut, shearing through the cartilage and meat even as she rolled and came to her feet.

Dull thumps carried across the lot, and two more men emerged from the alley, both armed with bloated black weapons something between a beetle and an assault rifle. Rounds thumped against metal as she hit the ground behind the closest car, too high-pitched – too light – to be regular bullets. Microdarts scattered across the ground on the other side of the vehicle.

Anger seethed as she recalled the prick in her neck, the hazy darkness as Shane Keene apologized, her last concrete memory before a months-long haze of blood and pain. The whispers crawled into the hot nugget of hate and flexed, and hot rage ravaged her psyche.

A breath.

Two.

A veneer of calm settled over her, professionalism and duty and loyalty to Marcia. The whispers raged beneath it, a nagging urge she refused to indulge. A brief glance around the front fender gave her three targets, two armed at the alley entrance, one kneeling, the other standing, using the wall for cover, faces obscured by black nylons. The third writhed on the ground clutching his knee, blood gushing through his fingers and soaking his jeans.

Between them Marcia lay on her side, white froth on her lips, eyes half-open with only the whites visible. Her pistol lay between her and the bleeding man.

Sakura tensed, then dashed to the next car, more to test the shooters' reaction time than to take better cover. Darts pinged off of metal, with only their travel time through the air saving her from getting stuck. Yanking a chrome hubcap from the front wheel, she hefted the flimsy plastic and rejected its use as a projectile.

It caught the sun, so she leapt up, turning the shining disk to blast sunlight into their eyes. As they recoiled she bashed open the car window and jerked on the handle. Hissing as her palm dragged across shattered glass, she dropped from sight as more darts peppered her position. Worming into the open door, she popped the car into neutral and pushed with her legs, turning the wheel to bank it out of the parking spot.

Her boots dug in as she heaved, rolling the left front tire over the bleeding man. His cries of pain became a wet, inarticulate gurgle, and the car jerked lower as his ribcage imploded under the pressure.

As fast as an Aug, but not nearly so tough.

Another push and the car rolled past Marcia, rubber millimeters from her head. Sakura reached underneath the car and pulled up Marcia's pistol, grimacing at the unfamiliar grip in her blood-slicked fingers, then pulled back and rolled right to keep the vehicle between her and her assailants.

As it scraped against another car and came to rest she dropped prone. One pair of legs skirted to her left, flanking, while the other held position at the corner of the building, just one calf visible. She raised the weapon, closed one eye, breathed out, and squeezed the trigger. It had more pull than she'd have preferred.

The pistol bucked with a bang, too loud, but she pulled the trigger again as her opponent fell to one knee. A red puff erupted from his wrist as his hand hit the ground, and he fell sideways.

She rolled right and raised the pistol as footsteps closed, pulling the trigger as the shadow appeared around the car. Bloody gobbets erupted from the last assailant's head even as he pulled the trigger. She grunted and pulled her shirt away from her chest, tearing free the trio of darts embedded there.

Her eyelids fluttered and she fell to her hands and knees. The world pulsed in time with her heart, a relentless beating that shook the pillars of reality. With each beat the whispers grew bolder, shrieking in sadistic elation.

It hurt to hold on. An endless agony of body and spirit, the world held nothing for her but duty, duty to a country that had used and sold her, to an organization that hated and feared her, to a man who respected her to the extent to which she remained useful. The pain of birth meant nothing to the pain of losing a child, and losing her daughter meant nothing next to the despair behind every waking breath.

A red film clouded her vision, bloody glass cracked with jade, and as it rent her vision something shifted in the space beyond.

"Mother."

Sakura sneered, ignoring the soft voice in her ear.

"Mother, you can't let her win."

The figure spread its wings, gossamer threads of emerald green shot through with the darkness between galaxies. It – she – held out her arms, a cruel smile on her face.

Sakura knew that cruelty. It had broken her body more times than she could count. She'd fought her entire life against it, sometimes embracing the darkness to destroy it, if only for a time. The demon in her mind sought to wrest control, and promised peace in return, and in that moment Sakura knew the terrible choice so many bonks had made.

Peace is an illusion except in death, and duty is a sword.

Screaming, she raised her eyes to the blue sky. Bile rose in her throat, and hot vomit spewed across the pavement. Chest heaving, she fell to the side. Each breath pulled burning needles in her throat and chest, and she struggled not to choke on the bile. Her muscles rippled and shifted over grinding bones, settling to mere humanity. The world resolved from jade to unending blue of the sky above, to cars in disarray, to kitchen staff gaping at the corpses in their parking lot. Marcia lay on the ground, a great purple bruise across her face, eyes closed.

Sirens wailed in the distance. Sakura rolled to her hands and knees, pocketed one of the darts, scooped Marcia into her arms and bolted for the street.

• • •

Four days later, Janet walked into Matt's office and dropped a plastic bag on his desk. The dart inside had been tagged with bright yellow plastic, signed by the forensic tech who'd analyzed it. He looked from it to her.

"What's the story?"

She chomped her gum a few times before responding. "It'll be a while. The lab weenies took a sample from the injector, nicked off a piece of the titanium to see if we can source it. Sakura's got a meeting later today with the Joint Chiefs – didn't give them much of a choice."

"What about Marcia?"

"Stein's gone dark. Sakura knows where, but won't even tell me."

He fought a forming scowl, schooled his face to professional neutrality. "What the hell were they thinking?"

"Supposed to be a recon gig. They weren't expecting combat."

He rolled his eyes. "If they knew she was being followed, they should have told me. I doubled the guard at home, but what if something happened?"

Janet sat on the edge of his desk, close enough to smell her perfume or shampoo – apple, which clashed with her peppermint gum. "Why would Marcia trust you? Just because Sakura does? The OPD is government, and so are you. So am I, and we both know Sakura trusts me about as far as I can throw her."

"There's too much going down here for us not to be on the same page. We have to trust each other – no secrets."

She chuckled. "That's asking a lot."

"It is." He held her gaze. "But it's as much as it has to be. We *have to* trust each other."

"Sure, bud." She tossed a manila folder on his desk. "Meantime, I got a call from President Williams. He has a job for us."

CHAPTER ELEVEN

The Patrick J Thomas Juvenile Justice Center's courtroom looked more like a conference room with a judge's bench, modern governmental blandness given physical form. As Matt perused the off-white walls and off-white rug under the fluorescent lights, a door opened behind the bench.

Matt turned as a portly bald man hurried around the wooden edifice, jamming glasses onto his face with one hand, tucking in his light blue shirt with the other. "Sorry! Sorry. Got a bit delayed. Mister Rowley?"

They shook hands, and Matt introduced Sakura, who gave a curt bow.

"I'm Tim. Justice Schwaeble. The Honorable, that is."

"Matt Rowley. What can you tell us?"

He blotted sweat from his head with a stained kerchief. "Well, I – do you want a seat? Some water?"

"No." They said it together.

Schwaeble leaned back into the prosecutor's table. "If it ain't the damndest thing I ever seen. We got eight juveniles here that, well, there's something wrong with them."

Matt waited for him to tell them something that hadn't been in their field briefing, while Sakura re-read the information on her phone.

"Females, age fourteen to sixteen, two black, three Rican, three white. All have priors – sealed, of course – from prostitution to possession with intent to distribute, affiliated with three separate gangs. Nothing violent, though one we caught with a butterfly knife. Thing is, each one turned themselves in in the past four days, confessed to murders we didn't even know about."

Matt pursed his lips. "Who'd they kill?"

"Boyfriends, mostly. One killed her step-uncle who was younger than her by a year, one her boyfriend and his best friend. These boys were violent offenders, dealers, pimps-in-training – ain't nobody nobody's going to miss, you hear me?"

Sakura grunted. Matt figured they had mothers and maybe siblings who'd miss them, but didn't bother pointing that out.

Instead he said, "Are we sure they're telling the truth?"

"Two was all covered in blood, but we ain't found any bodies yet. Should be nine in all."

Matt closed his eyes as the whispers cooed their approval, then opened them. "So how does this involve the Special Threats Bureau?"

The loaded question meant, 'How are fallen angels involved?'

Schwaeble swallowed. "I can't with definition say that it does, sir, but you got to understand, we got our worst neighborhood, a twelve-block area, that's seen a one hundred percent drop in crime – excepting these girls – in a day, and it's lasted nearly two weeks. Gift horses and mouths notwithstanding, it ain't natural, and it ain't possible. The FBI didn't do nothing, so I called Bob – President Williams – and he called you."

Sakura looked up from her phone. "You're on first-name basis with the president?"

"Yes, ma'am. We grew up together."

She exchanged glances with Matt. "That would have been nice to know."

"Well, I—" Schwaeble dug his vibrating phone from his pocket and held it to his ear. "Yeah?"

The voice on the other line, female and clipped, said, "Boss, we got another one. And she's got company."

George Needel ducked into the bathroom and read the text from Shane Keene.

'GO. '

A cold hand clutched his heart, the familiar pre-action jolt of adrenaline, new and exciting even after hundreds of missions. He took a breath, responded with a 'YES', sent another text to four prepaid cell phones, and rejoined the builders in the main hall.

For months he'd suffered through Jason Rees's blathering ministry, pretended to pray with the fanatics in the Adam cult while hiding bugs and explosives in the walls of their new church. The Office of Planning and Development had few staff for a government agency, but an extraordinary budget, and valued employee initiative within reason. Given several options, George had infiltrated the Adam cult.

A nearly rogue element, he couldn't allow Matt Rowley to maintain control of his son. That kind of power belonged in the hands of the United States government, and those loyal to her.

Matt followed the judge into booking and crinkled his nose at the smell. Three light-skinned, dark haired girls – probably sisters – in street clothes stood in front of three female cops, their bland smiles at odds with the blood and gobbets of flesh splattered across their clothes.

They turned as one to Matt and Sakura and, still smiling, opened their mouths. The cops shied back as sound erupted from the girls' spasming throats, a single voice of shrieks and wails and sounds of the streets – gunshots, sirens, traffic. "You are not welcome here. Go back to our daughter's embrace and trouble us no more."

Matt put up a hand, more to stop the cops from drawing their weapons than to keep Sakura from advancing. She had her combat knives, but they'd left the rest of their weapons in the car. He twitched his thumb and then his index finger, what he hoped Sakura would figure out as 'Guns. Go.' in American Sign Language. She disappeared out the door in a blur.

As Schwaeble and the cops stumbled back from the inhuman noise, Matt took a step toward the trio. "Sorry, whoever you are. These girls don't belong to you."

A thousand tortured voices responded with a growl that shook the walls. "You may not trespass on Shamsiel's Eden."

According to ancient writings on the Egregoroi, before following Shemjaza into damnation Shamsiel had guarded the gates to Eden and, once losing paradise on Earth, had tried to create his own before the Flood. Wherever the original garden of paradise might have once been, guarded by the archangel Uriel in the form of a flaming sword, Matt would bet anything it wasn't Omaha. "You've got the wrong continent, dumbass."

Their grins didn't flicker. "Eden is where I make it."

Matt raised his eyes to the policewomen behind the girls. "Get me someone in charge. Now."

• • •

Adam stood in the cart, hands on the edge, and giggled as Monica took the corner around the bread shelves a little too fast. She braked hard to avoid hitting an old lady, ignoring her indignant glare to give a sheepish grin to Aaron Walters, tall and imposing in his black suit and earpiece. Her security guard didn't meet her gaze and said nothing, though his lips twisted in the hint of a smile.

"Okay, little buddy," she said to Adam. "Time to calm it down a little."

"Okay." He sat, as well-behaved as any toddler could be, and let her fill the cart with their weekly wares, canned goods and cereal, Advil, fruit and veggies, two coloring books and a box of crayons, and three paperbacks from the bargain shelf. A few people stared sidelong at Aaron, and others whispered behind her back, but none abased themselves, none screamed out hymns to her son – which is why her detail picked a different Walmart every week, some as far as a hundred miles from White Spruce. She insisted on driving herself, but followed their white panel van without knowing or asking exactly where to.

Left to make their own decisions, she'd never go shopping at all, never visit her parents, never leave the house. Given a second chance at life, she refused to live it in a cage.

The cashier didn't seem to recognize her, and didn't even pay enough attention to realize Aaron looked more like a secret service agent than a typical shopper. Monica cringed at the total, two hundred and eighty bucks they could easily afford, old attitudes dying as hard as bad habits. She paid cash – a security protocol Aaron had insisted upon – and left the store.

Three steps from the curb, Aaron blocked her path with his arm, moving in the way to use his body. "Back inside. Now."

The van still sat next to her truck, exhaust trickling white-gray smoke into the chilly air. Red painted the spider-webbed windshield, obscuring the misshapen head slumped over the steering wheel.

Monica jerked the cart back as Aaron wrested a pistol from his shoulder holster, holding it two-handed and walking backward with his legs spread wide in an almost duck-like stance. As she dragged the heavy load back toward the store with her left hand, she fished around her purse for the pistol Matt had gotten her after the Kamen incident. Bigger than she'd have preferred, the Glock

4th Generation .357 semiautomatic had a custom grip, a 15-round magazine, and just enough weight to make the recoil easy to take.

Gunshots popped from behind her truck. Aaron spun and half-collapsed on the cart. Feet churning, he shoved them back through the automatic doors, falling to his knees before turning and returning fire.

Someone screamed. Glass shattered. Monica hoisted Adam from the cart and backed away toward the aisles. Her son settled on her left hip, it left her right hand free to wield the pistol, though not in the two-handed grip she'd trained with in the back yard. She aimed toward the car and fired twice, pistol bucking, not to hit anyone so much as to keep their heads down while Aaron shuffled on his knees behind a decorative column.

He looked up at her, eyes wide, and patted a hand against his massive chest before ejecting the magazine and slapping in a new one. His bullet-proof vest meant he'd maybe cracked some ribs but probably wouldn't die. Yet.

"Go!" He turned and fired, then rolled back as bullets peppered the ground.

She backpedaled past the registers, firing, sidestepping around abandoned carts and over terrified, cowering shoppers, to drop behind a display of Genuine Boston-Style Baked Beans. She shoved Adam behind her and shushed him. An old man in a cowboy hat lay on the floor to her left, the large revolver in his hands aimed out the door.

"Got your six, ma'am." He spoke around a gray beard smooshed to the side by the dingy white floor tile.

"My bodyguard—"

"I see him. He won't be a target."

The shooting stopped. She took aim around the display, waiting for a bad guy to show his face. "What you got for ammo?"

He spat. "Six. Wife's next door getting liquor. They come in here, she'll take 'em as they cross the lot."

"Good shot?"

"Better than me."

She fired as a head appeared, and the shot went wide. More fire erupted from the left and she cowered. Beans and shredded cans tumbled, slicking the floor, splattering across the back of her neck.

The cowboy yelled over the noise and fired once. "YOUR BOY'S IN TROUBLE!"

He fired again and the hail of bullets shifted to his position, so Monica popped up and fired three times. A man stumbled back from his position behind a car, then fell to his back. "AARON, GET IN HERE!"

Six more shots from her pistol peppered their position as Aaron bolted inside, diving behind a pallet of ice melt pellets and coming up with a twisted grimace. As she popped out the magazine and loaded her second, and last, a kid slid up behind her, skin squealing across the tile. His tan, collared shirt, olive shorts and light blue neckerchief emblazoned with an eagle identified him as an Eagle Scout, sixteen or seventeen years old.

"Ma'am." He pointed a .22 bolt-action long rifle out toward the parking lot, closing one eye to look down the iron sights.

"Jesus, kid, get out of here!"

He shook his head. "Dad says come back to sporting goods. Rest of the troop's fanning out. They ain't getting to you, no how."

"I am NOT putting you in danger!"

"No, ma'am, you're not." He pulled the trigger, rolled back out of sight of the front doors, and ejected the shell. "Those men out there did that. Now git."

The man in the cowboy hat nodded, so she scooped up Adam and ran, hunched to minimize her silhouette, toward the back of the store.

Sixteen deputies helped Matt and Sakura as they entered homes, rounded up their complacent and smiling residents, secured their arms with the giant zip ties they still called handcuffs, and deposited them on the curb under the watchful eye of twenty prison guards Matt had deputized for the purpose.

"Anything yet?" His helmet under his arm for PR purposes, he depended on Janet to relay Dragonfly data to his earpiece.

"Did I say there's anything yet?"

Sakura appeared in the doorway to a run-down two-story home with peeling blue paint on naked wooden slats that hadn't been primed prior to painting. She held up four fingers, then patted invisible heads while shaking her own.

Matt flagged down a deputy and pointed toward her. "Four people, no children."

They hadn't found a single child under fifteen or so, nor any adults who resisted or answered questions. Every single one had invited them inside, offered tea or coffee, and acquiesced to handcuffs with the same bland smile.

"C'mon, Shammy!" Matt's voice rang out down the street. "We going to have some fun here or what?"

The wind picked up, then faded – a natural rather than supernatural phenomenon.

"Dammit," he muttered. "Where is it?"

Five minutes and three houses later, Janet spoke up. "Got something, three blocks west. At the elementary school."

Matt pulled on his helmet and took off at a jog, Sakura at his side. "Get me the blueprints, please."

• • •

Four men in tan and olive hurried Monica behind the sporting goods counter even as they loaded weapon after weapon from the shelves. Shotguns, hunting rifles, .22s, dozens had already been laid out, and kids passed them two at a time to a man with bolt cutters who sheared the breech locks, then on to the kids at the ammo shelves.

Kids.

"I can't do this."

Adam turned from the boys loading weapons to the sporadic pops in the front of the store, then looked her in the eyes and nodded. She'd never felt such calm conviction, such self-assured warmth, not even in her husband's arms.

"Ma'am," one of the scoutmasters said. "Makes sense they're after you, so why don't you duck out the back while we hold them here? Wouldn't want—"

"THEY'RE COMING!" A roar split her eardrums as a teenager fired a shotgun, cocked it, and fired again.

Strong hands grabbed Monica and dragged her through the double-doors leading into the stock room, a concrete-floored cavern three stories high filled with pallets and shelves. A boy screamed, then cried out. "MOM! I WANT MY MOM!"

The pain in his voice tore at her heart. No one's babies should die to protect hers.

The scoutmaster shoved her toward the back door. "GO!" He turned, bolted out the doors, and stumbled back through as blood misted from his back. He fell to his side and lay there, unmoving, as red gushed from his chest and back.

She ran, Adam in her arms.

• • •

Children swarmed out of the elementary school, first dozens, then hundreds. They held furniture legs, meter sticks, fire extinguishers, baseball bats. Matt approached at a jog, shotgun slung across his back, hands raised with fingers spread wide, as unthreatening a gesture as he could manage. Smiles upon smiles greeted his gaze, the same blank, pleasant expression as the adults.

They approached at a lazy shuffle, closing ranks to block off entrance to the school.

Stepping back, Matt turned on his microphone to let the speakers in his helmet carry his voice at crowd-control volumes. "Awww, c'mon, Shamsiel. Hiding behind kids? Uriel's not such a coward, is he?"

As one the children sneered. Perfect.

"Oooh, did I hit a nerve? Are you jealous he took your job?"

Four steps and a leap would take him over most of them, two more steps to the flagpole, and using it to push off he should be able to clear the rest without ever contacting any of them.

"You can't even guard this one, Shammy, and it's a shithole, not a garden."

They raised weapons and approached at a jog.

Janet interrupted. "Cops behind you."

The IFF showed four deputies approaching his position, weapons out but pointed down. He turned, backpedaling. "Get back, dammit! We don't want to hurt these kids."

With a shriek the children charged.

Matt held up his hands. "WAIT!"

The cops opened fire.

* * *

"*Put the weapon down!*"

Monica shied back as the state trooper approached the employee entrance, pistol pointed at her face. Three squad cars blocked the back lot, lights flashing. With her left hand she pushed Adam further back into the building.

She let the pistol hang by the trigger guard, sank down with it held at arm's length.

He approached at a jog, which seemed off – cops used

that walk that made them look like Groucho Marx, because it allowed them to keep solid aim at a target while on the move. Studying his face, she'd seen it before, but not as a cop – tall, scruffy, he'd worked on Jason's church as a carpenter, had been there when Adam had saved Ted.

Undercover? And for who?

He wasn't sweating, and didn't even look nervous, even as the gunfight rattled behind her.

"Bring out the boy."

From his vantage point he wouldn't have been able to see Adam, even before she'd pushed him back inside. Her hand swept up, spinning the gun, rolling her body back to minimize his target.

He fired, and a fist punched her below the right breast. She squeezed the trigger twice and he stumbled back, the second round catching his shoulder outside his bullet-proof vest. His pistol clattered to the ground as she scrambled back inside and slammed the door.

Adam lay a hand on her and she jerked away, snarling, from the feeling of peace and well-being his touch brought. Blood gushed down her blouse, hot and sticky, as three scouts backed into the room, firing hunting rifles as fast as they could.

The doorknob jiggled, then warped in a hail of gunfire from outside.

The kids, white-faced and terrified, took cover behind pallets piled high with cardboard boxes, one of them whimpering, "Ohfuckohfuckohfuck."

"SURRENDER!" she yelled. "Don't die for me."

"We already tried," a boy hollered back. "Jim's dad threw down his gun. They killed him on his knees."

The back door banged open. The carpenter swung inside to the sound of a shotgun blast, and his head disappeared in a splatter of red against the wall. Someone moved behind him, but backed away as another shot tore through the empty space.

Monica grabbed the handle to the giant metal freezer, jerked it open with a groan. The pain in her ribs flashed white in her mind. She shook it off, shoved Adam into a stack of ice-rimed cardboard boxes. "COME ON!"

As she dragged it open, teeth gritted against the fire in her ribs, the boys backed toward her, shooting indiscriminately out both doors. She joined them, emptying her second magazine, pinning down their attackers long enough for everyone to retreat inside. At the last moment, two of them stopped outside the door.

"Hide in here with them, Steve. We'll draw them off."

Before the youngest could object, they closed the door, leaving Monica, Adam, and the blond-haired boy in the pitch black.

The freezer reeked of gunpowder and fear. Her chest throbbed, and each successive breath came out more of a wheeze. She dug out her phone and flipped on the light. A glance at the door handle and her stomach sank – a plain pull-bar, it had no lock, no pinning mechanism. Opening outward, they didn't even have a way to jam it so it wouldn't open.

"We're trapped," Steve said as yelling and gunfire receded from the freezer.

Monica backed as far as she could go, took shelter behind a pile of ice cream cartons. "Save your bullets for people breaching the door. If we make it bloody enough then maybe we can hold off until the real cops get here."

Steve sank to the floor and put his head in his hands. "I'm out of ammo."

"Me, too."

Adam hugged her leg, and put a hand on Steve's shoulder.

• • •

Matt slapped a pistol to the ground and punched another

cop in the chest, pulling back at the last moment so his fist didn't crush the man's chest. "RUN!"

As they stumbled away he turned on the mob of kids. They hit him at full speed, dragging at his clothes and armor, throwing themselves into his legs to try to drag him down.

But kids were just kids, and on a bad day Matt could bench-press a truck. He waded through them, throwing them off, shoving them aside, using ferocious speed and strength to spin, slap, and shake off anything that threatened to drag him down or grab at his grenades or ammo. He stumbled away from the last few and bolted for the school steps, taking them six at a time and flying through the front doors into the school.

An unimaginable reek permeated the building, a thousand years of pus and infections left to swelter in the midday sun. In the near-total darkness, his infrared vision picked up a massive glow down a hallway to the right, illuminating mud-streaked floors and walls, scattered books and papers, and doors left ajar. Impacts rang off the glass in the lobby behind him as his HUD overlaid the school blueprints with the scene in front of him.

Sakura appeared at his side, REC7 in her hands. "Doors are locked. Should keep them some time."

Matt clicked his COM in acknowledgment and moved out, footsteps soft along the hallway despite a strong suspicion that Shamsiel knew exactly where they were. They cleared rooms one at a time, not looking for kids or normals and instead focusing on the fallen angel. Matt trusted the whispers to warn him of anything behind them, and Sakura had proven time and again that she could take care of herself.

The smell grew as they approached the warm hall, sickly stench bad enough that Matt engaged his air filters. He rounded the corner and grunted.

"Janet, you getting this?"

Tendrils spilled from the gymnasium, filling the hallway with fat, mucus-covered tentacles. Several dozen children suckled on them, pulling fat pink nipples into their mouths to drink down the gray-green liquid leaking from countless others.

"Roger," Janet said. "Looks pretty gross."

Matt fell back around the corner and turned to Sakura, whose mirrored visor reflected his own in an infinity of images. "This thing is enormous. Advice?"

"Clear out what children we can, hit it with Hellfires."

"We can't—" Matt started.

"I'll clear it with the President," Janet interrupted. "I think we can 'Clear and Present Danger' this one pretty well. He's not going to want a Cholula-scale disaster on his hands."

"He may already have one." Matt closed his eyes, took a deep breath. "Yeah, scramble the drones, call the White House. And evacuate the area."

"You got it, bud."

• • •

Monica shifted her weight, more to slide the cold to another part of her ass than because of any muscular discomfort. The bleeding had slowed, but every breath came harder than the one before it. Her heart stuttered in time with the occasional gunshots outside, and her mind swirled with the sirens.

The frost from her breath coalesced, mingling with Adam's and Steve's, hanging in the air in impossible whirls and eddies like leaves in a windstorm frozen in time. She watched in amazement as the shapes resolved into feathers of silver and ice, and a familiar voice called out to her.

"Do not be afraid. All will be well."

She'd last heard it in the snows outside White Spruce, on the day Humans for Humanity had burned half the town, killed and injured her friends. They'd taken her captive, held her, drugged her, and had just started to rape her when her husband had burst in and killed every man and woman responsible, then hunted down the rest to find and rescue their child.

"Adam, baby, is that you?"

Her son snuggled into her, shivering, and the voice answered in her mind. "Yes and no. Not all who fell remained defiant, and—" a syllable shattered her mind, ringing like a gong through her being and wracked her body in ecstatic spasms, "—is forgiving. I'm sorry your Adam is the vehicle, but we have to hide from Her."

"We? Her? I don't understand."

"Shush. Be at peace."

"Lady," Steve whispered, "you need to shut the fuck up or they're going to find us."

The door handle rattled, and Steve's hands tensed on his empty rifle, fingers blue from the cold.

• • •

Matt sliced away another tentacle and pulled the last child free, this one a girl no older than six, licking her lips and smiling even as she reached out for another taste. He passed her back to Sakura and tried to peek past the writhing mass into the gym to see if there were any more.

Shamsiel, for its part, had yet to resist. The tentacles slithered away from their grasp, and a pathetic, mewling whine erupted from the gym as they cut the children free, but they'd encountered no violence they hadn't brought themselves. Sakura had her hands full keeping children from rushing back in once freed, electing to lock them in rooms further down the hall, and Matt's muscles ached from sawing through sticky, ropy nastiness.

The fleshy ropes crumbled to powder when severed, and he worked fast enough to kill them faster than they regrew, at least so far. With the last kid out of the way he waded in, hacking and slashing with razor-sharp knives, the ceramic-composite carbon fiber shredding ropy meat to dust in a blur of oddly dry carnage.

He reached the doorway, cracked his neck, and waded in. Shamsiel pulled back with a whine, tentacles collapsing farther and father in on themselves as they sought to escape his relentless advance. He stomped, cut, and hacked as the ball shriveled smaller and smaller, and wondered at what point the thing would decide to fight back.

The Dragonflies blipped, and the IFF lights in his HUD triggered on four bogeys swooping in from the South at two hundred miles an hour.

"Janet?"

"Not us. Flyboys say it isn't them, either."

"Don't suppose they want to intercept?"

"Offutt's pretty light on fighters and combat choppers. I'll see what I can do."

"Sakura?"

She charged in next to him, arms a blur as she sent dusty pieces of nothing across the room like a weed whacker set on 'annihilate'. A pattern emerged to Shamsiel's retreat – the tentacles collapsed toward the ventilation system in the rear of the gym. Matt unshouldered the shotgun, lifted it, and took aim.

"Sakura, see what you can do about cutting off that vent."

He pulled the trigger, and the fin-stabilized grenade plunged into the soft flesh before detonating. The tentacles collapsed in wisps of nothing, fading from view and IFF as if never there.

The building rocked, and fire bloomed outside.

"Company," Janet said.

Matt swore. "Sakura, get back here."

"It's in the basement. I'm going after it."

He shifted his feet to maintain balance as the building

rocked again. Dust rained from the ceiling, and Shamsiel's whimper turned into a nervous giggle.

"Just get back here." His voice rang funny in his ears.

The Dragonfly data disappeared in a pixelated fuzz.

"Janet?"

"I know, I see it."

The wall exploded inward, concrete and brick spraying across the room. Matt fired the AA-12 as the whispers rejoiced in his death at the hands of the monstrosities coming through, biomechanical suits ten feet tall and painted construction yellow. Yardley had almost killed him with one of these suits, but he hadn't been armed.

"Come get some." He fired high and triggered the frags to explode downward. The thing in front stumbled as red-hot fragments rained down around the human head mostly protected by a helmet stylized to look like a football helmet. It caught itself on the wall with a giant hydraulic claw, crumbling brick and slicing through rebar as it shifted to the side.

Matt took the delay to swap directional frags for depleted uranium-tipped sabot penetrators. The ultra-sharp darts lacked the fin-guided smart capabilities of the frags, but could punch holes in an Abrams tank.

A voice sounded over his COM. "You're getting expensive, Rowley. Just lay down and let the inevitable happen."

Keene. Shane Keene had posed as an FBI agent, set up Matt to die, and captured Sakura. He had to know Matt wasn't the surrendering kind.

The behemoths charged, and behind them shapes flickered in the dust and smoke, human silhouettes moving three times faster than the average man. Matt waited for the footballer to close, dove through its legs, and fired twice straight up, behind groin and buttocks and into the pressure pump powering the suit's motion.

Sakura's REC7 chattered somewhere below, her location obscured by the compromised Dragonfly system.

As the first behemoth sagged Matt rolled to his feet. The whispered chittered their precognitive disappointment as a target dove left to dodge his shot, so Matt pulled the weapon left and fired. The target dove, and the armor-piercing burst blasted most of his intestines into the wall behind.

Matt spun as bullets whizzed through the space he'd just occupied, grazing his abdomen.

"Fuck, they're fast," he muttered. They darted forward, flanking him. Using the disabled giant for cover, he shot the second behemoth through the chest, then the helmet. It stutter-stepped and froze in place.

Two tight bursts dropped another assailant, leaving three.

Whispers chittered. Turning—

The AA-12 tore out of his hands, along with most of his trigger finger. He stumbled back and yanked a grenade from his bandoleer left-handed, pulling the pin with his teeth. Ducking fire, he skittered it across the gym toward the man circling by the far bleachers.

Heat seared through his right thigh, then again, even as the whispers warned him. He stumbled, dove, as another round shattered his right knee. Rounds hammered his chest plate as he scrambled back toward the double-doors leading to the hallway. His visor cracked, a spider web of glitching pixels across his vision.

A woman dropped next to him, assault rifle aimed at his chest. Matt drew his pistol and rammed it into her stomach, the .50 caliber round exploding out her back even as she fell.

Bullets punched up his armor as he realized his mistake – pausing to eliminate her had left him open to the others. Flopping back under a wall of pain, he had to admire their professionalism: small caliber shots hammered his armor, solidifying the bullet-proof gel and bruising the flesh underneath without doing significant damage, while larger bullets reduced his legs and arms to ribbons and shattered bone.

Debilitating. Non-lethal.

He twitched and shuddered as electricity seared through his body. Head to the sky, panting, the world closed to only a hazy red sky and the whispers, rejoicing in his pain.

Adam put his hand on Steve's shoulder as the door opened. Monica felt the tension flood from his muscles even as she tensed, the fight-or-flight instinct trying to give her ravaged, weakened body enough adrenaline to move.

Two men stepped inside, masks and goggles obscuring their faces, sleek black outfits reducing their forms to shadow.

"Sir?" One turned around. "There's nobody in here."

Another person stepped in, jerked off his helmet to reveal a grizzled face pock-marked with old wounds, his bald head half-covered in mottled scar tissue. "Bullshit."

The subordinate stepped aside and gestured right at them. "Nowhere to hide, nowhere to run. They're not here."

The grizzled man threw boxes to the side, flipped a pallet in the small space, and roared while frozen produce tumbled off of Adam's wings. "YOU'VE GOT TO BE FUCKING KIDDING ME!" He took several breaths, eyes closed, before snapping them open. "I'm not telling Keene they got away. Clear the store again. Every fucking aisle. Now."

"We've already—"

"NOW!" He shoved both men out the door, and hollered over their protestations – the cops, the real cops, were already there, and more were coming.

They left the door open, and warmth streamed inside, turning the air into a thick fog. Steve twitched as if to move forward, and Monica squeezed him tighter.

"Not yet," she whispered.

"What... what just happened?"

"It's a miracle. Roll with it. And stay still."

Three men dragged Matt – or at least his head and torso – toward one of the four Sikorsky Super Stallion heavy-lift transport helicopters idling next to the playground. Sakura crept forward, a bandoleer of grenades in one hand, her REC7 in the other. As they carried Rowley up the ramp into the back of a helicopter, Sakura bolted forward and heaved.

"Now," she deadpanned. The grenades fell inside one helicopter. Someone screamed.

Hellfires streaked from above, slamming into another two as the grenades detonated.

Sprinting against the heat wash, she let the fourth machine shield her from the worst of the shrapnel, as she'd hoped it would shield Rowley. As fire billowed skyward she launched herself up the cargo ramp, her first two bursts pulping the head of the man holding Matt under the armpits.

The others dropped Matt and turned, reactions much faster than human. She shot one in the chest, kicked the other in the chin, and spun to avoid the knife-thrust from the first. It grazed her stomach, drawing a line across her armor, and he jerked back before she could break his elbow with a downward chop.

As the first drew a pistol she closed the distance, grabbed his wrist left-handed, and spun around it, using the momentum to drive the elbow of her rifle hand into his temple. He rolled with the blow but lost the gun, and as he flew away she pointed the REC7 at him one-handed and pulled the trigger.

The helicopter lurched.

A knife sank into her right shoulder and the rifle fell

from her grip. She threw herself back, slipped on Matt's blood, and fell, driving the knife the rest of the way in. Her opponent dove for the pistol and she smiled. No matter how fast a person could be, gravity was gravity, and Sakura was faster. She kicked out, drawing one of her own combat knives left-handed, and placed it pommel-down against the floor under the falling man's abdomen.

As it tore through his armor she drove him back into the wall, ripping the knife free through half of his stomach, turned, and threw it.

Her other opponent caught it in his neck, eyes wide in shock, and sat back down, so she yanked the knife from her shoulder and stalked to the cockpit, drawing her sidearm as she went.

The helicopter hovered twenty feet above the ground, the copilot turned with wide eyes to watch her approach. She shot him in the face and pressed the hot barrel against the pilot's temple. He winced as it hissed against his flesh.

"Put us down."

He pulled the stick, and the helicopter dropped. As it touched down he licked his lips. "I—"

She pulled the trigger, then wiped the blood from the barrel on his uniform before turning back to the cargo hold. "Requesting extraction."

"Roger. How's Rowley?"

Muscle and veins writhed around the shattered remains of bones, and his eyes had glazed over in unseeing pain. She kneeled and ran a hand over his forehead, an unfelt kindness she wasn't sure he could feel. "He's going to be hungry."

"Okay."

"And Janet? Call the White House. Tell them the angel got away."

"What? How?"

"Down the drain. It got… small."

Hours later, Monica dared to leave the freezer. Her gunshot had healed, a fact that should have surprised her but didn't.

A man in white overalls and a mask startled back as the door creaked open. He looked her up and down with eyes wide in shock. "WE'VE GOT SURVIVORS HERE!"

Approaching with hands outstretched, he stepped over the shattered body of a teenaged boy, his tan shirt stained dark red. "Ma'am, it's okay. You're going to be okay."

Tears rendered him blurry, obscured the body of the boy who had died protecting them, one of many. "No, no it isn't."

CHAPTER TWELVE

Rotors thrummed, a drumbeat of life a thousand times faster than his heart. The searing itch of regeneration overwhelmed all other sensation, and behind the wall of pain and shock the whispers promised him release if only he'd let go. Akash Rastogi smoothed his hand over Matt's head, warm and comforting. "Don't listen to them, eh? They're liars."

A million voices murmured their agreement, among them his son, the only one of the white whispers he knew to be alive.

"Are you here?"

Sakura answered, but in his ears rather than his mind. "Yes. Be still."

He let his useless eyes flutter closed and gritted his teeth against the itch, and the raw burn of her knife cutting eager new flesh away from slower-healing bone.

• • •

Monica sat on the wooden bench, Adam asleep beside her, his head on her thigh. Policemen and women rushed back and forth, the Macon County Sherriff's Department overwhelmed by a disaster of this magnitude. The lone TV in the corner, a 20" tube that might have been new in 1990, scrolled misspelled captions beneath a talking head on CNN, switching back and forth between the attacks and explosions in Tennessee, Nebraska, Virginia, and Texas.

Reporters lurked on the sidewalk next to the traffic circle in front of the building, cameras aimed inside or at bottle-blonde reporters yammering what they didn't know into microphones.

Steve huddled in the conference room, comforting his wailing mother. Numb and huddled in the freezer, he hadn't told Monica the boy who'd led their attackers away had been his older brother, nor that one of the scout masters had been their dad.

Had been.

Twenty-three dead, including nine scouts, five scout masters, the cowboy and his wife – who'd killed two assailants as they ran for the store before being gunned down – two civilians caught in the crossfire, and five attackers. An unknown number had escaped, taking with them the State Police vehicles and minivans caught on security cameras. The manhunt had spread across the state and into Kentucky.

Aaron Walters had been rushed to Nashville via helicopter with multiple gunshot wounds, and last she'd heard was still in surgery.

The thunder of a helicopter shook her out of her stupor, and Adam popped up from her lap.

"Daddy!"

A sad smile crossed her face, that Adam would associate helicopters with his father, an unwanted reminder of how much time Matt spent away.

He bolted for the front door and Monica took off after him, scooping him up into her arms before he made it more than a few steps. Her legs tingled, pins and needles from sitting too long on unpadded furniture, but she turned toward the commotion outside.

Matt limped up the steps, his black ICAP uniform a bloody tatters, bullet holes in the chest exposing the sleek armor underneath. Sakura stalked in front of him, clearing the steps, her helmet on and mirrored, a nightmare of menace in female form even without any visible weapons. They ignored reporters and cameras both, Sakura holding the door for Matt as he stepped inside, and shutting it behind them.

Red knots mottled his muscular arms and legs, the mostly hairless skin a sign of new growth. His light brown eyes blazed with equal parts fury and relief. As Adam squirmed and reached out for him, he forced a toothless smile, which broke into a real one as he tossed their son into the air and caught him in the crook of his arm.

Adam cackled as Steve's mother sobbed, and Monica's heart soared and broke in equal measure. She slid in under Matt's other arm and held her family, squeezing too hard, not nearly hard enough.

After a moment Matt shifted, a subtle tensing she wouldn't have noticed had she not been holding him.

"Hey," he said. "Turn that up."

She turned to look at the TV, a series of images of weird tentacled creatures and children with creepy smiles, a helmeted man – obviously her husband – using a stop sign as a battle-axe against a winged caveman-looking man. As the volume came up a woman's calm, newscaster voice droned on. "—were taken from the helmet cameras of a top-secret government division known as the Special Threats Bureau."

The picture changed to Ronald Kellett standing at a podium. Humans for Humanity's founder stood against the backdrop of dark blue banners emblazoned with H4H. His wrinkled, pale skin stood in stark contrast to his charcoal suit, complete with a dark-purple pocket square and matching tie. His hands trembled, but his voice rang out strong and clear. "My fellow Americans, there are those who might say I'm too old for politics. One of them might be me. But when our government funds, our President associates with, the demonic and unnatural, what are we to do? When beings from the ancient antediluvian days lay waste to cities and neighborhoods, what are we to do?"

The camera zoomed in on his clear gray eyes flecked with blue, something Monica had never seen before. They didn't shy away, and they didn't waver. "Despite being so very weary of this evil world and its evil ways, of evildoers and evil creatures, when God calls I must answer. And so I am declaring my candidacy for President of the United States."

He spoke for several more minutes, most of it about the Special Threats Bureau, led by 'demon wizard' Matt Rowley and 'heathen witch' Isuji Sakura, and answerable only to President Robert Williams. Matt reached up and turned the TV off.

"Fuck me, babe. What was that?" She stole a guilty glance at Adam, but if he'd heard he gave no indication, instead staring at the back of Matt's head.

He turned and threw up his hands. "I don't know, Mon. Something not good."

• • •

Sitting on the bed, Conor turned off the TV and Kellett's ramblings then ran his hands through the girl's black hair, taking no pleasure from the warmth of her mouth on his cock. Tiff or Tina or something, she'd joined his cult and his bed a willing victim, desperate to give everything for a hint of his adoration. The useless twat's soul held the same allure as the motel room she kneeled in, soaking up every nugget of faint praise, every suggestion of approval, a simpering void where he needed a font.

At climax she looked up at him, grinning, and swallowed. He lifted his legs and squeezed his thighs. With a shocked squeak her head burst, blood and brains gushing from the separated bone plates. He held her there long enough for struggling hands that didn't yet realize they were dead to smear her fluids across his stomach, then let her collapse on the floor.

His perfect body held not the slightest blemish. Stronger, taller, faster than before his death, he blazed with life and energy, an Adonis far too good for Aphrodite. But all food tasted like ashes, every touch a pale shadow of what had come before. He'd crossed the bridge, but left something of himself behind.

The bridge quivered in his mind. The things on the other side danced and scurried, fought and shoved to be near the front. They mewled and cajoled, begged and promised, demanded obeisance, offered fealty, if only he'd let them across. Far too much of him wanted to do it, a thought he still recognized as not his own.

Standing, he let flesh and fluid drain as he stretched, a human reaction that he didn't need and that didn't feel good, not like it used to. Some costs were better hidden than others.

"Dammit. Alive to jive, right?"

Instead of showering he opened the front door and stepped naked onto the stoop.

Hastings Shore didn't have much of a shore, just a smattering of decrepit docks that reeked of dead seaweed and old fish. Nineteen houses and a post office, its sixty-two residents depended on a gas station for overpriced groceries when they couldn't be bothered to drive twenty miles to somewhere smacking of civilization. None of them had eaten in days, or gotten their mail, or called their loved ones or families.

They stared at him in rapture from the parking lot, where they'd remained on their knees since he'd braided their souls and minds into a conduit for his will. Their incisions had festered in the damp environment, and ropes of bloody pus leaked down from the angry red lines in their scalps. Dehydrated and starving, not one had walked away, not one had resisted his will, and instead of empowerment he felt only disgust.

Creatures such as these had no place in the world, no place in the universe but as chattel, playthings, or food for higher beings. An insult to reality, they squandered their spirits on base things, television and gossip and envy. Not one knew the meaning of power, nor even thought to ask.

He circled around the first, put his hands on her shoulders, and cleared his mind. Black wind howled across the bridge, and against it he sent a trickle of jade. It wormed through the bore in reality and split into fine hairs, and split again and again, until sixty-two filaments groped across the span, fighting the wind's rage to wind ever closer to the eager creatures on the other side.

The first leapt, grabbing the closest filament, and screamed in triumph. Dissolving, it pumped up the jade strand like blood through an artery, screaming into existence as Conor jammed the other side into the woman's neck.

Her sigh contained finite regret, moments squandered from birth to now, as the demon infested her body. Its triumphant smile turned to shock as Conor grabbed her hair and lifted off her skullcap. He dove his hands into the glistening, rotting brain, and feasted.

The demon gibbered in panic as he stuffed chunks of the greasy organ into his mouth, chewed, swallowed. Its wail failed to nothing as he consumed its power into his near-mortal body, a churning oubliette for souls both human and demon. Across the bridge the others scattered, but too late. As jade filaments brushed them they froze, and whimpered, and gushed across the bridge in a fury of impotent betrayal.

Conor moved from host to host, choking down slimy gobbets of possessed human brain until he thought he might burst, and then did it again, and again. With each the bridge shuddered, shimmered, diminished, and his body shook with power.

The bridge shattered as he swallowed the last corrupted soul. His roar drowned out the ocean, and the Earth rumbled with his glory. Waves obliterated the dock, and wind tore houses from their foundations.

A thunderclap blasted him from his feet. He lay on his back, a smile on his lips, as the spell faded. Every nerve shot with ecstasy, every sensation an orgiastic banquet. He opened his eyes at the stars – he'd lost hours, but had an eternity to make up for it – and marveled at a beauty no human eyes could see.

Apotheosis. Godhood. Unimaginable power wrested from—

"Oh, silly boy." Her voice cut off his meanderings, and he snarled.

"Watch your tongue."

Her shadow blocked out moon, and then the stars, until emerald wings and jade eyes became his universe. Gerstner. Nyx. Bathsheba. Lilith. The last of the nephilim, she took many names, but he knew her form, knew her voice. It resonated with the universe and drowned him in majesty. "You think you know power, but what have you stolen? The lost looking for a way across the bridge? A few dozen souls? Trinkets."

He stood to look her in the eyes, and found his neck craned back. She stood as tall as the sky, an infinite shadow dwarfing him and everything around him. Glints of jade hinted at unimaginable beauty. Lust, a lost emotion he hadn't felt since murdering his sister in his early teens, consumed his mind.

She drew a fingernail down his neck, tenderly tore a jagged, bloody line through his skin. "You think you've achieved something, gained some kind of significant power. And I suppose for your kind you have. But you forget the bargain."

Conor sneered. "I made no bargain."

"Do you think I survived twelve millennia, bested all of my brothers and sisters, as a fool? All plans fail, so we make more than one. You traded power for servitude the moment you took me into your veins." Her smile brought a desperate need to please her, and he whimpered, choking it down to drown it in bile. It burned in his chest, undiminished, and another denial wouldn't form on his lips.

"I created you, Conor Flynn. Elevated you above men, led you to the dark places to find knowledge of bridges. All you are and all you've become is because of me. Belongs to me. Do you believe you did these things on your own? And do you believe I did this because I loved you?" Her hand sank lower, fingers pushing through his stomach into his abdomen, a horrible pain he never wanted to end. "Or have I misjudged you so poorly?"

"No!" The desperation in his voice disgusted him; desperate to keep his intestines where they belonged, desperate to feel her touch even if it killed him.

This isn't me. This isn't me. THIS ISN'T ME!

Words formed, his but not his. "I've felt you all along, guiding me."

"And what is my gift in return for my generosity?"

He licked his lips. "I am yours."

The lie became truth on his tongue, and at that moment he knew true damnation.

• • •

Otayba smiled at Levi. "Have you heard the tale of why blackfellas must never walk alone?"

Levi returned his grin, white teeth in a face too black for his name. "You going to go old wallaroo on me? Hit me with a boomerang and eat me?"

Otayba shook his head, then jutted his chin toward a girl stumbling down the country road toward them, one hand on a bottle of booze, the other holding her skirt out of the mud.

"You're going to hit her with a boomerang and eat her?"

Otayba shrugged. "Close enough."

Levi's nervous grin faded. "What do you—why?"

Otayba shrugged again. "Why did the wallaroo kill so

many? Because he could, because he needed to eat, because they were vulnerable."

"I'm not sure I get what you're saying, mate."

He grabbed Levi's wrist, felt the blood pulsing under the skin. "Aren't you hungry?"

"Sure, mate. I'm..." His confused grimace faded into blank nothingness. "Famished. But why her?"

"You don't see enough white people around here? This is our land, mate. Ours, not theirs. But here she comes, not a fear in the world. Like she owns the place."

Levi nodded. "Right, let's kill and eat her, then."

"Glad you're on board."

They stood as one, turned, and walked toward the stumbling girl.

• • •

The bartender looked up as the door opened, a rare enough occurrence at 2:30 AM in Polevskoy, and rarer still on a week night. The miners drank hard until midnight or so, but the bosses had no patience with hangovers or late arrivals when the trucks left in the morning – if you didn't show you didn't work, and if you didn't work you didn't get paid.

He sized her up – worn leather boots and a smudged white dress with a lizard embroidered on the breast, no jewelry or purse – before appraising her figure, petite but curvy in the right places, her black hair in a long braid that fell to her waist. Her light green eyes met his over a quirk of a smile, and he grunted.

"We're closed. But would you like a drink?"

She approached, a stream tumbling down the side of the valley. "Yes."

He grabbed two glasses and the vodka, poured shots, careful not to spill any. "I'm Pavel."

She downed her shot and set it next to the bottle. "Call me Az—Anzhelika."

He didn't bother to hide his smirk, at her strange accent or anything else. "The green eyes, the slip of the tongue. You think me a fool? Did Andrei put you up to this?"

"Andrei? You must introduce me to him. He sounds quite the trickster."

A wave of fatigue reminded him that he'd been on his feet almost sixteen hours, and as cute as she was he had little energy for a walking hoax about the girl from Azov Mountain. "Look, *Azovka* Anzhelika, I'm too tired for playing games. It's been a very long night and I must be up early."

"Oh, Pavel, I came because you are alone and I wished to speak with you. We have a job to do, and I need you to help me."

"A job?" Extra income came hard in the Urals, and he'd been looking for something to supplement his bartending wages.

Her fingertips brushed over his wrist, an electric thrill that shot to his throbbing heart. "Yes, Pavel. We're going to take back my mountains from the usurpers."

A small part of him worried that she wasn't speaking Russian, and that he knew no other language. But the rest fell under her spell, and downed his shot. "Okay, great. How are we going to do that?"

She leaned in until her lips brushed his ear, her breasts heaving against his arm. "You're going to free me, and then we're going to kill them."

Conor Flynn walked into the casino two hours from Oakland, California, and smiled. He'd always loved casinos. Rigged luck squelched the dreams of the rich and poor alike, brought in astounding wealth wrapped up in a semblance of freedom for a people that didn't, for all practical purposes, exist. The Mewok lived in worn-down trailers on land the government condescendingly allowed them to keep, and only a select few got rich from the white man's money.

That much resentment wouldn't need much of a push.

He walked up to the first employee he could find, a young man with light brown skin carrying a tray of drinks. He took a scotch, downed it, and set it back on the tray. "What say you and me steal the thunder, coyote?"

CHAPTER THIRTEEN

For the second time in far too little time, Matt disembarked onto the White House helipad, Sakura at his side. President Williams had demanded their presence the week before, but Matt had insisted on tripled protection for his family before leaving them in White Spruce, with a detail he picked himself – and that had taken four days.

They ducked into the entrance and surrendered their sidearms to the Secret Service before being marched through a warren of tunnels to a small, cluttered office barely big enough to fit Matt, Sakura, President Williams, and a worried-looking Air Force suit Matt didn't recognize, though his pair of stars made him a Major General. In contrast to the president's graying hair, clean shave and athletic build, the general sported an enormous black mustache and short, unruly hair to match on top of a beanpole frame almost six and a half feet tall.

The president nodded toward the chairs clearly set up for this meeting, and spoke before they'd finished sitting down. "Sergeant Rowley, you want to tell us what the hell is going on?"

"Pardon? Mister President."

"In here call me Bob." He turned his monitor around to show a map of the Earth dotted with red circles. "We've got insurrections in nine countries, each with supernatural support so it seems, and that doesn't even count Cholula or Nebraska. As the foremost expert on this shit, I was thinking maybe you could fill in the blanks."

Matt exchanged a glance with Sakura. "Begging your pardon, but I get my intel from the same channels you do, only you get a whole lot more of it."

The president looked at them, then at the general, then back at them. "Not anymore. Follow me."

They marched out, down the hall to an elevator, and rode it down an unknown number of floors before hopping on a one-car tram and whirring through lightless tunnels. With a nod from the president the general passed them a pair of folders from his briefcase.

"You've got clearance, but not for this. Well now you do, but you don't share it with anyone – we'll brief Janet LaLonde after this meeting. This is project FADE, the Federal Artefact Deconstruction Environment. I'm Major General Andrew Freudenberg, and I'm in charge. We've been around a long time in one form or another, about as long as the country, and..."

Matt turned a halfhearted ear, using his eidetic memory to store the conversation unless he needed to bring any of it up later, and flipped through the folder. Photocopies of microfiche slides set four to a page, it outlined a covert government entity tasked with identifying, monitoring, and if necessary eliminating supernatural threats to the sovereignty of the United States of America. Over two hundred years they'd debunked far more than they'd found, but had found a few items of concern – Native American shaman with supernatural abilities, demonic possession with verifiable powers.

As he read his ears picked up the subtle changes in pressure. They descended at least ten stories before he found their notes on a possible supernatural source for Jade.

"Why didn't we know about this?" Matt realized he'd interrupted, and didn't care. "We had a right to know."

Sakura flipped to the same page, read the slide, but said nothing.

The general clucked his tongue. "FADE's primary mandate is to observe, Mr Rowley, and if you read further we had no idea the Watchers were involved. Or that they even existed. Most people still doubt that they're fallen angels."

"Then what are they?"

Sakura cleared her throat then looked back and forth at them wide-eyed, an obvious ruse.

Freudenberg sighed. "Very old, very powerful beings that existed in prehistory until humans killed most of them off."

"And they're coming back now, because?"

"Because Gerstner, or whatever her name is, woke them up."

Matt remembered the fear in Gerstner's eyes when he'd figured out the crack in her plan. Some of the Nephilim had been allowed to survive the Great Flood as bodiless beings, to tempt mankind. By taking human form and imbuing the drug – and Gerstner Augmentations – with her essence she'd violated the compact with God. Whether FADE believed it, or the president, or whether or not it was even true, Gerstner had believed it, right up to the point where he'd blown her to pieces.

"Okay, that explains the egregoroi. What about the rest of this stuff?" The file filled in some details on recent unrest around the world, some of which held a kernel of truth. A cannibal cult had resulted in martial law across much of northern Australia; a string of unlikely earthquakes had buried towns all through the Ural mountains, and the survivors had been hacked to pieces; a charismatic preacher had gained an ever-larger following in the South through faith healing that actually seemed to work, and used it to buck local authorities and convert politicians; a neighborhood in New Delhi had drowned themselves in the Yamuna River, and reemerged to drown another before a military response reduced the bloated, walking corpses to inert pieces.

And less than a week earlier, nine shadows had stolen a nuclear weapon right off a missile near Truckee, California outside of Lake Tahoe, killing everyone in the silo by stabbing, strangling, or bludgeoning their shadows.

"Whoa, what is this?"

"That," the president tapped the paper, "is why we called you in. They left a note, thought maybe you could shed some light on it."

"A note?"

Freudenberg handed them a glossy, low-resolution black-and-white photograph of a missile pad. Under the missile, blood smeared the floor in Japanese Kanji, the same poem left in bodies at Lake Barnacle. "What does that poem mean to you, Sergeant?"

Matt closed his eyes. "The only thing it could mean is impossible. That Conor Flynn is alive. Again."

"Who the fuck is Conor Flynn?" the president asked.

The whispers urged Matt to tear off the President's head and beat the general to death with it. "Conor was my friend, or I thought he was. An Irish cop turned ICAP Aug, the best bonk killer that had ever lived. But he killed a lot of people, including his wife and child, and was heavily into the occult."

"And what happened to him?"

"I killed him."

Williams cleared his throat. "I'm going to need to see the files on this man."

"On it," the general said, swiping information into his phone.

"Conor, one 'n'," Matt said.

"Got it," Freudenberg deadpanned. After a minute he nodded. "Yeah, he's on our radar. His autopsy put him in the 'could have been dangerous but dead' file. What makes you think this is him?"

"A hunch." Matt pointed at the Kanji poem. "Someone left that exact poem – in body parts – at Lake Barnacle,

Georgia. It bears some semblance to the tattoos on Flynn's body, and ends with one of his favorite phrases."

The general dropped his phone into his pocket. "And you didn't think to include this in your report?"

President Williams rolled his eyes. "Come on, Freud. Would he have any reason to believe it? Or expect anyone else to?"

The car lurched to a stop and opened to a chrome steel door six feet wide, fitted with a thick glass porthole and a keypad with a retinal scanner.

Freud keyed in a password and let it scan his eye without getting out of the tram, then stepped back to allow the door room. As it opened metal claws grabbed the tram, preventing anyone on board from escaping in any kind of a hurry.

They stepped through an airlock, bare metal polished to a reasonable shine rather than the stark white of countless sci-fi movies, and into a cubicle farm that could have been anywhere, USA. High-definition plasma screens covered the walls, serving as windows to skyscapes that didn't quite substitute for natural sunlight.

Marcia Stein waited just inside the door, hands clasped in front of her. Her gray skirt-suit accentuated her femininity while projecting an air of 'don't push your luck'.

She shook the president's hand first, then the general's, before turning and hugging Sakura. "Good to see you."

Sakura returned the hug without expression, stepped back and bowed. "It's good that you're here. How long?"

"Since ICAP fell."

A hint of a nod from Sakura ended their conversation.

After a shake for Matt she turned and led them through the maze of cubicles, perhaps a third occupied by an employee, most of whom didn't bother to look up as they walked past. Matt wondered if they didn't notice the president, or found his presence unremarkable.

Marcia spoke while Freudenberg and Williams fell

back to whisper behind them. "FADE consolidated into three nearly-independent divisions after an exhaustive review showed cryptozoology to be a waste of time – if the Abominable Snowman is out there, he's not a national security threat. That leaves Corporeal Phenomena, Incorporeal Phenomena, and Application. CorPhen deals with things that we can see and touch, goblins and ghouls and swamp monsters and whatever. Incorps handles your ghosts, witches, psychics, the kinds of things that pop up time to time and threaten to destabilize cities or regions. Application is the geek wing. They mostly try to harness, control, or kill things in the purview of the other divisions.

"There's a lot of cross-work between them, and FADE brought me on to help manage interdepartmental process control. Except for a recent sabbatical, that's what I've been doing, and it's led me to one inescapable conclusion."

Freudenberg frowned. "What's that?"

"FADE is, for the most part, a giant waste of Black Ops money."

The general bristled, but the president calmed him with a hand on his arm. "Go on."

"In terms of intelligence, FADE is in the dark about almost everything. Massive occult libraries scanned into supercomputers have done nothing but show that almost all of it is garbage, hocus pocus, not worth anybody's time. Their track record at identifying genuine supernatural threats before they strike is pretty much zero, and Application has spent billions of dollars to yet develop a viable technology that couldn't be done cheaper and easier without magic. For every dollar—"

"Why are we here?" Sakura's scowl could peel paint from the walls.

Williams turned to her. "You're here because we're transferring the STB budget and authority to FADE." He held up a hand to stall Matt's objection. "You can still work from Nashville if you want, but in light of recent events we've decided to keep a lower profile with the public."

Matt snorted. "Kellett's got you running scared."

Williams flushed. "I don't think you understand the damage those tapes did. You had policemen shooting children, for God's sake."

"I didn't."

"On those tapes you did."

Managing not to put the president through a wall, Matt spoke through gritted teeth. "Those were chopped edits. I told them to run, and stopped them from firing. If you'd seen the entire feed—"

"I have. But the public hasn't, and the damage is done. This isn't a demotion, and you'll have the same operational authority you had before. Only difference now is that you'll work through General Freudenberg's office instead of SACLANT."

A lightbulb went off in his mind. "Oh. You're consolidating in-house. Does the UN realize this? NATO?"

Feet shuffled in the uncomfortable silence. Williams scowled. "Not yet."

Sakura crossed her arms. "There are two Augs. The United States only has authority over one."

"We were hoping you'd be on board, Miss Sakura." Freudenberg kept his face strictly neutral, something that wouldn't work at all on Sakura's ability to read microexpressions. "While our main focus will be the security of the United States of America, we know we're more secure when the world is more secure. As Bob said, you'll have the same operational authority you had under the STB. All we ask is complete transparency in your dealings with the supernatural."

President Williams – Bob – cleared his throat. "I'd hoped this would be a foregone conclusion. We have a missing nuclear weapon, and it looks like your dead friend took it."

Sakura raised her eyes from the floor and bored them into Williams's. "For this, yes. After, we'll have to see."

Freudenberg tipped his nonexistent hat. "Deal.

Meantime, let's show you how to kill shadows."

Matt interrupted. "After I take care of my family."

"We are not moving to Washington, DC." Monica pushed away from the counter and stomped into the living room, flopping down on the couch to stare at the fireplace her husband had built. "This is our house, our home, and there are, like, thirty guards outside. We ain't going to be safer for moving."

Matt let an angry reply roll over him unsaid, then spoke. "The government's not going to maintain this much security, and God knows we can't afford it on our own. There's a safety in anonymity that guns can't provide."

"I ain't stupid, baby, and I hear what you're saying. I'm just saying 'no' to it."

Okay, time for the nuclear artillery.

"Have you talked to Steve Laako lately? Or his mother?" She flushed and looked at the floor so, feeling like an asshole, he pressed it. "They're dead because we're a danger to be around. We didn't ask for this, and we sure as hell don't want it, but we have to look at what is—"

"—not what we want to be." She finished her dad's favorite saying as he dropped on his knees in front of her.

"I'm sorry, Mon. I don't want this, either."

Her tears tasted like eyeliner as he kissed them away, and he let her squeeze his neck hard enough to hurt a normal man, and bawl. Eventually the sobbing stopped, and she pulled back, eyes red and puffy.

"I don't appreciate your using other people's safety to manipulate me. But I get it, and you're right. We'll go away, at least for now, let this whole thing blow over a while. On one condition."

Oh, boy. "What's that?"

"When he gets out of the hospital, I want Aaron Walters to run our security."

"I'm sure I can make that happen. He's a good man, and already cleared." The rising church spire across the road reflected in her eyes, and he kept his thoughts on 'a while' to himself. Two thousand fanatics from all over the country now lived in White Spruce, and worshipped in the unfinished church going up just off their property, and grew more fanatical with every passing week. "I'm sorry, babe."

"Me too, baby."

• • •

Matt loaded the last of the suitcases in the black panel van and tried to ignore the roars of screaming adulation from across the street. A quick guesstimate put the throng at a thousand people, maybe more, packing every inch of church grounds, plus the new sidewalks right up to the white-and-orange construction sawhorses serving as a police cordon. They chanted and sang songs, wailed and cried, held signs about Jesus or Adam or Armageddon, but mostly yelled and screamed in a desperate attempt to draw any of the Rowley's attention.

He didn't know who had leaked the news that they were leaving White Spruce, which was probably for the best – he didn't much feel like killing anyone today, at least not in front of his wife, and knowing the responsible party might have made that happen. So instead he closed the rear door and banged on it, then gave the driver a thumbs-up in the side-view mirror. The van rumbled to life, so Matt stepped back to the SUV backed up to the porch steps.

The twenty-year-old Ford Excursion had sixty thousand miles on it. With a thousand pounds of armor, inch-thick polycarbonate laminate windows that wouldn't roll down, and run-flat tires, it had protected American diplomats in Cairo for most of its life before being retired stateside for high-profile Witness Protection duties. He requisitioned it on STB's budget, one of the last official acts before DHS shut the Bureau down, at the cool price of two hundred grand.

He opened the rear door and waved at the house.

As Monica opened the front door, Ted in her arms, Adam at her heels, the crowd surged. Sawhorses fell, and policemen in riot gear stumbled back. Canisters tumbled from black-gloved hands, and Matt could only express thanks that the police were there – his guards carried no gas, no stun guns, only pistols designed and purposed to cripple and kill. They pushed back against the crowd and forced a path out of the driveway.

Monica hurried down the steps, then plopped Ted on the floor as Matt lifted Adam and put him in his seat. They got in, and she buckled their son in before the cars rolled.

The crowd broke as the choking gas dispersed through the air, and the masked policemen had to drag retching bodies from in front of the lead vehicle. A few die-hard fanatics braved the gas and pawed at their windows, red eyes wide and full of tears, mouths ululating nonsense cries of religious elation or gasping pain.

Matt scowled at the lone figure blocking the road, his black shirt unadorned with a white priest's collar, blue jeans torn and stained like he'd spent the week camping. His normally-shaved head sprouted tufts of dark hair that avoided his forehead and the circle on top. Jason stood with his arms crossed, ignoring the gas, ignoring the approaching police even as they drew their batons. Even choking on the gas he found a way to shout.

"YOU HAVE A DUTY TO BRING PEOPLE TO GOD!"

Matt opened the door and jumped out, slamming it before too much tear gas could discomfort his family. The irritants, a combination of aerosolized OC and CS – pepper spray and tear gas – couldn't assault his mucus membranes and eyes as fast as his body healed, so the unpleasant itch did nothing but turn his foul mood ever fouler. The car was insulated but not quite air tight so Ted would likely suffer the worst, and he had no tolerance for anything that hurt his dog.

"Get out of the road, Jason."

Head held high, Jason spread his arms wide. "You have a duty to the Almighty. Here, in White Spruce. You can't leave."

"We're leaving, so get out of the way."

"I can't do that."

Matt advanced, hands balled into fists.

"I've seen it, Matt. The Lord will not let—"

He broke into a run.

Jason stepped back, then backpedaled, as Matt closed the distance at breakneck speed. Jason's defiant, righteous expression fractured as Matt turned his shoulder, and vanished upon impact. Pulling the hit at the last moment, Matt left just enough 'oomph' to maybe crack something non-vital.

The fallen priest landed on his back, limbs askew, and skidded ten feet across gravel and stone. Matt didn't give him a chance to stand on his own.

Matt's fingers tangled in greasy hair, and Jason came off the ground before grabbing Matt's wrist to mitigate the pressure on the sparse roots. Feet kicking open air, he grunted and squirmed but offered no significant fight even as Matt tossed him over the ditch into a gaggle of his followers. They fell in a heap, and Matt waved the cars past.

The crowd held their ground as he advanced, so he tilted his head forward to look at them under his brow, spread his arms like a predator's claws, and let instinct cow them. He crossed the grass at a deliberate walk, and now Jason's followers shied back. The priest only dusted himself off, grimacing with the effort – probably the result of a cracked rib or two – and glared with eyes ablaze, a worm of blood squirming on his fattening lip. "You dare defy the will of God?"

Matt rolled his eyes at his onetime friend and projected as much contempt as he could into his reply. "Don't presume to threaten me."

Head high, again, Jason rallied the crowd around him, calling them forward with his fingers. "It is not I who threatens you. We have no power in this world. You squander your God-given gift to wallow in the sin and violence of Satan, and the Lord God will not withhold His judgment."

The crowd muttered, "Amen."

Matt sneered as he said aloud what he'd shied away from thinking about for three years. "You of all people know where my gifts came from, how my son got twisted by tainted magics. Adam's no saint, and neither is my wife. The world's going to shit, and you're not helping."

Jason's eyes fell. "It isn't this world that concerns me, but the next."

The crowd said, "Amen."

"Yeah, I got that. Meantime, I'm taking my family where you can't reach them, and we're not coming back to this town, ever. So enjoy the view from your fucking church."

The crowd rumbled, and Jason shushed them. "Peace, brothers and sisters! Do not give the devil a reason to use this man to his violent ends. He means us no harm, but only has difficulty accepting what we already know."

A smile had never felt so cold. "I think I mean you a little harm. Anybody want to go first?"

Every one of them met his challenging glare, but not one stepped forward.

"Are there only cowards among your flock, Rees?"

Matt held no illusions of beating up a thousand people, even with his speed, strength, and reflexes, but it would never come to that. The fight-or-flight instinct tilted only one direction when one faced an insurmountable foe and had room to run, and panic remained the most contagious of human conditions. He stalked forward, shifting his path as the crowd shied away, always advancing toward the closest person – except Jason, who didn't move.

As their spirit broke he turned and put a hand on Jason's shoulder from behind, an echo of their former friendship, an innocence burned to ashes in the furnace of obsession and fanaticism. He leaned in close and spoke just loud enough for his words to carry. "She's out of your reach now. Let her go, or you're going to learn what the wrath of God really looks like. We both know our parents still live here. They have nothing to do with this, so if you touch them, if your people touch them, if they ever even make them feel unsafe, I'm going to kill every single one of your pathetic followers and snap your neck on the burning embers of your church. Do you understand?"

Jason said nothing for a moment, then, "You've threatened me before."

Matt dug his fingers into muscle just enough to hurt, and the whispers cajoled him to keep going, tear Jason's arm off at the shoulder and wade into the rest of the crowd. "Yeah, back when I thought you might try to fuck her again. This is different, and you know it. Leave my family alone. Leave her family alone. This is your last and only chance. So please, tell me you understand."

"I understand."

Matt let go and walked away, turning his jog into a sprint to catch up with the retreating cars. He very much doubted Jason understood anything, least of all the conviction behind his threat.

• • •

Matt carried their bags into the safe house, a two-story modular home with vinyl siding, one of dozens just like it on the same cul-de-sac in Sterling, Virginia. The plain furniture looked new enough, and cinnamon potpourri mostly covered the smell of dust and old pizza. Ted trotted into the middle of the beige carpet and flopped on his side, exhausted from most of a day staring out the car window.

"This place is a hole." Hostile disappointment tinged every one of Monica's words.

"A temporary hole." He set the bags on the floor and closed the door after Jake Martin, the bodyguard assigned until the morning shift. As the security here depended on secrecy they would have only two guards on shift at any given time, one at the front door and one at the back.

A young man in a suit a little too big, Jake ran a hand through his sandy brown hair and gave them a constipated smile. "No need to worry about anything, Mrs Rowley. This place has got state-of-the-art security, and the hall closet upstairs is really a panic room. Come hell or high water, we'll keep you safe as can be."

"Splendid," she deadpanned, turning to unbuckle Adam from the car seat. He yawned as she picked him up and gave Matt a sleepy smile over her shoulder.

"Pantry's full," Jake continued, either oblivious or ignoring her mood as he showed them the first floor. "So's the fridge. You've got food for at least a week, and if there's anything you want special we can make that happen."

Next to the kitchen he opened a door, stepped in and turned on the light. Food loaded three high shelves, everything from cereal and pasta to canned goods and soda. Against the back wall sat two cases of cheap beer and two boxes of wine. Monica whirled away, and Adam's head banged off of the doorframe.

"Fuck!" she said, as Matt pointed at the booze.

"Martin, get that shit out of here. Don't you know she's an alcoholic?"

Adam blinked and raised a hand to his head, and tears brimmed in his eyes. "Sorry, Momma."

"Oh, no, baby." She kissed his head and her lips came away red. "It was Mommy's fault." Her tone snapped as she looked at Matt. "Can you get me some paper towels? And the baby bag?"

He found a roll of towels on the counter, pulled it off the holder and tossed it to her, then went into the living room to get the bag. Jake passed him on the way out, carrying half the alcohol in one trip, the other guard on his heels with the rest, both red-faced. Jake passed off a smile more constipated than happy. "I'll stash this in the garage until morning. Don't worry, we'll keep it under guard. I… I'm sorry."

Matt held his gaze, bag in his hand. "You guys need to do your homework."

Jake nodded and pushed through into the garage, the other guard right behind. Matt joined Monica in the kitchen, set the bag down next to her. As she rummaged for bandages and Neosporin he took the bloody paper towels – only a small dot of red – and tossed them in the garbage.

An hour later they'd gotten the crib set up and Adam laid down, and had settled into a strange bed in a strange house, Monica fast asleep a minute after her head hit the pillow. He didn't want to tell her he had to leave in the morning, but it beat telling her now.

Jake Martin pulled the bloody tissue from the garbage and inverted his latex glove, tying it closed to contain the sample. He put it in a cooler of ice, set it in his car, then sent a text: 'I left the mail on the porch'.

That gave him sixteen hours to deliver the sample to General Freudenberg, the first six of which would be standing guard over the most dangerous family in the world.

CHAPTER FOURTEEN

The ICBM complex in Truckee, California had never been on any official maps, and nuclear disarmament talks had never included it or, presumably, a thousand more just like it hiding under the landscape of the United States. It housed four units comprising three buildings each – the missile silo, the access staircase, and the control center with sleeping quarters, each connected to the others by corrugated metal pipe like the kind you'd find in drainage culverts, only much bigger.

They accessed the broken arrow through its only entrance, a ten-inch thick steel hatch buried in the hillside that led to a metal staircase descending into the artificial depths. Lieutenant-Colonel Buck Jones led them past several unoccupied murder holes, their walls still stained with blood that looked dark brown in the washed-out fluorescent lights. Fifty-something with salt-and-pepper hair and deep bags under his eyes, he spoke with an Alabama drawl and looked like he hadn't skipped a meal in decades.

They ignored the blast lock leading to the control center and accessed the blast door to the 'cable way', a steel-floored hallway lined with cables and wire, the only way in or out of the silo itself. The hall should have ended in another airlock-style blast door, but instead a jagged, torn-out circle of concrete opened into the silo. Sixty feet across, the launch shaft descended over ten stories down, most of that space filled with an enormous white missile, the top of which had been torn open in jagged sheets of metal.

"That the warhead?" Matt nodded toward the damaged tip.

Jones smoothed his mustache and pretended to spit. "MIRV. Held twelve warheads, now it's got eleven."

"Why did they take only one?" Sakura asked.

"Don't reckon I know, Miss Sakura. Seems they loaded the one on a truck, and didn't have another truck."

"How'd they get it out of there?" Matt asked.

"Cameras don't look at the top of the missile, but as far as we can tell they peeled the capsule like an orange and removed the slice."

"Plates on the truck?" Sakura's eyes didn't leave the gash in the missile.

"They already found it down near the res."

"Res?" Matt asked.

"'Bout five hundred Miwoks own a bit of land down near Shingle Springs. Ain't much there but the casino and a wellness center. They ditched the truck right outside the casino parking lots, past where the cameras see. Ain't nothing—"

The ground shook, and dust rained from the ceiling. Jones steadied himself on the wall, Sakura and Matt rode out the tremor for ten seconds.

Matt touched his COM. "Janet, was that an earthquake?"

Jones shook his head. "You're in a giant Faraday Cage sixty feet underground. You're not going to get any kind of signal unless we go back upstairs."

"Yeah," Matt said. "Let's do that."

As they popped the access hatch his COM pinged and a waiting message played automatically. Janet's voice said, "Check in *now.*"

He tried again. "Janet?"

"We've got a political insurrection in San Francisco. A group of insurgents kidnapped the mayor and his family and sent a tape to the news promising earthquakes if their demands aren't met. The first one hit the moment the guy on the video promised a warning to make sure the authorities know they're serious. Looks bad."

"Sounds bad." Matt stared westward toward a city and ocean too far away to see. "What do they want?"

"Nothing much, just sovereignty over the greater Bay Area and two billion dollars in restitution."

He closed his eyes. "Let me guess. Miwok Indians."

Marcia Stein broke in. "What do you know that we don't?"

"Getting there, Stein. Clear the channel." The annoyance in Janet's voice could cut a man in half.

"Nothing," Matt replied. "We just learned the truck they used to take the bomb was swapped for another ride at the Miwok Reservation. You want us there or the city?"

"The city, but you'll need a chopper. The bridges are out of commission and traffic is a fustercluck."

"Roger that. We'll—"

"This is a trap."

He opened his eyes, looked at Sakura, who still stared into the distance.

"Wreck the bridges, bait us in, set off the bomb. Flynn's been toying with you, and already knows he can't take you in a fair fight. Doubly so with me here. It's a trap."

Jones looked from Matt to Sakura, back to Matt. "Do you really think he'd nuke a city just to kill you?"

Matt nodded. "He'd probably nuke a city just to kill a million people. Add killing me into the mix? No question."

"Fuck." Jones grabbed his hair with both hands, and all the blood drained from his face.

"How big is this warhead?"

Jones dropped his hands. "The W92 is tactical, four hundred and seventy five kilotons, like the W88. Call it a million people killed or crippled, give or take. Plus fallout."

"Great. What's an Aug's chance at close range?"

Jones snorted. "I'm no doctor, but within a mile you're dead, four miles most people are dead and you're going to be very, very hurt. And maybe worse, the W92 doesn't exist – it's not covered by SALT II or any other treaty, because nobody knows we have them, especially not in twelve-clutster MIRVs. This thing goes off, or gets identified, we're in for a world of shit."

Nodding to cover how little he cared about the political ramifications of the United States violating its own treaty, Matt said, "So how do they detonate it?"

"Step one is know a lot about nukes. You program it, and when the conditions hit, boom."

"What conditions can you program?"

"Modern nukes need GPS and at least one other condition – air pressure, altitude, impact force. The W92, you have to calibrate all of those conditions, and impact isn't an option. The priority being that it only goes off where and when you want it to."

"Roger that. So how do we diffuse it? Cut the red wire?"

Jones shook his head. "They're precision machines, and they're not going to go off from a fire or impact. Sufficient damage should trigger the disabling failsafes without the weapon detonating, and that'll render it inert."

"That's good."

"But," he put a finger in Matt's face, "if you breach either of the cores you're going to have a hot mess on your hands, radiation-speaking."

"Could I survive it?"

He spat, for real this time. "You're the superman. Did ICAP do any studies of augmentation versus radiation?"

Sakura shook her head. "I don't think so."

"Then your guess is as good as mine."

"Great."

• • •

Terry looked out the window at the cars and their flashing lights, the SWAT vans and the snipers on the rooftops, all circling the wrong buildings half the city away. The weight of his body dragged him down, sluggish and impotent, and the mewling whine of the fifteen-year-old boy grated down his spine. "Can somebody please shut him the fuck up?"

"Scalp him," Coyote said. A dangerous man who'd taught them ancient magic, Terry had no doubts about Coyote's authenticity or sincerity – had had none. Irish through and through in looks and accent, he promised them too much and respected their culture too little. They were being used, but Terry held out hope they were using him in turn.

"Miwoks aren't scalpers."

Coyote turned, white teeth flashing in the yellow city lights. "Miwoks *weren't* scalpers, right is right. It's never too late to pick up a hobby."

Terry bristled as the boy's whimpers turned to blubbering sobs. "We are wolves and eagles, a noble people that once ruled this land. We will not debase ourselves to your racist stereotypes."

"Racist, am I? A wolf, are you? I think I can arrange that."

Black words poured from Coyote's mouth, and Terry faded. The world brightened as he grew dim, and the smells of the night assaulted his consciousness. A shrieking, incoherent intelligence settled in the crannies of his consciousness. Blood lust clawed at his belly, and the hearts of the mayor's family beat in his ears.

"Not here, ya dog, we need these ones a bit. Go outside where you belong, and don't hunt too close."

Terry slunk to the door on all fours, drool dropping from his jaws to evaporate in the light that streamed across the floor from the hall.

"Take your friends."

The pack of shadow wolves bolted downstairs, slipping through the crack in the door into the night, their howls a silent call to the blood red moon. Terry led them south and east toward the bay, far from the police and their useless guns. Not to find more worthy prey, but more tender.

A twinge of guilt tore at his heart as the dark thing in his mind chose their hunting ground, a false memory of another life. Had he had children of his own, before Coyote came into the casino and promised him unimaginable power? No. That belonged to a softer thing, a colder thing, a thing of meat and blood. And now the white man would pay for centuries of theft and oppression with blood of their own.

Guilt drowned in anticipation as he slipped under the loading dock door into the UCSF Benioff Children's Hospital.

• • •

Sakura dropped from the speeding helicopter ten feet from the hospital roof. As gravity brought her down she tucked into a ball around her REC7. Her shoulder hit first and she rolled to her feet, took four skidding steps to arrest her momentum, turned, and hopped backward off the roof, rifle now in her right hand. Ten feet down the fingers of her left hand caught the granite edge above the sixth-floor window. With a jerk she spun inward, smashing through the glass into the blood-streaked hallway.

It smelled of gore and shit and bleach and antiseptic – the four horsemen of combat and her daughter's death. Fluorescent lights buzzed overhead, courtesy of the hospital's generators. A black woman in pink nurse's scrubs gaped up at her from the floor, her hands wet and slick from trying to hold in the ragged remains of her entrails. Her mouth worked but no sound came out, only bubbles of spit and blood.

She snapped the woman's neck with her boot on the way by, as close to mercy as she could offer in a world this cruel, and stalked down the hall in the wake of a flurry of

Dragonflies. Her HUD blipped on two probable friendlies hiding in a closet and a hot infrared spike at the nurse's station down the hall. The drone closest to it vanished, its datastream disappearing from the cloud of information, and a low rumble carried through her ear bud as its speakers shuddered and then failed.

She touched the new button on the side of her helmet and FADE's weird strobe bathed the area in white-blue. Subtlety irrelevant in light of it, she charged the desk and the beast hiding behind it. The wolf-thing rose on its hind legs, standing to a full height of almost seven feet tall, its muzzle of serrated teeth dripping with red. Sparks crackled between black strands of nothing-fur, highlighting taut muscles and long, hooked claws.

A shiver ran down her spine at its silent howl – this was no yama-inu, the wolf-spirit that haunted the mountains of ancient Japan, but more something out of Transylvania. Pragmatics slammed down over her nerves, the cold iron cage of duty and a job that needed doing. She pulled the trigger and spat ceramic death at its center of mass.

It took the hits without dodging and stumbled back, eyes wide in surprise. She fired again and it disappeared behind the desk. As she came over the top, it lunged.

She jammed her palm under its chin, knocking its jaw closed before it reached her neck. The impact knocked her over the counter, and claws raked down her right arm, tearing the rifle from her grasp. She landed on her feet while drawing her sidearm and put three bullets in its shoulder before it could take cover. The .357's stopping power barely made the thing lurch, but she wanted to hurt it, not kill it.

It bolted down the hall, limping heavily, streams of hot black nothing dribbling from its fur to evaporate on contact with the floor. She followed, firing a double-tap over its head as it hit the stairwell, then scooped up her rifle on the way by.

"Matt, coming your way," Janet said in the COM.

Blood leaked from Sakura's arm, the wound throbbing in time with her heartbeat. Kneeling next to an overturned cart, she grabbed a roll of elastic bandage and wrapped it from wrist to elbow and back. "We may have a problem."

"Go ahead," Matt said, his voice clipped.

Weapon up, she kicked open the stairwell door and walked inside, clearing each landing at a sprint. "It clawed my arm. Regenerates are slow, if working."

"That's fun," Janet said. "Try not to die."

In the corner of her HUD, Matt's screen showed a creature fragment into wisps of nothing from a volley of fragmentation rounds. "Two down," he said. "Let the others run."

She broke out onto the street and circled the building. Three shadows bolted toward the highway, almost white in the infrared. The strobe didn't penetrate the darkness nearly that far, so she lowered the rifle and stopped. Her arm burned, and ached, but didn't itch.

"Where are they going?"

"Northwest," Janet said. "Downtown, if that's what they call it. Where all the tall buildings are."

"You sure about this, Matt? If Flynn still has Augs, he sees what we see. He'll know we can track them."

"There's no way that asshole won't set off a bomb if he went through the trouble to get it. He likes killing far too much."

She paused. "Yeah. I'll meet you running."

• • •

Between the Dragonflies and a CIA satellite tasked to finding the broken arrow Matt had no problem following the wolves, blazing white in the infrared. Sakura joined him halfway to downtown, a regular grid of skyscrapers. No cars patrolled the streets, with almost every business closed due to the power outage.

"If we die, I'm haunting you."

He chuckled. "How's your arm?"

"Bleeding has slowed."

"Should be healed by now."

"I know."

On the HUD, the remaining wolves entered a rectangular building with reflective windows, thirteen stories tall. He stopped Sakura with a hand on her shoulder.

"Jones said an air burst would be worse than a ground burst. Have you ever known Flynn to do anything halfway?"

"No." She looked up at the Transamerica building, and he shook his head. She turned, taking in the view. "I see it."

Half the city away, mostly obscured by trees, stood a giant cross on top of a hill.

"There's no way he's going to waste that kind of symbolism. He's going to make sure we're in the building with the goons, then he's going to detonate the bomb."

"I told you it was a trap."

"Yeah. Let's go break it."

• • •

Matt counted four hostiles and three civilians, the latter hung by steel cables from the hundred-foot cross. They approached upwind, and none of the three wolves stirred from the base of the cross. Conor Flynn stood naked next to the nuke, a conical dunce cap on top of the cross. He held a circuit board that connected to the nuke via several long wires.

Operating on the assumption that Flynn lived had not prepared him for the sight. Flynn had died two years earlier when Matt separated his skull with a butcher's knife and pulped his brain with his own hands. Matt had attended the autopsy and the cremation.

"What's that thing made of?" he muttered.

"Concrete," Janet replied. "Nothing you're going to knock down."

"How does the Navy feel about cruise missiles?"

"Against a landmark cross in a populous city? Give me a couple weeks, I might be able to convince them not to arrest you for suggesting it."

"Sakura, how's your aim?"

"He moves too much, but I can hit where the wires connect to the device. If Jones is right, should shut it down."

"On my mark." He raised his right hand to the side of his head, ready to trigger the strobe, and pulled a grenade from his bandoleer with his left, hooking the pin with his thumb. "Three… two… one… mark."

The report battered his helmet, but he waited for the spark off the nuke to bolt forward. The grenade flew, spoon spiraling to the ground ten feet in front of him, and the strobe lit up the lounging wolves. The frag landed and one dove on top of it, shattering into a million wisps. Matt pulled the AA-12 but they charged too fast.

Claws raked across his chestplate. He brought the shotgun up, cracking a jaw with the metal stock. The brutes grappled his arms, wrenching them to each side with inhuman strength. He strained, and they shifted their feet, dug in, opened their mouths to expose enormous, serrated teeth.

Shots rang out, two bursts in rapid succession. His left arm slipped free.

He spun while Sakura advanced on the other wolf, still firing.

The wolf-thing ducked his awkward haymaker and bit his thigh.

Fingers tangled in its scalp, he pulled, screaming through gritted teeth as meat tore with a wet rip. Reaching across his body he yanked free his WildStang, put the .50 caliber pistol against the thing's head. Muscle separated from bone, sending shockwaves through his body. He pulled the trigger. The pistol bucked.

Gunpowder mingled with singed fur as the creature

collapsed. A naked young man fell to the ground, head a pulped mess. He couldn't have been more than twenty. The wound in his leg burned, a searing contrast to the familiar itch of regenerates doing their work.

The whispers cackled. Matt turned, but couldn't put weight on his leg. He fell, and rolled. The warhead smashed into the ground with a wet thud where his body had been.

Flynn stomped where his head had been, then again and again. Matt stopped and caught his foot one-handed, twisted, extended his left arm and pulled the trigger.

Flynn's knee caught the pistol, knocking it to the side as he spun away. He spread his arms, oblivious to or ignoring the gunshot wound that obliterated his cock and balls, already stitching closed. "C'mon, Matt. You kill me, you break my toys, now you take my tallywhacker? Rude."

"Incoming," Sakura said in his ear. A dozen white-hot shadows loped through the trees. "I'm on them. Janet, air support."

Groaning, Matt forced himself to his feet. His leg throbbed, and blood soaked his pants and sloshed in his boot. Flynn had always healed faster, and he needed to buy time. He dropped the dented pistol and pulled a knife, cracking his neck for effect. "What's the end-game here, Flynn?"

Flynn shrugged. "I just got back, haven't given it much thought, past killing you, of course."

"Back from where?"

His eyes glazed, and every emotion drained from his face. "It's not like you think. You think it's a place you can badass yourself to the top. But there is no top, and these things know suffering like you can't even imagine."

A cautious step sent a jolt up Matt's spine. He hopped back toward the AA-12, and the world spun, lightheaded from blood loss for the first time in a decade.

Flynn blinked, his eyes focused. "You want that gun, yeah? Think it can kill me thrill me?"

Another hop, and he swooned. He stopped, breathing hard. "I think I can give it the old college try. Will you stay dead this time?"

"Not planning on it."

A helicopter thudded in the distance. Matt dove.

Flynn hit him as he landed, knee crushing his fingers against the gun. His head rang as a fist impacted his helmet.

He drove a knife-hand into Flynn's gut, and his fingers bounced off of taut muscle.

Flynn punched again. A crack split his helmet.

He dug his fingers into Flynn's knee, jamming his thumb behind the cap, and tore.

His helmet came off as Flynn fell back. With broken fingers he turned the AA-12 and fired. Flynn ducked the round and dove. His forearm exploded as Matt pulled the trigger again. Bone, blood and shrapnel peppered Matt's face, and blood leaked into his eyes.

Flynn tore the gun from his hand and spun. Stars exploded as the stock took him in side of the face. He fell to his hands and knees, the agony in his thigh muted by the concussion. The gun came down again and Matt slumped to the ground, the world swimming. Light flashed in front of his eyes, sparkling off of his combat knife.

Flynn flipped it to an overhand grip, held it over Matt's head. "My turn, you burn. Eat shit, Rowley."

His head evaporated a moment before the report hit, a continuous roar from the helicopter's GAU-17A minigun. Matt watched, unable to move, as fifty rounds a second converted Flynn's torso to a red, pulpy mass indistinguishable from the mud on which it lay.

The stream of fire banked away, and he heard Sakura in his ear, her voice authoritative but unintelligible. A minute later he struggled to a sitting position, blood flow finally slowing from the wound in his thigh.

Sakura sauntered up, helmetless, REC7 over her shoulder, her suit a mess of tattered, bloody rags and exposed impact-gel plates. "Two got away. Chopper's hunting. I gave them my helmet for strobing."

She nudged Conor's disembodied leg. "Even came back with the tattoos. What do you think it means?"

"I don't know. I just hope we don't have to kill the fucker again."

"Okay, kids," Janet broke in. "Air Force is coming in to secure that bomb, and SWAT's en route to cut down the mayor and his family, so try to look non-threatening. They're bringing some FADE techs for Flynn's body, or what's left of it."

"We should burn it." Sakura looked from Matt to the body and back. "Those tattoos have some kind of power, or he wouldn't reproduce them."

"No," Janet said. "We're bringing it in for analysis."

"I'll get gasoline." As Sakura turned, Matt grabbed her wrist.

"No. Burning didn't stop him last time. Maybe we can learn something."

She turned her body, invaded his personal space, to hide her hands from Dragonflies. 'I don't trust her. I don't trust FADE.'

The rapid-fire sign language would have been hard for a camera to process even if they'd caught it.

'We have to trust someone.'

Her eyes flared in anger. 'Your mistake, not mine.'

'I'll own it.' He dropped his hands and spoke aloud. "Roger that, Janet. Just get us a ride out of here, will you?"

"You got it, bud."

• • •

They landed at Joint Base Anacostia-Bolling nine hours later, as the sun rose over Washington, DC. Still filthy but fully healed, they disembarked carrying their broken weapons and equipment, and a FADE forensics team carried Flynn's remains in an airtight body bag. Matt's thigh had taken three times longer than usual, and had hurt more than anything since augmentation, like a bad infection gone red with inflammation. Even now a dull ache remained.

A convoy of three black SUV's met them on the tarmac each with a driver, the foremost with General Freudenberg riding shotgun. Matt got in the back of that one, and Sakura joined him.

"'Sup, Freud?" Matt patted the general on the shoulder.

The driver's eyes widened, but he said nothing.

Freudenberg flushed, but moderated his expression well. "In private you're welcome to call me Andrew, but in front of others I'd appreciate it if you use my title."

"Cool, Andrew. What are we doing with this body?"

He answered as the car pulled away. "We're going to study it, see what we can learn, and then cremate it."

"To what end?" Sakura asked.

"This man came back from the dead. If we can figure out how he did that, maybe we can keep it from happening again. Meantime we can monitor the body for signs of regeneration, or whatever process brought it back."

Matt shook his head. "No, Flynn had been cremated. I watched. I carried eleven pounds of remains – bone fragments – out of the morgue and buried them myself. That grave hasn't been disturbed."

"So we don't understand what happened here. All the more reason to study it. Miss Stein will be heading the team."

"Begging your pardon, General," Janet broke in on the car's speakerphone, which Matt hadn't realized was active. "I'd like the lead on this one. He was our man. His wife was my friend."

Sakura kicked Matt's boot, signed, 'No.' Matt replied with a tiny shrug.

"Marcia?" Freudenberg asked. "You okay with that?"

"Fine by me. I'll expect reports, same as anyone."

"Settled, then."

They headed into downtown DC and turned into a parking garage, where a false wall receded to allow them into the FADE complex. Sakura rolled her eyes, and Matt had to grin as he read her mind. Americans were parodies of themselves, and American spies the worst of the bunch.

The driver dropped them in another parking garage, who knows how far underground, and after they got out Freudenberg led them to an elevator with a security camera but no buttons. It opened for them, and as they entered Matt grinned harder, because there were no buttons on the inside either.

It lurched, going up, and opened a minute later into FADE HQ, a warren of activity with men and women of all ages clicking away at computers, monitoring screens, and rushing back and forth between stations. All the secrecy seemed pretty stupid to Matt – any organization with this many people had to have humint leaks, which made the rest of the precautions about their location mostly if not entirely moot.

A twentysomething man in an impeccable olive suit hurried by them, eyes widening at their torn-up, bloody appearance. He almost got his hand up enough to salute the general, but didn't stop to pay him the proper respect.

"Seems busy," Matt said.

"Well," Freudenberg said, "three minutes ago an eight-point-nine hit right under Mount Davidson, and we're trying to figure out if it's a coincidence."

Sakura muttered something in Japanese.

"Pardon me, sir!" A graying woman with a Texas twang drew their attention. "The Miwok just reiterated their demands with a letter to CNN. It's postmarked yesterday."

"Thank you." He gave her a curt nod, then turned to walk into his office. "You two shower, then we're going to see the President."

• • •

President Williams ran his hands through his hair, elbows planted on the Oval Office desk. "Somebody want to tell me what the fuck is going on here?"

Matt stood behind Freudenberg, who in turn stood behind the Joint Chiefs, who actually got to sit on the leather loveseats set out in a ring around an unreasonably large coffee table. Sakura had declined to participate in the meeting to sit outside and read, and nobody wore ear buds. Only important people got to sit: the Joint Chiefs, the Director of Homeland Security Suzanne Fraser, dour and businesslike despite her wild mane of silver-gray hair, and Secretary of State John Marks, a fat, red-faced man who looked primed for a heart attack at any moment. In the legion of suits and uniforms behind them, Matt recognized only Freudenberg and Colonel Eugene McGrath, the Deputy Undersecretary of Defense conspicuous in his wheelchair, his face a knotted mass of scar tissue along the left side.

Fraser spoke without consulting the iPad she held in her lap. "The Confederated Umatilla Tribes declared solidarity with the Mewoks and claimed the Columbian Plateau for their own, plus both sides of the Umatilla River and the city of Pendleton. They burned the court house to the ground, and the governor sent in the National Guard. Things… went south, setting off a chain reaction through Oregon, Washington, and into Utah – Native Americans are slaughtering anyone they find on 'their land', which seems to be, by their definition, the continent."

"Ridiculous," McGrath said, his gruff, grizzled voice even more pronounced in person. "They can't hope to win. In just those three states we have more cops than they have people."

She continued over the top of his final words. "At least four hundred are dead in Baton Rouge, in what looks like coordinated violence from the followers of Black Hawk, a Sauk chieftain from Illinois who died in 1838. They wear gris-gris, amulets that appear to render them all but immune to, among other things, tear gas and bullets, both rubber and lead."

Marks chuffed. "What does a dead Illinois Indian have to do with Baton Rouge?"

"Certain voodoo spiritualists consider him their intercessor with the divine. May I continue?"

She detailed six more declarations of secession and sovereignty: native tribes in Oklahoma and New Mexico, a New Hampshire militia that appeared to have at least one tank, and megachurches in Alabama, Georgia, and Texas who declared 'Dominion over the New Promised Land over the Forces of Babylon' in their press release, which also proclaimed solidarity with the 'Church of the Current Divine' in White Spruce, Tennessee. "Which I believe," she finished, "is right across the street from your house, Mr Rowley."

Everyone turned to look at him.

"Yeah. They think my son's an angel and my wife a saint."

The president waved his hand, almost dismissive. "This is about that incident on the Mall, right?"

"It started there, sir. Yes."

"But didn't end there?"

"No, sir."

Fraser continued. "Adam Rowley has been documented on video twice, and in dozens of anecdotes, performing miraculous acts, none of which have presented a security threat to the United States. He bears watching, especially in the light of the rest of this, but I don't think he's relevant at this time, especially considering he's currently in government custody."

"My family is in a safe house "

"Same thing." She smiled for the first time, lips a tight line across her teeth. Then she turned to Williams. "Which answers your question, Mr President – you have about a dozen mini Civil Wars going on, all of them more successful than they should be, all of them with a religious component, and all of them with a lot of innocent civilians at ground zero. They appear to be unrelated and even in opposition – I don't think the megachurch folks will truck much with the pagan Amerinds – but if the timing's a coincidence I'll eat my shirt. Mr President."

"Do we have a cause?"

"No, sir."

"All right." He looked around the room. "This would be a shitstorm even if it weren't an election year. Do we have any solutions?"

McGrath cleared his throat. "I've got authority to speak for Jim, here. The only response to insurrection is to crush it. I don't care what kind of hoodoo nonsense these traitors have, they're not going to stand up to the United States military. Quash this idiocy early, and others won't start."

Williams bemoaned the use of violence. Someone else objected on constitutional grounds, and Matt tuned out. He followed orders, he didn't give them, and nobody in this conversation would listen to him anyway.

"Sergeant Rowley," the president said at some point. "Intelligence suggests that you're familiar with the head of this church in White Spruce. Is that correct?"

He nodded.

"What's the nature of your relationship?"

Matt ran his tongue over his upper teeth. "Jason Rees was my best friend until he slept with my wife. Sir. Some years later he assisted in the destruction of ICAP, and then a combat operation against a cult in Georgia. He left the church after the incident on the Mall, and we speak if and when we must."

"Do you think you can talk him down from this ledge?"

"I'm not sure what you mean, sir."

"These churches, these… insurrectionists, they seem to look up to him. Do you think he can talk them into giving up this insanity? Before others join them?"

Matt shrugged. "Rees isn't violent by nature, but he's not my biggest fan, either." He breathed out, long and low. "I think my wife might be able to. Sir."

"Then that's settled. National Guard for New Hampshire and to back up the BIA, and Sergeant Rowley will handle the Christians. Anything else?"

No one said anything, so he added, "Dismissed."

As they shuffled out the president held back the Joint Chiefs. Freudenberg hurried Matt out of the room, murmuring, "That's a different sort of mission for you, isn't it?"

Sakura stood as they came out, killed her e-Reader, and put it in her back pocket.

"Yes," Matt said. "It'll give Sakura a chance for some R&R, and let me actually spend a little time with my family. I'm almost looking forward to it," he lied.

"To what?" Sakura asked.

"Bossing Rees around."

• • •

General Marco Valdez marched into President Robles's office, flanked by six of the president's guards. Robles looked up from his desk, and the topless secretary kneeling in front of him ducked out of the way, wiping her mouth with the back of her hand, her sly grin a counter to the president's outraged bluster.

"Do we no longer knock, Marco?"

Valdez flicked a finger at the girl, and the guards put their hands on their sidearms. "Matias, please stand and zip up your pants."

She bolted toward the door, panties in one hand, blouse and bra in the other, revealing a tight body closer in age to the president's daughter than his wife. A guard grabbed her arm and threw her down, then kicked her in the ribs hard enough to lift her from the ground. Robles shot daggers at Valdez as the girl gagged and coughed blood onto the carpet.

"What is the meaning of this?" He stood, zipped his fly, and buckled his belt. "Do you forget who you're speaking to?"

Valdez pulled an unloaded .38 revolver from his pocket and tossed it across the desk. Robles caught it, turned it around in his hand, and looked up, brow scrunched in confusion.

With a nod, the guards opened fire. As Robles dropped, Valdez clicked his radio twice. Gunfire popped in the courthouse next door and though he couldn't hear it, a similar scene played out in parliament down the street. "Prepare the media room for an address to the people. Leave us."

The guards backed out and closed the doors. Valdez tangled his fingers in the secretary's hair and pulled her to her feet. He grew hard at her whimper, and harder still as her fingernails drew red runnels down his hand.

"Tell me, little girl." He licked her face, from chin to temple, and whispered the rest in her ear. "What can you do that makes you worth keeping?"

Sobbing, she stopped clawing to run her hands down his arms, down his chest, to fumble at the buttons on his shirt.

For a moment his vision flared jade, and a sliver of thought shrieked that something else had control. Weakened but not weak, Ometeotl crushed the errant worry and faded back into the undercurrents in Valdez's psyche, content to let the general's animal drive for power serve his needs.

• • •

"You're not going to leave our side, either of you." Matt loaded Adam into the car seat strapped into the Apache helicopter while Sakura helped Monica with her straps. "We're just going to talk to him, and then we're going to leave. No side trips, no distractions – the OPD is still out there, and we don't know what assets they have where."

"They won't dare do nothing with you right here, will they?" The worry in her voice broke his heart.

"No." *I don't think so.* "I think they've wasted enough hardware on Sakura and I to think twice before they try again. Besides," he plopped small earmuffs over his grinning son's head, "nobody knows we'll be home."

They lifted off and Monica looked out the window, knuckles white on the holy shit handle by the door but her eyes wide with wonder. He'd always loved helicopters, and it warmed his heart to see her share that joy. Adam giggled and clapped his hands, squirming against his restraints to get a better view, but his unbridled joy faded, and an hour out he'd fallen asleep.

When they crossed the Tennessee line Matt tapped Monica on the knee. She rolled her eyes, triggered her microphone, and dialed. Matt eavesdropped as the noise-canceling mic did its best to muffle the thundering rotors.

Rees picked up on the third ring. "Hello?"

"Hey, Jason."

"Hey, yourself. You in a helicopter?"

"Yup."

"Cool. Your husband know you're calling?"

"Yup."

"What do you want, Mon?"

Matt looked out the window to hide a twitch as Rees used her nickname, an old familiarity he no longer deserved.

"You remember the gravel pit out on Eight? Past Blechley's stand?"

"Sure."

"Meet me there. Just you. Don't tell anyone."

"Will it be just you?"

"Yeah. Me and Adam."

"Okay. When?"

"Half an hour."

His annoyance carried perfectly over the line. "I have a meeting in a half an hour."

"Cancel it. This is life or death." The line clicked dead, and she gave Matt a sheepish grin. "I didn't want to give him time to argue."

"Lord knows he'll do that."

"You just remember to stay back. I'll talk to him, you listen. If you don't like what you hear, pull up your big girl panties and get over it."

He patted her knee. "I remember the arrangement."

They came in low over the mountains, where almost nobody would see them and the echoes would obscure their location. Touching down woke Adam, who rubbed his eyes and yawned, then gave Matt a happy smile. Matt helped Monica out of the helicopter, took her ear muffs, but left the ear bud in, fluffing her hair to hide it.

She slapped his hand away and arranged it herself, checking it with a compact mirror from her purse. "And I don't look like a poodle."

The gravel pit would make a great kill box – a single winding road barely wide enough for two cars, steep earthen walls on two sides, and tall trees – and an even better meeting place at the spur of the moment. Even if the Office of Planning and Development knew they were coming, they wouldn't have had time to set up anything, so those high vantage points served as perfect walls. Sakura vanished into the trees.

"Don't take too long." He kissed Monica's cheek then swatted her ass as she walked away.

"Yeah, yeah, yeah," she muttered into the COM. She stopped a hundred feet away, at the far side of the pit, arms crossed.

A few minutes later Jason rounded the corner in a white Malibu, a smile dying on his face when he locked eyes with Matt. They exchanged nods, and Matt made sure to keep his face neutral as he drove past. He stopped next to Monica, fiddled with something in his lap a moment, then got out.

They shook hands, an awkward gesture at the best of times, then stood there a moment with their hands clasped in front of their bodies. Standoffish. Nervous.

"I thought you were alone."

"We are alone," she replied. "They're way over there. We can talk private."

"They?"

"Matt's with the boy, Isuji's in the woods somewhere. I don't know what she's doing, but she doesn't like to sit still."

"Sakura's here, too?" He looked up at the trees, then toward the entrance.

Matt narrowed his eyes as Jason put his hand in his pocket, fingers working. Matt keyed his COM to go only to Sakura and the pilot. "Keep sharp. He's way more nervous than he should be."

"Yeah," Monica said. "Why, is that a problem?"

Jason shook his head. "No, no, of course not. So I'm here. What's this about?"

"You heard about them churches."

"Sure, yeah, yeah. Hard not to. What about them?" His rapid-fire speech raised the hair on the back of Matt's neck.

"They're going to call in the military to deal with them. A lot of people are going to get hurt if they don't quit what they're doing and turn themselves in. They sent me here in the hopes that maybe—"

Sakura spoke over the top of her. "Three trucks coming hot. Twenty people maybe."

"—our relationship. So were hoping that you could talk to them, get them to stand down or whatever."

Jason patted her shoulder. "Yeah, sure. Good to see you, Mon. I got to go."

Matt hopped into the cabin, yanked his kit out, jumped down and closed the door. "Sam, take my boy up. Something's not right here."

The motor whined as Matt kneeled, popping the hatches to reveal several load-outs of ICAP kit. He holstered the WildStang and on second thought picked up an AA-12.

Jason jumped in his car. His starter screeched, then the engine thrummed to life. His tires spit dust as the trucks careened around the corner into the pit, dusty old pickups loaded with men. Matt turned, slapped a drum magazine of frag rounds into the shotgun, racked it, and stepped in the way of the trucks – and of Jason's car.

Two thirds of the men were strangers, a few he'd seen around town after Jason's church had started going up, but it broke his heart to see people he knew and loved. Tony Palermo, bartender and longtime friend; Old Man Finster, a grizzled, octegenarian vet who'd helped them against Humans for Humanity only a year before; Bob Vallimont, whose daughter he'd saved in the grocery store parking lot that same month. All of them armed with long guns, all of them ruddy-faced and eager.

Matt put up a hand, fingers splayed wide. Jason rolled to a stop to avoid running him over, forming an L with the trucks, which rolled to a stop, the front one twenty feet from him.

"What's going on here, Rees?" He had to yell over the quickening rotors.

"Just brought some backup is all, in case something fishy was going on."

Sakura appeared beside Matt, a knife in each hand. "He's lying."

"I know."

Jason licked his lips. "Look, just let us be on our way, and nobody needs to get hurt."

Matt nodded. "That sounds like a great—"

"WE AIN'T LEAVING HERE WITHOUT THE BOY!"

Bob Vallimont yelled. A chorus of agreement rose from the trucks, along with some "Amens!" and "Hallelujahs!" Bob revved the motor and the truck lurched, then settled. "WE DON'T MEAN HIM NO HARM, BUT HE NEEDS TO TAKE HIS RIGHTFUL PLACE!" More "Amens!" More "Hallelujas!" And a "Fuck yeah!" from the rear truck.

Matt kept the AA-12 pointed at the dirt, and spoke without moving his lips, trusting the COM to carry his voice where it needed to go. "Mon, hide. Get behind that gravel pile and don't come out until I get you." She edged away as he raised his voice, drawing attention to himself. "Bob, you back those trucks down that road and call it a day, and we'll call this no harm no foul."

Old Man Finster spit out the passenger's side window. "He needs guidance! It's Satan's work, keeping him from us!"

"He's my son—"

"SATAN'S WORK! There's no negotiation with the devil."

In his peripheral vision, Monica inched closer to cover.

"I'M NOT NEGOTIATING!" He yelled to be heard, but carefully schooled his face and actions to be as nonthreatening as possible. "You back on out of here right now!" He looked at Jason, willed him to understand. "Diffuse this."

Jason got out of the car, hands outstretched, one toward the truck, one toward Matt. "Brothers, we made a mistake. Let's just turn around and head back to the church. No one has to—"

"SHE'S GETTING AWAY!"

Monica bolted. The chopper left the ground.

Someone fired, the bullet ricocheting off the fuselage. The whispers cried their disappointment as a dozen bullets passed through the space Matt occupied.

"No!" Matt dove for a tree and opened fire, beating the fanatics by a hair's breath. A bullet punched through Matt's boot and the foot inside.

Pieces of men rained from the truck bed, six men torn to ribbons as they pulled their triggers. Sakura appeared next to Finster and a red jet gushed from his neck. Bob Vallimont gaped as his hand fell from his wrist, and Sakura disappeared behind the front vehicle.

"HOLD YOUR GODDAMNED FIRE!" Matt screamed.

Jason, back in the car, gunned the gas, backward, toward Monica's hiding place. Bullets sprayed Matt's position, raining chunks of bark and wood around him. He stood erect, arms at his sides, to minimize his profile behind the tree. Rees's car disappeared as the shooting stopped.

Matt bolted, sparing a glance toward the other vehicles. Sakura had moved through them like the Angel of Death, bathed in blood; a dozen men dead in a fourth as many seconds, blood spraying in every direction before a body had hit the ground.

He ran after Rees.

• • •

Jason screeched around the gravel pile, opened the car door and stepped out, hands in the air, eyes wide, tearful. "Monica, please! I didn't mean for this to happen!"

"Oh, I believe that." She poured accusation into her voice, palming the rock she'd picked up in her left hand. "You never do."

"I—I didn't think anyone would get hurt. I just meant… I mean I meant…"

She stepped toward him and tried to speak through a voice cracking with heartbreak, at the boy she'd known, at the man she'd loved. Another step. She owed him more than Matt would ever know, more than any person should owe another. "I know, JJ. You only meant to take my son."

He fell for her feint, shying left to avoid a knife-hand to his trachea. Her foot contacted his temple and he dropped, face-down in the dirt. She fell to her knees next to his squirming body, rock over her head, and brought it down on his ratty skull. The dull 'thunk' surprised her – she'd expected something more dramatic, something with more of a crack. The second one felt like the first, and the third softer.

Strong hands grabbed her wrists and lifted her, stopping the fourth, and she kept screaming her incoherent rage at the blood leaking from his ear.

"Monica, hey! Baby! It's over, we're okay."

She screamed and kicked at his shins, kneed his groin and chest, but Matt wouldn't let go. She stopped struggling, but had a few seconds of hateful scream left in her.

Sakura appeared next to Jason, felt for a pulse, looked up at them. "He lives. Is this what you want?"

"Yes," Matt said as Monica said, "No."

He wrapped her and held her, his strong, loving arms a prison from which she couldn't escape, didn't want to escape, and he whispered in her ear with the tender confidence she'd always loved. "You're not a murder, Mon. He's down, he can't hurt you, none of them can hurt you. If he lives, he lives. But he'll never touch you again."

She broke into sobs, and let Matt carry her back to the chopper.

• • •

"Ambulance is coming," the pilot said. "We waiting or going?"

Matt ran a hand over his scalp. "We have to stay. How many casualties?"

"Sixteen," Sakura said.

"Injured?"

"Three, and the priest if he lives."

Sakura had bound wounds and delivered CPR. Bob Vallimont lay unconscious, gray-faced, his hand next to his wrist, the bleeding stopped with a tourniquet made from a strip of denim and a stick. The other two he didn't recognize, and didn't spare a second thought. Instead he approached the slaughtered men, destroyed with meticulous precision to save his son.

Tony Palermo lay on his side, a massive bruise on his temple, blood in his open left eye and puddled in his ear, his mouth open in shock or surprise. Matt sat next to him, ran his hand across the thinning hair on his scalp. He beat away memories of hunting crawdads in the creek, building snowmen, playing football on Friday nights.

"I'm sorry, man. It didn't have to be like this."

Anger flared at the fallen priest, a deep rage filling his chest with honest, wholesome hate. Rees's eyes had dilated fully and didn't respond to light. They'd raised his legs and treated him for shock, and he hadn't died yet. Left to the EMTs he might yet live, might not even have permanent brain damage.

Matt stood, walked over to him, looked down at his almost peaceful face. A twinge of jealousy rippled through him, that Monica had bashed in Jason's skull and not him. His fists clenched.

Commotion fluttered behind him, his son yelling, his wife cooing calming words. He turned.

Monica huddled in the helicopter, trying to shield Adam from the violence he'd already witnessed, while Adam screamed and cried for "Unca Rees" and reached for the door handle. Icy wind howled through the pit, kicking up dust devils and peppering the helicopter with rocks. Matt shielded his eyes and shook his head, and when Monica wouldn't relent Adam calmed, so did the wind.

Sirens blared in the distance. He sat with Sakura and Sam by the helicopter, the weapons deployed in the fight on the ground twenty feet away, the rest packed away in the helicopter, and waited.

They were polite but adamant with the police, who realized straight-away that they were dealing with not only government agents but the last two Augs, and the miracle mother and child, and gave them far more deference than they deserved. He answered questions as patiently as he could, next to the helicopter with Sakura and Sam, far enough away to let the county and state forensics teams do their work.

Hours passed, and the sun crept toward the treetops. At long last the moment he'd feared came.

As a news van rolled around the corner, Matt turned away from the Sherriff. "Sorry, Sherriff, but looks like we're not going to be here when the FBI comes after all. You've got my number. Call me when you have to."

He left the man gaping as Sam hopped aboard. They went around the far side, invisible to cameras, and got in. The Sherriff banged on the door, hollering, which they ignored.

"Are we going?" Monica asked, face smudged but no longer damp with tears.

"Yeah. We're going."

They lifted off moments later, headed back for DC.

• • •

A blip in his COM woke him to a dark cabin and overcast skies.

"Yeah, go ahead," he said, voice low so as not to wake his exhausted wife and child, somehow not preposterous in a helicopter moving at a hundred and eighty miles an hour.

Janet's voice rang well too loud in his ear. "Two things. First, thought you might want to know we got the DNA back on Flynn's remains. He's a chimera, a mix of Conor Flynn and Ben Case. Even his fingerprints are a mix of the two."

"That's fucking weird."

"You're telling me. The lab weenies are all atwitter over

it, and Stein's got a microscope up my keister looking for anything else that might be fun."

"Glad you've settled into a productive working relationship. What's number two?"

"Looks like your pal Williams ordered US forces under SACLANT back to US command. LC Smith refused, and so far the men are following him, not the Commander in Chief."

"Jesus. Do we know why?"

"The world's going to hell in a handbasket if you haven't noticed. Nineteen new insurrections today just in Africa, three in the Middle East. The Ural Mountains are a no-go zone right now, Delhi's on fire, Mexico just had a coup and is mobilizing troops toward the cartel land on their northern border, and the media's reporting hopping freaking vampires on the Yangtze. I think he wants more troops at home in case the shit hits the fan."

"I meant why did Smith refuse? He's a dick, but seems a 'takes orders' kind of guy."

"Hard to say, bud. The official line is that our obligations to NATO still stand. Unofficial line is that the Joint Chiefs scuttled the order through back channels. Rumor has it his first tried to strip him of command and Smith had him executed."

"Seriously?"

"No confirmation on that, but some chatter that went silent pretty fast, yeah."

"That might explain a little something about dissolving the Special Threats Bureau, pulling us closer to home as far as Chain of Command."

"I thought that, too. Pretty ugly. Anyway, see you in a few hours."

"Yeah." He killed the line and leaned his head back against the cold, vibrating metal.

"Everything okay?" Monica asked.

"Sure. As okay as they can be. We're still an hour or so out, so get some rest."

"Okay."

Adam stared at him, his gentle brown eyes icy pinpricks in the dark cabin.

CHAPTER FIFTEEN

The helicopter slowed as they approached Joint Base Anacostia-Bolling. Monica's eyes fluttered open to look down at Washington, DC below. The bags under her eyes had only grown in the trip back from White Spruce, but Matt loved her all the more for her disheveled appearance. She yawned and leaned her head against the window. "Is that the base?"

Matt followed her gaze. "That's Reagan. Abab is across the river."

She frowned. "Why do they call it an Air Force Base if it doesn't have any runways?"

"It's mostly support and ceremonial stuff now. Marine One, the Air Force Band, some other stuff. They have a helipad, though."

"Couldn't any big parking lot be a helipad?"

"Sure, Mon. But in—"

A burst of light accompanied the whispers. Matt unhooked his harness and turned. Sakura dove across and covered Adam with her body, hands twisted in the restraints to his car seat. The helicopter rocked with a bang, and the sound of the rotors dropped to a lower register.

"We're hit." Sam's voice came clipped and tight over the radio.

They listed to the right and drifted clockwise, rotating ever faster as they fell. Matt grabbed the strap and door handle on either side of Monica, wrapping her with his body to take the bulk of the impact.

"Hold on!" Sam said in their headsets. They leveled out at the last second above the Defense Intelligence Institute, a huge, industrial-looking building just shy of the helipad. Sam skimmed the higher roof, dropped and twisted, jerking them back and forth, before passing over the building and dropping straight down.

"Close your mouth, Mon!"

Monica jerked her tongue back and clacked her teeth shut a split second before a jarring crunch shocked up Matt's legs. A shriek of metal shuddered down Matt's spine and through his teeth, the chopper tilting as the landing skid gave way. They bounced hard, and her forehead rebounded off his shoulder.

As the machine skidded to a halt Sakura tossed him his AA-12 and a satchel of magazine; he still wore his pistol from the conflict in White Spruce. He popped the door shielded by the rest of the building, speaking into the COM with controlled authority.

"Sam, get my family out of here. Across the road! Sakura, on me."

Alarms wailed in the building, and lights flashed in bright, white pops. Whatever had mangled the tail rotor had punched clean through without exploding, a kinetic-kill weapon or a dud, and whoever had shot it had tremendous aim.

He bolted around the building toward the AA fire, hoping to draw fire away from Monica and Adam. His calf twinged as every running step re-tore something before it could heal. With Janet home for the night and no Dragonflies they had no tactical advantage, and no notion of the forces allayed against them.

Figures boiled out of the far side of the DIA – Matt bet they'd expected a closer crash, and said a silent prayer of thanks for Sam's flying. He set the AA-12 to range off of the laser sight and opened fire, spraying the mass of... commandos? Soldiers? He had no idea.

The semi-guided munitions exploded as they hit their target or reached their proscribed range. Some dodged with impossible leaps and spins, sheltering behind the slower 'normals'. Others died, stumbling, falling, a few missing limbs or chunks of their heads.

A rumble drowned out the whispers as he pulled back, large-caliber bullets chipping brick and mortar from the building's facade. A .50 caliber machine gun designed to take out light vehicles could make mincemeat of an Aug, and the M2A1 barely needed to reload.

"Sakura, what do you have on that M2?"

"On a Jeep."

Matt didn't have time to sit still, pinned down while his opponents out-maneuvered him. "Anything you can do about it?"

"In minutes, not seconds."

Shit. "Do it."

He backed up to a side entrance and smashed the window with the butt of his AA-12, tearing through the steel mesh in the safety glass. Reaching through, he hit the crash bar and pulled, then spun around the door to take cover behind the reinforced steel. A grenade tumbled around the corner, too far and too wide to be much of a concern. He fired twice, rounds set to pass the building and explode left.

Hot metal dug into his right eyebrow, but four men stumbled and fell around the corner, the only visual casualties.

Two more shots for good measure, then he bolted inside and up the stairs, swapping out his magazine for another drum. A massive office building, he'd never visited DIA headquarters and had no idea where any hallway led – but if pursuing him kept their attackers away from Monica and Adam he'd gladly trap himself in a maze of hallways.

Sakura circled the firefight perimeter at a full sprint, ducking between apartment buildings and dashing through groggy crowds of annoyed residents, men and women in underwear and robes peering toward the conflict with more curiosity than worry.

An older black man wearing an Army hat with gold oak leaf on the front frowned at the scene with dark, intelligent eyes. She stopped in front of him, letting the rush of air billow the towel around his waist before speaking, though it startled him anyway.

"Not an exercise. Matt Rowley and his family are in danger. Only two friendlies, him and me."

He opened his mouth, but she took off, weaving through the growing crowd faster than they could react. Their attackers had planned well – had the helicopter landed where they'd hit it, none of them would have survived. By putting them down on the other side of the building Sam had turned their crossfire ambush into a chase and left several elements out of position.

The Jeep crept forward, the gunner searching for a target near the DIA building with a pair of night vision binoculars. She approached at a run, boots rolling across asphalt as close to silently as possible without sacrificing speed. Ten feet from the vehicle she threw her first knife. The gunner stiffened as it sunk into his neck.

Boot on the bumper, she leapt, landing in the back seat. Two swipes with the knife and the soldiers on either side of her grinned red smiles from their necks. Before their blood fell she reversed her grip and jammed the blade into the driver's carotid artery, then leapt up to the machine gun.

As blood gushed across her shoes she snatched the twitching gunner's ear bud from his head and put it in her right ear, then pulled the trigger and swept left. The tang of gunpowder and hot metal mingled with the smells of blood and gasoline. White tracers lanced from the bucking gun into the squad of men taking shelter behind a brick wall. With no cover and nowhere to run, they fell like grass.

"Regent Four, hostile on your three o'clock. Engage." The calm, confident male voice sent a shiver up her spine, cold terror and white-hot hatred her only emotions since he'd taken her from woods of Centralia. Shane Keene.

She turned the M2 left, still firing, as a metal bay door exploded outward with a hideous shriek. Twin mechanical behemoths charged from a hundred feet away, hydraulics clanking as the ten-foot humanoids built up to speed. Parodies of human form, they sported enormous, stylized helmets decorated with huge serrated jaws jutting out from skulls that shined a metallic black.

Paint peeled and metal dented as she concentrated fire on the rightmost, walking the tracers into neck, groin, knees, and elbows. With a harsh clack the M2 ran dry.

Crouching, she pulled her knife from the driver, and leapt as they hit the Jeep. The impact rolled it. She ran across the now-horizontal door and up the battered one's arm, jamming the knife into the crack between its helmet and shoulder pauldron. It jerked her to a stop, and she jammed an incendiary grenade between the jaw and helmet—while the magnets didn't stick, the gap left plenty of room to insert the device and pull the pin. Huge hands reached up and it whirled, grabbing for her but unable to bend enough.

Feet against its back, she let go of the knife and pushed off.

The thermite ignited with a white flash that turned the night into day. Boiling metal and cooking meat sizzled under the dying shrieks of the woman inside. She hit the ground, pulled another incendiary, and smiled at the other beast.

It reached up, tore off the decorative jaw that had doomed its partner, and circled her.

• • •

Matt had seen those web-guns before, when they'd rescued

Sakura. Stubby like a grenade launcher, they fired a sticky goo that hardened into extremely strong filament moments after impact. Four men carried them, their movements sleek and inhuman, each leading a squad of three more armed with HK416 carbines, short-barreled assault weapons favored by Special Forces.

They lifted their night-vision goggles in response to the fire alarm strobes, a worst-case mix for night blindness on unaugmented eyes. In the ultraviolet the LED strobes made an annoying flicker, nothing more, and registered not at all in the infrared. Even half-blind, they fanned out through the third-floor, clearing cubicles and hallways with methodic, professional precision, communicating with US military hand signals.

He kept the handle of the office door turned and closed it, slowly, to make as little movement as possible, then turned the lock. It wouldn't stop them, but he didn't need a lot of time. The plastic rolly chair behind the desk was useless, but the wooden desk chair had sufficient heft and durability to meet his needs. Damned office windows wouldn't open more than six inches, which wouldn't even fit his thigh.

The glass shattered as the chair sailed through, tearing out the miniblinds in a flutter of cheap plastic. Then he stepped back into the coat closet and closed the door, holding it shut with his left hand, WildStang in his right.

The office door blew inward. He counted to three, let the whispers cheer his death and in doing so give him the locations of his would-be killers, then broke out, pistol raised.

The squad leader turned, faster than human, almost as fast as Sakura – and not fast enough. Matt pulled the trigger at point-blank range, splattering brains across the other three. As they flinched back he pistol-whipped one hard enough to crack his skull, shot a second, and kicked the third in the chest. He flipped over the desk and his thighs slammed down on the broken window, plate glass embedded deep in the muscle.

Matt leapt, tearing the injured man off of the glass and manhandling him underneath as they fell. His chest cavity imploded as it absorbed the impact of Matt's boot, and Matt rolled out of the collision to come up on his feet, weapon raised and firing. Men scattered back from the broken window, and Matt bolted for the corner of the building, denying them line of sight to return fire.

The whispers giggled as his skull popped like a melon hit with a sledgehammer.

He ducked and slid around the corner. A massive hydraulic claw shattered the brick over his head. He punched the WildStang into the behemoth's groin and double-tapped, wincing as the second armor-piercing bullet shattered against the thick plate, spraying hot shards of tungsten and ceramic into his face. Wet liquid ran down his left cheek, his eye totally blind. He leapt up, turning to keep the thing in sight.

Red fluid gushed from between its legs, and it sagged against the wall. He spun, scanning for targets. Men with web guns piled out of the doorway. He ran thirty steps across open ground before a whine drew his attention. Another behemoth lurked behind a dumpster across the parking lot, the minigun on its shoulder spinning up. With nothing but empty all around, he charged, firing.

• • •

Sakura danced back, schooling her breath to the calm necessary to maintain proper focus in a combat situation. Scrapes and dings along joints were the only signs that she'd made contact with her opponent, bonk-killer rounds and frags as ineffective as her knives against the thing's armor. It might as well have been a human tank for all it cared, but like a tank she had no problem getting out of the way of the massive claws and feet that could crush or dismember with a single stroke.

Without the stupid jaw it had a tiny head, almost comical compared to its upper body, but that left her nowhere to put another incendiary grenade. Ponderous and bulky in appearance, on open ground it could beat her foot speed and had stunning maneuverability. Escape seemed as elusive as destroying the thing, so she circled, feinted and dodged, and inched toward the storage sheds near the water.

In her ear Keene told it to keep her there until reinforcements arrived, reported Rowley engaged with Reaper, and coordinated the hunt for Monica and the child. She listened for any clue to his whereabouts, but heard none.

Twenty feet from the sheds she bolted, counting on inertia to slow the enormous machine enough for her to get out of sight. She rounded the corner between two small buildings and sprinted for the far end.

A pair of men swung out, one on either side, and took aim with snub-nosed guns. She leapt as they fired, using her speed to run up the wall, but an orange strand nicked her foot. Her next step brought more of the web around her ankles. She fell, .357 already out of its holster and firing, but they'd disappeared behind the walls.

She hit the ground, kicking at her boots, but the stretchy mess clung to her legs and turned rock hard. Straining, something tore in her hip, but the substance didn't give.

A shadow blocked the lights from the city. Behind her, the behemoth lumbered forward, claws spread wide to scrape against the alley walls. She fired twice before more orange strands entrapped her arms and hands, settling like splattered paint between her fingers and limbs before solidifying.

Panting, she fumbled the pistol. Her great strength couldn't budge the orange gunk, couldn't turn the pistol toward her own head, couldn't pull the trigger.

An endless stream of cruel machinery cutting and slicing her flesh, crushing limbs, burning skin and muscle and organs, rending chunks of meat from bone, slicing off ears and nose and breasts, popping eyes. The visions – the memories – wouldn't stop, and unbidden a scream escaped her mouth, silencing only long enough for her to suck in a breath before it came again, and again.

• • •

Matt made it three steps before the minigun opened fire, the pummeling thunder of high-velocity shells mingling with Sakura's sudden shrieks in his ear. He ducked left, keeping his good eye toward the target, leaping the deadly spray of high-velocity metal. It swept back as he closed the distance. Dropping prone, the line of death swept over his head even as he scrambled up and closed with the metal monster.

Gasping, he fell, the remains of his right calf blown across the parking lot. Incomprehensible agony overwhelmed conscious thought as his left femur shattered. Through a haze of jade clouds he trained the pistol two-handed on the thing and fired. It bucked four times before clicking empty, and a hydraulic claw closed on his arms, severing them at the elbow.

Lightheaded, he fell back.

• • •

Throat raw, Sakura's screams had fallen to silence by the time they'd loaded her into an unmarked white panel van with Virginia plates. Athletic men in black combat suits had used electrical devices about the size and shape of Tasers to cut the orange webbing, freeing her from the pavement and wall without allowing the slightest struggle. They left the .357 in place, a sign of either their confidence in the technology or nervousness of what she'd do with a free hand.

Shame accompanied the slamming doors, that she'd choose suicide over imprisonment, even by monsters such as these. Any given human life held no value except that given to it by loved ones, and she had no loved ones… but she had a duty and a debt and the honor to carry them with every last breath.

"I'm sorry." Keene's low voice scraped rusty nails down her spine. It came from her left, his presence obscured by the hardened webbing. "I know what they did to you. What they're going to do. It's inhuman and it's wrong, and nobody deserves it, least of all you."

She wouldn't beg, unless it bought her time to tear his lungs from his chest.

"… but you don't understand the stakes, what we're fighting against and what we need to destroy it. Your power can't be left in the hands of two, or even a dozen or a hundred. We need it, and that means we need you, and though you have no reason to believe me, I respect your sacrifice even if it's unwilling."

The back doors opened, and hope died.

Matt's bloody torso landed on the gurney next to her, blue lips open to reveal a blue tongue, tourniquets on all four severed limbs. Alive, then, but soon he'd wish he weren't. She closed her eyes, licked her lips, spoke through a jaw she could just move.

"You don't need him. You have me, and you can use me as you used me and I will not complain or attempt escape. Just let him go."

"You honor your ancestors," Keene said. Then his voice turned hard. "But you have no cards to play." He hopped out, replaced by a guard in urban camouflage, his young face dusted with a hint of dark stubble.

The van rolled, rocking her back and forth, before smoothing out to a steady acceleration, wind whistling through a cracked window she couldn't see. Her ears popped. Unable to turn, she rolled her eyes to the side to look at Matt.

The blue in his lips and tongue had faded to a purple-pink, and the shredded muscles past his tourniquets writhed and grew.

"You must undo the bands and cut away the meat as it heals over the bone, else he will heal at odds and need reamputation."

"Be quiet," the guard said. "Or I'll make—"

The van lurched, brakes shuddering as the computer struggled to keep the tires from locking. Small arms popped outside, and glass shattered. They stopped with a shriek of crunching metal.

"Report!" Keene yelled through the guard's radio.

"We're under attack!"

The back door flew open to a series of gunshots and the guard twitched, falling out of sight as bullets riddled his torso, one punching through his neck in a spray of blood almost black in the dim van.

An older black man stepped inside, stooping to remain standing in the cramped space, his eyes wide under bushy gray eyebrows. He tipped his hat – the same one with the gold oak leaf – and looked around. "How do we free you?"

"No. Take him first. Get him to safety."

"Beg pardon, ma'am, but—"

"GO!"

He stepped aside and Matt's gurney wheeled out of the van with a crash.

A man's voice cried out, "Major! We've got company!"

"Okay, ma'am, how do we get you out?"

"The guard has an electric device." Automatic weapons chattered outside the van. "It cuts the restraints very easy."

He crouched out of sight, then popped up with the remote control-sized object in his right hand. "Got it!" Clicking the buzzer, an arc of blue light shot between the electrodes, lighting up his beaming smile. "Now let me just—"

His teeth exploded through his lips, spraying a red mist across her face and neck. He tottered, then collapsed to the side. The door creaked and a calm, careful voice said, "It's all clear, sir."

Keene replied. "Get her out of there – we're going for the other van."

Rage burned in Sakura's chest, fueled by a hatred for her own impotence, and a deeper hatred for Shane Keene. She struggled, muscles straining hard enough to tear ligaments and tendons, to crack the bones of a normal woman. Her restraints wouldn't budge.

• • •

Matt's eyes fluttered open to a night sky the hazy orange of sodium vapor lights. A deep ache wracked his body, a consuming, eternal agony that unconsciousness, shock, or death was supposed to spare the human mind. Every bounce, every jiggle sent hammer-blows through his brain, and unbidden he let out a low moan.

"God, you're tough."

Shane Keene. His face twitched, the only response he could muster to the desire to drown the man in his own blood. With herculean effort he managed to tilt his head back, rolling his eyes to assess the man pushing his gurney.

Dark bags under his eyes, blood in his gray beard, a red split down his bottom lip, Keene's worried scowl turned the grizzled man's expression downright dour. His eyes flashed back and forth, ignoring Matt for the time being.

But Matt couldn't capitalize, couldn't even lift his head to assess how badly he'd been hit.

"Lie still, Rowley. You aren't in any position to be a threat, so save your energy." A thick strand of blood gushed from his nose to darken his mustache. He reached up, touched it with two fingers, pulled them away. "Shit."

His grunt turned into a snarl and he stumbled out of sight. The gurney rolled to a stop, then shuddered as Keene crashed back into it. Blood leaked from his nose and eyes, dribbled from his mouth into his beard. He slammed the heel of his palm into his jaw, once, twice, three times, as his facial muscles twisted and contorted, bones cracking and popping as they reshaped and reformed.

All at once the tension rushed out of him, and the gush of blood stopped. Matt almost didn't recognize the face staring down at him, but the eyes betrayed the owner more than Keene's beard and mustache could hide him.

Conor Flynn grinned with Keene's nicotine-stained teeth. "It's really not something you want to do again, right is right."

"Sir?" a hesitant voice said. "Are you all right?"

Flynn booped Matt's nose with a fingertip. "Minute, sir."

He disappeared, and someone screamed. The air filled with gunpowder, then a sharp explosion, likely a grenade. Matt's eyes stung as the acrid smoke drifted over him. A body slammed into Matt, tumbling him from the gurney, and the white-hot nothing blanked out the world.

His vision returned in fireworks of red, just in time to see Flynn tear a man's throat out with his bare hands. Another of the fast men charged in, feinting with a combat knife. Flynn stepped into the feint, let the knife scrape off Keene's body armor, and shattered the man's nose with a vicious head butt.

He stumbled back, hand to his forehead. "Riches and bitches, this body isn't used to that."

The fast man buried the knife in Conor's neck. His responding knife-hand strike crushed his opponent's trachea, and he turned, scooping up a webbing gun and firing into a charging behemoth. The enormous metal humanoid shredded through the orange filament and reached out with a massive claw.

The massive metal blades closed, severing Flynn's head from his shoulders. It tumbled into the dirt as the body collapsed, and the features relaxed into a hybrid of Keene and Flynn.

A fast man's cough turned into bright red vomit, splattering his shoes as his squad mates scattered back. He clutched his gut and fell to his knees, moaning, then rose, haughty and proud, Conor with olive skin and rich, black hair. He turned on the behemoth, grabbed a hydraulic line from between two armor plates and yanked, spraying red-brown fluid across the ground. As the thing sagged Flynn swung up onto its shoulders, lifted off its helmet, and ran his hands through the pilot's hair.

"How do you drive this thing? Levers and gears?"

He shook his head. "No. Y-you just move, and it moves with you. It's all sensors."

"Brilliant, brilliant." Conor twisted and pulled. The pilot's low, furious scream turned into a shriek as most of his scalp and face came off in Flynn's hands.

Flynn sagged, dropping to the ground and landing on all fours. He looked up, face red from exertion. "Bridges. They take a lot out of you."

Clanking metal and whirring gears heralded the arrival of another behemoth. Conor grinned. "You've got to admire their stick-to-it-iveness, don't you, Rowley? They just keep coming."

His chest evaporated as a recoilless rifle shook the air.

• • •

Behind the van, Sakura concealed a snarl as a fast man appeared over her, Taser-thing in front of her eyes. He licked his lips and flicked the switch. "I can get you out but you have to help us. That man, that thing, he's killing everyone, and every time he dies he just comes back. You got to stop him."

"Hai. Yes. I'll help you."

With efficient slashes he disintegrated the bonding material. As the last piece fell away Sakura punched the .357 into her rescuer's neck and pulled the trigger twice. He stumbled and fell to the ground, jerking and flopping as his brain processed his body's death. She kneeled, scooped up the web gun and his pistol – a Glock 9mm much more suited to law enforcement than their line of work – and ran around the van.

Conor Flynn whirled and struck in combat with two fast men and a circling behemoth, twenty feet from where Rowley lay, his arms and legs slithering masses of muscle overgrowing bone. Slower than she remembered, Flynn stood half a head taller and had thick brown hair instead of shaved black or maybe a hint of stubble. His wild swings spoke of lazy arrogance, but also fatigue.

She watched from the shadows, assessing the new development. Flynn ducked a haymaker and hyperextended his opponent's knee with an open-palm strike, then twisted to block a knife thrust toward his back and kidneys. The behemoth swiped down, shattering Flynn's wrist, and the man with the injured knee punched him hard in the solar plexus.

He fell to his hands and knees, and the behemoth stomped. Flynn's abdomen burst, and the combatants stumbled back, eyes wide, circling, looking for threats.

Blood leaked out of the behemoth's helmet, and it reached up with a massive claw to tear it off. Flynn looked down at the fast men, with short blond hair and a smear of red down his too petite, too elfin face. Unprepared, the fast men didn't see the arms that crushed them to the ground, breaking their bodies against the pavement.

Flynn turned to Matt. "Brilliant. I think I'm getting the hang of this, Rowley. As long as the world doesn't run out of killers and thrillers, I think I…" He staggered sideways, braced himself against a building with a hydraulic claw.

"Wow. Doozy of a woozy there a minute, innit?"

He took a deep breath, then another, then stood up tall, nearly ten feet in the massive chassis. "Right, then. Time to die, Rowley."

Sakura rushed him, leaping at the last moment, and brought the butt of the web gun down on his skull. It crumbled under the impact, and the mechanical monster housing the body didn't even twitch. Hopping down, she crouched next to Matt and pulled a knife.

"I have to cut away muscle. It will hurt."

He blinked, licked his lips. "Careful. He… back."

She shushed him, but her head tilted forward a few degrees, as close as she could come to a nod without giving up the game. He gasped as she carved away superfluous meat on his thigh, his eyes wide and glassy under the orange city lights. Sawing and hacking with brutal efficiency, she cleared his bones and moved up to his arms.

The expected shadow appeared in the reflection of Matt's eyes. She let it move up, faster than human but so very much slower than Conor Flynn before he died, and only at the last second scooped up the web gun and fired it over her shoulder. She spun, kicked the man over, and fired twice more, covering the front of his body in the sticky goo.

A face almost Flynn's but also Asian and terrified snarled and snapped and spit venomous curses that hurt her mind, but his struggles against the hardening fibers slowed and then stopped. Kazuko hummed under his curses, soothing the mental barbs away into ephemera, dying out only when he stopped. Kneeling next to him, Sakura slashed a knife along the back of his hand. Blood welled in viscous beads, then stopped. The cut healed, leaving the skin smooth and pink.

Flynn chuckled, then spoke, his cheek mashed against the asphalt. "You can't kill me and no prison can hold me, so what's your endgame, Sakura?"

With sirens in the distance heralding the arrival of armed men with dubious loyalties, she loaded Matt into the other OPD van, tossed Flynn face-down next to him, and drove down to the river, killing the engine several kilometers from the commotion. Matt's legs had healed into twisted, useless knots, so she pulled a knife and kneeled.

Then she pivoted so that the knife hovered above Flynn's back.

It entered at his shoulder, twisting around to free the joint from muscle and other connective tissue. He groaned, and laughed, and sobbed, and laughed again, but fell silent as she swapped the knife for the electronic device and trimmed the webbing from his almost-disconnected arm.

"What are you doing to me, you crazy bitch?"

Knee on his back, she grabbed his arm just above the elbow, twisted, then leaned into the bend until the bone popped out of the joint.

Another string of venomous invectives streamed through his clenched teeth, and even as she worked the limb free new sprouts of muscle wormed their way into the air, entwining and grappling to form ever-larger tissues. A tangled collection of metal tools lay on the floor. She picked up a handful and jammed the grapefruit-sized bundle into the joint, holding it while muscle healed around it. As the wet, messy tissue grappled her fingers she pulled away with a sucking wound.

She turned to Matt. A few moments of work cleared the muscle from around the tips of the bones protruding from his arms and legs, and then she repeated her work with Conor's right arm. The psychotic killer had shut up except for gasps and groans, a miracle in itself, and she could only hope that he had an inkling of what she had planned for him.

More junk went into the second shoulder joint – pebbles and a broken beer bottle from the ground outside, an empty Glock 9mm pistol from the floor, a chunk of shredded fender she tore from a wrecked car in the brush – then she checked on the first arm. Flynn healed unbelievably fast.

The foreign objects had served as a perfect obstacle, and the muscle had grown in knotted, twisted tangles around it, leaving fingers and wrist bones jutting at random, useless angles. She weaved the second arm toward the first, entangling the slippery, skinless hash into a single chaotic braid, stopping here and there to tend to Matt.

A shot with the web gun locked the misshapen, twisted limbs into immobility with the rest of Flynn's body, so she started on his legs, digging deep to access the ball joint in his hip. After a time his stream of black curses faded to incoherent blubbering punctuated by sharp breaths. She worked in the relative silence with methodical diligence, stopping only to collect litter and bits of the abandoned car.

Three hours later Matt had sat up and could flex his new left hand, though his right arm had barely progressed past his elbow. Flynn had become a torso surrounded by misshapen, horrific tangles of muscle and bone, his stolen body's best attempt to cope with damage blocked by obstruction and deliberate manipulation.

The van contained no snacks, no food, and she wouldn't leave Flynn unattended just to feed Matt. He'd be weak and starving even after wholly healed, but it served no purpose to bemoan what couldn't be helped. Flynn held power she didn't understand, and she'd take no chances with it.

"What are we going to do with him?"

She looked up at Matt's question, but Flynn answered first.

"You're going to watch while I skull-fuck that pretty son of yours, you son of a bitch."

"Be silent," Sakura said.

"You, too, you sad cunt."

With a flick of her knife she removed Flynn's lips, along with much of the flesh around his nose and chin. As he tried to jerk back out of the way she took his left ear, and for spite removed his eyes with two efficient jerks of the blade. The orbs dangled from the optic nerves until she grabbed them with one hand and popped them the rest of the way out.

As Flynn shuddered and twitched she leaned in close to his remaining ear. "Be respectful or I'll get more rubbish and you won't ever speak, hear or see again."

"Jesus," Matt said, his wide eyes darting from Flynn's ruined face to her stare and back.

With a nod she wiped the blade clean on Flynn's shirt. "He comes back, so we can't kill him. The lab, where they held me? It had cryo units, banks of them."

"Sure."

"The OPD had several former bonks frozen. Even without augmentation they still lived. If they can be kept indefinitely, then so can Flynn."

Matt smiled. "FADE confiscated that equipment."

"I am aware, and this is what we should do. But secret. We keep this from everyone."

"Freudenberg will have to know."

"Okay, but only him. Not Marcia, and especially not Janet."

His scowl held no weight – he must have known better than to question her resolve, even when he disagreed with it. "Okay."

"I'll call the General."

"Good. And once we take care of this, we find the OPD and kill them all."

CHAPTER SIXTEEN

Monica groped across the nightstand and pulled the buzzing phone to her face, read the number through sleep-blurred eyes. Matt lay too still next to her in the FADE basement apartment, wide awake at the slightest disturbance despite the trauma of the night and his arrival just a half hour prior. He'd crashed into bed and fallen immediately asleep, a level of exhaustion she hadn't seen since his post-Gerstner hospital stay.

Her mother's number flashed on the screen, so with heart in her throat she hit 'Talk' and held it to her ear.

"Momma, what's wrong?"

"You get your husband up here right now to talk some sense into these pagans!"

"Pagans?"

"Rees's flock! They's going crazy up and down the street with signs and whatnot, every day, blocking traffic and causing a nuisance."

"At four in the morning?"

"Poppa just caught one creeping round the chicken coop, had to go out confront him with a shotgun!"

Monica took a deep breath, happy there didn't seem to be any imminent danger. "Is he okay?"

"Well, yeah and no. Broken nose and he peed himself when Poppa knocked him down and pointed both barrels at him, but he'll recover, sure. Deputy Broadbent's coming around to cart him off soon as he takes care of something else."

"I meant – it don't matter." Her accent always slipped

a little deeper into the trailer park whenever she spoke to her parents. "As long as Poppa's okay it *doesn't* matter. You want me to call Jason?"

"Oh, that boy ain't the problem. He tried to talk 'em down, but they ain't listening to him no more, 'cept maybe at that demonic pulpit. They're out of control, and we need something done. Mayor Schenk's called a town meeting for eight this morning about how we're going to take back this town, and would you believe he's got Wilkinson agreeing with him? This is gonna get out of hand and you know it. We'd like your husband here to talk some sense into everyone, maybe put a little government fire under their backsides."

Matt pulled the pillow from under his head and held it over his face, muffling his voice under layers of cloth and down. "I usually talk sense with a shotgun. What do they expect me to do here?"

Monica repeated the question into the phone. Her mothers' rambling escalated into a rant. She held the phone away from her ear. "You getting this, baby?"

He let loose an affirmative-sounding grunt.

"So you're going, yeah?"

After a moment he pulled the pillow from his face, keeping his voice too low to carry over the phone. "These people have a right to picket or protest, and if they break the law the county should handle it. We've got people working around the clock digging up the OPD, and once we find them they're not going to stay somewhere long. I can't go. Tell them to be safe and get on without me."

She patted the taut muscle across his belly, then put the phone back to her ear. "He's not going to make it, Momma."

• • •

Matt got up at six, put on sweat pants and a wife-beater that showed off his inhuman physique, and wandered down to the FADE cafeteria. In line between the only other two people up and about at this hour, he helped himself to a mounded plate of eggs, twelve strips of bacon, four sausage patties, a stack of pancakes and a half-dozen 'Maple Flavored Syrup' packets.

"Holy shit," the younger, dark-haired man said. "I heard you can eat, but seriously?"

Matt grinned with a collegiality he didn't feel – he hadn't expected company and didn't want it, but these people were his coworkers and it would smooth things for his family if they were liked. "Got in a bit of trouble last night. Regeneration makes you really hungry."

The guy chuckled as he wandered to the closest table and set down his tray. "You must have lost a limb."

Matt sat next to him. "Four of them." He stuck out his hand. "Matt Rowley."

They shook. "Emilio Cruz, Director of Advanced Imaging."

"What's that mean?"

The older man set his tray down on Matt's left. "It means he runs the labs that develop camera systems to look for ghosts and magic."

"That's possible?" Matt asked.

"Not so far," they said in unison. The older man shook Matt's hand. "Dean Flowers, Director of Acquisitions. I'm the guy who turns $800 toilets into guns and airplanes and laboratories."

"So you picked up all the OPD equipment." Matt shoveled eggs and bacon into his mouth while Dean responded.

"After your raid on the OPD facility we seized all of the assets found, yes. It's not that hard to strip assets from an organization that essentially doesn't exist on paper."

"Essentially."

"That's right. They have an office and nineteen official employees, all but two of whom have been detained – they're on the lam. The rest, well, President Williams declared them terrorists and had them renditioned to somewhere under Freud's control."

Matt spoke around a mouthful. "Does he know you call him 'Freud'?"

"All the old timers call him Freud." Emilio took a ginger bite of sausage and chewed thoroughly.

"I see," Matt said. "So what makes you think 'advanced imaging' will work?"

Emilio shrugged. "Nothing. I was hired to help the geeks go to town on it, get them what they need and try to keep frivolous spending down. I don't think those Ghost Hunter shows are real, and most of our engineers are skeptics; but they're being paid to try hard with serious ideas, in case some day it pays off."

"Do you have any reason to believe it will?"

Dean answered. "We live in the age of miracles. You yourself can predict the future, going out a split second or so, and rumor has it that Dawkins could do far more. We have fallen angels forming kingdoms all over the world, insurgencies using black magic to infiltrate and control their enemies. Why not wizards and ghosts and cameras that can capture ectoplasmic energy?" He framed the last words with air quotes.

"So FADE's working on what, everything?"

Dean smiled. "After a fashion. What it comes down to these days is that if it doesn't sound like complete and utter bullshit, we're looking into it. And if it does, we're thinking about looking into it. Our R&D teams have created miracles, and we're likely to create more as time goes on."

Matt hid a frown behind a piece of French toast, shoved whole into his mouth. ICAP, except for the top brass, had believed that Jade and Augmentations were based on science, but they were being used by Gerstner, a sacrifice of hundreds of millions of drug users to blast open the prison that held the egregoroi, ancient, angel-like creatures who considered her their last remaining daughter. He couldn't help but worry that FADE had a similar hidden patron, if not the same one.

"Well if you develop something that will calm a pissed-off wife, let me know." Matt looked down the empty plates on his tray, considered another run, and decided against it. He stood, tipped a nonexistent hat, and said his goodbyes to meet with Marcia Stein in the exercise room.

In a bright purple halter top and black yoga pants she cut an impressive figure for a normal, already running on an inclined treadmill by the time he'd arrived. Taut, lean muscle without a hint of fat, she moved with a graceful efficiency that defied the encroachment of age. Matt got on the treadmill next to her and set it to twenty miles an hour, more for nostalgia's sake than for the exercise he didn't need.

"Everything set?" he asked.

"Yes. The general agreed to transfer your security detail, and they've been granted clearance. I've got direct command."

"Good, thanks. What about OPD?"

She threw up her hands, then grabbed the rail to keep from falling back. "We're working on some leads. You didn't leave us any survivors last night, any that didn't get away, anyway. Hard to interrogate the dead."

"Are we getting cooperation from the Justice Department?"

"Sure, if you can call it that. They deny any knowledge of the OPD, and it's possible they really were that in the dark. We've got the NSA, FBI, and forensic accountants trying to trace the equipment buys to build those robot guys – most of it is impossible to trace, but the microchips are state-of-the-art, and somebody had to have made them. There's a trail, and we're going to find it."

"What about the White House? Can they grease the skids, here?"

She shook her head. "Williams is in full campaign mode, and he's losing. The polls have Kellett up almost twenty points – that 'Jesus wants us to exterminate the demonic pagans' thing has a lot of appeal right now. You've got millions of pissed-off people registering to vote for the first time, and it's skewing hard toward 'burn the witch'."

"Great. Well, keep me posted." He killed the machine and hopped off onto the side rails.

"That's it? You didn't even break a sweat!"

"I never do."

• • •

Dean Flowers knocked on the door to Matt's new office. He looked up from the stacks of banker's boxes, ushered Flowers in, and closed the door.

"The general spoke to you?"

"He did." Flowers kept his hands in his suit pockets. "We're installing the unit you've requested in a facility off-site. It draws power from a nearby high-use building without anything going on any books anywhere, and will be secure indefinitely. All records will be expunged."

"Excellent, thank you."

He hesitated, hands in his pockets. "May I ask what it's for?"

"No."

Flowers nodded as if that was the expected answer. "Is that all, then?"

"Yes, thank you."

• • •

Two days later, Matt waited under the shadow of Mount Mitchell, several miles outside the North Carolina state park that bore the same name. Fir and Hemlock trees stood in half-barren stands, ravaged by acid rain and some insect or another, but the area smelled of clean earth and pine needles. Except for a higher tick on the thermometer, it could have been home.

An hour after the last FADE employee had left, the white OPD van rolled into view, Sakura's grim face behind the windshield. Matt hopped on, grabbing the driver's side door handle to steady himself, and let her roll into the shaft of the ruby and sapphire mine, long-closed since it ran dry in the 1980s. They followed the chemical glow sticks left behind for the purpose, winding deep inside the earth past a thousand side passages before arriving at the cryo unit, a room-sized steel cube somehow powered via a thick cable put through the wall.

Matt hopped down and patted the thick black insulation and then the wall it went through. "What do you think's on the other side?"

"Politician hideaway for nuclear war. This far underground, with black money? Only thing that makes sense."

He grunted in agreement, circled the van, and opened the back door. Stepping back, he cringed away from the smell of vomit, shit, and old, rotting blood. "Holy shit, how can you stand to be in there?"

Instead of Sakura answering, Flynn did. "Not much of a choice, you bastard. What say you let us go and be done with this mess?"

Sakura dragged the gurney out, and Matt stifled a gasp. Under her ministrations, Flynn's flesh had grown around the bed and legs, a nightmare of twisted flesh and protruding bone that reached almost to the wheels. There was no chance that such treatment wouldn't have driven anyone utterly insane.

"Not the prettiest girl at the ball, am I, Rowley?

"You never were." He looked at Sakura. "Let's do this."

He opened the massive metal door and held it while Sakura wheeled Flynn inside. Once there they hooked him up to the pump, per instructions, two dozen needles in two dozen veins, all hooked to a small box the size of a filing cabinet. Flynn yammered the whole time, about doors and bridges and the impossibility of mortality, but if Sakura paid him any more heed than Matt did, she made no indication of it. He flicked the switch. White-blue fluid flowed into Flynn's veins, and blood flowed out.

For the first time since he'd known him, Flynn's eyes widened with worry and fear. "What is this, Matt?"

"If we didn't replace your blood, your cells would rupture and you'd never survive the freeze. Can't have you dying on us and coming back again, not for a few centuries or so."

Flynn looked around, eyes darting from featureless steel wall to featureless steel ceiling. "You can't do this. You can't leave me alone with her. Not like that. You can't."

"With her?"

Flynn closed his eyes. "Gerstner. She won't leave me alone."

"What is she, in your head?"

His face twitched, then calmed. "Soul. She's got me caught in a loop where I can't stay and I can't go back, and every life I take belongs to her. I think that's true for you, too. You serve her, same as me."

"Sure." Matt walked over to the wall and dropped the knife switch, triggering the compressor that would drop the room – and Flynn's body temperature – to forty degrees below zero. "Meantime, sleep tight."

Flynn screamed and cursed as they exited, waffling between rage and panicked pleas until Sakura closed the door, cutting off the sound. They jogged to the surface. Two minutes later the detonators went off, burying the room behind a wall of rubble a mile deep.

Matt looked from the stinking van to Sakura and back. "How do you feel about a run?"

"To Virginia?"

"Out of here. Leave the van to rot, catch a ride from the next city. No stink, and all the evidence stays here."

She took off, slowing enough to let him keep up.

"That's him." Janet tapped the fuzzy blob on the projector screen with a bright green fingernail. "Eighty-three percent."

The grainy parking lot security camera made the man's face a grotesque, pixilated jack-o-lantern. Black and white, Matt had a hard time even determining his race.

"You've got to be kidding me." Marcia looked from the screen to Freudenberg to Matt and back in naked disbelief. "That could be anyone."

"As he enters and exits the image changes enough so that even at this resolution we have an eighty-three percent confidence that this is Walter Jenkins, the jeep driver Sakura killed two weeks ago." Janet flipped to the next slide, a shot inside a crowded bar with a bombshell blonde's face circled. "Taken two days later, this is Jasmine Bero, girlfriend of Nick Burgess, who Matt shot inside. This bar is eight blocks from that Walmart."

Another slide depicted Shane Keene in high definition, three-piece suit at odds with his biker's beard, mouth open in mid-word to a similarly-dressed Asian man carrying a black briefcase. "These two gentlemen entered the uptown Berkshire Credit Union four days before the attack and transferred eighty million dollars to and from various accounts, all of which we are now monitoring."

"Who's the Asian?" Freudenberg asked.

"He's Chinese," Sakura said, arms crossed.

"We have no idea." Janet zoomed in on his face. "But he went back the day after the attack, without Keene."

"So they're operating out of Cleveland," Matt said. "Cleveland."

"Looks that way, bud. Vaguely central, easy to smuggle stuff in and out of the country across the lake, lots of open space outside the city for covert air fields. And it's a shithole, so there are a lot of abandoned buildings and the rents are dirt cheap."

"Okay, let's go to Cleveland." Two steps toward the door he turned, looked at everyone still sitting at the conference room table. "What?"

"We have assets in place," Freudenberg said. "But we have to do this right. If we're going to root them out and destroy them we need to uncover everything – their funding, leadership, and bases of operation at the very least. If we don't do this right then we won't get them all, and that's going to take some time."

Matt closed his eyes, took a deep breath, then opened them again. "They tried to kill my family."

"Kidnap," Sakura said. "If they wanted us dead they'd have blown the helicopter."

"And if they took my wife and son, would they have done what they did to you?"

She nodded. "Probably."

"So close enough. They have to die."

The general put his hands up. "I'm not saying they're not going to. We just need to proceed cautiously or we're going to force them the rest of the way underground."

Janet snorted. "You bullshit us and we walk, General."

"Excuse me?"

"Oh, come on. This place has been a throbbing hard-on for two weeks just based on the tech we ganked out of the DIA parking lot. The neural enhancers alone is a multibillion-dollar coup for the military, not to mention the webbing compound and the exo-suits. You want caution because you want their toys."

"Degrading and destroying the OPD's operation is your number one priority, and I'm content to let that stand for the time being. But yes, securing technology that can help us against the supernatural has always been FADE's focus."

Matt kept his face neutral. "So we twiddle our thumbs while you make sure you can secure the assets. I don't think I like that."

Freudenberg leaned back in his chair, eyes rolling to

the ceiling before snapping back to Matt. "We are on the same team here, Rowley, but let me be clear about this." He jabbed his finger at the empty space between them. "Even if we weren't on the same team, you are under my command and my protection. We're doing what we can to protect your family, but we're going to use you as we see fit to defend and protect the United States of America. Sakura we can deport, but if you start bucking orders you'll go to jail."

He swiveled in his chair and jabbed the finger at Janet. "That goes for you, too, Miss LaLonde. This is not a fucking democracy."

She held up her hands, eyes wide and mouth open in mock terror, then formed her fingers into pistols and shot him with both. "We're civilian employees on US soil, daddy-o. On a war footing on foreign soil you could maybe court martial us for disobeying chain of command, but right here, right now, the only person you can order around is Matt, and that's only if you officially recall him to military service first. So if you don't like the way I do things you can fire me, but you sure as shit can't put me in jail."

Freudenberg ran a hand through his hair. "I'm sorry, let's start over. I'm not trying to throw anybody in jail, I'm just trying to get us all on the same page. You want to destroy the OPD, and so do we, but there is a larger mission here as well, and you all need to understand that the secondary objective, your objective, is subordinate to the first."

"If you'd have said that in the first place—"

He slammed his hand on the table, cutting Janet off. "I'm not going to tolerate flippancy, Miss LaLonde. You have an impressive set of skills, but you're not irreplaceable, so if you're going to continue working here you will address me with an enhanced sense of respect. Is that clear?"

"It is. Sir." She sat down, smoothed her skirt over her thighs, and blinked at him.

He waited, she said nothing.

"What?"

"You're in charge, sir, and I'm done with my briefing, so I'm just waiting to be told what to do."

"You're dismissed. Rowley, stay here."

Marcia and Janet packed up their folders and walked out without a word. Matt stayed in his chair, and so did Sakura.

"You're dismissed, Isuji."

She shook her head. "If you're speaking to him I'm staying."

"I second that," Matt said. "We're partners, and we don't keep anything from each other anyway."

As the door clicked closed he leaned forward, almost conspiratorial. "How set are you on working with Miss LaLonde?"

"I don't trust her," Sakura blurted.

"I do." Matt tried not to glare at either one of them. "Without reservation. We've been through a lot together, and she's sacrificed a great deal to do the right thing."

As far as he knew, nobody outside Janet, Matt, and Sakura knew that the largest Jade dealer in the world, Dawkins, had been an ex-ICAP agent and Janet's brother.

"Marcia doesn't. Says she's cagey, standoffish."

"Oh," Matt said. "She's got the people skills of a pissed-off grizzly bear, but she's a wizard with tech and one of the best engagement coordinators I've ever worked under. We won't be as effective without her."

Freudenberg hesitated. "It's unfortunate you feel that way, Sergeant, because we're letting her go."

"You're kidding."

"No. She's not a good fit for our organization, and—"

"She's *my* employee, goddammit. You—"

"Have the prerogative to hire and fire anyone under FADE's purview, up to and including people who've been here for forty years. I've considered the real possibility of pissing you off and discussed the ramifications with President Williams."

Raw fury boiled under his skin. "You already decided."

Freudenberg nodded. "This meeting only reinforced that I'd made the right decision. She'll land on her feet."

He stood; Sakura didn't. "This is a mistake."

"Your opinion has been noted, Sergeant."

Matt walked out, managed not to slam the door, and stormed down the hall to Janet's office. Always impeccable, only her computer sat on it, and on top of that her ID, which also served as a keycard to get into the building.

"You missed it," Marcia said behind him. "They escorted her out the moment she left the building."

He whirled, pulled her into Janet's office, and slammed the door. "You knew this was coming."

She shook her head. "I didn't, but I recommended it and I'm glad it happened."

"If you had a problem with her you could have come to me."

"I did, multiple times, but you wouldn't hear it. Isuji suggested that we bring our concerns to the general, so we did."

The world grew dark with his anger. "Sakura, too."

"Yes, though he'd heard from others, too. Everyone but you, really. That woman is toxic, and we can't trust her. Between you, me, and the wall, she's got something very, very, bad between her ears, something so much worse than just being a prickly bitch, and we don't want to be anywhere near it when it breaks free."

"You're wrong."

"It's possible, Matt, but I've never been more sure about a gut feeling in my entire life. I'm sorry it happened this way, but I'm not sorry it happened."

"When we need her and she's not there, we're going to regret it."

Marcia patted his shoulder. "Sorry, Matt."

CHAPTER SEVENTEEN

Janet LaLonde showed her ID to the secret serviceman standing guard outside the Humans for Humanity headquarters in Martonville, Texas. The annex could have rivaled any cathedral, were it not in the shadow of the several-acre megachurch over which Ronald Kellett presided, six-stories tall and almost large enough to hold an NFL stadium. On any given Wednesday afternoon only a hundred cars dotted the parking lot, a tiny fraction of what the prosperity preacher drew for Sunday service. But this Wednesday cars stretched off into the distance in every direction.

She pulled her white BMW sedan up next to the handicapped spot – rows upon rows of blue squares with white wheelchairs in them – and into the spot marked 'Reserved for J LaLonde'. The large, black doorman she'd first met under far different circumstances, Phil, rushed to open her door and take her bag. He glanced down her shirt and his breath caught, an involuntary response to the soul trap that hung there. A swirling gemstone of green and blue, it remained cold against her skin and left a slimy, unclean feeling wherever it touched, the spiritual residue of Ronald Kellett's soul as it shrieked and blubbered and begged to be set free. He met her eyes and, after she flashed her credentials to the Secret Service guard, let her in.

Stacy, the busty, bottle-blonde receptionist greeted her as she walked by, and if the security cameras from the past six weeks told the truth, probably flipped her off behind her back. In a month and a half she'd become Ronald Kellett's most trusted advisor, and by playing down the white trash act and playing up the cutthroat professional she'd won the respect of his campaign staff and the hatred of this one jealous woman. Her first order of business had been to end Stacy's constant flirtations – Kellett hadn't been able to carry on an affair for at least a decade, but he looked like he could, and they didn't need an October Surprise rumor damaging the evangelical vote.

To that end Janet never met him outside the office, plane, or bus, and always with other functionaries around. A slave to her will as long as she wore the necklace, she let him have enough autonomy to do anything but defy her, in letter or spirit. A gentle word or hushed whisper served, and when not in his presence she had bloodier, messier ways of making her will known.

She followed the royal purple carpet past statues in alcoves and paintings on the walls, every one of them as religious as they were mediocre to a discerning eye, and let herself in through a modest door into an office anything but modest and bubbling with joyous excitement. The octogenarian candidate sat at his giant mahogany desk surrounded by aides and advisors, already in makeup for the journalists scuttling around the room. An enormous screen blocked the garish painting of himself he'd had commissioned decades before when his scam of a church had suckered its first millions from the pockets and wallets of pious morons who could little afford it.

The amulet squirmed between her breasts and desperation oozed from it; for release, for repentance, to please her. It radiated a conviction that Janet LaLonde had been sent from the almighty to punish Kellett, his own personal purgatory so that he might earn redemption before joining the Lord in his almighty righteousness above. Weak and foolish, his tattered spirit couldn't handle the simple truth: God didn't care one way or another, and his predicament arose when his usefulness brushed against her pragmatism.

She approached through the excited gaggle of functionaries and campaign volunteers, avoiding some, brushing against others she might someday find useful. The screen above the desk blinked, drawing her eyes from the soon-to-be President Elect.

Exit polls showed a pending electoral landslide, even in the war-torn Pacific Northwest. Running on a platform of God, Borders, and Culture, Kellett's campaign seized the religious, xenophobic mania sparked by magic-fueled indigenous revolts domestic and foreign, and forged it into an iron-hard hammer to bludgeon the milquetoast, business-as-usual candidates from both of the major parties. He had promised no compromise, but only the righteous wrath of God, and had all but declared war on fallen angels, idolaters, witches and warlocks, pagans, heathens, and Satanists.

In a matter of hours Humans for Humanity – Janet – would win the White House, control of the world's largest military, and the country's deepest secrets, of which she cared about only one.

• • •

"Did you see this?" Monica muted the volume on the remote as Matt's cell rang.

Military, but he didn't recognize the number.

He glanced over, smiled at his son asleep under the plastic Christmas tree FADE had provided, still up almost a week after New Year. Then he raised his eyes to the TV.

The wide screen blared high-definition scenes from Paris, the streets packed with people chanting psalms and singing music with familiar tunes and unfamiliar words. White-eyed men in red robes stood on the steps of Notre Dame cathedral, a monstrous gothic construction in white marble, twin towers reaching skyward over three enormous archways. On the grainy, zoomed-in images, legions of people shuffled forward, kneeling, eyes cast heavenward, to have their throats slit by priests before acolytes dragged them to the side and dumped them in the river. Clogged with bodies, the Seine ran pink under the midday sun.

On the third ring he hit 'Talk'.

"Rowley, go ahead."

"Sergeant Rowley," a clipped female voice said, "you are to report to Guantanamo immediately using STB transport and, once there, await further instructions."

"On whose orders, please?"

"Lieutenant-Colonel Smith's, Sergeant."

"I have a pending mission, it will have to wait."

"You're under orders—"

"I'm already under orders, from the Commander in Chief. Whatever it is, Gitmo is going to wait."

Smith's voice replaced hers. "Sergeant Rowley, Williams is a lame duck with fourteen days left in office. I'd consider my loyalties very carefully, given what's coming."

"Given what's coming?"

"Don't be naive, Sergeant. The country is fracturing, and the only thing that's going to hold it together is people like you and me."

Matt snorted. "A little bird told me that you defied orders to return to Patuxent and executed several of your own officers to keep the men in line. Doesn't sound like keeping the homeland safe to me."

"Those men were traitors."

"I'm sure their wives and families will understand, sir."

He hung up and dialed General Freudenberg.

"Yes?" Even over the phone, FADE's director sounded exhausted.

"I just got the weirdest call, thought maybe you could help me parse it." Matt relayed the conversation word for word.

The line remained silent. On the TV, refugees streamed down from the Ural mountains, not a single man among them.

Freudenberg sighed. "Yeah, belay that order, obviously. Smith has gone off the reservation, and a lot of assets are moving in that direction."

"Doesn't he have command of nuclear subs?"

"He did, but only the surface fleet went with him. The strike subs RTB'ed as ordered."

"Thank God. So what's the move?"

"I have no idea. Our focus is still supernatural threats, and as far as we can tell, even with two-thirds of the Atlantic fleet under his command, Smith's just a traitor."

"Huh."

The TV switched to riots somewhere in Africa.

"Yeah. So I've got a present for you."

Matt raised an eyebrow Freudenberg had no way of seeing. "Oh?"

His phone blipped. He pulled it away from his face, opened the message. A satellite photo of a city by a lake popped up, then zoomed in to a building in the city center. A hot knife of anticipation scraped down his spine. "OPD?"

"Yeah, dead to rights. We have confirmation of heavy equipment in and out, and infrasonic telemetry shows one massive tunnel leading to a warehouse abutting Burke, the airport by the lake."

"When do we go in?"

"Tomorrow afternoon. We've got intel their bigwigs are meeting to discuss the change of power in Washington. I've called in Miss Sakura and we're briefing tomorrow 8 AM. This is going to be a big operation, and we don't want to hurt any civilians if we can avoid it."

"How big?"

"*Terror from the North* big. Yesterday we pulled the 1st Battalion, 24th Marines from Detroit, dropped them into Erie for the 174th Arctic Warriors Joint Training Exercise.

Tomorrow they learn they've got an actual mission on their hands."

"The whole battalion?"

"With support. Current strength is nine hundred and sixty-four marines and sailors, eighteen beach-assault hovercrafts, nine helicopters, fourteen combat drones including yours, and eight 1126-SPARX amphibious battle suits to take on their big guys." Slower and four times as massive as the OPD's behemoths, SPARX towered over tanks and carried twice as much firepower, but could maneuver in much tighter spaces.

"Holy shit. What's our role?"

"The Marines are going to hit them hard, pen them in and terminate with prejudice. We figure that will force them into the tunnel they'll hope we don't know about, and you'll meet them there."

"Roger that. Two questions."

"Go ahead."

"First, how is this legal, and second, with that many people involved how can we insure secrecy?"

Silence. Then, "Yeah, as to the second, not even their commanders are going to know the plan until we give it to them at zero-minus-three hours. They'll be keyed up and ready for another evening of training, but they're marines, so they'll get it. As to the first, why don't you let Williams worry about that?"

An image flashed in his mind, his wife and son holding on for dear life as the helicopter fell from the sky.

"Yeah, good enough for me."

• • •

Monica followed Matt out of their tiny apartment in the FADE basements, down the hall to the T intersection. Right led to the cafeteria, gym, and pool, so she swatted his butt as he cut left, then let him blow her a kiss before turning down the other hall. Her heart always ached to see him go, and she said a little prayer of gratitude that most of the time she had no idea what kind of danger his day might bring.

The fluorescent lights buzzed as she pushed Adam up over the small lip that led into the gym. She hadn't seen the sun in over a week, and in the back of her mind a maelstrom of shrieking souls swirled over an endless plain of broken needles. Parking Adam in front of the TV, she warmed up where she could keep an eye on him, then wheeled both of them into the dojo annex.

"Oh, shit, there she is." Pete Marshall's grin lit up his dark brown face. Tall, handsome, and well-built, the martial arts instructor waited for her in red shorts and a white t-shirt, both too small for sufficient modesty. The shirt rippled over his massive biceps, almost as large as Matt's, stretching out the 'One Mind, Any Weapon' logo of a fist under a crossed knife and rifle. The MCMAP instructor bobbed on the balls of his feet and worked his hands together, a contrast in almost every way to her Sifu, Chris Malec, one of the few people besides her parents she missed since their decision not to return to White Spruce until things calmed down.

Adam tumbled from the stroller as she unhooked him, somersaulting across the padded floor with a cackle.

She shut the door behind them, turned, and cracked her neck. "Here I am. What's on deck today?"

"Savate."

She frowned. "I don't know what that is."

"French kickboxing. We use elements of it in MCMAP training, because it emphasizes foot kicks instead of ankle or shin, and works well in shit kickers. It's a different animal than your northern-style kung fu. I think you'll like it."

"All right, let's kick each other to death."

He nodded toward a pair of small combat boots by the door, polished to a shine. "Should be your size."

• • •

Drenched with sweat and covered in bruises, Monica shuffled down the hall back toward their apartment, combat boots still on her feet. More leaning on the stroller than pushing it, she reveled in the burning muscles and extreme fatigue from the intense workout.

As they reached the apartment door Adam shot up, whirling, his eyes wide.

"No, Mama." He put his hand on the door and shook his head. "Don't."

Suddenly cold, she bent to one knee next to him, bored her eyes into his. "What do you know, little man?"

He kept his voice low, like hers. "Bad man. Don't go in."

With a sneer she pushed him back, turned, and put her hand on the doorknob.

"Mama, no."

"You stay right here, baby. Momma's going to take care of this."

She turned the knob, slowly, and opened the door. Well-oiled, it didn't creak.

Just inside, the bathroom door stood open. She'd closed it when she left, as she always did, to keep Adam from getting into any toilet or bathtub-related trouble. A soft step brought the 'bad man' in focus – huge, with broad shoulders, he moved with a graceful efficiency she hadn't seen since the shootout at the grocery store. Aaron Walters, her presidential bodyguard, stripped the hair from her brush and put it in a bag, then stuffed it into his pocket.

Red fury washed over her vision. She strangled it, buried it under discipline and focus.

Then she cleared her throat.

His hands snapped to the sink, turning it on. "Hey, Mrs Rowley?" he called, the deep rumble of his voice carrying over rushing water. "I'll just be a second."

With a forced smile she opened the apartment door and pulled Adam inside while Aaron toweled off his hands and stepped out of the restroom. She hugged him, forcing down the gag reflex, and pulled back keeping his damp hands in hers.

"Well, look at you! You look fantastic!"

He grinned. "Back on full duty. They said you requested me, so thank you for that."

"You saved my life."

"Just doing my job."

She nodded, heart pounding in her chest. "That's why I asked you here, wanted you protecting my family." His smile died as she continued. "Is that what the hair's about? Just doing your job?"

He flushed, cast his eyes to the floor. "Shit. It would have been better had you not seen that."

"Who's it for? What's it for?"

Massive shoulders rolled up, then down; a shrug. "My orders are to protect you and your family even at the cost of my own life… and to collect samples. I'm sorry, but you and your son are too valuable not to study."

The world blurred through tears, and despite herself her voice cracked. "You could have asked, you son of a bitch."

"We did, ma'am. Your husband said, 'no'."

A snarl tore from her throat. "You could have asked *me*. That's *my* hair you've got in your pocket. *I'm* the one who came back from the dead. *I'm* the one who sees that fucking place every goddamned time I close my eyes."

"Place?"

She heard the shift in his tone, from careful defensiveness to curiosity and sympathy, and whether fake or not she resented it. "Yeah. An expansive plane stretching as far as the eye can see, full of none of your fucking business get out of my apartment."

Wiping the tears away she advanced, small steps on the balls of her feet, not quite hostile.

"Mama, no!"

She ignored her son and inched closer, planning her

moves in the confines of the short hallway. "Now. I'm not asking."

Aaron stood tall, squaring his shoulders to fill the space. He dwarfed her, with biceps as big as her thighs, his torso a solid wall of muscle under the black suit. As their eyes met he stepped back – she saw no fear in them, only hesitation, but she couldn't parse the nature of it.

Another step back, and he paused with his hand on the doorknob. "Ma'am, if I may offer a word of advice. These people are loyal first to their country, and then to mankind as a whole. Folks like you and me and even your husband rate far lower, except insofar as they think they can use you."

She waited, he said nothing and didn't move. "So what's the advice?"

"Know your place and your priorities." He opened the door. "You have a good day, ma'am."

As the latch clicked shut she rushed to the bedroom and yanked her suitcase from the closet. Three changes of clothes for her and six for Adam, the emergency cash they hid in the drop-down ceiling, topped by her .357 and his 1911 and several boxes of ammo for each. Adam watched her from the doorway, ancient eyes tracking her movement with scrutiny nothing like childhood curiosity.

"Get in your stroller, baby boy. We're leaving."

"No," Adam said, his high voice weary well beyond its years. "They won't let us."

She slammed the suitcase as closed as it would go, then sat on it to force the buckles close enough to latch. "You can't know that."

"If you run they'll hurt you."

She dropped to her knees and wrapped him in a hug. "Don't you understand, little man? It's only you I care about. Only you."

His tiny lips brushed her ear as he whispered, "What they'll do to me is so much worse."

Strength left her, and she sagged against the wall. "Oh, baby boy. How can you know so much?"

"Can we have pannakes for dinner?"

"Sure, little man. We can have pancakes."

"Chockit chips?"

"With chocolate chips."

She wiped the wet from his cheeks, stood, and turned to the suitcase. With a sigh she put it in the closet, still packed.

CHAPTER EIGHTEEN

The Terror from the North descended on Cleveland with a whisper. Hovercrafts and boats encroached on the shoreline at a few knots, just enough speed to avoid succumbing to the incessant, eastward nag of the waves. Given the option, Matt chose to ride a hovercraft with forty marines trained in search and destroy – they would wait five minutes and then follow the augs into the tunnel connecting the beach to the Office of Planning and Development's secret headquarters five blocks away.

If they had anything to mop up, he and Sakura were dead, so FADE had kitted them out from the Special Threat Bureau's armory – ceramic composite 'bonk killer' ammo and four spare AA-12s with dozens of drum magazines with both fragmentation grenades and tungsten-tipped armor-piercing sabot rounds. Neither of the latter wouldn't benefit from guidance from the Dragonfly network and IFF software, but in a pinch could still put big holes in things they needed dead.

Their orders were simple: nothing leaves the tunnel.

Dragonflies lifted off from the foremost boats, rising above the frosty waves, and ahead of them the city washed in a sea of colors in Matt's heads-up display. Civilians blipped orange and then faded to pale green – suspected but unconfirmed non-hostiles. The marines shone bright green, and as the swarm of semi-intelligent drones approached the suspected OPD headquarters guards popped up in red double-triangles – armed hostiles within the attack perimeter.

Dozens, then hundreds, popped red in the block surrounding the complex, with clustered bunches on rooftops in the buildings surrounding.

"Are you getting this?" Matt asked no one in particular.

"Rah, Sergeant," someone said in the COM. "Those are some fancy toys you have there."

Matt grunted. "Fog of war is so 2015. Welcome to the new age."

"Roger that," she replied. "They'll be dead before they realize they're under attack. Proceed as planned."

They approached the beach at twenty knots. Ahead of them, the SPARX unfolded from the water, humanoid monstrosities fifteen feet tall. Water sloughed from their hulking frames, sheeting off of hydrophobic plates thicker than tank armor as they accelerated to a run. They hit the beach at forty miles per hour, feet churning up massive explosions of rock and sand as they covered the distance to the streets.

Lines of fire streaked from the sky, and orange-red flames blossomed from the rooftops as red triangles went dark on the HUD. The hovercraft leapt from the water in a blast of sand, then lurched to a halt in front of the 'escape tunnel'. A trio of limousines sat parked next to what looked for all the world like a parking garage. Next to them their tuxedoes chauffeurs lay face down, hands zip-tied behind their backs, a pair of marines with assault carbines standing over each.

Matt leapt as the hovercraft slowed, feet churning to keep his forward momentum, then slowing to avoid impact with the bay doors. A glimmer of dragonflies hovered around the unopened doors. He put a hand on the cool metal and spoke into the COM. "Why aren't these open?"

The same female voice replied. "The plan requires that the targets flee into the tunnel. We didn't want to tip them off that we knew it's here, and can't breach without triggering the alarm."

"Can't you disable it?"

"This isn't the movies, Sergeant."

He turned to the marines crowding the beach behind him. "I need sappers, now."

The voice in his ear interrupted. "They've already been rigged and are awaiting your orders. Analysis of the situation suggests you wait eighteen more seconds before alerting the targets by blowing the doors."

"Detonate on zero."

"Roger that, Sergeant. Sixteen... Fifteen..."

He backpedaled, and waved back the marines coming to the fore. With a nod to Sakura he got in the driver's seat of one of the limos, a lumbering vehicle with half-inch bullet-proof glass and, judging by the weight, armor in the doors. She appeared beside him, hitting the button to roll down her window and propping her REC7 on the side-view mirror. The engine roared when he turned the key, and when the voice in his ear said "four" he floored it. At zero the HUD flashed white, and shrapnel pinged off the windshield, leaving spiderweb cracks in the first layer of filament-coated glass.

They blasted through the falling tangle of twisted metal at twenty miles per hour, Sakura's weapon raised as she scanned for hostiles. Dragonflies zipped ahead of them, skimming along the eight-foot ceilings along the concrete passageway, sensors lighting the way through the pitch-black. The car rocked as shockwaves shuddered through the ground, hellfires or something bigger detonating on the surface forty feet above.

A mile ahead figures scrambled out of a doorway toward two SUVs and another limousine, their outlines popping bright red on the HUD as the dragonflies closed within sensor range. Four hostiles moved too fast for humans, and another two far too slow to be anything but very old men or women.

Matt floored it.

They closed before the hostiles had finished getting in their cars. A hundred meters out Matt whipped the wheel to the side, shrieking to a skidding halt across the narrow passage.

Sakura opened fire. Even muffled by his helmet the REC7's chatter deafened him, sensation returning after each burst as his regenerates healed the damage and muffled the agitated nerves. Three tight bursts took the closest targets. An old woman using a walker and two bodyguards fell. The rest scrambled, several diving into an SUV and slamming the doors, others taking cover behind their vehicles.

Matt leapt out of the limo, rolled to his feet, and opened fire with his AA-12. Fin-guided munitions exploded behind the limo, shredding limbs and pulping organs without the slightest regard to conventional notions of defilade. Tires shrieked as the occupied SUV rocketed toward them.

"Got it." Sakura became a streaking blur headed straight at the approaching vehicle. She veered right, skimming past the tires a few feet from the ground, then appeared stock-still behind it, remote detonator in her left hand, knife in her right. As her thumb twitched the tunnel shuddered, and the vehicle hopped, skidded, flipped.

Rolling, a door popped open and two shapes flew out. Whispers urged Matt to tear and rend them, gorge on their bloody organs and choke to death on the meat. He fired instead, grenades flitting in slow motion toward the impossibly fast targets that dodged and darted forward. Sakura appeared behind one, REC7 raised, and shot him in the back of the head from a meter away. As he stumbled and fell, eyes wide in shock and pain, the other hit Matt.

The world rocked as his helmet cracked into their limo like a rifle shot, and he rolled left to avoid a fist that dented the fender. The AA-12 tore from his hands and a fist pounded into his chest. Ribs cracked and the wind left his lungs even through the body armor.

With a brutal slash his monofilament knife raked across his assailant's wrist. Cloth parted, and skin, but the knife lodged in bone far stronger than anything he'd encountered in a human opponent. His adversary twisted and the knife tore free, flying into the darkness to pop blue on the HUD as a Dragonfly found and tracked it.

Grabbing the cut wrist, Matt slammed the heel of his palm into it sideways.

The shocking jolt shot up to his elbow, rupturing ligaments in a wrenching heat. He pulled back, and winced as his helmet tore from his head.

In the infrared his opponent shone blue and black, colder than room temperature. In the ultraviolet he blazed hotter than a furnace. Gossamer wisps of tattered cloth hung from bones that stretched out twenty feet, enormous skeletal wings that did and didn't exist. Claws raked down Matt's face, tearing his cheeks to strips of tattered flesh.

As the hot, meaty taste of blood filled his mouth he jerked the WildStang from its holster and pulled the trigger. Chunks flew from the egregoroi's abdomen and it stumbled back, laughing. He fired again as it dove behind the limo, form collapsing to human-sized.

Face a mass of sticky itches, he scooped up the AA-12 and swapped drum magazines for armor-piercing tungsten sabots, then circled the vehicle.

• • •

Isuji Sakura turned from the dead man and approached the occupied SUV at a run, tossing a grenade as she did so. It skittered underneath and detonated, lifting the front end inches from the ground. Tires squealed as she slid, dropping below the bumper and punching upward with a knife, savaging metal, plastic, and rubber with equal abandon. Frigid liquid that stank of oil and antifreeze gushed over her as the car pulled away.

She caught the rear bumper left-handed and used it to flip to her feet, landing as the SUV stuttered and died. The front doors popped open as the grenades left her fingertips. They passed through the widening gap as the guards inside started to roll out, weapons coming up, fingers on the triggers. They died in a mess of fire and bloody shrapnel before their young faces had registered any danger.

A figure exploded out the back window, short black hair and a Navy dress blues all she had time to register. She blocked two punches before dropping and driving her fingers into her opponent's thigh. He pulled back before she could puncture muscle and shatter bone, and she flipped forward, striking hard, forcing him to defend his groin from the unrelenting onslaught.

His knee caught her shoulder and knocked her sideways. She sprinted into the stumble and his strike at her neck caught only air. Using her momentum she ran up the wall, and flipped down, steel-toed boot aimed at where his vertebrae met his skull. He spun, knocked her leg sideways, and grunted as she bounced off his shoulder, both of them landing in a crouch.

A grim satisfaction stole over her, wisps of memory from the dojos of her youth. Since augmentation she'd had few opponents fast enough to be anything more than fighting dolls, and most of those had died before they'd realized how much her speed outmatched theirs. Her opponent scrambled back as her punches became kicks became a standing flurry of strikes, but none of them landed.

He backed into the limo and rolled left, arms raised to block anticipated attacks.

She ripped the 9mm from her holster and quadruple-tapped him in the head.

As the bullets ricocheted and skimmed off his skull he turned, smirked. "Surprise."

His jaw unhinged, impossibly wide, huge canines black with rot growing from the extended bone. Hell poured from it.

White-hot streamers of liquid fire followed her across

the artificial cavern, reducing concrete and steel to molten slag in her wake. She zig-zagged around him, swapping the magazine for AP rounds, flipped feet-over-head over a stream of shimmering, white-hot air, and pressed her pistol against the left side of his neck. High-velocity tungsten entered his carotid artery and exited near his spine.

The backwash melted her armor to her skin, and her ammo detonated under the heat.

The gun exploded, carrying with it fingers and chunks of her palm. She jammed her truncated pinky into his – its – neck and tore forward. A shower of blood sprayed out as muscle ruptured outward. A knife-hand strike to its spine broke her middle and ring fingers on her right hand, so she head-butted her reeling opponent before he could recover.

Stumbling, stars filled her vision. Weaponless and missing much of her right hand, she scrambled back. It turned, laughing, a smoky mass of black nothing jerking and jetting from its shoulder blades to form black wings darker than the void between galaxies. Ramiel hunched under the low ceiling, his eyes glowing embers against the darkness, every bit as alive as the day Matt had killed him.

• • •

Matt turned at the blast of heat from down the tunnel and opened fire at the thing hulking over Sakura. Plumes of flame erupted where the bullets punched through flesh, and the efrit stumbled sideways under the barrage. The magazine clicked dry so he popped it out and reached for another.

The black thing swarmed over the limo. Matt turned, ducked a swiping claw, and brought the butt of the shotgun up into its jaw. Metal kinked with the impact, but the bone shattered. It roared in his face, so he jammed a thermite grenade in its mouth left-handed, shattering teeth and breaking his own knuckles with the impact. It bit down, savaging his wrist as claws raked at his armor. Thumb hooked on the pin ring, he pulled it free and dropped as far as he could from its head.

His helmet darkened as the bright flash illuminated the tunnel. A faint sensation that might have been pain replaced the feeling below his left elbow. He fell, catching himself with his right hand, trying not to look at the charred, red-black stump of his left.

The egregoroi wobbled then dropped to its knees, no blood gushing from the flash-cauterized remains of its neck. It stayed there, an unmoving supplicant with hands in its lap, as Matt loaded the AA-12 one-handed, picked it up, and braced the kinked stock against his shoulder.

Ramiel struggled to his hands and knees. Sakura fumbled with her pistol, forcing swollen, bent fingers around the grip and through the trigger guard. Matt braced and pulled the trigger, walking his aim down to blast chunks of white-hot demon against the floor and wall, arcing side to side to pulp the demon's hips and skull. As he reloaded Sakura advanced, firing, each shot into the inferno that passed as the egregoroi's brain.

It stopped moving, and their eyes met. "You killed this one before."

He nodded. "Or one that looked just like it."

She nodded, then took up position to cover the lone door on this side of the tunnel.

"It was Ramiel." The weak voice stuttered from inside the upright SUV. Matt circled, shotgun raised, to point in the back seat where a familiar face stared back at him between two shredded bodies. Gaunt, with deep bags under his eyes made worse by the blood running down his face and neck, Nigel Rush had had his teeth replaced since last Matt saw him yammering on TV in his northern Georgia drawl, the pearly whites an improvement over the brown rot. Maggot-pale, his lips formed a thin, pink-white line across them.

"Mister Rush," Matt said. "You seem… out of place, here."

Rush coughed and struggled to undo his seatbelt, sagging back when his hand wouldn't cooperate. "It seems my expertise led to a certain notoriety. The Office of Planning and Development took note and recruited me in their efforts to close the gate. They were willing to overlook my religious proclivities, and I, in turn, found out that they were right and I was wrong. It appears in their enthusiasm to recruit they gathered in some powerful moles."

"Gate."

"Watchers escape with every passing month. Killing them sends them back for a time, but as you just witnessed it's all too short and growing shorter. With every bridge, Nyx's Gate – y'all call her Gerstner, like this contemporary name holds any significance to a being of such age – widens. There are perhaps sixty Watchers freed thus far, yet thousands ascend from the depths to cross into our world. When Semjaza slouches towards Bethlehem to be reborn, no force on Earth will stop him, and he will reward his daughter-mother with dominion over all."

"These bridges, how does she open them?"

Rush jerked back, surprise scrunching across his emaciated features. "With death." The unspoken 'duh' rang loud in Matt's mind. "Every death she causes, every person killed by an Aug or a Jade overdose, for you were both her creations, births a strand. Enough strands create a braid, and when it's strong enough it bores a hole from there to here."

A coughing spasm wracked his body, and his eyes fluttered. Matt pulled the first aid kit from his satchel, removed a syringe of adrenaline, and stabbed it into Rush's thigh. His eyes popped wide and he gasped, gagging on his own tongue, before settling back into the seat.

"How do we close them? How do we break the strands?"

Rush rolled his head left, to his dead companion. "This is Avery Jackson. Or was, before you killed him. His office is upstairs, 13-B. In it you will find detailed accounts of the sacrifices necessary to stop Gerstner, which have been done and which remain. A terrible task they gave themselves, to save the world by sacrificing the almost-innocent, but they would have succeeded had you not intervened, and we would all be safe."

"Sacrifices?"

His eyes fluttered closed. "You. Isuji Sakura. Your cursed wife and blessed son. Every aug and Jade user, their children. When no trace of Nyx's influence remains, her spell will fail, and her Gate will close. The egregoroi will fall back to the Pit, and drag the last of the Nephilim with them. You have to..."

His eyes closed.

"You have to kill them all."

His chest fell a final time. The whispers gasped out an elated babble, and Matt dropped to his knees behind the limo.

The world rocked and his eardrums burst. The door upstairs blew from the wall in a gout of flame, spinning end over end to crash into the concrete on the far side. Stumbling around falling debris, he scrambled toward Sakura's broken body, dashed across the floor and battered against the SUV by the force of the explosion.

He scooped her up and ran for the exit as the concrete cracked and crumbled around him. A dozen laser sights painted him as he approached the column of marines, now falling back in an ordered retreat from the collapsing structure. They exited onto the beach, awash in warm orange light, where many marines already stood and stared, gaping, a continuous blast of grit-filled air whipping their clothes toward the city.

Matt turned, and his heart fell. A mushroom cloud rose over the city, and around it the Cleveland skyline lay in ruins, the bones of buildings crumbling to the ground in a torrent of broken concrete and twisted steel. Shattered glass littered the streets, and bloody civilians stumbled and wailed over the bodies of loved ones.

"Was that nuclear?" Matt asked no one in particular.

"Negative," the calm female from before said, choking up as she continued. "Radiation is zero. Conventional weapon, several kiloton range."

"Casualties?"

"Fuck Jesus, they're all dead. Most of the 24th 1st, who knows how many civilians. A quarter million? Twice that?"

A roar rumbled through the city, greater than the rushing wind pulled toward the rising fireball. Streaks of flaming light shot from the mushroom cloud, rising into the night sky in great glowing arcs, first three, then ten, then a dozen. They banked and turned on enormous wings, flying ever higher and farther away, and their elation drowned out reason and hope.

At his feet, Sakura sat up, flexing the fingers on her intact hand, brushing sand from the wounds in the other.

"What did we do?"

Matt grunted. "We removed a threat to my family."

Her eyes rolled up to his, blazing with reflected light from the fireball. "At what expense?"

"Too big of one."

• • •

They debriefed via radio on the ride back to DC, a conversation that degenerated into an argument far too fast.

"We can't kill millions of people to save the world," Matt repeated.

"I'm not saying we can and I'm not saying it's the right thing to do," Marcia said. "I'm just saying that if any of that is even partly true, we need to know how much and what. We've got forensics techs going through the rubble, hoping for a needle in the haystack, but if they don't find anything we need to find out where we can learn more."

"And I don't want to say this," General Freudenberg added, "but we can't rule it out. If the only way to stop Gerstner is to remove her influence, then we need to keep that option on the table."

"YOU'RE TALKING ABOUT MY GODDAMNED FAMILY!"

"Which is why you can't be objective, Rowley, and I understand that. I'm just asking you to understand it, too. Put yourself in my shoes."

"He's right," Sakura said. "They must consider it."

"You're never going to imagine a world where your family has to die so that everyone else can live," Freudenberg added, "but goddammit if that's the case then somebody has to imagine it."

Matt banged his head against the metal wall behind him. "Rush was lying."

"He wasn't." Sakura's shattered hand had mostly healed, the skin fresh and pink in contrast to the creamier brown of her bicep. "He believed every word as it came from his mouth."

"All the more reason I need to get my family out of DC, then. General, we're leaving tonight."

"No, you're not."

Matt closed his eyes, let the thrum of the rotors buffet his murderous impulse. The whispers chittered and mewled, psychic background noise urging him to give in. "Excuse me, General, but did I hear you right? Are you kidnapping my family?"

"No, Sergeant, we are not. But we *are* holding them in protective custody for as long as we need to in order to determine that they are not a threat to the whole human race. And frankly, with the Kellett administration on the horizon, we're the only friends you've got."

"We're friends, but my wife and son can't leave your facility."

"Correct, Sergeant. We will do everything we can to make them feel safe and welcome, just as we have these past weeks, but we're no longer pretending to ignore the elephant in the room. Your son is extranormal, and we don't have a sufficient handle on the extent of the threat. In light of that, we're going to hold your son and wife until we're satisfied they're safe outside of our custody, but in all other ways we're going to allow them the rights of any other United States citizen."

Matt's heart broke in a million pieces, shards of honor and manhood that could never fully heal. He sucked in a breath, swallowed, and spoke. "Yeah, I get it. But. But if you want to prevent violence, there are going to have to be ground rules."

"Of course."

Matt told him the first three, and the rest would wait until he spoke to his wife.

CHAPTER NINETEEN

"Was this you?"

Matt looked up at Monica's words, then shifted his eyes from her to the TV. The devastated buildings of Cleveland's downtown stood in stark contrast to the beauty of the lake beyond. Streams of civilians overwhelmed hospitals and mobbed both Red Cross and FEMA tents, and a flood of first responders poured through the wreckage in search of survivors. Matt knew that a more focused team searched through the epicenter, not for the living or even the dead, but for information.

She had some notion that she couldn't leave the building without an escort, and had revealed that FADE was spying on their family, going so far as to collect hair and skin without their knowledge and permission, but had consented to the continued arrangement on reassurances from Matt that he only half-believed.

He snatched up the remote and unmuted the TV when President Kellett came on, a day after what was supposed to have been a triumphant inauguration but had instead been a private-but-televised affair inside the Oval Office. He looked healthy despite his age, with no sign of tremor or illness, and his voice carried the calm assurance of a skilled orator.

"My fellow Americans." He swept the speech from the podium and looked straight at the camera. "It pains me to come before you on what should be a day of celebration. This act of terror on our shores is unprecedented in

American history, a catastrophe of terrible magnitude that extinguished the lives of half a million of our fellow citizens.

But it is not a man-made catastrophe, oh no. This Office has learned that mere minutes before five hundred thousand souls were stuffed from existence, the diabolical creature in human form known as Matt Rowley descended into the depths below the epicenter with his pagan cohort, the fiend Sakura Isuji. These creatures, these demons, conspire to rob us of our liberty, of our lives, of our souls. And in that they are not alone.

"Deep in the bowels of your government – *your* government – lurks a cult. A cult! This secret society amasses to it all knowledge of the profane and unholy, and with that knowledge seeks to steal from the Almighty the keys to the divine. And God, God our Savior, he will not stop them if we do not. We must gird ourselves with the Shield of Faith, the Helmet of Salvation, and the Sword of Truth, which is the Word of God.

"And with that Sword we must purge the wicked, root out the spiritual cancer in our midst, cleanse our nation of the perverse, the vile, the satanic, so that God may again make our country great!" He pounded on the podium – the pulpit – and continued in a much softer tone.

"My fellow Americans. It pains me to do this, but I have instructed the military to root out those elements of society that bring us harm, that have opened the gates to Tartarus and let bleed through the black creatures that plague our world. We know now that that scourge, that darkness, that evil that was the drug Jade is not just harmful, oh, no, it is demonic! And those who have used it, though recovered, are irrevocably tainted. Fellow citizens, you must bring them to us, all of them, so that we might shine God's light upon them and purge them of the wickedness that has taken root in their hearts."

He spoke for twenty minutes, declaring war – literal war – against all 'demonic' and 'unholy' forces, referencing

Matt and Adam Rowley not once or twice but on four separate occasions. He called for proactive self-defense, and encouraged all "true Americans" to take up arms against their spiritual oppressors, to capture or kill any and all who sought to bring the world to ruin. And in the end he declared martial law, with the Joint Chiefs standing behind him to give the unconstitutional, immoral action the semblance of legitimacy.

"Fuck, baby," Monica said, mouth still open. "We got to get our folks the hell out of White Spruce."

He rubbed her shoulder. "They've got nothing to worry about, Mon. Marcia's manning all our security now – she'll send some people to make sure they stay safe."

• • •

Kellett stepped off the stage and shuffled over to Janet LaLonde. The bauble between her breasts tugged at him, strangled his will, encased his mind in a fog of terrible truth: that by virtue of his actions he had fallen beneath God's notice, to wallow in the devil's playground of rank, fetid humanity. To know that the Almighty exists and to persist eternally outside of His grace… he didn't know of any greater punishment, and only after LaLonde had entered his office that summer day did he truly understand the meaning of hell.

"Great speech." Her smile would have driven the old him to fury, but outside of God's love he held no passion, not even for the creature that had enslaved him. Her voice lowered and she leaned in to whisper. His heart caught in his throat at a glimpse of the orb that contained his wretched soul, a swirling cascade of brilliant colors more beautiful than anything on the cursed Earth. "Beg off for the evening as soon as is expedient. We have a date."

He smiled, shook her hand, a cold worm that scraped across his flesh with a million microscopic barbs. "Thank you, Janet. Could you please cancel my meetings for this evening? I have some pressing business to attend to."

"Of course."

She slid away, yet the fog remained. The useless, sinful meat of his body went through the motions of an after-speech analysis, pointless wonkism for people interested in being anything other than a true sword of truth, prevaricators and triangulators who sought to maintain power through deceit and pander.

They spoke of Russia and China leaving the UN, of that traitor Smith declaring himself Eternal Emperor of the Bahamas and Florida Keys, of riots throughout the South and West in reaction to his speech. And they stank of cologne and lust for domination, though his stomach would not roil. After a time he excused himself without explanation, and met Janet on the White House helipad.

He didn't ask where they were going, because he didn't care, couldn't care. Curiosity, creativity, faith, devotion – all the positives of existence, all the blessings of the Almighty hung trapped in her cleavage, leaving him nothing, worse than nothing.

They raced across the landscape at hundreds of miles an hour, exchanging pleasantries with the Secret Service details sharing the cabin of Marine One, a sixteen-passenger stealth helicopter with a million bells and whistles he could neither name nor care about. Below them towns burned, gunshots popped, people died and babies were born, sinners sinned and God damned them for it. After some hours they landed, and the Secret Service fanned out, one of them interrogating the grizzled old man driving the tracked mining vehicle that awaited their arrival.

At Janet's suggested Kellett ordered the man left alone, so they boarded the monster with one agent and descended into a hole in the ground. Treads kicked up rock dust as they delved ever lower into the mountain, but he couldn't summon the wherewithal to cough or cover his nose. She directed their driver with small whispers, directing him through the winding network with quiet confidence.

At last they arrived at a pair of blast doors, massive steel things big enough to let in a tank, emblazoned with the Seal of the President of the United States. A camera and computer screen lurked next to them, mounted in the rock wall as if the most normal thing in the world. Janet looked at him and then at it.

He got out and approached. It blipped awake, formed a pair of eyes, and a soft female voice said, "Retinal Scan Required."

Leaning in, he let it scan his eyes, and the doors rumbled open. The driver hopped out, then dragged a steel pick from the trunk. Janet, Kellett, the driver, and the guard walked inside a network of rooms reminiscent of a submarine, though much larger. Janet led them through the warren with confident steps until at last they reached a rock wall with a black cable snaking through it. She put her hand on the wall, closed her eyes, and sighed.

"So close."

"Pardon?" the agent asked. He hadn't said much throughout their journey, but eyed the president and his chief advisor with a burning curiosity.

"Nothing," she said. "Break it down."

The miner stepped up and swung the pick, putting a small chip in the wall.

"Begging your pardon, Mr President, but what's all this about?" The secret serviceman scowled at the brawny, bearded man hammering his way through a solid stone wall.

Janet whispered in the President's ear, and he spoke. "That's enough, son. Now give me your gun."

"Excuse me?" The guard stepped back and put his hand on his holster.

"You heard me, son. You won't be needing it, and we don't need an accident when you see what's on the other side of that wall."

"Do it," Janet snapped. Rock crumbled behind them.

The agent looked from her to the president, scowling, but produced his weapon and handed it over. The grip felt rough and too cold in his hands. Kellett had never liked weapons, and resented living in a world where a holy man needed armed guards. He flicked the safety with his thumb on the way up and shot the agent in the face.

The driver whirled, wall forgotten, and met the same fate. His brains sprayed through the opening he'd wrought, and his body tumbled out of the way.

Janet smiled and patted Kellett's cheek, her lizard touch bringing a shiver of anticipation. "Well done, Mr President."

She lifted his soul from her breasts by the chain, slipped it over her head, and put it around his neck. The light in the orb died, and Kellett cried out as emotion flooded back into to his heart. Hundreds of thousands dead and a looming civil war that would take countless more, innocents driven to acts of inhuman barbarity by the words that had spilled from his lips. Already damned, he had nothing left to lose.

He raised the gun, put it to his temple, and pulled the trigger.

• • •

Janet triggered the warming protocols on the cryogenic unit and waited forty minutes for the light to go from red to green. The door hissed open and she stepped inside, smiling down at the twisted, tube-punctured, grinning blob of meat with Conor Flynn's face.

"Sore eyes and nice thighs, LaLonde. Been a minute."

She held up the orb, watched his eyes flash from curiosity to fear. "This doesn't have to be unpleasant. Just tell me everything you know of bridges."

• • •

Six hours later, Marcia Stein opened her door with a surprised grunt. Janet LaLonde barreled into her apartment and set a briefcase on the coffee table, then tore off her coat, exposing a bright pink halter top and olive miniskirt more suited to a Disney star turned slut than an advisor to presidents. Marcia's mouth went dry at the enormous emerald cross that stretched from shoulder to shoulder and all the way down her spine, an intricate piece of delicate swirls and spirals that managed to distract even from her incredible curves.

She turned around, a predatory smile on her face, and Marcia's eyes drifted down her long neck to the dull gray orb hanging from a chain between her breasts.

"I've seen you look at me," Janet said. "Let's do something about that."

BONUS NOVELLA

BONKED

FROM:
SNAFU: Hunters
Now available from Cohesion Press

BONKED

Patrick Freivald

Four bonks?" Lieutenant Washington ran a hand over the wispy stubble on his dark-skinned head. "Are they stupid?"

Matt Rowley tried not to sigh, and for the most part succeeded – the resulting noise more of a dissatisfied grunt.

Conor Flynn, just as bald as Washington but pale as milk, grinned at Matt across the giant conference room table emblazoned with the eye-and-thunderbolt logo of the International Council on Augmented Phenomena, the elite organization founded through UN-NATO cooperation to combat the threat of Jade and unregulated Gerstner Augmentation. "FNG got an opinion?"

Jeff Hannes froze in his thousand-dollar suit and glared at all of them, his thumb over the 'advance slide' button. "Are you implying there are non-stupid Jade users, Washington?"

"Point, sir. But they have to know they're playing with fire. I mean, look what Gerstner Augs did to the Russian military. A gang's not going to have that kind of firepower."

Flynn spoke without taking his eyes from Matt. "Maybe that's what the other three are for. One goes bonk, the other three take it down before it wrecks the neighborhood. Somebody else Augs up; lather, rinse, repeat."

Washington pounded a fist on the manila folder that contained his mission briefing. "Are we equipped to deal with that kind of oomph?"

While avoiding Flynn's unwavering gaze, Matt replied. "Yeah, we are, according to the analytics. If they don't know we're coming." Matt turned to Jeff. "They don't know, do they?"

Hannes threw up his hands. "Unless they've got a mole in this room, they're clueless, just another Jade gang hopped up on power. The biggest, sure, and they've seized way too much territory, but they're just a gang. And besides, to have a mole they'd have to know we're operating on American soil."

Flynn quirked an eyebrow at Matt. "Dibs for fun on the pointy one, New Guy." His Irish mumble would have been incomprehensible if not for a decade's friendship, which made the 'New Guy' treatment all the more absurd. Their units had fought together in overseas operations and they'd kept in touch in the years since. That Flynn had signed up for ICAP two years before Matt didn't erase that history, so shouldn't change their friendship.

Matt glanced from Flynn to the photo jacked from a nightclub security camera, splayed large across the white wall that served as a screen. The largest of the four bonks had augmented himself beyond anything Matt had seen before. At least ten feet tall with hands the size of Christmas hams, he loomed over the scene behind giant sunglasses, massive arms crossed over his naked chest. In lieu of hair, steel studs protruded from the top of his skull in a regular grid. Metal spikes protruded from his forearms, ending in cruel barbs sharpened to a razor sheen.

Flynn stroked his chin with an air of too much theater. "He's prettier than me. I can't let that stand."

Turning to Jeff, Matt tapped the picture. "How has he

not bonked out already? Nobody can tolerate that level of Augs." Bonks had gotten their nickname – which Conor found particularly funny – from the inevitable psychosis that overtook chronic Jade users, the superhuman threat that ICAP had been founded to confront. The more you took, the bigger and badder you got, until the whispers drove you into a killing frenzy you never come out of.

And Jade is addictive, with a recidivism rate over ninety-nine percent.

Psychotics are bad. Psychotics that can shrug off bullets and throw cars are rather worse. The Russian military wouldn't be a threat for at least a generation.

And now it's a street drug.

Hurya al-Azwar answered with a roll of her pale-blue eyes. "It's a matter of time, Rowley. You know it, I know it, he has to know it. Which just makes him that much more dangerous." A scar ran from her left temple back into her short blonde hair. It, and the missing quarter-inch off the top of her ear, spoke of a life on the streets of Detroit before two tours as a Marine in the sand box, before Jade and augmentation and ICAP, before the regenerates that would heal any damage short of death without mark or scar and in seconds or minutes instead of months.

Five years his senior in ICAP, she'd seen dozens of her colleagues bonk out, had to put far too many of them down, and her first-generation regenerates put her at a higher risk than any of them. Augmentation protocols had improved as scientific understanding increased, but everyone in the room ran the risk of psychotic, ravening insanity. Everyone but their boss.

Jeff's constipated grimace pulled them away from the picture. "Look, we've got four heavily-augmented threats and at least sixteen who might be normals, or might just not be showing. I'm bringing in Platt and Karle," he raised his voice over their groans, "and giving Karle operational discretion on this one."

"Why do you hate us?" Flynn asked.

Jeff ran his tongue over his teeth. "Karle's got a better success rate than any of you. I want you all back alive, and there's something about this," he waved his hand at the scattered pictures, "I don't like at all."

Washington sighed without looking up. "Feel the love, man."

• • •

Matt eyed the sunglasses in Flynn's proffered hand and shook his head. "Those make me look like a cop."

"You are a cop. Were a cop. Pretending to be a cop. Whatever you did in Tennessee."

"No need to advertise it."

"Eat your bones." Flynn tossed the shades into the back seat and fastened his seatbelt, then ran his hands over the fake leather dash above the late-model Impala's glove box. "Brilliant. These American-made autos really spice up the sex life, Rowley. We'll fit right in."

At two hundred and forty pounds and one percent body fat, Conor Flynn looked every bit the cop, or ex-military, as Matt. His skin-tight gray t-shirt did nothing to dispel the effect, and his square sunglasses screamed, 'I am a Government Agent. Do not speak to or trust me.'

Flynn raised an eyebrow at the naked appraisal. "What?"

Matt just shook his head and put the car into gear.

They cruised through the suburbs, past an endless stream of one-story ranches and dingy, sun-faded plastic swimming pools. The smells of the city filtered through the air conditioning, street food and salt water and sweat and garbage rotting under the blazing summer sun. Matt considered grabbing the shades from the back seat, but wouldn't give Flynn the satisfaction. Chain link replaced white pickets, and vinyl siding blurred into graffiti on decaying brick.

They pulled up to a stoplight and idled next to a cluster of young men, baggy street clothes and wary brown faces sweltering in the midday heat. This far south it took a special kind of stupid to wear pants if you didn't have to, which might explain why half of them hung on their thighs or even lower. The pale yellow bandanas around foreheads, necks, wrists, or ankles identified them as Camino Reals. Heroin dealers and thieves, they lay outside ICAP's jurisdiction even with their new domestic operations protocols.

Flynn held a hundred-dollar bill up with two fingers, but no one approached the car, their lack of attention as conspicuous as staring.

"Oy, boys." Flynn waved the folded bill in the air. "I could use some information." They glowered at the ground, at the sky, the telephone poles, anywhere but at the car. "Brilliant, lads. Thanks for nothing." The light turned green and Matt pulled away, eyes on the mirrors, watching them watch him with wary eyes.

"No love from the South-Side Banana Hammocks." Flynn chuckled and slipped the money back into his pocket. "Told you we look like cops."

"If you're so worried about it, why are we the ones going?"

"I didn't say I was worried. It's just going to be hard to pick a fight if they know we're the law."

"We're not here to pick–"

Babbling whispers slithered through his mind, a mad cacophony of thoughts bent on murder and pain, the worst side effect of Gerstner Augmentation. Matt took the warning from the Late-Second Precognition but ignored the lurching desire to tear Flynn's face from his skull and stuff it into his mouth. Jerking the wheel, he hit the brakes then the gas to bring them around ninety degrees, then floored it before the jeeps rounded the corner behind the run-down convenience mart.

Flynn laughed and reached down, but stopped when Matt shook his head.

"You won't need the pig-sticker, they're just running us off." He down-shifted to pick up speed, then jammed the car into higher gear, gas pedal to the floor. The motor whined, a cicada with an internal-combustion mating call.

Flynn took his hand off the hilt of his katana, leaving it on the floor between the seats. The titanium and carbon nanofiber blade had yet to see use in combat, but Matt had watched Flynn dice up a car in the practice arena without breaking a sweat. Why an Irishman fought with a katana Matt would never understand.

Flynn jerked his thumb toward the back. "You want me to get the trunk?"

Matt shook his head. The REC-7 carbine and Auto-Assault 12 combat shotgun could stay where they were, in the trunk under lock and key. If worse came to worse he had his personal Glock 9mm in the glove box. But it wouldn't. They'd been made as cops in a no-go zone, but hadn't done anything to justify a murder, even from a gang as vicious as the Camino Reals.

They blew through two red lights, the jeeps swerving and honking behind, but as they passed from one turf to the next the pursuit broke off and didn't return.

"You sussed those out pretty fast. Precog, yeah?" Flynn asked.

Matt nodded without taking his eyes from the road.

"Brilliant, brilliant. They wouldn't clear me for it, said I'd had enough. I'm thinking what's the harm, right?"

"The harm is you go bonk and kill everything around you until other people like you put you down."

Flynn chuckled. "That's what I mean, right? The side effect is 'fun.'"

"Just keep your pants on."

"Aye, Sergeant."

Ten minutes later they rolled past the Marquee, a modern glass-and-steel structure at odds with the dilapidated neighborhood. The fading day washed the neon lights to a pale glow but did nothing to hide the ultraviolet paint across the front windows, a cartoon shark swimming through a golden crown that would be invisible to unaugmented eyes.

"See that?" Matt asked.

Flynn nodded. "Fancy. You think the Shades don't have blacklights?"

Matt shrugged. "One cop in fifty might have augged vision, maybe. Not like the Mako Kings don't know the police know where they hang out, anyway. As long as they think we're just cops, we'll–"

Flynn popped his handle and stepped out, the car still rolling at fifteen miles an hour. He hooked a parking meter with his right hand and used it to spin himself around, stopping with a flourish with his toes balanced on the edge of the curb. As Matt slammed on the brakes and swore under his breath, Flynn took a bow to the wide-eyed onlookers. Flynn waited behind the car for Matt to pull over, put on the brake and get out.

People milled the streets, heading home from work or out for a Friday on the town. As one they gave the car a wide berth, eyeing both newcomers with open suspicion or naked hostility.

Matt stepped up to his friend with his jaw clenched in frustration. "Dammit, Conor, we're supposed to be scoping the place, not painting bullseyes on our heads."

A seven-foot tall bouncer, rippling with muscles impossible through normal exercise, eyed them from the front door across the street. Taking in the sea of Hispanics, all either staring or trying too hard not to stare, Flynn ran a hand over the stubble on his pasty scalp. "See, we fit right in, sunnies and all." He put on his shades and sauntered across the street.

Music trickled out behind the double-doors, Latin horns over a hip-hop beat, death-metal Spanish growling from a microphone. They approached, cop-casual, Matt two steps behind. The bouncer moved to intercept them. His voice rumbled an octave lower than a normal man's, his accent a blend of Mexican and south Florida. "Can I help you, gentlemen?"

"Yes," Matt said. "We–"

"Looking for a drink and twirl is all." Flynn spun, an elegant pirouette that ended in a curtsey. He held the pose and looked up under his brow into the bouncer's eyes. "Heard the Marquee had it happening, am I right?"

"You're not our target clientele, ese." The bouncer put his hands on his hips so that his massive frame blocked most of both doors. Matt winced as Flynn's eyes flashed, an almost imperceptible twitch that showed not the slightest hint of fear. The bouncer put his hand on Flynn's chest, fingers splaying almost to his shoulders. "You're going to have to leave."

"What, because I'm white? You discriminating here? You think the Irish haven't faced–"

Matt put his hand on Flynn's shoulder. "We're not here to pick a fight, Conor."

"–their share of discrimination, you racist prick? Why don't you make me leave, big guy?"

To his credit, the bouncer didn't take the bait. Much. He extended his arm, slowly, forcing Flynn several steps back on the sidewalk. "Move along, little man. This isn't the place for you." He extended his fingers and Conor stumbled back two steps.

Matt moved between them and Conor rebounded off of his back. "We're sorry, sir. We'll be on our way." He stepped back, bumping Flynn toward the street, then turned and backed him off the curb and into the road. Through gritted teeth he mumbled, "The point was to maintain surprise, moron."

Flynn almost frolicked toward the car, locking eyes with anyone and everyone who dared challenge his right to be there. "Nah, there's no fun in that, and he thinks we're cops or feds or something anyway. The point was to size that meathead up. You see what I saw?"

Matt recalled the scene, his eidetic memory enhancements bringing to crystal-clear focus details he hadn't seen in real time. "Tracks?"

"Right is right. He's on the H, not just Jade. We follow him home, wait for him to snow out, bangers and mash," he mimed tossing a flash-bang grenade. "Black bag over the head, voila. New toy for the intel department."

Matt tried not to smile as he gunned the engine. "Call it in."

"We could just–"

"Call it in, Conor." He pulled away from the curb and took a left toward the expressway.

The dash shook as Flynn banged his fist on it. "Karle's a pussy. We've got an opportunity here, and you know he'll–"

Matt sighed. "Twelve years a Royal Marine, decorated six times for valor, awarded the Victoria Cross for insane but admirable stupidity in the Kandahar valley. . . What rank were you when you left the force to join ICAP?"

Flynn mumbled.

"Say again, Corporal?"

"Cor-por-al." He emphasized every syllable. "And you know it."

"And why not a Sergeant? A Warrant Officer? Lieutenant?"

They said it together. "A history of unpredictable behavior and violent tendencies uncurbed by disciplinary measures."

"ICAP wanted a killer," Flynn mumbled again, "so they can't complain when they get one."

"Right. But right now we need to be smart. We're on US soil, and have limited mission parameters. If Karle sanctions the move, we–" His eyes widened as the whispers shrieked blood-soaked charnel houses into his brain. Before it happened a shadow separated from the wall, crushing the Impala and tumbling it end over end into the sidewalk grocery.

Late-second precognition made Rowley and a select few other Augs impossible to surprise, at least while awake. The whispers gave warning, but not much. Matt swerved, taking the bonk head-on.

He squeezed his eyes shut as the airbags deployed, gritted his teeth against the impossibly loud crunch, and yanked the 9mm from the glove box. Two pulls of the trigger deflated the airbag and caused the massive shadow dwarfing his vision to stagger. His eardrums healed as fast as the explosions shredded them, and the car lurched sideways. Gasping in a breath of chalky white dust and the tang of gunpowder, he tore off his seatbelt.

Flynn had disappeared, his door hanging ajar on a crumpled hinge.

A monster lifted the car by the front, a wall of muscle and spikes with jet black eyes, teeth filed to cruel points, threaded steel studs protruding from its head in a regular pattern. The bonk roared and Matt's world overturned, the roof imploding as it impacted the asphalt. Neck tilted almost to ninety degrees, he fired twice out the spider-webbed windshield.

Hot red blood exploded from the bonk's enormous black sneaker, a chunk of leather torn free from the glancing shot. Matt pushed with his legs, straining against the seat as massive fingers gripped the hood under the car and lifted. If the bonk had felt the gunshot, it made no sign of it. Matt's stomach lurched as the car raised up. He pushed harder, bracing his hands on either side of the steering wheel for leverage.

The seat snapped and he fell back, his face sliding across the upholstered roof as the car smashed into the ground again, trapping him in a sandwich of crumpled metal.

BONKED

Conor Flynn rolled right as gunfire peppered the sidewalk. His heart soared as civilians screamed, the adrenaline rushing through his veins in an orgy of pending violence while his augmented heart beat at a steady seventy beats per second. He hit the facade of the brick building at a full sprint and ran straight up it, using his momentum to gain traction on the vertical surface.

Twenty feet up he grabbed the roof lip and jerked, sailing over the top in a graceful arc. One knife had already left his hand, sinking to the hilt into his first opponent. Conor ignored the dead man as he drew and threw the second knife left-handed.

Shooter number two held his HK53 like a movie gangster, the stock collapsed, relying on arm strength to bring and hold the weapon to bear. He jerked as the knife hit, glancing off the gun instead of finding purchase in his flesh.

Conor landed, crouched low, grinning in the thrill of battle. Bullets zoomed over his head as the gangbanger's weapon jerked high. Three steps brought Conor in range, so he drew the katana and spun. The ancient bone fragment hidden in the hilt sang to him, urged the blade forward, thirsted for the death that it had brought in life. He resisted and pulled back at the last second. The monofilament blade took the man in the bridge of the nose without the slightest resistance, a spray of red gore joining the near-silent steel breeze. Stepping in as the man dropped the weapon to bring his hands to his face, Conor shouldered him off the roof.

He fell with gurgling wail that cut off in a wet thump on the pavement.

Picking up the carbine, Conor looked down at the overturned car and the giant bonk slamming it into the pavement. "Oh, Matt, you silly boy. I called dibs."

He dove sideways as the roof access door banged open, bullets tearing through the air where he'd just stood. Three men armed with ARs fanned out as Conor scrambled behind an air conditioning unit. They moved with an uncoordinated, nervous energy, to make room for a dark-skinned bonk in a black trenchcoat, like Wesley Snipes's Blade enlarged on a photocopier.

A sharp itch shot up from his ankle, and he looked down to find his cuff darkening with spreading blood just above his boot.

The pain hadn't hit him, and wouldn't before the wound healed.

"Brilliant, lads. Let's play."

• • •

Automatic weapons-fire punctuated the mind-rattling crunch as the bonk beat the car into the ground. Matt squirmed to the back, popped down the latch to access the trunk, and pulled the case containing his AA-12 combat shotgun into the back seat. His stomach lurched as the car lifted and he ran his thumb over the biometric lock.

The car slammed down and a searing, white-hot pain shot up his leg into his spine.

He popped open the case and slid out the weapon, the drum magazine already loaded with fin-stabilized fragmentation rounds. He turned, his left leg making a sloppy ripping sound as it tore free from the jagged chunk of metal that used to be the gearshift, and took aim.

The car came up, and in the four-inch space between the dash and the remains of the roof the bonk's abdomen came into view, rippling muscle barely contained in a baby-blue t-shirt. Matt fired, the roar deafening in the confined space.

He held the trigger as the bonk whirled to the side and only one microgrenade found its mark, the others deactivating automatically as they missed the intended target. As it exploded the world disappeared from view and the car crashed down onto the pavement with a final crunch. Matt squirmed back and crushed the latch on the trunk with a knife-hand, tearing it free with a wince. Ignoring the bloody mess he'd made of his fingers he launched himself out, weapon raised toward the rooftops.

He fired and swept right over three targets, wishing for his tactical helmet with its Friend-or-Foe identifier and smart projectile guidance system. A man's head exploded, raining bloody brains and chunks of skull from the rooftop before pitching back out of sight, but the other two took cover, unharmed. Shots rang out from the roof across the street, though at what target he couldn't tell.

Footsteps rang behind him. On his back, he rolled his head to take aim at the charging bouncer, eight-hundred-plus pounds moving at twenty-something miles an hour. He triggered the rounds to explode 'downward' toward the sky and pulled the trigger. The weapon barely recoiled against his shoulder, and a dozen shots flew in two seconds. The depleted uranium-tipped rounds punched into the bonk's legs and abdomen and then erupted in a bloody mist. The massive thing stumbled mid-stride, left femur and part of its hip exposed by the rapid disintegration of intervening flesh.

Matt fired twice more, punching up under the fused bones of its ribcage to pulp the heart and lungs. With any luck the trauma would be enough to bring it down.

The whispers tittered in hateful glee and he jerked his legs up, but his injured left knee didn't respond. The shredded remains of his Impala came down on top of it in an explosion of wet red pain, erasing everything below his lower thigh in a gory smear across the concrete. Black spots formed in his vision, but he jerked up the shotgun – and found no targets. Blue sky and scattering civilians filled his vision over the demolished car.

As the arteries pumping life from his body closed and meat formed around undeveloped bone, he lay back and panted, trying to circumvent the unbearable, itching agony of bleeding, knitting flesh. His vision darkened, but he forced his eyes to remain open and trained on the rooftop. His view remained empty, devoid of targets.

In the distance, sirens wailed.

He slid to a sitting position, his right hand on the stock of the AA-12, and looked down at the tattered remains of his leg. The muscle writhed, ropy masses weaving together only to split, bleeding, as the bone grew between them.

A shadow crossed his vision. He looked up.

Conor shook his head, frowning, every inch of him covered in bright red blood. He smiled, white teeth glinting like the metallic sheen on his sword in the fading sunlight. "You let him get away. You going to do your job or what?"

Biting back his vulgar reply, Matt allowed his head to drop to the sidewalk, filling his vision with clear blue sky. "Call it in. And put that damned sword away – the cops are en route."

• • •

Hurya al-Azwar stepped down from the helicopter and surveyed the carnage wrought by Conor Flynn. Five dead men sprawled across the rooftop, policemen already marking evidence with little yellow tags – shell casings, severed limbs, discarded weapons. Red stains marred the gravel in an expanding spiral that ended in the shredded remains of a giant black man, a third of his head three meters further away, remaining eye wide open in unending shock, mouth open to reveal serrated steel teeth bolted into his jaw.

"How many did they get?" She nodded toward the corpse.

Sergeant Karle frowned down at the dead bonk. "Two, plus nearly a dozen normals. All fatalities. Conor's unhurt, Matt will be fine in an hour or so if we stuff enough food in him."

"This was recon. What the hell happened?"

Karle held up his hands. "Conor Flynn happened. Matt said he picked a fight."

"Remind me to never do that." She nudged the dead bonk with her toe. "Intel didn't even know about this one. What's a big black guy doing Augging-up in a Latin gang?"

Karle grunted. "Tell Platt and Washington to make nice with the locals. I'm going to see if we can't get Conor and Matt out of custody."

"Aye, sir."

• • •

The map appeared on Matt's HUD as Karle spoke in his ear piece. The Mako Kings controlled a nine-block area just outside of downtown, and ruthlessly crushed any and all opposition regardless of whether or not they were law enforcement, rival gangs, or even the cartels. Pioneers in nationwide Jade distribution, they'd partnered with Dawkins's organization to spread like a virus from Chicago to both coasts and everywhere in-between. With an irresistible product and superhuman augmentation they destroyed their competition and carved out an empire from the ashes of burning ghettos.

A network of Dragonflies gave Matt real-time data of the Mako Kings's turf, the quad-copter drones blanketing the area with sonar, visual, and infrared surveillance. Coupled with his own infrared and ultraviolet vision, the HUD removed the fog of war and replaced it with stark, robotic clarity. The overlay projected an image that saw through brick walls and even assessed the likelihood that any particular person was a target or a civilian.

Pointy, as Conor had taken to calling him, had left a blood trail from the wreckage of Matt's rented Impala through the back alleys to an abandoned shopping plaza now known as 'Spanish City', a lawless haven for derelicts, junkies and people who didn't want to be found. A wall of wrecked vehicles surrounded the parking lot and included a crude gate made out of the burned-out carcass of a double-decker bus rigged to an old crane.

The reek of unwashed bodies, burning garbage, and urine combined into something not unlike ammonia-soaked charred bananas left to rot in the sun. Matt couldn't imagine what it smelled like in the midday heat and humidity.

Dozens of people wandered the asphalt, or warmed themselves at fires set in rusted steel drums. Junkies lay on the ground, or on each other, sharing needles and pills and body heat in the midnight chill. Sentries wandered the rooftops, armed with long rifles and binoculars that may or may not be night-vision capable.

Too many civilians. A squad of Augs could make mincemeat of the hostiles without the use of heavy ordnance, but the civilians would pay a heavy toll. Besides, if Jade wasn't involved it wasn't their purview, and while some Jade dealers found their way to Spanish City it was not, according to their intel, a pipeline worthy of ICAP's attention. Yet.

Karle had operational control – former rank meant nothing in ICAP – but ultimately the plan came from Washington. Washington, Karle, and Flynn would storm the gates, loud and proud, with flash-bangs and drone support to crack a hole in the wall. As the civilians ran and the guards engaged, Rowley, Platt, and al-Azwar would eliminate Pointy. Conor had complained, citing "dibs" which Washington ignored, mollifying him with a chance at the fifth bonk the Dragonflies had pegged near the gate.

Mission parameters authorized deadly force for the bonks and anyone identified as a Mako King. Between the baby-blue bandannas and facial recognition, the quad copters had added eleven human-sized targets in addition to the two bonks. Matt's HUD outlined them with double red triangles, the suspected civilians with orange triangles, and his own team with green circles. In the age of Jade, collateral damage had become a price of law enforcement, and the DHS hoped the joint UN/NATO strike force would bring so much firepower to bear that they could minimize or at least contain the destruction . . . but this somehow wasn't a 'military operation'.

Peace through superior bureaucracy.

The timer hit zero, and the bus-gate disintegrated in a roar, the fireball rising skyward as the drone banked toward home.

Screams. Panic. Weapons-fire pinging off the wreckage from jittery, untrained gangbangers wasting their ammo—and precious time reloading.

Pointy's hulking form, bright yellow on the infrared, bolted from his mattress in the abandoned Macy's sales floor, joined by several others. The huge blob raced through the open space toward the loading dock a hundred feet from their position.

Platt charged, screaming, before the bay door had opened. Matt opened his mouth to countermand, and closed it, angry. Platt came to a halt inches from the unmoving metal.

Pointy's blob faded, then disappeared.

"What the hell?" Platt put his fist through the loading-dock's side door, pivoted, and ripped it off its hinges. Staccato pops sounded from inside, and chips of cinderblock lashed into Platt's face.

"Hold position!" Matt moved up, his HUD tracking for targets simultaneously on the Dragonfly feed and the helmet camera, the 'Identify Friend or Foe' lighting up at several weapon profiles sticking out from around pillars and decrepit, half-burned display cases.

He fired three times on approach, eschewing the Groucho technique he'd learned as a Tennessee police officer in favor of a thirty-mile-per-hour sprint and superhuman strength to keep the recoil-suppressing weapon aimed true. The fin-stabilized microgrenades auto-aimed toward the identified targets, skimming past the makeshift defilade and exploding downward and sideways. Men screamed. A pair of legs kicked out from behind a cracked marble pillar, the IFF fading from red to black as a pool of blood spread across the filthy tile.

He grunted as a round rocked his shoulder back, the gel under the dragon skin hardening to dissipate the energy before turning soft again. Behind him, al-Azwar's NATO-issue REC7 chattered, spitting ceramic composite 'bonk killer' rounds with unerring accuracy.

Matt's visor automatically dimmed over the continuous muzzle-flash as Platt fired full auto and swept inside, following the bullets through the doorway with a roar that carried over the intercom. Matt and al-Azwar came in behind, al-Azwar keeping their targets pinned down with tight, controlled bursts while Matt killed them with the directional grenades.

Seconds later the room fell quiet, the FoF indicating no living targets.

"Here!" al-Azwar cried, flipping up a metal access hatch with her boot. Without waiting she stepped in and dropped out of sight, carbine pointed down as she fell through the hole.

Platt and Rowley whirled as a pair of men ran in, gaped wide-eyed at the carnage then fled in panic. Matt stepped up and looked inside the hole. A series of rebar handles led into the darkness, which in the UV spectrum resolved into a ladder descending several stories to a concrete floor. IR signatures showed faint signs of passage, but the tunnels glowed too warm for much more.

Platt nodded at the hole. "You first."

Matt stepped inside, pressing his boots against the walls to slow his descent enough not to break his legs when he hit the ground. Above him, Platt stepped in and grabbed a rung.

Platt hissed as his fingers separated from his hand in a flash of silver. He turned, groping for his carbine left-handed. Another flash and his helmet toppled down the shaft, his head still inside, neck spurting steaming red blood. A block of plastic bricks followed Platt's dead body down the hole, a red light blinking in the darkness.

Matt fired a burst up the shaft and pulled his feet back, falling the last twenty feet before impacting hard on the concrete floor. He leapt. With a spin he just managed to pull himself behind a metal door before the room erupted.

Heat washed over him in a deafening, blinding white, crushing him between the wall and the door. His armor crackled, the HUD went dark. He held his breath for as long as he could, then gasped in air that seared his throat, scorched his lungs. Gagging, he stumbled to his knees and tore off his helmet. His hair shriveled in the fading heat, and he kept his eyes squeezed tight.

A moment passed, and a breeze tickled his skin as more air rushed back into the room. He gasped in a breath, cleaner now, and opened his eyes.

Flecks of blackened skin fell from his hands, the only part of his body exposed to the explosion. He flexed his fingers as the skin knitted over and through the damaged tissue – he'd have to cut it away later to let blemish-free skin grow. If there was a later.

Dust and smoke obscured his vision, but from his vantage point he could just make out the pile of demolished concrete that had once made up the shaft, and next to it the smoldering remains of one of Platt's boots, a chunk of bone sticking out of the ruined meat. Matt stood and looked down at the bandoleer of drum magazines for the AA-12. The smoking leather had protected the munitions just enough. Had they detonated, he'd be a dead man.

He rounded the corner, weapon up, and left the room, his useless helmet lying next to Platt's boot. "Hurya, do you copy?"

Static burst through his ear bud, intermingled with what might have been al-Azwar's voice.

"I'm on your six. Platt's dead."

"–ay again, Rowley." Karle's deep voice reverberated through his ears. "Y– king up."

"Karle, Platt's dead, hostile unknown. We're underground." He rounded a corner and snarled at the uselessness of his IR; the floor and walls glowed a uniform red, an afterimage from the explosion, or perhaps from a subterranean heat source. "al-Azwar, I'm on your six, copy."

The indecipherable noise that followed left him no idea whether or not they'd understood, or if Hurya had heard him at all.

• • •

Bullets pinged off of the bus-gate as Conor leapt through the holes left by the trio of AGM-176 Griffin missiles, the drone-capable, candy-ass little brothers of Hellfire missiles designed to limit collateral damage. His ears filled with the melodious sounds of rifle shots and screaming panic, and in his mind his katana sang of unending bloodshed as he drew it from its sheath.

He ignored the scattering civilians, and the whispers' nagging encouragement to cut them down. They didn't tell him anything he didn't already know, and there were bigger, more challenging prizes to pursue.

Karle and Washington took position behind the gate and fired short, controlled bursts from their M4s, letting the IFF targeting system guide the electronically-controlled flechette rounds to their targets. They couldn't shoot around corners, but in Conor's opinion, 300-meter shots without bothering to aim just scoured all the joy out of combat.

Conor leapt, taut muscle launching him twenty feet in the air and straight at the bonk charging their position.

Smaller than Pointy, the nine-foot monstrosity wore

full body armor, matte black carbon fiber over enormous metal plates, and wielded a battered stop sign like an axe. A mane of black hair flowed down her back from a topknot that gave her a vaguely Mongolian look, though she bore the extended brow and thick facial structure of bonks everywhere. Enormous claws extended from her left hand, the gleaming metal bolted to or through the bone and stretching half a meter from her fingertips.

Conor swung, two-handed, but without purchase he couldn't put enough force into the blow to threaten such a creature. She didn't take the feint. Faster than he believed possible, Scratchy sidestepped and swung. He twisted to take the blow on his hip as the stop sign swatted him from the air. He took the landing on his left hand, cartwheeled, and came up swinging.

The monofilament blade sparked against the sign inches from his head, skittering up the handle to bite into the reflective sheet metal. Scratchy twisted, tearing the blade from Conor's hands, and swiped low with her claws.

Laughing, Conor stepped into the swipe, using her elbow for a foothold to spin-kick her in the face. The steel toe caught her in the temple, the shock of metal on thick bone reverberating up Conor's left leg as the blow arrested his momentum. The reinforced steel in his boot crumpled with the impact, crushing his toes.

Scratchy dropped the sign and stumbled back, shaking her head like a dog.

Conor dove into a roll, grabbing the hilt of his blade on the way by. The metal shrieked as he wrenched the sword free. He spun, weapon up, and gave her a nod of respect.

"C'mon, lassie. You've got some fight in you."

Scratchy swept up the sign and advanced, makeshift axe and claw whirring almost too fast for his augmented eyes to follow. Metal clanged against metal as he backpedaled, limping, sword flashing to deflect the blows before either crushed or sliced him to pieces.

His back hit the wall. Scratchy swung.

Hurya al-Azwar closed her eyes, but heard only the soft trickle of water in the distance, the echo washing it out to white noise in the sewer tunnels. She muttered a soft prayer of thanks that sanitation services had long-since failed in this part of the city, and only the ghosts of odors remained to haunt her senses. All said, the sewers smelled much better than the mall above.

Her COMMs produced nothing but occasional static, like her GPS and the IFF linked through the network of Dragonflies, though because of intervening metal or deliberate jamming she couldn't say. Pointy – despite Conor's childishness, a lack of known identity had ensured that the name stuck throughout operational planning – had vanished down the twisting corridors, and the heat from the walls kept her from tracking him with IR vision.

The tunnels had rocked a few minutes earlier, in what she'd hoped had been a deliberate explosion set by Platt or Rowley, and since then her world had condensed to long, dark corridors rendered bright by augmented eyes, dripping water, and the desiccated memories of ancient shit.

She waited. Rats squeaked in the distance, their feet scrabbling across the stone-and-mortar hallways, too far and too quiet for human ears to hear.

Something Pointy's size couldn't move through these corridors without making noise, and her augmented ears could pick up a pin dropping at ten meters. A scrape of boot on the floor, a shoulder brushing against the wall. If he moved, she'd hear it, and she'd have him.

A bead of sweat trickled down the back of her neck, tickling from her hairline until it hit the collar of her undershirt, the white cotton soaked under her armor in the oppressive heat. She tightened her grip on the carbine, textured handle proof against her sweaty palms, and took one careful step, rocking from the ball of her foot to her toes. Silent, she regulated her breathing to the barest motion, letting not even that betray her presence.

Her ears pricked at a soft scrape. She turned, rotating soundlessly on the balls of her feet, breath held. It came again, closer, from a hall on the left. She lifted the REC7 and crept two careful steps back. The FoF highlighed a potential target, blue for an unconfirmed type. Another step back, and–

She jerked up, too late. The giant shape landed on her, thick, sinuous muscle crushing her arms to her chest. Pain exploded in her trigger finger as it snapped sideways in the guard. Hot runnels of fluid streamed to the floor as serrated barbs sank deep into her flesh. She stomped with the strength of a dozen men, driving her heel down onto the foot below.

Pointy only squeezed harder. Her ribs, fused as part of augmentation, cracked. Slamming her head back, she hit thick muscle instead of teeth or nose. She gasped in a breath, but her lungs wouldn't inflate. Held in the air, she found no purchase. The grip tightened, and the fire in her chest strangled hope. Bones shifted, her infrared vision blurred.

Her fingers walked along the black leather of her belt to the loop holding the grenades. She fumbled for the pin, the spoon, any part of it, something she could drop and kick behind them, shred the monster from the back.

She groaned out the last of her air.

Her finger touched metal.

Blood and organs vomited from her mouth as her ribcage collapsed, the hot, meaty taste her last sensation before the world went black.

• • •

Conor spun right as the wall next to him disappeared in a puff of concrete dust, Scratchy's claws reducing the brick facade to chunks and powder. He slashed downward, and the sword's psychic scream pumped energy into his exhausted muscles. It drank deep, pulling blood and life from the bonk's thigh, cutting through muscle and bone with an ease that technology couldn't account for.

What ICAP didn't know wouldn't hurt them.

He danced away in a hot arterial spray, Scratchy's muscles already knitting in ropy, purple masses. One mass formed a lump-like, writhing tentacle. Conor smiled. First Generation Regenerates had their own set of problems, so he decided to have some fun.

She charged, a limping rhinoceros's trundling attack, brute force and sharp steel at forty miles an hour.

Eschewing the sword, he drew his 9mm pistol and fired, emptying the fifteen-round magazine into her face and arms in a series of little red holes and streaks of shredded tissue. Small caliber rounds wouldn't do anything but annoy a bonk of her size, but it would tax her system just enough for his next–

–she slammed into him, carrying him to the ground in a gridiron tackle that blasted the air from his lungs, but he kept his blade pointed out and maintained his grip. She bit down on his shoulder. The armor absorbed the brunt of her iron hard teeth. The increase in pressure didn't restrict his movements any more than her arms already had.

Fabric tore. The pressure increased.

He let her squeeze, and worked the katana back and forth across her exposed wrist. Even without leverage the razor-sharp blade sliced through the meat without effort. His teeth clenched against the growing pain in his shoulder; Conor worked the katana up and down in a rough sawing motion, the best he could manage with his arms pinned to his side.

She grabbed his thigh with her claws and squeezed. The bone gave way with a burning rush of endorphins and heat, and Conor fought to remain conscious through the unbearable, itching agony. He slid the blade up, and then down.

Up. Down.

Muscle parted. Metal scraped against bone. Scratchy dragged her teeth free then slammed her head into Flynn's helmet, again and again, stars exploding across his vision. Something cracked, and cracked further, then white supernovas streaked through his skull. Still he sawed.

Her grip slackened against the blade, just enough to free his arm. Conor pulled a combat knife from his belt and jammed it between metal plates, through carbon fiber and meat into the junction between her leg and groin. He propped the pommel against the metal plate on his abdomen and used her leverage to shove it farther in. Hot, sticky fluid gushed over his hand.

Her squeeze became a squirming, frantic push, but he straightened his good leg to lift against her weight, jamming the blade deeper until it met bone, and then a little further. As the knife sank between the ball and socket he twisted with every ounce of his augmented strength. The joint popped free.

Roaring, she let go and rolled off of him.

He stood.

Tearing off his helmet and letting it drop to the ground, he whirled, blade slicing through the air and her mid-spine without slowing. Her claws tore into the asphalt, desperately scrabbling across the pavement, limp legs trailing behind.

Conor hobbled after her, unable to put much weight on his left leg. The sword bit down, slicing armor and meat once, twice, three times, tracing deep gashes across her shoulders and upper arms. Purple masses writhed across the wounds as she dragged herself away from him, legs twitching as her spine began to knit.

She rose to all fours.

He cut across the back of her knee, severing tendons and ligaments, the wound welling black under the sodium-vapor sky. As she fell he drove the blade into one kidney, leaning in to punch it through to her armor on the other side. He pulled it out and did the other.

She swung, an ineffectual batting with her claws that he hopped way from. He took several of her fingers. They fell to the ground in a gush, and as she reared to her knees he took her right ear. The contrast highlighted the difference between first and second-generation regenerates: his thigh itched as muscle and bone knitted under his armor, but it still wouldn't take his weight. She healed much faster, but the unstable flesh molded and twisted her body into something less than human.

He stabbed her again, avoiding her heart to target her right lung. Once. Twice. Then her stomach, just to the left of her spine.

No reason to keep you down too long, darling.

She fell back to her hands and knees. He took the time to slice the side of her neck, just enough to prick the artery. Blood gushed in erratic spurts across the decaying asphalt, and she collapsed to her face, shaking, as the wound slithered and squirmed.

Her whole body shuddered, and a mad, keening growl erupted from her throat.

"There it is."

The whispers slithered through his mind, calling to their sister, entwining her, embracing her in an unending maelstrom of madness and carnage. She thrashed on the ground, a half-ton child in a temper-tantrum, denied her favorite toys.

He glanced up long enough to see Washington and Karle advancing toward the mall without taking fire, then looked back down at Scratchy's transformation. First-generation bonks made for the best bonk-outs. *Tee-hee.*

Tentacles oozed from her shoulder, and a mouth gnashed with serrated teeth from the wound in her neck. He limped back with too much theater for the benefit of the

Dragonflies and took shelter in the shadows by the wall, his smirk hidden in the shadows.

Scratchy erupted in a mountain of writhing flesh, suckered tentacles and ropy masses of muscle almost obscuring her humanoid form. Her scream couldn't come from human lungs, an animalistic rage purer and more potent than the worst that men could devise.

And better than most, Conor Flynn knew what men could devise.

Karle and Washington turned and opened fire as the bonked-out mountain of flesh charged them. His voice admirably calm, Karle called for air support and then addressed Conor. "Flynn, you alive?"

He coughed for effect. "Barely. Be a minute."

"Well, step on it. We've got company."

"Aye, sir." From the shadows, Flynn smiled, and watched.

Washington drew a pair of combat knives and took the charge head-on. He disappeared in an avalanche of psychotic, ravening meat. Blood fountained up from the hideous abomination, though from his squad-mate or the monster Conor couldn't tell.

He tried his leg. An electric jolt shot up his spine, but it held his weight and didn't get any worse. Satisfied, he limped right, around the side of the building. Karle bellowed in the distance, and staccato gunfire echoed across the parking lot. Conor found a manhole, popped it up with his foot, and cocked his head.

Far beneath him, a bloody mess stained the ground, just hotter than the walls and floor. In what little streetlight hit the bottom he could just make out the remains of an ICAP uniform, too small to be Rowley or Platt. Organs and steaming chunks of viscera spilled out of the helmet, a viscous glob of jellied entrails that crisscrossed al-Azwar's unmoving chest in a pattern his mind had to and wouldn't recognize. The eldritch symbol lanced through his head, seeking a foothold he would never allow it to find. He snuffed it out and opened eyes he hadn't realized he'd closed.

Overhead, streaks of orange fire lit up the sky. The earth rocked a moment before the explosions hit Conor's ears, and Karle's bellow of triumph brought a small shake to his head.

What's your hollering about, big man? He'd never understand the valor in a drone strike, the glory in killing by remote control. The warriors of antiquity wouldn't recognize this dispassionate barbarity. The bone shard hidden in the hilt of his sword cooed its agreement. He laughed, and it took that moment of empathy to attack.

Daggers of black thought lanced into Conor's mind, seeking dominance and control, freedom from the eternity of death and the enslavement of soul. It surged forward, triumphant, exultant in the ease in which it invaded his mind. Instead of fighting, Conor let it in, deeper and deeper in its orgiastic triumph, until it came at last to the center of his being. He laughed at the panicked retreat from what it found there, then cut it off and strangled it with his will.

You serve me. And you will serve.

Cowed, the sword mewled in his mind, but it would find no mercy, no sympathy in its new master. A tremor of despair vibrated through the blade, and turned to a single, pathetic, razor thought: *Hungry.*

Conor patted the blade, a reflexive gesture with no emotion behind it. He grabbed a rung and climbed down, careful not to mess his boots any further on the slippery, stinking remains of Hurya al-Azwar.

• • •

Ten minutes after he found al-Azwar's shattered body, Matt stopped with a mental grunt. Pointy's bloody tracks marked the floor in the ultraviolet spectrum like highlighter, disrupted only by spotty patches of urine – rat or mouse by the look of it – and the acrid smell of the place. Pointy's tracks led into a small room made of dark brick, and then straight under the steel door on the far side, a bulkhead-type monstrosity with a gasketed rim and a rusty, wheeled, double-bar lock.

Pointy had gone inside, so it couldn't be flooded, but Matt doubted he'd be able to open it without giving away his presence. He sniffed the axle and detected no trace of WD-40 or grease, nothing to keep it from screaming like a banshee if he tried to open it.

If you're going to be loud...

Matt pulled a fist-sized wad of C4 from his combat pouch, split it into two pieces and pressed it into and around the latching mechanism on either side of the door. The detcord came next, clothesline-like material impregnated with PETN that burned at four miles a second, not so much a fuse as a linear explosive. He pushed the nylon-like material into and around the gasket, as well as through the wads of C4. Last, he added a blasting cap and set the detonator to radio signal.

Sixty feet down the hall he rounded the corner into a side passage. He set the detonator's remote on the floor twenty feet from the intersection, gripped his shotgun in both hands, and backed up. Then he ran.

A typical ICAP Aug could maintain a three-minute mile indefinitely, and run a hundred meters in eight seconds. Matt's personal record topped out at seven point seven-two. Legs pumping, he tried to beat it.

The impact as he stepped on the red button rocked the world sideways, and the shockwave buffeted him back just before he reached the main hallway. Legs pumping, he ran halfway up the far wall, muscles straining to turn him ninety degrees at such speeds, and fired a three-round burst of fragmentary projectiles toward the remains of the door and anything that might lie behind it.

Still glowing from the aftermath, chunks of shredded metal and broken brick littered the small room, and the resulting hole opened up not into a sewer tunnel but a metro line. A pair of tracks led left and right, and hazy orange sodium-vapor lights dotted the walls amid generations of overlapping graffiti.

The whispers chittered in anticipation of the slaughter. *As Matt rushes through the door, Pointy drops from the arced ceiling, a thousand pounds of muscle and brute force crushing him to the floor and pulping his head with one double-fisted crush.*

Matt tucked into a roll as he flew through the doorway, pulling the trigger as Pointy's gigantic form came into view. Two slugs impacted on the ceiling. Three found flesh.

Gore spattered Matt's face as he finished the roll and spun, firing again. Pointy slapped the shotgun out of the way and punched, telegraphing the move without the slightest bit of finesse. Matt rolled with it, taking the impact on his shoulder. His armor stiffened with the blow, reducing the punch to a solid hit with a Louisville Slugger.

He backpedaled as Pointy advanced, the hole in the bonk's leg knitting closed even as he picked up speed. A center-of-mass burst failed to penetrate skin, and the fragmentary rounds shredded Pointy's pectoral muscles to expose a gore-covered solid mass beneath. Half-blind, face streaming blood from a thousand gouges, the bonk dove, arms outstretched to catch Matt as he tried to flee.

Instead, Matt dropped prone and rolled left. He screamed as Pointy stomped, crushing his knee to the ground right through the ceramic composite. Matt fired, and two rounds caught the bonk in the stomach before he slapped the AA-12 hard enough to dent the barrel and send it flying from Matt's grip.

Chunks of meat and organs sprayed them both.

Matt scrambled back, his shattered knee a bonfire of itching, squirming flesh. He drew his official-issue pistol, a .50 caliber Barrett WildStang with ICAP-custom SLAP rounds. The depleted uranium core and tungsten carbide tip combined with a nanofiber composite sabot and fifty grains of powder to produce a bullet that would go through just about anything. It kicked like a mule, and took superhuman strength to fire with any accuracy.

Two shots took Pointy in the bloody meat over his heart, and another two ricocheted off of his forehead.

Pointy charged, strings of intestines flopping out of his abdomen to trail behind him.

Matt fired four more times as he rose to his feet, and two more before the bonk crushed him against the wall.

Blood erupted from Matt's mouth as his ribs imploded. A giant hand smashed the gun against the wall, denting the metal in a shower of brick dust.

Pointy stepped back for another body check. Matt let his knees buckle, dropping to the floor, and tore at the exposed viscera, fingers digging into slippery organs, wrenching them out to splatter on the ground.

The dark tunnel exploded in stars as Pointy's knee caught him in the side of the head. Deafened by the ringing in his ears, he scrambled to the side and whirled, pistol raised. A six-car double-decker train shimmied down the tunnel at forty or so miles an hour, its light catching Pointy's right side, washed in bright red gore.

The abomination's abdomen had closed, cutting off the dead intestine and sealing over with fresh skin. It took a tentative, wobbly step forward. The train's horn reverberated through the tunnel, too loud.

Matt took inventory: three combat knives, two 32-round magazines for a broken gun, no functional firearms. His knee no longer itched, but Pointy stood moments from full health.

As the train flashed between them, Matt bolted alongside, grabbed a handle and jerked himself aboard. He landed with his toes on the lip of the entry, pried the door open left-handed, and stepped inside. A half-dozen shocked faces gaped at his blood-spattered face and body armor.

"Go to the front car." They stared, wide-eyed, but nobody moved. "NOW!"

The train lurched.

"GO!" Matt tore a stainless steel pole from the car and ran toward the back of the train. Ignoring the squeals of panic behind him, he stood alert, ready for bear.

Pointy's head appeared in the rear window. Matt moved to dive forward, and the whispers chittered their approval as his body crushed into the rails, his brain splattering into the ground. Instead he backpedaled, shouldered open the door between cars, and gripped the handle to the coupling mechanism. The back door came off in a shriek of twisted metal, and Pointy threw it to the side.

Matt heaved, and the cars separated with a lurch.

The bonk pulled himself up onto the trailing car, quickly falling away into the distance, an almost quizzical look on his blockish face. Matt sighed in frustrated relief, alive but without his quarry.

And then the train braked, hard.

Matt shifted his weight to maintain balance as the other car gained ground, momentum carrying it forward as the train slowed to a stop. If the conductor didn't have the sense to keep going, Matt would have to lead the bonk from the civilians on the train. He looked down at the pole, the best weapon he had, and suppressed a grimace. *Better than nothing, but not by much. Not against that.*

As the train ground to a halt he leapt out the back then darted left toward a side tunnel.

• • •

Miguel Salido watched the man in black armor fade into the distance, wielding a metal pole like a Ninja Turtle. He growled in curious frustration.

The high pitched squeal of brakes brought a low tremor to his throat; a laugh. The whispers rejoiced, a slithering, pernicious cacophony of psychotic bloodshed that got harder to ignore with every passing day, and though he couldn't understand them, they urged him to slaughter every man, woman, and child on the train.

He crushed them to a disappointed mewling, forced himself to think like a rational person.

The man in black armor, the woman he'd crushed, Miguel had never encountered anyone like them. Through years of street fighting, standing guard over drug deals, rising in the ranks of the Mako Kings despite being Cuban, not Mexican, Miguel had always been bigger, tougher, more of a *cabron* than any bastard around. When Jade hit the streets and everyone started getting bigger, Miguel pushed the limits of musculoskeletal enhancement and backed it up with surgically-added barbed spikes in his wrists and titanium alloy plates under his skin.

But this man, not much bigger than most, had almost taken him down. One crazy gun and some kickass bullets helped balance the score, almost too much.

Since growing up in the shantytowns of Arroyo Naranjo, swiping fruit from stalls at the mercado to stave off scurvy and starvation, he'd come to appreciate the big things in life. In coming to the United States, his time with the Mako Kings had given him almost everything: a bachelor's degree in Business Administration from the University of Miami – despite his size he'd never had the team spirit for football – a mansion, three cars, all the gold, drugs, and pussy he could ever want. But since Jade, since augmentation, they couldn't give him a challenge.

Sometimes it took the little things to bring a smile.

Miguel took off at a run. At twelve hundred pounds he couldn't sprint much faster than your average Olympian, even with no body fat. But he knew these tunnels, had operated in Spanish City for two years, and his prey hadn't. That had to count for something.

He slowed, approached the train at a jog, and cut left at the smell of the man, subtle deodorant and gun oil and blood tinged with an underlying spice he couldn't quite place, like Jade but not. He followed the scent until it reached an access door, and stopped. Sized for normal men, it would constrict him, keep him from using his reach or bringing his full strength to bear. A perfect place for an ambush.

• • •

Conor Flynn watched as Pointy approached the doorway. The hulking monstrosity moved with a smooth grace at odds with its blocky form, silent in giant, almost comical basketball shoes. It cocked its head and waited, one hand on the door, listening or feeling for vibrations or something.

Stepping to the side, it pulled open the door, which squeaked on old hinges. It winced, waited again, and after a long, long pause, went inside.

Conor followed through the open door, sword drawn. Darkness swallowed him.

• • •

Something thrummed through the floor and walls, a breathing shudder too low-frequency for even Matt's ears to hear. He drew a mental map to al-Azwar's body. Her REC7 carbine didn't pack the punch of his AA-12, but it beat the hell out of combat knives, and he wasn't likely to beat Pointy with his fists and elbows.

He jogged down the dark hall until it ended at a T intersection, on a hunch took a right, and a few minutes later when the hall took another right, farther away from al-Azwar, he backtracked to the intersection and headed left.

• • •

Miguel paused. The man's scent tracked in both directions.

The right-hand path led back to the railway, and past that, deeper into downtown. The left-hand path led to Spanish City, the Mercado Royale, and a warren of smaller access tunnels under the city's west side.

Where are you going?

He chuckled, a low rumble with more growl than mirth. A smart man would try to get back to his allies, back to whatever blew the gate to the parking lot, back to guns and backup. With a shrug, he turned left – if Miguel caught him before he got out, it wouldn't matter.

The scent grew in intensity, the sharp tang of Old Spice, the underlying notes of blood and gun oil. He froze at a realization. In the chemical miasma that permeated his enhanced nose he noted the lack, the utter absence, of anything approaching fear. Running, hunted, through unfamiliar tunnels, the man smelled of predator, not prey.

A tingle of excitement ran up Miguel's spine, a shiver of apprehension. *How are you not afraid?*

• • •

Matt knelt over al-Azwar's shattered body, ignoring the pungent reek of shit to rifle through her kit. Someone had stripped her of her carbine, pistol and combat knives, but had left her first aid kit, which all ICAP agents carried in case an innocent or suspect needed saving. That it had soaked with urine when her system had let go had probably discouraged close inspection, and he gladly took the morphine autoinjector.

He looked up at the ladder embedded into a short tunnel that terminated in a round steel hatch. Heaving on it bent a rung on the ladder but did nothing to budge the portal.

He tried the COM again. "This is Rowley, come in."

Nothing. However they built this place, it made far too good of a Faraday Cage.

He climbed down, listened for any signs of pursuit then hatched a plan.

• • •

Conor Flynn let Matt creep off, waited a full minute then approached the body. Matt had hidden the tripwire under Hurya's exploded viscera, a clever move that would reduce detection but make it less likely that Pointy would trip it in the first place. Matt had wrapped his remaining det cord around the magazines for his ridiculous shotgun, thirty-two-round drums loaded with smart, direction-triggerable microgrenades, enough raw explosives to make mincemeat out of anyone who tripped the switch.

He knelt, ran his finger just above the wire, and pulled the detonator from the cord.

"What the hell are you doing?" Matt's whisper clawed down his spine like fingernails down a chalkboard.

Conor plastered on a half-grin, the charming mask he'd worn for over thirty years. Matt gave him a slack-jawed stare, trust and suspicion warring in his eyes. The sword begged him to cut Rowley to ribbons, and the whispers cajoled their elated agreement.

"Not now," he growled.

Matt hesitated. "What do you mean?" His wary stance betrayed too much caution, and Conor suppressed a chuckle at the misunderstanding.

He whispered back, "I called dibs. Not my fault you blighters don't listen, is it? So let's kill this thing."

"Are… are you insane?"

Conor hid the truth behind the truth. "That's why they hired me, am I right?"

• • •

"Put it back," Matt said. He took a step toward his friend, for the first time wary around the enthusiastic psychopath.

"Oil of palm, Rowley." Flynn replaced the detonator, though Matt had no idea what 'oil of palm' meant in these circumstances. His wife, Monica, had said that rhyme slang was much more of a cockney rather than an Irish thing, but either way Matt had yet to find Conor's flippant word games particularly comprehensible.

"Are you–" he cut himself off from asking the same question again. "Get over here and watch our six. These bastards killed Platt and al-Azwar, and I'm not about to let them get away with it."

Flynn sauntered over, thumbs hooked in his belt loops, katana slung at his waist in exactly a non-Japanese manner.

"What have you got for weapons?"

Flynn pulled his pistol, identical to Matt's. "Just this and the sword. Couple knives. Here, take it." He held it out grip-first.

Matt took it and holstered it.

Flynn smiled, but kept his voice at a barely audible whisper. "I'll go up. You can be bait." Before Matt could argue he'd scampered up the ladder to crouch in the darkness overhead, wedged in place like a movie action hero, left palm pressed against one wall, feet against the other. He drew his katana and winked. "Run along, little birdie. And tweet a little, would you?"

Chirp, chirp.

• • •

The scents mingled, the man's combining with someone else's, sharper, a cold, metallic bite reminiscent of dentist's offices and morgues. Miguel hesitated, then peeked around the corner. The body still lay where he'd left it, though her weapons were missing. Nothing moved, and nothing registered in the infrared.

He stepped out, approaching the body in a silent walk, and the cold smell grew stronger, more dominant. An infrared glow filtered down from the access hatch, normal in the daytime but out of place at night. Miguel tried not to roll his eyes at the soft scrape from the end of the hall.

There had never been a time, not since puberty, that people hadn't underestimated his mind. Only Calloway had seen through the lump of meat, lifted him up and made him a true player in her organization. The Mako Kings had no idea what they'd gotten themselves involved in, and she kept them rolled in enough cash to keep them blind, but she trusted Miguel, and used his shrewd mind to cement her ties with the Latin gang.

If you want a bull...

Miguel charged, as they'd expect him to, but at the last second leapt, punching into the overhead tunnel, driving his massive fist and barbed metal spikes into hard armor and soft flesh. The hidden man let out a strangled grunt as his abdomen imploded, and as Miguel tore away he went slack. Miguel's foot came down, slipped on the body, and the world went white.

• • •

The whispers cooed their disapproval as Matt rounded the corner too late for the explosion to shred his flesh. The bonk had stumbled to one knee, a mass of charred skin smeared with red where the mass of fragmentation grenades had sheared through. Pale metal shone through the injuries, an enhancement Matt hadn't expected.

Conor dropped from the shaft, hairless skin golden and shiny from the intense heat, and hit the ground on his knees and elbows, too hard. And stayed there, gagging.

Matt fired, a single round straight to the forehead. The bonk jerked sideways and the bullet ricocheted off, gouging the skin but otherwise doing no damage. As burnt flesh knitted over metal, it looked healthier than when they'd started.

Holy shit.

The bonk leaned forward and drove a fist down, crushing Flynn to the floor. His pelvis shattered and his legs twitched, but he didn't scream.

Matt charged, firing, as the bonk raised his fist again. The impacts should have driven it back, but instead it lunged forward, rising to its feet in an athletic leap. It stumbled as Flynn lashed out. His composite blade caught it in the knee, slicing through the meat to lodge in the joint.

Flynn held on, two-handed, as it dragged him another half-step and then fell, unable to drag its other leg underneath it.

Matt stepped forward and aimed, point-blank, at the top of its head. The single shot rang out and the bonk dropped, hot red fluid pulsing from the hole. He let out a breath, pointed down, fired twice more into the fractured skull.

Kneeling, Matt put his hand on Conor's shoulder. "You alive?"

Conor's hand twitched, and his thumb extended.

Matt patted the top of his head. "Sorry about the dibs. You maniac."

• • •

Six hours later they landed in D.C., Karle and Flynn still on stretchers, al-Azwar, Platt, and Washington in body bags. Matt shook Jeff Hannes's hand on the tarmac, Jeff's tie lashing in the downwash from the propellers.

Jeff pinned Flynn with his eyes and spoke as the chopper lifted off. "What the hell was that, Flynn?"

Karle held up a hand. "We already discussed it, sir. Flynn thought he'd taken down his target, so once he'd recovered from his injuries he'd redirected to assist in the hunt for, um, for Pointy."

Jeff looked from Flynn to Karle, his anger fading to his

familiar grimace. "We lost three Augs taking down four, with drone support. How did that happen?"

Matt licked his lips. "We're still not sure. Something ambushed us on the way down, killed Platt and isolated al-Azwar so that Pointy could take her out. We looked at the Dragonfly feeds, and IR picked up a signature, but not much of one, and it disappeared into the crowd before we'd finished the sweep."

"What are you saying?"

Karle answered. "We… we don't know, sir. Alpha, Bravo, and Charlie squads came in on cleanup, and we vetted everyone before we released them or turned them over to metro PD for warrants. Nobody flagged, not even as suspicious, though way too many tested positive for Jade – nothing serious yet, just junkie-level cut crap."

Jeff looked at each of them in turn. "Well, in that case, I think you have a new mission."

MORE COHESION PRESS TITLES
ON THE FOLLOWING PAGES

FATHOMLESS BY GREIG BECK

SEPTEMBER 2016

FATHOMLESS BY GREIG BECK

Carcharodon megalodon – the largest and most fearsome predator to have ever existed on our planet. Rumors of its existence in our modern oceans have persisted for centuries. Now, in a new adventure, the rumors explode into brutal and terrifying reality in *Fathomless* by Greig Beck.

Baranof Island, Gulf of Alaska, 1952

Jim Granger is searching for a place of legend. Known as 'Bad Water' by the island's elders, it's reputed to be home to many dangerous creatures. Through a seam in a cliff face, Jim finds what he seeks. He also finds, too late, that the water demon he was warned about is horrifyingly real.

Today, Cate Granger is following in her grandfather's footsteps. Along with a team of scientists and crew, she accidentally releases a creature from Earth's primordial past into today's oceans. The giant Megalodon shark follows its instinct and a genetic memory of a home that once existed millions of years ago along the Californian coast. Nothing is safe on or below the water as the monster stakes its claim on the world's oceans.

Now Cate and her team must do battle with a creature that has no rival, knows no fear, and regards humans as nothing more than prey.

In FATHOMLESS, the greatest predator the world has ever known is coming home in 2016.

"... combines the terror of Benchley's JAWS with the primordial horror of Alten's MEG in an adventure that is the best of both."

—Matthew Summers, Smash Dragons Book Reviews.

SNAFU: UNNATURAL SELECTION

AVAILABLE NOW

SNAFU: UNNATURAL SELECTION

Man versus Nature.

In the 70s and 80s, animals ruled. Anacondas, piranha, giant crocodiles/alligators/lizards, mutated bears near nuclear power stations, prehistoric sharks all featured heavily in books and films, when bio-horror was at its modern peak.

This anthology of military-bio-horror stories is inspired by those classic days.

Think Greg McLean's Rogue, Lake Placid, Eight-legged Freaks, Anaconda, Meg, Prophecy, Deep Blue Sea, and other films/books where people (in this case soldiers) are fighting against mutated, weird, or ultra-dangerous animals.

Join some of the best writers working today, along with some SNAFU favourites, for an unnaturally good time.

Table of Contents:

INTO THE MIST BY LEE MURRAY

"Cinematic and evocative, Into the Mist *is a tension-packed expedition into primordial terror.*

Murray's writing had me feeling the damp of the forest, seeing the mist curling through the fern fronds, and sensing the danger lurking there.

Ancient myths, military men and scientists placed in remote, primordial locations – it had all the right ingredients for me, and it didn't disappoint for a moment.

Lee Murray is an author to watch."

– Greig Beck, best-selling author of the Arcadian series

When NZDF Sergeant Taine McKenna and his squad are tasked with escorting a bunch of civilian contractors into Te Urewera National Park, it seems a strange job for the army.

Militant Tūhoe separatists are active in the area, and with its cloying mist and steep ravines, the forest is a treacherous place in winter.

Yet nothing has prepared Taine for the true danger that awaits them. Death incarnate.

They backtrack toward civilisation, stalked by a prehistoric creature intent on picking them off one by one. With their weapons ineffective, the babysitting job has become a race for survival.

Desperate to bring his charges out alive, Taine draws on ancient tribal wisdom. Will it be enough to stop the nightmare? And when the mist clears, will anyone be left?

"Creepy and addictive, Into the Mist *is an irresistible tapestry of military action, dark myths, and an ancient and terrifying horror. A must read for speculative fiction fans."*

– Matthew Summers (Smashdragons)

SNAFU: BLACK OPS

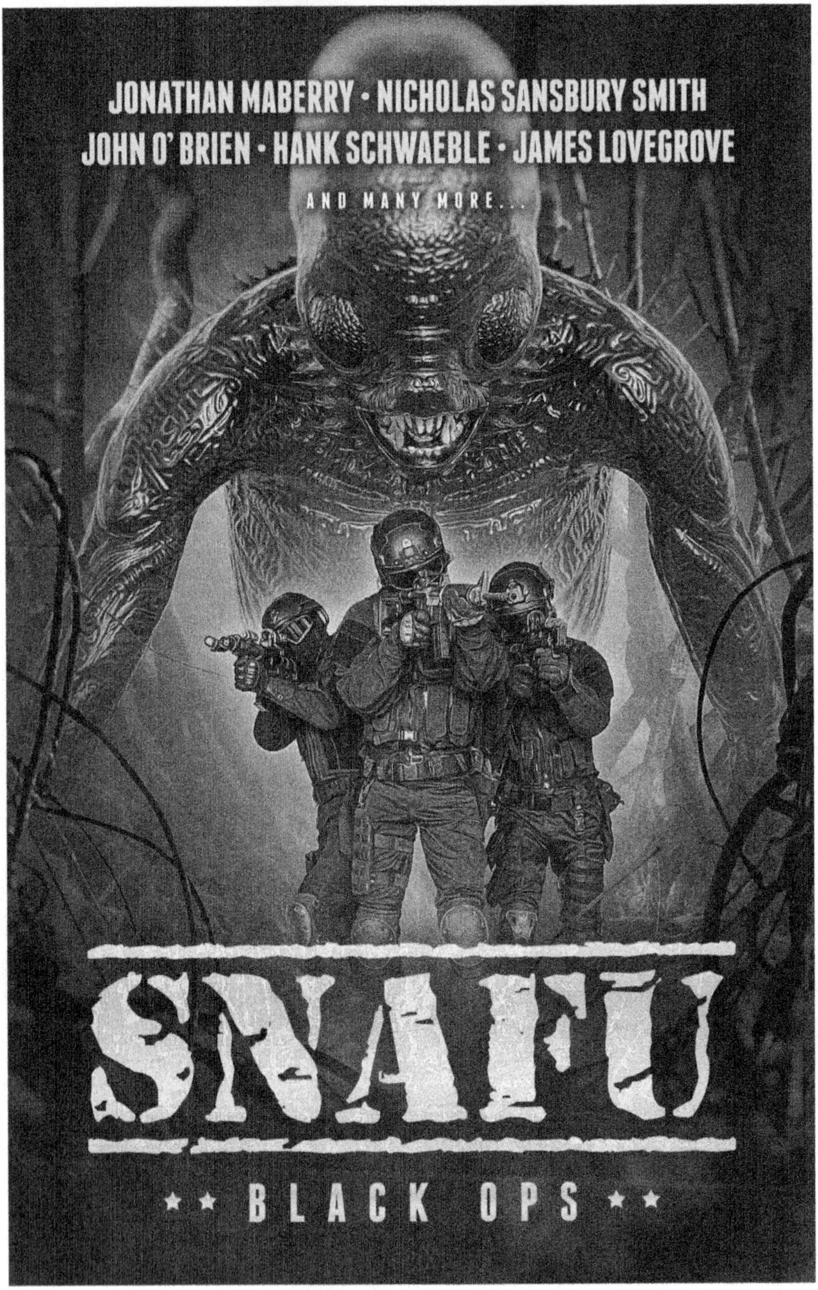

COMING NOVEMBER 2016

SNAFU: BLACK OPS

Special Forces.

The best of the best.

SEALs, Rangers, Operational Detachment Delta. The greatest fighters the modern world has seen.

In Black Ops, these ultimate warriors square off against the most dangerous opponents they have ever faced.

Sworn to protect and serve their countries, these men and women go beyond the call of duty to ensure that we can sleep safe at night, in our beds.

Featuring some of the best writers in the genre, this anthology takes it further than any previous SNAFU.

Sometimes all it takes is all you've got, and the only easy day was yesterday.